Metzov smiled, a gloss... bly cordial voice, confi... Ensign, back on Old Eart... you could always persuade the army to shoot the navy, or vice versa, when they could no longer discipline themselves."

"Mutiny!" said Miles, startled out of his resolve to speak only when spoken to. "I thought the issue was poison exposure."

"It *was*. Unfortunately, due to Bonn's mishandling, it's now a matter of principle." A muscle jumped in Metzov's jaw.

"Principle, sir, what principle? It's *waste disposal*," Miles choked.

"It's a mass refusal to obey a direct order, Ensign." The sergeant lined the grubs up in a crossfire array around the stiff-standing techs, and barked an order. They aimed their weapons at the techs.

"Strip," Metzov ordered through set teeth. "When you are again ready to obey your orders," Metzov continued in a parade-pitched voice, "you may dress and go to work."

. . . . Fifteen naked men started to shiver violently as the dry snow whispered around their ankles. Fifteen bewildered faces began to look terrified and their eyes shifted toward the nerve-disruptors trained on them.

Metzov's eye fell on Miles. "Vorkosigan, you can either take up a weapon and be useful, or consider yourself dismissed."

When Miles made no move, the sergeant walked over and thrust a nerve disruptor into Miles's hand. *This isn't going to be a mutiny. It's going to be a massacre . . .*

Baen Books by Lois McMaster Bujold

THE VOR GAME

LOIS
MCMASTER
BUJOLD

THE VOR GAME

This is a work of fiction. All the characters and events portrayed in this book are fictional, and any resemblance to real people or incidents is purely coincidental.

Copyright © 1990 by Lois McMaster Bujold

A signed, limited hardcover edition of this bok has been published by Easton Press.

All rights reserved, including the right to reproduce this book or portions thereof in any form.

A Baen Books Original. A portion of this novel appeared in *Analog* magazine in slightly different form as "The Weatherman."

Baen Publishing Enterprises
P.O. Box 1403
Riverdale, NY 10471

ISBN: 0-671-72014-7

Cover art by Gary Ruddell

First printing, September 1990
Fifth printing, September 1999

Distributed by Simon & Schuster
1230 Avenue of the Americas
New York, NY 10020

Printed in the United States of America

For Mom.

And with thanks to
Charles Marshall
for firsthand accounts
of arctic engineering, and
William Melgaard
for comments on war and wargames.

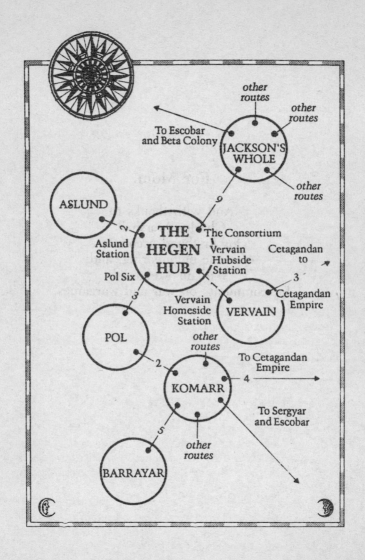

other
routes

other
routes

To Escobar
and Beta Colony

JACKSON'S
WHOLE

9

other
routes

ASLUND

2

THE
HEGEN
HUB

The Consortium

Aslund
Station

Vervain
Hubside
Station

Cetagandan
to

Pol Six

3

Vervain
Homeside
Station

3

Cetagandan
Empire

POL

VERVAIN

other
routes

2

To Cetagandan
Empire

KOMARR

4

5

other
routes

To Sergyar
and Escobar

BARRAYAR

CHAPTER ONE

"Ship duty!" chortled the ensign four ahead of Miles in line. Glee lit his face as his eyes sped down his orders, the plastic flimsy rattling slightly in his hands. "I'm to be junior weaponry officer on the Imperial Cruiser *Commodore Vorhalas*. Reporting at once to Tanery Base Shuttleport for orbital transfer." At a pointed prod he removed himself with an unmilitary skip from the way of the next man in line, still hissing delight under his breath.

"Ensign Plause." The aging sergeant manning the desk managed to look bored and superior at the same time, holding the next packet up with deliberation between thumb and forefinger. How long had he been holding down this post at the Imperial Military Academy? Miles wondered. How many hundreds—thousands—of young officers had passed under his bland eye at this first supreme moment of their careers? Did they all start to look alike after a few years? The same fresh green uniforms. The same shiny blue plastic rectangles of shiny new-won rank armoring the high collars. The same hungry eyes, the go-to-hell graduates of the Imperial Services' most elite school with visions of military destiny dancing in their heads. *We don't just march on the future, we charge it.*

Plause stepped aside, touched his thumbprint to the lock-pad, and unzipped his envelope in turn.

"Well?" said Ivan Vorpatril, just ahead of Miles in line. "Don't keep us in suspense."

1

"Language school," said Plause, still reading.

Plause spoke all four of Barrayar's native languages perfectly already. "As student or instructor?" Miles inquired.

"Student."

"Ah, ha. It'll be galactic languages, then. Intelligence will be wanting you, after. You're bound off-planet for sure," said Miles.

"Not necessarily," said Plause. "They could just sit me in a concrete box somewhere, programming translating computers till I go blind." But hope gleamed in his eyes.

Miles charitably did not point out the major drawback of Intelligence, the fact that you ended up working for Chief of Imperial Security Simon Illyan, the man who remembered *everything*. But perhaps on Plause's level he would not encounter the acerb Illyan.

"Ensign Lubachik."

Lubachik was the second most painfully earnest man Miles had ever met; Miles was therefore unsurprised when Lubachik zipped open his envelope and choked, "'ImpSec. The advanced course in Security and Counter-assassination.'"

"Ah, palace guard school," said Ivan with interest, kibbitzing over Lubachik's shoulder.

"That's quite an honor," Miles observed. "Illyan usually pulls his students from the twenty-year men with rows of medals."

"Maybe Emperor Gregor asked Illyan for someone nearer his own age," suggested Ivan, "to brighten the landscape. Those prune-faced fossils Illyan usually surrounds him with would give *me* depressive fits. Don't let on you have a sense of humor, Lubachik, I think it's an automatic disqualification."

Lubachik was in no danger of losing the posting if that were so, Miles reflected.

"Will I really meet the emperor?" Lubachik asked. He turned nervous eyes on Miles and Ivan.

"You'll probably get to watch him eat breakfast every day," said Ivan. "Poor sod." Did he mean Lubachik, or Gregor? Gregor, definitely.

"You Vorish types know him—what's he like?"

Miles cut in before the glint in Ivan's eye could materialize into some practical joke. "He's very straightforward. You'll get along fine."

Lubachik moved off, looking faintly reassured, rereading his flimsy.

"Ensign Vorpatril," intoned the sergeant. "Ensign Vorkosigan."

Tall Ivan collected his packet and Miles his, and they moved out of the way with their two comrades.

Ivan unzipped his envelope. "Ha. Imperial HQ in Vorbarr Sultana for me. I am to be, I'll have you know, aide-de-camp to Commodore Jollif, Operations." He bowed and turned the flimsy over. "Starting tomorrow, in fact."

"Ooh," said the ensign who'd drawn ship duty, still bouncing slightly. "Ivan gets to be a *secretary*. Just watch out if General Lamitz asks you to sit on his lap, I hear he—"

Ivan flipped him an amiable rude gesture. "Envy, sheer envy. I'll get to live like a civilian. Work seven to five, have my own apartment in town—no girls on that ship of yours up there, I might point out." Ivan's voice was even and cheerful, only his eyes failing to totally conceal his disappointment. Ivan had wanted ship duty too. They all did.

Miles did. *Ship duty. Eventually, command, like my father, his father, his, his* . . . A wish, a prayer, a dream . . . He hesitated for self-discipline, for fear, for a last lingering moment of high hope. He thumbed the lock pad and unzipped the envelope with deliberate precision. A single plastic flimsy, a handful of travel passes. . . . His deliberation lasted only for the brief moment it took him to absorb the short paragraph before his eyes. He stood frozen in disbelief, began reading again from the top.

"So what's up, coz?" Ivan glanced down over Miles's shoulder.

"Ivan," said Miles in a choked voice, "have I got a touch of amnesia, or did we indeed never have a meteorology course on our sciences track?"

"Five-space math, yes. Xenobotany, yes." Ivan absently scratched a remembered itch. "Geology and terrain evaluation, yes. Well, there was aviation weather, back in our first year."

"Yes, but . . ."

"So what have they done to you this time?" asked Plause, clearly prepared to offer congratulations or sympathy as indicated.

"I'm assigned as Chief Meteorology Officer, Lazkowski Base. Where the hell is Lazkowski Base? I've never even heard of it!"

The sergeant at the desk looked up with a sudden evil grin. "I have, sir," he offered. "It's on a place called Kyril Island, up near the arctic circle. Winter training base for infantry. The grubs call it Camp Permafrost."

"*Infantry?*" said Miles.

Ivan's brows rose, and he frowned down at Miles. "Infantry? You? That doesn't seem right."

"No, it doesn't," said Miles faintly. Cold consciousness of his physical handicaps washed over him.

Years of arcane medical tortures had almost managed to correct the severe deformities from which Miles had nearly died at birth. Almost. Curled like a frog in infancy, he now stood almost straight. Chalk-stick bones, friable as talc, now were almost strong. Wizened as an infant homunculus, he now stood almost four-foot-nine. It had been a trade-off, toward the end, between the length of his bones and their strength, and his doctor still opined that the last six inches of height had been a mistake. Miles had finally broken his legs enough times to agree with him, but by then it was too late. But not a mutant, not . . . it scarcely mattered any more. If only they would let him place his strengths in the Emperor's service, he would make them forget his weaknesses. The deal was understood.

There had to be a thousand jobs in the Service to which his strange appearance and hidden fragility would make not one whit of difference. Like aide-de-camp, or Intelligence translator. Or even a ship's weaponry officer, monitoring his computers. It had been understood, surely it had been understood. But infantry? Someone was not playing fair. Or a mistake had been made. That wouldn't be a first. He hesitated a long moment, his fist tightening on the flimsy, then headed toward the door.

"Where are you going?" asked Ivan.

"To see Major Cecil."

Ivan exhaled through pursed lips. "Oh? Good luck."

Did the desk sergeant hide a small smile, bending his head to sort through the next stack of packets? "Ensign Draut," he called. The line moved up one more.

Major Cecil was leaning with one hip on his clerk's desk, consulting about something on the vid, as Miles entered his office and saluted.

Major Cecil glanced up at Miles and then at his chrono. "Ah, less than ten minutes. I win the bet." The major returned Miles's salute as the clerk, smiling sourly, pulled a small wad of currency from his pocket, peeled off a one-mark note, and handed it across wordlessly to his superior. The major's face was only amused on the surface; he nodded toward the door, and the clerk tore off the plastic flimsy his machine had just produced and exited the room.

Major Cecil was a man of about fifty, lean, even-tempered, watchful. Very watchful. Though he was not the titular head of Personnel, that administrative job belonging to a higher-ranking officer, Miles had spotted Cecil long ago as the final-decision man. Through Cecil's hands passed at the last every assignment for every Academy graduate. Miles had always found him an accessible man, the teacher and scholar in him ascendant over the officer. His wit was dry and rare, his dedication to his duty intense. Miles had always trusted him. Till now.

"Sir," he began. He held out his orders in a frustrated gesture. "What *is* this?"

Cecil's eyes were still bright with his private amusement as he pocketed the mark-note. "Are you asking me to read them to you, Vorkosigan?"

"Sir, I question—" Miles stopped, bit his tongue, began again. "I have a few questions about my assignment."

"Meteorology Officer, Lazkowski Base," Major Cecil recited.

"It's . . . not a mistake, then? I got the right packet?"

"If that's what that says, you did."

"Are . . . you aware the only meteorology course I had was aviation weather?"

"I am." The major wasn't giving away a thing.

Miles paused. Cecil's sending his clerk out was a clear signal that this discussion was to be frank. "Is this some kind of punishment?" *What have I ever done to you?*

"Why, Ensign," Cecil's voice was smooth, "it's a perfectly normal assignment. Were you expecting an extraordinary one? My job is to match personnel requests with available candidates. Every request must be filled by someone."

"Any tech school grad could have filled this one." With an effort, Miles kept the snarl out of his voice, uncurled his fingers. "Better. It doesn't require an Academy cadet."

"That's right," agreed the major.

"Why, then?" Miles burst out. His voice came out louder than he'd meant it to.

Cecil sighed, straightened. "Because I have noticed, Vorkosigan, watching you—and you know very well you were the most closely-watched cadet ever to pass through these halls barring Emperor Gregor himself—"

Miles nodded shortly.

"That despite your demonstrated brilliance in some areas, you have also demonstrated some chronic weaknesses. And I'm not referring to your physical problems, which everybody but me thought were going to take you out before your first year was up—you've been surprisingly sensible about those—"

Miles shrugged. "Pain hurts, sir. I don't court it."

"Very good. But your most insidious chronic problem is in the area of . . . how shall I put this precisely . . . subordination. You argue too much."

"No, I don't," Miles began indignantly, then shut his mouth.

Cecil flashed a grin. "Quite. Plus your rather irritating habit of treating your superior officers as your, ah . . ." Cecil paused, apparently groping again for just the right word.

"Equals?" Miles hazarded.

"Cattle," Cecil corrected judiciously. "To be driven to your will. You're a manipulator par excellence, Vorkosigan. I've been studying you for three years now, and your group dynamics are fascinating. Whether you were in charge or not, somehow it was always your idea that ended up getting carried out."

"Have I been . . . that disrespectful, sir?" Miles's stomach felt cold.

"On the contrary. Given your background, the marvel is that you conceal that, ah, little arrogant streak so well. But Vorkosigan," Cecil dropped at last into perfect seriousness, "the Imperial Academy is not the whole of the Imperial Service. You've made your comrades here appreciate you because here, brains are held at a premium. You were picked first for any strategic team for the same reason you

were picked last for any purely physical contest—
these young hotshots wanted to win. All the time.
Whatever it took."

"I can't be ordinary and survive, sir!"

Cecil tilted his head. "I agree. And yet, sometime,
you must also learn how to command ordinary men.
And be commanded by them!

"This isn't a punishment, Vorkosigan, and it isn't
my idea of a joke. Upon my choices may depend not
only our fledgling officers' lives, but also those of the
innocents I inflict 'em on. If I seriously miscalculate,
overmatch or mismatch a man with a job, I not only
risk him, but also those around him. Now, in six
months (plus unscheduled overruns), the Imperial
Orbital Shipyard is going to finish commissioning the
Prince Serg."

Miles's breath caught.

"You've got it," Cecil nodded. "The newest, fastest, deadliest thing His Imperial Majesty has ever
put into space. And with the longest range. It will
go out, and stay out, for longer periods than anything
we've ever had before. It follows that everyone on
board will be in each other's hair for longer unbroken periods than ever before. High Command is
actually paying some attention to the psych profiles
on this one. For a change.

"Listen, now," Cecil leaned forward. So did Miles,
reflexively. "If you can keep your nose clean for just
six months on an isolated downside post—bluntly, if
you prove you can handle Camp Permafrost, I'll
allow as how you can handle anything the Service
might throw at you. And I'll support your request
for a transfer to the *Prince.* But if you screw up,
there will be nothing I or anybody else can do for
you. Sink or swim, Ensign."

Fly, thought Miles. *I want to fly.* "Sir . . . just
how much of a pit is this place?"

"I wouldn't want to prejudice you, Ensign Vorkosigan," said Cecil piously.

And I love you too, sir. "But . . . infantry? My physical limits . . . won't prevent my serving if they're taken into account, but I can't pretend they're not there. Or I might as well jump off a wall, destroy myself immediately, and save everybody time." *Dammit, why did they let me occupy some of Barrayar's most expensive classroom space for three years if they meant to kill me outright?* "I'd always assumed they were going to be taken into account."

"Meteorology Officer is a technical speciality, Ensign," the major reassured him. "Nobody's going to try and drop a full field pack on you and smash you flat. I doubt there's an officer in the Service who would choose to explain your dead body to the Admiral." His voice cooled slightly. "Your saving grace. Mutant."

Cecil was without prejudice, merely testing. Always testing. Miles ducked his head. "As I may be, for the mutants who come after me."

"You've figured that out, have you?" Cecil's eye was suddenly speculative, faintly approving.

"Years ago, sir."

"Hm." Cecil smiled slightly, pushed himself off the desk, came forward and extended his hand. "Good luck, then. Lord Vorkosigan."

Miles shook it. "Thank you, sir." He shuffled through the stack of travel passes, ordering them.

"What's your first stop?" asked Cecil.

Testing again. Must be a bloody reflex. Miles answered unexpectedly, "The Academy archives."

"Ah!"

"For a downloading of the Service meteorology manual. And supplementary material."

"Very good. By the way, your predecessor in the post will be staying on a few weeks to complete your orientation."

"I'm extremely glad to hear that, sir," said Miles sincerely.

"We're not trying to make it impossible, Ensign."

Merely very difficult. "I'm glad to know that too. Sir." Miles's parting salute was almost subordinate.

Miles rode the last leg to Kyril Island in a big automated air-freight shuttle with a bored backup pilot and eighty tons of supplies. He spent most of the solitary journey frantically swotting up on weather. Since the flight schedule went rapidly awry due to hours-long delays at the last two loading stops, he found himself reassuringly further along in his studies than he'd expected by the time the air-shuttle rumbled to a halt at Lazkowski Base.

The cargo bay doors opened to let in watery light from a sun skulking along near the horizon. The high-summer breeze was about five degrees above freezing. The first soldiers Miles saw were a crew of black-coveralled men with loaders under the direction of a tired-looking corporal, who met the shuttle. No one appeared to be specially detailed to meet a new weather officer. Miles shrugged on his parka and approached them.

A couple of the black-clad men, watching him as he hopped down from the ramp, made remarks to each other in Barrayaran Greek, a minority dialect of Earth origin, thoroughly debased in the centuries of the Time of Isolation. Miles, weary from his journey and cued by the all-too-familiar expressions on their faces, made a snap decision to ignore whatever they had to say by simply pretending not to understand their language. Plause had told him often enough that his accent in Greek was execrable anyway.

"*Look at that, will you? Is it a kid?*"

"*I knew they were sending us baby officers, but this is a new low.*"

"*Hey, that's no kid. It's a damn dwarf of some sort. The midwife sure missed her stroke on that one. Look at it, it's a mutant!*"

With an effort, Miles kept his eyes from turning

toward the commentators. Increasingly confident of their privacy, their voices rose from whispers to ordinary tones.

"*So what's it doing in uniform, ha?*"

"*Maybe it's our new mascot.*"

The old genetic fears were so subtly ingrained, so pervasive even now, you could get beaten to death by people who didn't even know quite why they hated you but simply got carried away in the excitement of a group feedback loop. Miles knew very well he had always been protected by his father's rank, but ugly things could happen to less socially fortunate odd ones. There had been a ghastly incident in the Old Town section of Vorbarr Sultana just two years ago, a destitute crippled man found castrated with a broken wine bottle by a gang of drunks. It was considered Progress that it was a scandal, and not simply taken for granted. A recent infanticide in the Vorkosigan's own district had cut even closer to the bone. Yes, rank, social or military, had its uses. Miles meant to acquire all he could before he was done.

Miles twitched his parka back so that his officer's collar tabs showed clearly. "Hello, Corporal. I have orders to report in to a Lieutenant Ahn, the base Meteorology Officer. Where can I find him?"

Miles waited a beat for his proper salute. It was slow in coming, the corporal was still goggling down at him. It dawned on him at last that Miles might really be an officer.

Belatedly, he saluted. "Excuse me, uh, what did you say, sir?"

Miles returned the salute blandly and repeated himself in level tones.

"Uh, Lieutenant Ahn, right. He usually hides out—that is, he's usually in his office. In the main administration building." The corporal swung his arm around to point toward a two-story pre-fab sticking up beyond a rank of half-buried warehouses at the edge of the tarmac, maybe a kilometer off. "You can't miss it, it's the tallest building on the base."

Also, Miles noted, well-marked by the assortment of comm equipment sticking out of the roof. Very good.

Now, should he turn his pack over to these goons and pray that it would follow him to his eventual destination, whatever it was? Or interrupt their work and commandeer a loader for transport? He had a brief vision of himself stuck up on the prow of the thing like a sailing ship's figurehead, being trundled toward his meeting with destiny along with half a ton of Underwear, Thermal, Long, 2 doz per unit crate, Style #6774932. He decided to shoulder his duffle and walk.

"Thank you, Corporal." He marched off in the indicated direction, too-conscious of his limp and the leg-braces concealed beneath his trouser legs taking up their share of the extra weight. The distance turned out to be farther than it looked, but he was careful not to pause or falter till he'd turned out of sight beyond the first warehouse-unit.

The base seemed nearly deserted. Of course. The bulk of its population was the infantry trainees who came and went in two batches per winter. Only the permanent crew was here now, and Miles bet most of them took their long leaves during this brief summer breathing space. Miles wheezed to a halt inside the Admin building without having passed another man.

The Directory and Map Display, according to a hand-lettered sign taped across its vid plate, was down. Miles wandered up the first and only hallway to his right, searching for an occupied office, any occupied office. Most doors were closed, but not locked, lights out. An office labeled Gen. Accounting held a man in black fatigues with red lieutenant's tabs on the collar, totally absorbed in his holovid which was displaying long columns of data. He was swearing under his breath.

"Meteorology Office. Where?" Miles called in the door.

"Two." The lieutenant pointed upward without turning around, crouched more tightly, and resumed swearing. Miles tiptoed away without disturbing him further.

He found it at last on the second floor, a closed door labeled in faded letters. He paused outside, set down his duffle, and folded his parka atop it. He checked himself over. Fourteen hours travel had rumpled his initial crispness. Still, he'd managed to keep his green undress uniform and half-boots free of foodstains, mud, and other unbecoming accretions. He flattened his cap and positioned it precisely in his belt. He'd crossed half a planet, half a lifetime, to achieve this moment. Three years training to a fever pitch of readiness lay behind him. Yet the Academy years had always had a faint air of pretense, We-are-only-practicing; now, at last, he was face to face with the real thing, his first real commanding officer. First impressions could be vital, especially in his case. He took a breath and knocked.

A gravelly muffled voice came through the door, words unrecognizable. Invitation? Miles opened it and strode in.

He had a glimpse of computer interfaces and vid displays gleaming and glowing along one wall. He rocked back at the heat that hit his face. The air within was blood-temperature. Except for the vid displays, the room was dim. At a movement to his left, Miles turned and saluted. "Ensign Miles Vorkosigan, reporting for duty as ordered, sir," he snapped out, looked up, and saw no one.

The movement had come from lower down. An unshaven man of about forty dressed only in his skivvies sat on the floor, his back against the comconsole desk. He smiled up at Miles, raised a bottle half-full of amber liquid, mumbled, "Salu', boy. Love ya," and fell slowly over.

Miles gazed down on him for a long, long, thoughtful moment.

The man began to snore.

After turning down the heat, shedding his tunic, and tossing a blanket over Lieutenant Ahn (for such he was), Miles took a contemplative half-hour and thoroughly examined his new domain. There was no doubt, he was going to require instruction in the office's operations. Besides the satellite real-time images, automated data seemed to be coming in from a dozen micro-climate survey rigs spotted around the island. If procedural manuals had ever existed, they weren't around now, not even on the computers. After an honorable hesitation, bemusedly studying the snoring, twitching form on the floor, Miles also took the opportunity to go through Ahn's desk and comconsole files.

Discovery of a few pertinent facts helped put the human spectacle before Miles into a more understandable perspective. Lieutenant Ahn, it seemed, was a twenty-year man within weeks of retirement. It had been a very, very long time since his last promotion. It had been an even longer time since his last transfer; he'd been Kyril Island's only weather officer for the last fifteen years.

This poor sod has been stuck on this iceberg since I was six years old, Miles calculated, and shuddered inwardly. Hard to tell, at this late date, if Ahn's drinking problem were cause or effect. Well, if he sobered up enough within the next day to show Miles how to go on, well and good. If he didn't, Miles could think of half a dozen ways, ranging from the cruel to the unusual, to bring him around whether he wanted to be conscious or not. If Ahn could just be made to disgorge a technical orientation, he could return to his coma till they came to roll him onto outgoing transport, for all Miles cared.

Ahn's fate decided, Miles donned his tunic, stowed his gear behind the desk, and went exploring. Somewhere in the chain of command there must be a conscious, sober and sane human being who was actually doing his job, or the place couldn't even function on this level. Or maybe it was run by corporals, who knew? In that case, Miles supposed, his next task must be to find and take control of the most effective corporal available.

In the downstairs foyer a human form approached Miles, silhouetted at first against the light from the front doors. Jogging in precise double time, the shape resolved into a tall, hard-bodied man in sweat pants, T-shirt, and running shoes. He had clearly just come in off some condition-maintaining five-kilometer run, with maybe a few hundred push-ups thrown in for dessert. Iron-grey hair, iron-hard eyes; he might have been a particularly dyspeptic drill sergeant. He stopped short to stare down at Miles, startlement compressing to a thin-lipped frown.

Miles stood with his legs slightly apart, threw back his head, and stared up with equal force. The man seemed totally oblivious to Miles's collar tabs. Exasperated, Miles snapped, "Are all the keepers on vacation, or is anybody actually running this bloody zoo?"

The man's eyes sparked, as if their iron had struck flint; they ignited a little warning light in Miles's brain, one mouthy moment too late. *Hi, there, sir!* cried the hysterical commenter in the back of Miles's mind, with a skip, bow, and flourish. *I'm your newest exhibit!* Miles suppressed the voice ruthlessly. There wasn't a trace of humor in any line of that seamed countenance looming over him.

With a cold flare of his carved nostril, the Base Commander glared down at Miles and growled, "*I* run it, Ensign."

*   *   *

Dense fog was rolling in off the distant, muttering sea by the time Miles finally found his way to his new quarters. The officers' barracks and all around it were plunged into a grey, frost-scummed obscurity. Miles decided it was an omen.

Oh, God, it was going to be a long winter.

CHAPTER TWO

Rather to Miles's surprise, when he arrived at Ahn's office next morning at an hour he guessed might represent beginning-of-shift, he found the lieutenant awake, sober, and in uniform. Not that the man looked precisely well; pasty-faced, breathing stertoriously, he sat huddled, staring slit-eyed at a computer-colorized weather vid. The holo zoomed and shifted dizzyingly at signals from the remote controller he clutched in one damp and trembling palm.

"Good morning, sir." Miles softened his voice out of mercy, and closed the door behind himself without slamming it.

"Ha?" Ahn looked up, and returned his salute automatically. "What the devil are you, ah . . . ensign?"

"I'm your replacement, sir. Didn't anyone tell you I was coming?"

"Oh, yes!" Ahn brightened right up. "Very good, come in." Miles, already in, smiled briefly instead. "I meant to meet you on the shuttlepad," Ahn went on. "You're early. But you seem to have found your way all right."

"I came in yesterday, sir."

"Oh. You should have reported in."

"I did, sir."

"Oh." Ahn squinted at Miles in worry. "You did?"

"You promised you'd give me a complete technical

17

orientation to the office this morning, sir," Miles
added, seizing the opportunity.

"Oh," Ahn blinked. "Good." The worried look
faded slightly. "Well, ah . . ." Ahn rubbed his face,
looking around. He confined his reaction to Miles's
physical appearance to one covert glance, and, perhaps deciding they must have gotten the social
duties of introduction out of the way yesterday,
plunged at once into a description of the equipment
lining the wall, in order from left to right.

Literally an introduction, all the computers had
women's names. Except for a tendency to talk about
his machines as though they were human, Ahn
seemed coherent enough as he detailed his job, only
drifting into randomness, then hung-over silence,
when he accidently strayed from the topic. Miles
steered him gently back to weather with pertinent
questions, and took notes. After a bewildered brown-
ian trip around the room Ahn rediscovered his office
procedural disks at last, stuck to the undersides of
their respective pieces of equipment. He made fresh
coffee on a non-regulation brewer—named "Geor-
gette"—parked discreetly in a corner cupboard, then
took Miles up to the roof of the building to show
him the data-collection center there.

Ahn went over the assorted meters, collectors, and
samplers rather perfunctorily. His headache seemed
to be growing worse with the morning's exertions.
He leaned heavily on the corrosion-proof railing surrounding the automated station and squinted out at
the distant horizon. Miles followed him around dutifully as he appeared to meditate deeply for a few
minutes on each of the cardinal compass points. Or
maybe that introspective look just meant he was getting ready to throw up.

It was pale and clear this morning, the sun up—
the sun had been up since two hours after midnight,
Miles reminded himself. They were just past the
shortest nights of the year for this latitude. From

this rare high vantage point, Miles gazed out with interest at Lazkowski Base and the flat landscape beyond.

Kyril Island was an egg-shaped lump about seventy kilometers wide and 160 kilometers long, and over five hundred kilometers from the next land of any description. *Lumpy and brown* described most of it, both base and island. The majority of the nearby buildings, including Miles's officers' barracks, were dug in, topped with native turf. Nobody had bothered with agricultural terraforming here. The island retained its original Barrayaran ecology, scarred by use and abuse. Long fat rolls of turf covered the barracks for the winter infantry trainees, now empty and silent. Muddy water-filled ruts fanned out to deserted marksmanship ranges, obstacle courses, and pocked live-ammo practice areas.

To the near-south, the leaden sea heaved, muting the sun's best efforts at sparkle. To the far north a grey line marked the border of the tundra at a chain of dead volcanic mountains.

Miles had taken his own officers' short course in winter maneuvers in the Black Escarpment, mountain country deep in Barrayar's second continent; plenty of snow, to be sure, and murderous terrain, but the air had been dry and crisp and stimulating. Even today, at high summer, the sea dampness seemed to creep up under his loose parka and gnaw his bones at every old break. Miles shrugged against it, without effect.

Ahn, still draped over the railing, glanced sideways at Miles at this movement. "So tell me, ah, ensign, are you any relation to *the* Vorkosigan? I wondered, when I saw the name on the orders the other day."

"My father," said Miles shortly.

"Good God." Ahn blinked and straightened, then sagged self-consciously back onto his elbows as before. "Good God," he repeated. He chewed his lip in fascination, dulled eyes briefly alight with honest curiosity. "What's he really like?"

What an impossible question, Miles thought in exasperation. Admiral Count Aral Vorkosigan. The colossus of Barrayaran history in this half-century. Conqueror of Komarr, hero of the ghastly retreat from Escobar. For sixteen years Lord Regent of Barrayar during Emperor Gregor's troubled minority; the Emperor's trusted Prime Minister in the four years since. Destroyer of Vordarian's Pretendership, engineer of the peculiar victory of the third Cetagandan war, unshaken tiger-rider of Barrayar's murderous internecine politics for the past two decades. *The* Vorkosigan.

I have seen him laugh in pure delight, standing on the dock at Vorkosigan Surleau and yelling instructions over the water, the morning I first sailed, dumped, and righted the skimmer by myself. I have seen him weep till his nose ran, more dead drunk than you were yesterday, Ahn, the night we got the word Major Duvallier was executed for espionage. I have seen him rage, so brick-red we feared for his heart, when the reports came in fully detailing the stupidities that led to the last riots in Solstice. I have seen him wandering around Vorkosigan House at dawn in his underwear, yawning and prodding my sleepy mother into helping him find two matching socks. He's not like anything, Ahn. He's the original.

"He cares about Barrayar," Miles said aloud at last, as the silence grew awkward. "He's . . . a hard act to follow." *And, oh yes, his only child is a deformed mutant. That, too.*

"I should think so." Ahn blew out his breath in sympathy, or maybe it was nausea.

Miles decided he could tolerate Ahn's sympathy. There seemed no hint in it of the damned patronizing pity, nor, interestingly, of the more common repugnance. *It's because I'm his replacement here,*

Miles decided. *I could have two heads and he'd still be overjoyed to meet me.*

"That what you're doing, following in the old man's footsteps?" said Ahn equably. And more dubiously, looking around, "Here?"

"I'm Vor," said Miles impatiently. "I serve. Or at any rate, I try to. Wherever I'm put. That was the deal."

Ahn shrugged bafflement, whether at Miles or at the vagaries of the Service that had sent him to Kyril Island Miles could not tell. "Well." He pushed himself up off the rail with a grunt. "No wah-wah warnings today."

"No what warnings?"

Ahn yawned, and tapped an array of figures— pulled out of thin air, as far as Miles could tell—into his report panel representing hour-by-hour predictions for today's weather. "Wah-wah. Didn't anybody tell you about the wah-wah?"

"No. . . ."

"They should have, first thing. Bloody dangerous, the wah-wah."

Miles began to wonder if Ahn was trying to diddle his head. Practical jokes could be a subtle enough form of victimization to penetrate even the defenses of rank, Miles had found. The honest hatred of a beating inflicted only physical pain.

Ahn leaned across the railing again to point. "You notice all those ropes, strung from door to door between buildings? That's for when the wah-wah comes up. You hang onto 'em to keep from being blown away. If you lose your grip, don't fling out your arms to try and stop yourself. I've seen more guys break their wrists that way. Go into a ball and roll."

"What the hell's a wah-wah? Sir."

"Big wind. Sudden. I've seen it go from dead calm to 160 kilometers, with a temperature drop from ten degrees cee above freezing to twenty below, in seven minutes. It can last from ten minutes to two days. They almost always blow up from the northwest, here, when conditions are right. The remote station on the coast gives us about a twenty-minute warning. We blow a siren. That means you must never let yourself get caught without your cold gear, or less than fifteen minutes away from a bunker. There's bunkers all around the grubs' practice fields out there." Ahn waved his arm in that direction. He seemed quite serious, even earnest. "You hear that siren, you run like hell for cover. The size you are, if you ever got picked up and blown into the sea, they'd never find you again."

"All right," said Miles, silently resolving to check out these alleged facts in the base's weather records at the first opportunity. He craned his neck for a look at Ahn's report panel. "Where did you read off those numbers from, that you just entered on there?"

Ahn stared at his report panel in surprise. "Well— they're the right figures."

"I wasn't questioning their accuracy," said Miles patiently. "I want to know how you came up with them. So I can do it tomorrow, while you're still here to correct me."

Ahn waved his free hand in an abortive, frustrated gesture. "Well. . . ."

"You're not just making them up, are you?" said Miles in suspicion.

"No!" said Ahn. "I hadn't thought about it, but . . . it's the way the day smells, I guess." He inhaled deeply, by way of demonstration.

Miles wrinkled his nose and sniffed experimentally. Cold, sea salt, shore slime, damp and mildew. Hot circuits in some of the blinking, twirling array of instruments beside him. The mean temperature, barometric pressure, and humidity of the present moment, let alone that of eighteen hours into the future, was not to be found in the olfactory information pressing on *his* nostrils. He jerked his thumb at the meteorological array. "Does this thing have any sort of a smell-o-meter to duplicate whatever it is you're doing?"

Ahn looked genuinely nonplussed, as if his internal system, whatever it was, had been dislocated by his sudden self-consciousness of it. "Sorry, Ensign Vorkosigan. We have the standard computerized projections, of course, but to tell you the truth I haven't used 'em in years. They're not accurate enough."

Miles stared at Ahn, and came to a horrid realization. Ahn wasn't lying, joking, or making this up. It was the fifteen years experience, gone subliminal, that was carrying out these subtle functions. A backlog of experience Miles could not duplicate. *Nor would I wish to,* he admitted to himself.

Later in the day, while explaining with perfect truth that he was orienting himself to the systems, Miles covertly checked out all of Ahn's startling assertions in the base meteorological archives. Ahn hadn't been kidding about the wah-wah. Worse, he hadn't been kidding about the computerized projections. The automated system produced local predictions of 86% accuracy, dropping to 73% at a week's long-range forecast. Ahn and his magical nose ran an accuracy of 96%, dropping to 94% at a week's range. *When Ahn leaves, this island is going to experience an 11 to 21% drop in forecast accuracy. They're going to notice.*

Weather Officer, Camp Permafrost, was clearly a more responsible position than Miles had at first realized. The weather here could be deadly.

And this guy is going to leave me alone on this island with six thousand armed men, and tell me to go sniff for wah-wahs?

On the fifth day, when Miles had just about decided that his first impression had been too harsh,

Ahn relapsed. Miles waited an hour for Ahn and his nose to show up at the weather office to begin the day's duties. At last he pulled the routine readings from the substandard computerized system, entered them anyway, and went hunting.

He ran Ahn down at last still in his bunk, in his quarters in the officers' barracks, sodden and snoring, stinking of stale . . . fruit brandy? Miles shuddered. Shaking, prodding, and yelling in Ahn's ear failed to rouse him. He only burrowed deeper into his bedclothes and noxious miasma, moaning. Miles regretfully set aside visions of violence, and prepared to carry on by himself. He'd be on his own soon enough anyway.

He limp-marched off to the motor pool. Yesterday Ahn had taken him on a scheduled maintenance patrol of the five remote-sensor weather stations nearest the base. The outlying six had been planned for today. Routine travel around Kyril Island was accomplished in an all-terrain vehicle called a scat-cat, which had turned out to be almost as much fun to drive as an anti-grav sled. Scat-cats were ground-hugging iridescent teardrops that tore up the tundra, but were guaranteed not to blow away in the wah-wah winds. Base personnel, Miles had been given to understand, had grown extremely tired of picking lost anti-grav sleds out of the frigid sea.

The motor pool was another half-buried bunker like most of the rest of Lazkowski Base, only bigger. Miles routed out the corporal, what's his name, Olney, who'd signed Ahn and himself out the previous day. The tech who assisted him, driving the scat-cat up from the underground storage to the entrance, also looked faintly familiar. Tall, black fatigues, dark hair—that described eighty percent of the men on the base—it wasn't until he spoke that his heavy accent cued Miles. He was one of the sotto voce commenters Miles had overheard on the shuttlepad. Miles schooled himself not to react.

Miles went over the vehicle's supply check-list carefully before signing for it, as Ahn had taught him. All scat-cats were required to carry a complete cold-survival kit at all times. Corporal Olney watched with faint contempt as Miles fumbled around finding everything. *All right, so I'm slow,* Miles thought irritably. *New and green. This is the only way I'm gonna get less new and green. Step by step.* He controlled his self-consciousness with an effort. Previous painful experience had taught him it was a most dangerous frame of mind. *Concentrate on the task, not the bloody audience. You've always had an audience. Probably always will.*

Miles spread out the map flimsy across the scat-cat's shell, and pointed out his projected itinerary to the corporal. Such a briefing was also safety SOP, according to Ahn. Olney grunted acknowledgment with a finely-tuned look of long-suffering boredom, palpable but just short of something Miles would be forced to notice.

The black-clad tech, Pattas, watching over Miles's uneven shoulder, pursed his lips and spoke. "Oh, Ensign *sir.*" Again, the emphasis fell just short of irony. "You going up to Station Nine?"

"Yes?"

"You might want to be sure and park your scat-cat, uh, out of the wind, in that hollow just below the station." A thick finger touched the map flimsy on an area marked in blue. "You'll see it. That way your scat-cat'll be sure of re-starting."

"The power pack in these engines is rated for space," said Miles. "How could it not re-start?"

Olney's eye lit, then went suddenly very neutral. "Yes, but in case of a sudden wah-wah, you wouldn't want it to blow away."

I'd blow away before it would. "I thought these scat-cats were heavy enough not to."

"Well, not *away*, but they have been known to blow *over*," murmured Pattas.

"Oh. Well, thank you."

Corporal Olney coughed. Pattas waved cheerfully as Miles drove out.

Miles's chin jerked up in the old nervous tic. He took a deep breath and let his hackles settle, as he turned the scat-cat away from the base and headed cross-country. He powered up to a more satisfying speed, lashing through the brown bracken-like growth. He had been what, a year and a half? two years? at the Imperial Academy proving and re-proving his competence to every bloody man he crossed every time he did anything. The third year had perhaps spoiled him, he was out of practice. Was it going to be like this every time he took up a new post? Probably, he reflected bitterly, and powered up a bit more. But he'd known that would be part of the game when he'd demanded to play.

The weather was almost warm today, the pale sun almost bright, and Miles almost cheerful by the time he reached Station Six, on the eastern shore of the island. It was a pleasure to be alone for a change, just him and his job. No audience. Time to take his time and get it right. He worked carefully, checking power packs, emptying samplers, looking for signs of corrosion, damage, or loose connections in the equipment. And if he dropped a tool, there was no one about to make comments about spastic mutants. With the fading tension, he made fewer fumbles, and the tic vanished. He finished, stretched, and inhaled the damp air benignly, reveling in the unaccustomed luxury of solitude. He even took a few minutes to walk along the shoreline, and notice the intricacies of the small sea-life washed up there.

One of the samplers in Station Eight was damaged, a humidity-meter shattered. By the time he'd replaced it he realized his itinerary timetable had been overly optimistic. The sun was slanting down toward green twilight as he left Station Eight. By the time he reached Station Nine, in an area of mixed tundra and rocky outcrops near the northern shore, it was almost dark.

Station Ten, Miles reconfirmed by checking his map flimsy by pen-light, was up in the volcanic mountains among the glaciers. Best not try to go hunting it in the dark. He would wait out the brief four hours till dawn. He reported his change-of-plan via comm-link to the base, 160 kilometers to the south. The man on duty did not sound terribly interested. Good.

With no watchers, Miles happily seized the opportunity to try out all that fascinating gear packed in the back of the scat-cat. Far better to practice now, when conditions were good, than in the middle of some later blizzard. The little two-man bubble shelter, when set up, seemed almost palatial for Miles's short and lonely splendor. In winter it was meant to be insulated with packed snow. He positioned it downwind of the scat-cat, parked in the recommended low spot a few hundred meters from the weather station, which was perched on a rocky outcrop.

Miles reflected on the relative weight of the shelter versus the scat-cat. A vid that Ahn had shown him of a typical wah-wah remained vivid in his mind. The portable latrine traveling sideways in the air at a hundred kilometers an hour had been particularly impressive. Ahn hadn't been able to tell him if there'd been anyone in it at the time the vid was shot. Miles took the added precaution of attaching the shelter to the scat-cat with a short chain. Satisfied, he crawled inside.

The equipment was first-rate. He hung a heat-tube from the roof and touched it on, and basked in its glow, sitting cross-legged. Rations were of the better grade. A pull tab heated a compartmentalized tray of stew with vegetables and rice. He mixed an acceptable fruit drink from the powder supplied. After eating and stowing the remains, he settled on a comfortable pad, shoved a book-disk into his viewer, and prepared to read away the short night.

He had been rather tense these last few weeks. These last few years. The book-disk, a Betan novel of manners which the Countess had recommended to him, had nothing whatsoever to do with Barrayar, military maneuvers, mutation, politics, or the weather. He didn't even notice what time he dozed off.

He woke with a start, blinking in the thick darkness gilded only with the faint copper light from the heat-tube. He felt he had slept long, yet the transparent sectors of the bubble-shelter were pitchy black. An unreasoning panic clogged his throat. Dammit, it didn't matter if he overslept, it wasn't like he would be late for an exam, here. He glanced at the glowing readout on his wrist chrono.

It ought to be broad daylight.

The flexible walls of the shelter were pressing inward. Not one-third of the original volume remained, and the floor was wrinkled. Miles shoved one finger against the thin cold plastic. It yielded slowly, like soft butter, and retained the dented impression. What the *hell* . . . ?

His head was pounding, his throat constricted; the air was stuffy and wet. It felt just like . . . like oxygen depletion and CO_2 excess in a space emergency. Here? The vertigo of his disorientation seemed to tilt the floor.

The floor *was* tilted, he realized indignantly, pulled deeply downward on one side, pinching one of his legs. He convulsed from its grip. Fighting the CO_2-induced panic, he lay back, trying to breathe slower and think faster.

I'm underground. Sunk in some kind of quicksand. Quick-mud. Had those two bloody bastards at the motor-pool set him up for this? He'd fallen for it, fallen right in it.

Slow-mud, maybe. The scat-cat hadn't settled

noticeably in the time it had taken him to set up this shelter. Or he would have twigged to the trap. Of course, it had been dark. But if he'd been settling for hours, asleep . . .

Relax, he told himself frantically. The tundra surface, the free air, might be a mere ten centimeters overhead. Or ten meters . . . *relax!* He felt about the shelter for something to use as a probe. There'd been a long, telescoping, knife-bitted tube for sampling glacier ice. Packed in the scat-cat. Along with the comm link. Now located, Miles gauged by the angle of the floor, about two-and-a-half meters down and to the west of his present location. It was the scat-cat that was dragging him down. The bubble-shelter alone might well have floated in the tundra-camouflaged mud-pond. If he could detach the chain, might it rise? Not fast enough. His chest felt stuffed with cotton. He had to break through to air soon, or asphyxiate. Womb, tomb. Would his parents be there to watch, when he was found at last, when this grave was opened, scat-cat and shelter winched out of the bog by heavy hovercab . . . his body frozen rictus-mouthed in this hideous parody of an amniotic sac . . . *relax.*

He stood, and shoved upward against the heavy roof. His feet sank in the pulpy floor, but he was able to jerk loose one of the bubble's interior ribs, now bent in an overstrained curve. He almost passed out from the effort, in the thick air. He found the top edge of the shelter's opening, and slid his finger down the burr-catch just a few centimeters. Just enough for the pole to pass through. He'd feared the black mud would pour in, drowning him at once, but it only crept in extrusive blobs, to fall with oozing plops. The comparison was obvious and repulsive. *God, and I thought I'd been in deep shit before.*

He shoved the rib upward. It resisted, slipping in his sweating palms. Not ten centimeters. Not twenty.

A meter, a meter and a third, and he was running short on probe. He paused, took a new grip, shoved again. Was the resistance lessening? Had he broken through to the surface? He heaved it back and forth, but the sucking slime sealed it still.

Maybe, maybe a little less than his own height between the top of the shelter and breath. Breath, death. How long to claw through it? How fast did a hole in this stuff close? His vision was darkening, and it wasn't because the light was going dim. He turned the heat tube off and stuck it in the front pocket of his jacket. The uncanny dark shook him with horror. Or perhaps it was the CO_2. Now or never.

On an impulse, he bent and loosened his boot-catches and belt buckle, then zipped open the burr by feel. He began to dig like a dog, heaving big globs of mud down into the little space left in the bubble. He squeezed through the opening, braced himself, took his last breath, and pressed upward.

His chest was pulsing, his vision a red blur, when his head broke the surface. Air! He spat black muck and bracken bits, and blinked, trying with little success to clear his eyes and nose. He fought one hand up, then the other, and tried to pull himself up horizontal, flat like a frog. The cold confounded him. He could feel the muck closing around his legs, numbing like a witch's embrace. His toes pressed at full extension on the shelter's roof. It sank and he rose a centimeter. The last of the leverage he could get by pushing. Now he must pull. His hands closed over bracken. It gave. More. More. He was making a little progress, the cold air raking his grateful throat. The witch's grip tightened. He wriggled his legs, futilely, one last time. All right, now. Heave!

His legs slid out of his boots and pants, his hips sucked free, and he rolled away. He lay spread-eagled for maximum support on the treacherous surface, face up to the grey swirling sky. His uniform jacket and long underwear were soaked with slime, and he'd lost one thermal sock, as well as both boots and his trousers.

It was sleeting.

They found him hours later, curled around the dimming heat-tube, crammed into an eviscerated equipment bay in the automated weather station. His eye-sockets were hollow in his black-streaked face, his toes and ears white. His numb purple fingers jerked two wires across each other in a steady, hypnotic tattoo, the Service emergency code. To be read out in bursts of static in the barometric pressure meter in base's weather room. If and when anybody bothered to look at the suddenly-defective reading from this station, or noticed the pattern in the white noise.

His fingers kept twitching in this rhythm for minutes after they pulled him free of his little box. Ice cracked off the back of his uniform jacket as they tried to straighten his body. For a long time they could get no words from him at all, only a shivering hiss. Only his eyes burned.

CHAPTER THREE

Floating in the heat tank in the base infirmary, Miles considered crucifixion for the two saboteurs from the motor pool from several angles. Such as upside-down. Dangling over the sea at low altitude from an anti-grav sled. Better still, staked out face-up in a bog in a blizzard. . . . But by the time his body had warmed up, and the corpsman had pulled him out of the tank to dry, be reexamined, and eat a supervised meal, his head had cooled.

It hadn't been an assassination attempt. And therefore, not a matter he was compelled to turn over to Simon Illyan, dread Chief of Imperial Security and Miles's father's left-hand man. The vision of the sinister officers from ImpSec coming to take those two jokers away, far away, was lovely, but impractical, like shooting mice with a maser cannon. Anyway, where could ImpSec possibly send them that was worse than here?

They'd meant his scat-cat to bog, to be sure, while he serviced the weather station, and for Miles to have the embarrassment of calling the base for heavy equipment to pull it out. Embarrassing, not lethal. They could not have—no one could have—forseen Miles's inspired safety-conscious precaution with the chain, which was in the final analysis what had almost killed him. At most it was a matter for Service Security, bad enough, or for normal discipline.

He dangled his toes over the side of his bed, one of a row in the empty infirmary, and pushed the last of his food around on his tray. The corpsman wandered in, and glanced at the remains.

"You feeling all right now, sir?"

"Fine," said Miles morosely.

"You, uh, didn't finish your tray."

"I often don't. They always give me too much."

"Yeah, I guess you are pretty, um . . ." The corpsman made a note on his report panel, leaned over to examine Miles's ears, and bent to inspect his toes, rolling them between practiced fingers. "It doesn't look like you're going to lose any pieces, here. Lucky."

"Do you treat a lot of frostbite?" *Or am I the only idiot?* Present evidence would suggest it.

"Oh, once the grubs arrive, this place'll be crammed. Frostbite, pneumonia, broken bones, contusions, concussions . . . gets real lively, come winter. Wall-to-wall moro—unlucky trainees. And a few unlucky instructors, that they take down with 'em." The corpsman stood, and tapped a few more entries on his panel. "I'm afraid I have to mark you as recovered now, sir."

"Afraid?" Miles raised his brows inquiringly.

The corpsman straightened, in the unconscious posture of a man transmitting official bad news. That old they-told-me-to-say-this-it's-not-my-fault look. "You are ordered to report to the base commander's office as soon as I release you, sir."

Miles considered an immediate relapse. No. Better to get the messy parts over with. "Tell me, corpsman, has anyone else ever sunk a scat-cat?"

"Oh, sure. The grubs lose about five or six a season. Plus minor bog-downs. The engineers get real pissed about it. The commandant promised them next time he'd . . . ahem!" The corpsman lost his voice.

Wonderful, thought Miles. Just great. He could see it coming. It wasn't like he couldn't see it coming.

*   *   *

Miles dashed back to his quarters for a quick change of clothing, guessing a hospital robe might be inappropriate for the coming interview. He immediately found he had a minor quandry. His black fatigues seemed too relaxed, his dress greens too formal for office wear anywhere outside Imperial HQ at Vorbarr Sultana. His undress greens' trousers and half-boots were still at the bottom of the bog. He had only brought one of each uniform style with him; his spares, supposedly in transit, had not yet arrived.

He was hardly in a position to borrow from a neighbor. His uniforms were privately made to his own fit, at approximately four times the cost of Imperial issue. Part of that cost was for the effort of making them indistinguishable on the surface from the machine cut, while at the same time partially masking the oddities of his body through subtleties of hand-tailoring. He cursed under his breath, and shucked on his dress greens, complete with mirror-polished boots to the knees. At least the boots obviated the leg braces.

General Stanis Metzov, read the sign on the door, *Base Commander.* Miles had been assiduously avoiding the base commander ever since their first unfortunate encounter. This had not been hard to do in Ahn's company, despite the pared population of Kyril Island this month; Ahn avoided everybody. Miles now wished he'd tried harder to strike up conversations with brother officers in mess. Permitting himself to stay isolated, even to concentrate on his new tasks, had been a mistake. In five days of even the most random conversation, someone must surely have mentioned Kyril Island's voracious killer mud.

A corporal manning the comconsole in an antechamber ushered Miles through to the inner office. He must now try to work himself back round to Metzov's good side, assuming the general had one. Miles

needed allies. General Metzov looked across his desk
unsmiling as Miles saluted and stood waiting.

Today, the general was aggressively dressed in
black fatigues. At Metzov's altitude in the hierarchy,
this stylistic choice usually indicated a deliberate
indentification with The Fighting Man. The only
concession to his rank was their pressed neatness.
His decorations were stripped down to a mere modest three, all high combat commendations. Pseudo-
modest; pruned of the surrounding foliage, they
leapt to the eye. Mentally, Miles applauded, even
envied, the effect. Metzov looked his part, the combat commander, absolutely, unconsciously natural.

*A fifty-fifty chance with the uniform, and I had to
guess wrong,* Miles fumed as Metzov's eye traveled
sarcastically down, and back up, the subdued glitter
of his dress greens. All right, so Metzov's eyebrows
signaled, Miles now looked like some kind of Vorish
headquarters twit. Not that that wasn't another
familiar type. Miles decided to decline the roasting
and cut Metzov's inspection short by forcing the
opening. "Yes, sir?"

Metzov leaned back in his chair, lips twisting. "I
see you found some pants, Ensign Vorkosigan. And,
ah . . . riding boots, too. You know, there are no
horses on this island."

None at Imperial Headquarters, either, Miles
thought irritably. *I didn't design the damn boots.* His
father had once suggested his staff officers must need
them for riding hobbyhorses, high horses, and night-
mares. Unable to think of a useful reply to the general's sally, Miles stood in dignified silence, chin lifted,
parade rest. "Sir."

Metzov leaned forward, clasping his hands, abandoning his heavy humor, eyes gone hard again. "You
lost a valuable, fully-equipped scat-cat as a result
of leaving it parked in an area clearly marked as a
Permafrost Inversion Zone. Don't they teach map-
reading at the Imperial Academy any more, or is it

to be all diplomacy in the New Service—how to drink tea with the ladies?"

Miles called up the map in his mind. He could see it clearly. "The blue areas were labelled P.I.Z. Those initials were not defined. Not in the key or anywhere."

"Then I take it you also failed to read your manual."

He'd been buried in manuals ever since he'd arrived. Weather office procedurals, equipment tech-specs . . . "Which one, sir?"

"Lazkowski Base Regulations."

Miles tried frantically to remember if he'd ever seen such a disk. "I . . . think Lieutenant Ahn may have given me a copy . . . night before last." Ahn had in fact dumped an entire carton of disks out on Miles's bed in officers' quarters. He was doing some preliminary packing, he'd said, and was willing Miles his library. Miles had read two weather disks before going to sleep that night. Ahn, clearly, had returned to his own cubicle to do a little preliminary celebrating. The next morning Miles had taken the scat-cat out. . . .

"And you haven't read it yet?"

"No, sir."

"Why not?"

I was set up, Miles's thought wailed. He could feel the highly-interested presence of Metzov's clerk, undismissed, standing witness by the door behind him. Making this a public, not a private, dressing-down. And if only he'd read the damn manual, would those two bastards from the motor pool even have been able to set him up? Will or nill, he was going to get down-checked for this one. "No excuse, sir."

"Well, Ensign, in Chapter Three of Lazkowski Base Regulations you will find a complete descrip-tion of all the permafrost zones, together with the rules for avoiding them. You might look into it, when you can spare a little leisure from . . . drinking tea."

"Yes, sir." Miles's face was set like glass. The general had a right to skin him with a vibra-knife, if he chose—in private. The authority lent Miles by his uniform barely balanced the deformities that made him a target of Barrayar's historically-grounded, intense genetic prejudices. A public humiliation that sapped that authority before men he must also command came very close to an act of sabotage. Deliberate, or unconscious?

The general was only warming up. "The Service may still provide warehousing for excess Vor lordlings at Imperial Headquarters, but out here in the real world, where there's fighting to be done, we have no use for drones. Now, I fought my way up through the ranks. I saw casualties in Vordarian's Pretendership before you were born—"

I was a casualty in Vordarian's Pretendership before I was born, thought Miles, his irritation growing wilder. The soltoxin gas that had almost killed his pregnant mother and made Miles what he was, had been a purely military poison.

"—and I fought the Komarr Revolt. You infants who've come up in the past decade and more have no concept of combat. These long periods of unbroken peace weaken the Service. If they go on much longer, when a crisis comes there'll be no one left who's had any real practice in a crunch."

Miles's eyes crossed slightly, from internal pressure. *Then should His Imperial Majesty provide a war every five years, as a convenience for the advancement of his officers' careers?* His mind boggled slightly over the concept of "real practice." Had Miles maybe acquired his first clue why this superb-looking officer had washed up on Kyril Island?

Metzov was still expanding, self-stimulated. "In a real combat situation, a soldier's equipment is vital. It can be the difference between victory and defeat.

A man who loses his equipment loses his effectiveness as a soldier. A man disarmed in a technological war might as well be a woman, useless! And you disarmed yourself!"

Miles wondered sourly if the general would then agree that a woman armed in a technological war might as well be a man . . . no, probably not. Not a Barrayaran of his generation.

Metzov's voice descended again, dropping from military philosophy to the immediately practical. Miles was relieved. "The usual punishment for a man bogging a scat-cat is to dig it out himself. By hand. I understand that won't be feasible, since the depth to which you sank yours is a new camp record. Nevertheless, you will report at 1400 to Lieutenant Bonn of Engineering, to assist him as he sees fit."

Well, that was certainly fair. And would probably be educational, too. Miles prayed this interview was winding down. *Dismissed, now?* But the general fell silent, squinty-eyed and thoughtful.

"For the damage you did to the weather station," Metzov began slowly, then sat up more decisively—his eyes, Miles could almost swear, lighting with a faint red glow, the corner of that seamed mouth twitching upward, "you will supervise basic-labor detail for one week. Four hours a day. That's in addition to your other duties. Report to Sergeant Neuve, in Maintenance, at 0500 daily."

A slight choked inhalation sounded from the corporal still standing behind Miles, which Miles could not interpret. Laughter? Horror?

But . . . *unjust!* And he would lose a significant fraction of the precious time remaining to decant technical expertise from Ahn. . . . "The damage I did to the weather station was not a stupid accident like the scat-cat, sir! It was necessary to my survival."

General Metzov fixed him with a very cold eye. "Make that six hours a day, Ensign Vorkosigan."

Miles spoke through his teeth, words jerked out

as though by pliers. "Would you have preferred the interview you'd be having right now if I'd permitted myself to freeze, sir?"

Silence fell, very dead. Swelling, like a road-killed animal in the summer sun.

"You are dismissed, Ensign," General Metzov hissed at last. His eyes were glittering slits.

Miles saluted, about-faced, and marched, stiff as any ancient ramrod. Or board. Or corpse. His blood beat in his ears; his chin jerked upward. Past the corporal, who was standing at attention doing a fair imitation of a waxwork. Out the door, out the outer door. Alone at last in the Administration Building's lower corridor.

Miles cursed himself silently, then out loud. He really had to try to cultivate a more normal attitude toward senior officers. It was his bloody upbringing that lay at the root of the problem, he was sure. Too many years of tripping over herds of generals, admirals, and senior staff at Vorkosigan House, at lunch, dinner, all hours. Too much time sitting quiet as a mouse, cultivating invisibility, permitted to listen to their extremely blunt argument and debate on a hundred topics. He saw them as they saw each other, maybe. When a normal ensign looked at his commander, he ought to see a god-like being, not a, a . . . future subordinate. New ensigns were supposed to be a sub-human species anyway.

And yet . . . *What is it about this guy Metzov?* He'd met others of the type before, of assorted political stripes. Many of them were cheerful and effective soldiers, as long as they stayed out of politics. As a party, the military conservatives had been eclipsed ever since the bloody fall of the cabal of officers responsible for the disastrous Escobar invasion, over two decades ago. But the danger of revolution from the far right, some would-be junta assembling to save the Emperor from his own government, remained quite real in Miles's father's mind, he knew.

So, was it some subtle political odor emanating from Metzov that had raised the hairs on the back of Miles's neck? Surely not. A man of real political subtlety would seek to use Miles, not abuse him. *Or are you just pissed because he stuck you on some humiliating garbage detail?* A man didn't have to be politically extreme to take a certain sadistic joy in sticking it to a representative of the Vor class. Could be Metzov had been diddled in the past himself by some arrogant Vor lord. Political, social, genetic . . . the possibilities were endless.

Miles shook the static from his head, and limped off to change to his black fatigues and locate Base Engineering. No help for it now, he was sunk deeper than his scat-cat. He'd simply have to avoid Metzov as much as possible for the next six months. Anything Ahn could do so well, Miles could surely do too.

Lieutenant Bonn prepared to probe for the scat-cat. The engineering lieutenant was a slight man, maybe twenty-eight or thirty years old, with a craggy face surfaced with pocked sallow skin, reddened by the climate. Calculating brown eyes, competent-looking hands, and a sardonic air which, Miles sensed, might be permanent and not merely directed at himself. Bonn and Miles squished about atop the bog, while two engineering techs in black insulated coveralls sat perched on their heavy hovercab, safely parked on a nearby rocky outcrop. The sun was pale, the endless wind cold and damp.

"Try about there, sir," Miles suggested, pointing, trying to estimate angles and distances in a place he had only seen at dusk. "I think you'll have to go down at least two meters."

Lieutenant Bonn gave him a joyless look, raised his long metal probe to the vertical, and shoved it into the bog. It jammed almost immediately. Miles frowned puzzlement. Surely the scat-cat couldn't have floated upward. . . .

Bonn, looking unexcited, leaned his weight into the rod and twisted. It began to grind downward.

"What did you run into?" Miles asked.

"Ice," Bonn grunted. " 'Bout three centimeters thick right now. We're standing on a layer of ice, underneath this surface crud, just like a frozen lake except it's frozen mud."

Miles stamped experimentally. Wet, but solid. Much as it had felt when he had camped on it.

Bonn, watching him, added, "The ice thickness varies with the weather. From a few centimeters to solid-to-the-bottom. Midwinter, you could park a freight shuttle on this bog. Come summer, it thins out. It can thaw from seeming-solid to liquid in a few hours, when the temperature is just right, and back again."

"I . . . think I found that out."

"Lean," ordered Bonn laconically, and Miles wrapped his hands around the rod and helped shove. He could feel the scrunch as it scraped past the ice layer. And if the temperature had dropped a little more, the night he'd sunk himself, and the mud re-frozen, would he have been able to punch up through the icy seal? He shuddered inwardly, and zipped his parka half-up, over his black fatigues.

"Cold?" said Bonn.

"Thinking."

"Good. Make it a habit." Bonn touched a control, and the rod's sonic probe beeped at a teeth-aching frequency. The readout displayed a bright teardrop shape a few meters over. "There it is." Bonn eyed the numbers on the readout. "It's really down in there, isn't it? I'd let you dig it out with a teaspoon, ensign, but I suppose winter would set in before you were done." He sighed, and stared down at Miles as though picturing the scene.

Miles could picture it too. "Yes, sir," he said carefully.

They pulled the probe back out. Cold mud slicked the surface under their gloved hands. Bonn marked the spot and waved to his techs. "Here, boys!" They waved back, hopped down off the hovercab, and swung within. Bonn and Miles scrambled well out of the way, onto the rocks toward the weather station.

The hovercab whined into the air and positioned itself over the bog. Its heavy-duty space-rated tractor beam punched downward. Mud, plant matter, and ice geysered out in all directions with a roar. In a couple of minutes, the beam had created an oozing crater, with a glimmering pearl at the bottom. The crater's sides began to slump inward at once, but the hovercab operator narrowed and reversed his beam, and the scat-cat rose, noisily sucking free from its matrix. The limp bubble shelter dangled repellently from its chain. The hovercab set its load down delicately in the rocky area, and landed beside it.

Bonn and Miles trooped over to view the sodden remains. "You weren't in that bubble-shelter, were you, ensign?" said Bonn, prodding it with his toe.

"Yes, sir, I was. Waiting for daylight. I . . . fell asleep."

"But you got out before it sank."

"Well, no. When I woke up, it was all the way under."

Bonn's crooked eyebrows rose. "How far?"

Miles's flat hand found the level of his chin.

Bonn looked startled. "How'd you get out of the suction?"

"With difficulty. And adrenalin, I think. I slipped out of my boots and pants. Which reminds me, may I take a minute and look for my boots, sir?"

Bonn waved a hand, and Miles trudged back out onto the bog, circling the ring of muck spewed from the tractor beam, keeping a safe distance from the now water-filling crater. He found one mud-coated boot, but not the other. Should he save it, on the off-chance he might have one leg amputated someday? It would probably be the wrong leg. He sighed, and climbed back up to Bonn.

Bonn frowned down at the ruined boot dangling from Miles's hand. "You could have been killed," he said in a tone of realization.

"Three times over. Smothered in the bubble shelter, trapped in the bog, or frozen waiting for rescue."

Bonn gave him a penetrating stare. "Really." He walked away from the deflated shelter, idly, as if seeking a wider view. Miles followed. When they were out of earshot of the techs, Bonn stopped and scanned the bog. Conversationally, he remarked, "I heard—unofficially—that a certain motor-pool tech named Pattas was bragging to one of his mates that he'd set you up for this. And you were too stupid to even realize you'd been had. That bragging could have been . . . not too bright, if you'd been killed."

"If I'd been killed, it wouldn't have mattered if he'd bragged or not," Miles shrugged. "What a Service investigation missed, I flat guarantee the Imperial Security investigation would have found."

"You knew you'd been set up?" Bonn studied the horizon.

"Yes."

"I'm surprised you didn't call Imperial Security in, then."

"Oh? Think about it, sir."

Bonn's gaze returned to Miles, as if taking inventory of his distasteful deformities. "You don't add up for me, Vorkosigan. Why did they let you in the Service?"

"Why d'you think?"

"Vor privilege."

"Got it in one."

"Then why are you here? Vor privilege gets sent to HQ."

"Vorbarr Sultana is lovely this time of year," said Miles agreeably. And how was his cousin Ivan enjoying it right now? "But I want ship duty."

"And you couldn't arrange it?" said Bonn sceptically.

"I was told to earn it. That's why I'm here. To prove I can handle the Service. Or . . . not. Calling in a wolf pack from ImpSec within a week of my arrival to turn the base and everyone on it inside-out looking for assassination conspiracies—where, I judge, none exist—would not advance me toward my goal. No matter how entertaining it might be." Messy charges, his word against their two words— even if Miles had pushed it to a formal investigation, with fast-penta to prove him right, the ruckus could hurt him far more in the long run than his two tormentors. No. No revenge was worth the *Prince Serg*.

"The motor pool is in Engineering's chain of command. If Imperial Security fell on it, they'd also fall on me." Bonn's brown eyes glinted.

"You're welcome to fall on anyone you please, sir. But if you have unofficial ways of receiving information, it follows you must have unofficial ways of sending it, too. And after all, you've only my word for what happened." Miles hefted his useless single boot, and heaved it back into the bog.

Thoughtfully, Bonn watched it arc and splash down in a pool of brown melt-water. "A Vor lord's word?"

"Means nothing, in these degenerate days." Miles bared his teeth in a smile of sorts. "Ask anyone."

"Huh." Bonn shook his head, and started back toward the hovercab.

Next morning Miles reported to the maintenance shed for the second half of the scat-cat retrieval job, cleaning all the mud-caked equipment. The sun was bright today, and had been up for hours, but Miles's body knew it was only 0500. An hour into his task he'd begun to warm up, feel better, and get into the rhythm of the thing.

At 0630, the deadpan Lieutenant Bonn arrived, and delivered two helpers unto Miles.

"Why, Corporal Olney. Tech Pattas. We meet again." Miles smiled with acid cheer. The pair exchanged an uneasy look. Miles kept his demeanor absolutely even.

He then kept everyone, starting with himself, moving briskly. The conversation seemed to automatically limit itself to brief, wary technicalities. By the time Miles had to knock off and go report to Lieutenant Ahn, the scat-cat and most of the gear had been restored to better condition than Miles had received it.

He wished his two helpers, now driven to near-twitchiness by uncertainty, an earnest good-day. Well, if they hadn't figured it out by now, they were hopeless. Miles wondered bitterly why he seemed to have so much better luck establishing rapport with bright men like Bonn. Cecil had been right, if Miles couldn't figure out how to command the dull as well, he'd never make it as a Service officer. Not at Camp Permafrost, anyway.

The following morning, the third of his official punishment seven, Miles presented himself to Sergeant Neuve. The sergeant in turn presented Miles with a scat-cat full of equipment, a disk of the related equipment manuals, and the schedule for drain and culvert maintenance for Lazkowski Base. Clearly, it was to be another learning experience. Miles wondered if General Metzov had selected this task personally. He rather thought so.

On the bright side, he had his two helpers back again. This particular civil engineering task had apparently never fallen on Olney or Pattas before either, so they had no edge of superior knowledge with which to trip Miles. They had to stop and read the manuals first too. Miles swotted procedures and directed operations with a good cheer that edged toward manic as his helpers became glummer.

There was, after all, a certain fascination to the clever drain-cleaning devices. And excitement. Flushing pipes with high pressure could produce some surprising effects. There were chemical compounds that had some quite military properties, such as the ability to dissolve anything instantly including human flesh. In the following three days Miles learned more about the infrastructure of Lazkowski Base than he'd ever imagined wanting to know. He'd even calculated the point where one well-placed charge could bring the entire system down, if he ever decided he wanted to destroy the place.

On the sixth day, Miles and his team were sent to clear a blocked culvert out by the grubs' practice fields. It was easy to spot. A silver sheet of water lapped the raised roadway on one side; on the other only a feeble trickle emerged to creep away down the bottom of a deep ditch.

Miles took a long telescoping pole from the back of their scat-cat, and probed down into the water's opaque surface. Nothing seemed to be blocking the flooded end of the culvert. Whatever it was must be jammed farther in. Joy. He handed the pole back to Pattas and wandered over to the other side of the road, and stared down into the ditch. The culvert, he noted, was something over half a meter in diameter. "Give me a light," he said to Olney.

He shucked his parka and tossed it into the scat-cat, and scrambled down into the ditch. He aimed his light into the aperture. The culvert evidently curved slightly; he couldn't see a damned thing. He sighed, considering the relative width of Olney's shoulders, Pattas's, and his own.

Could there be anything further from ship duty than this? The closest he'd come to anything of a sort was spelunking in the Dendarii Mountains.

Earth and water, versus fire and air. He seemed to be building up a helluva supply of yin, the balancing yang to come had better be stupendous.

He gripped the light tighter, dropped to hands and knees, and shinnied into the drain.

The icy water soaked the trouser knees of his black fatigues. The effect was numbing. Water leaked around the top of one of his gloves. It felt like a knife blade on his wrist.

Miles meditated briefly on Olney and Pattas. They had developed a cool, reasonably efficient working relationship over the last few days, based, Miles had no illusions, on a fear of God instilled in the two men by Miles's good angel Lieutenant Bonn. How did Bonn accomplish that quiet authority, anyway? He had to figure that one out. Bonn was good at his job, for starters, but what else?

Miles scraped round the curve, shone his light on the clot, and recoiled, swearing. He paused a moment to regain control of his breath, examined the blockage more closely, and backed out.

He stood up in the bottom of the ditch, straightening his spine vertebra by creaking vertebra. Corporal Olney stuck his head over the road's railing, above. "What's in there, ensign?"

Miles grinned up at him, still catching his breath. "Pair of boots."

"That's all?" said Olney.

"Their owner is still wearing 'em."

CHAPTER FOUR

Miles called the base surgeon on the scat-cat's comm link, urgently requesting his presence with forensic kit, body bag, and medical transport. Miles and his crew then blocked the upper end of the drain with a plastic signboard forcibly borrowed from the empty practice field beyond. Now so thoroughly wet and cold that it made no difference, Miles crawled back into the culvert to attach a rope to the anonymous booted ankles. When he emerged, the surgeon and his corpsman had arrived.

The surgeon, a big, balding man, peered dubiously into the drainpipe. "What could you see in there, ensign? What happened?"

"I can't see anything from this end but legs, sir," Miles reported. "He's got himself wedged in there but good. Drain crud up above him, I'd guess. We'll have to see what spills out with him."

"What the hell was he doing in there?" The surgeon scratched his freckled scalp.

Miles spread his hands. "Seems a peculiar way to commit suicide. Slow and chancy, as far as drowning yourself goes."

The surgeon raised his eyebrows in agreement. Miles and the surgeon had to lend their weight on the rope to Olney, Pattas, and the corpsman before the stiff form wedged in the culvert began to scrape free.

"He's *stuck*," observed the corpsman, grunting. The body jerked out at last with a gush of dirty water. Pattas and Olney stared from a distance; Miles glued himself to the surgeon's shoulder. The corpse, dressed in sodden black fatigues, was waxy and blue. His collar tabs and the contents of his pockets identified him as a private from Supply. His body bore no obvious wounds, but for bruised shoulders and scraped hands.

The surgeon spoke clipped, negative preliminaries into his recorder. No broken bones, no nerve disruptor blisters. Preliminary hypothesis, death from drowning or hypothermia or both, within the last twelve hours. He flipped off his recorder and added over his shoulder, "I'll be able to tell for sure when we get him laid out back at the infirmary."

"Does this sort of thing happen often around here?" Miles inquired mildly.

The surgeon shot him a sour look. "I slab a few idiots every year. What d'you expect, when you put five thousand kids between the ages of eighteen and twenty together on an island and tell 'em to go play war? I admit, this one seems to have discovered a completely new method of slabbing himself. I guess you never see it all."

"You think he did it to himself, then?" True, it would be real tricky to kill a man and *then* stuff him in there.

The surgeon wandered over to the culvert and squatted, and stared into it. "So it would seem. Ah, would you take one more look in there, ensign, just in case?"

"Very well, sir." Miles hoped it was the last trip. He'd never have guessed drain cleaning would turn out to be so . . . thrilling. He slithered all the way under the road to the leaky board, checking every centimeter, but found only the dead man's dropped hand light. So. The private had evidently entered the pipe on purpose. With intent. What intent? Why go culvert-crawling in the middle of the night in the middle of a heavy rainstorm? Miles skinned back out and turned the light over to the surgeon.

Miles helped the corpsman and surgeon bag and load the body, then had Olney and Pattas raise the blocking board and return it to its original location. Brown water gushed, roaring, from the bottom end of the culvert and roiled away down the ditch. The surgeon paused with Miles, leaning on the road railing and watching the water level drop in the little lake.

"Think there might be another one at the bottom?" Miles inquired morbidly.

"This guy was the only one listed as missing on the morning report," the surgeon replied, "so probably not." He didn't look like he was willing to bet on it, though.

The only thing that did turn up, as the water level fell, was the private's soggy parka. He'd clearly tossed it over the railing before entering the culvert, from which it had fallen or blown into the water. The surgeon took it away with him.

"You're pretty cool about that," Pattas noted, as Miles turned away from the back of the medical transport and the surgeon and corpsman drove off.

Pattas was not that much older than Miles himself. "Haven't you ever had to handle a corpse?"

"No. You?"

"Yes."

"Where?"

Miles hesitated. Events of three years ago flickered through his memory. The brief months he'd been caught in desperate combat far from home, having accidently fallen in with a space mercenary force, was not a secret to be mentioned or even hinted at here. Regular Imperial troops despised mercenaries anyway, alive or dead. But the Tau Verde campaign had surely taught him the difference between "practice" and "real," between war and war games, and that death had subtler vectors than direct touch. "Before," said Miles dampingly. "Couple of times."

Pattas shrugged, veering off. "Well," he allowed grudgingly over his shoulder, "at least you're not afraid to get your hands dirty. Sir."

Miles's brows crooked, bemused. *No. That's not what I'm afraid of.*

Miles marked the drain "cleared" on his report panel, turned the scat-cat, their equipment, and a very subdued Olney and Pattas back in to Sergeant Neuve in Maintenance, and headed for the officers' barracks. He'd never wanted a hot shower more in his entire life.

He was squelching down the corridor toward his quarters when another officer stuck his head out a door. "Ah, Ensign Vorkosigan?"

"Yes?"

"You got a vid call a while ago. I encoded the return for you."

"Call?" Miles stopped. "Where from?"

"Vorbarr Sultana."

Miles felt a chill in his belly. Some emergency at home? "Thanks." He reversed direction, and bee-lined for the end of the corridor and the vidconsole booth that the officers on this level shared.

He slid damply into the seat and punched up the message. The number was not one he recognized. He entered it, and his charge code, and waited. It chimed several times, then the vidplate hissed to life. His cousin Ivan's handsome face materialized over it, and grinned at him.

"Ah, Miles. There you are."

"Ivan! Where the devil are you? What is this?"

"Oh, I'm at home. And that doesn't mean my mother's. I thought you might like to see my new flat."

Miles had the vague, disoriented sensation that he'd somehow tapped a line into some parallel universe, or alternate astral plane. Vorbarr Sultana, yes. He'd lived in the capital himself, in a previous incarnation. Eons ago.

Ivan lifted his vid pick-up, and aimed it around, dizzyingly. "It's fully furnished. I took over the lease from an Ops captain who was being transferred to Komarr. A real bargain. I just got moved in yesterday. Can you see the balcony?"

Miles could see the balcony, drenched in late afternoon sunlight the color of warm honey. The Vorbarr Sultana skyline rose like a fairytale city, swimming in the summer haze beyond. Scarlet flowers swarmed over the railing, so red in the level light they almost hurt his eyes. Miles felt like drooling into his shirtpocket, or bursting into tears. "Nice flowers," he choked.

"Yeah, m'girlfriend brought 'em."

"Girlfriend?" Ah yes, human beings had come in two sexes, once upon a time. One smelled much better than the other. Much. "Which one?"

"Tatya."

"Have I met her?" Miles struggled to remember.

"Naw, she's new."

Ivan stopped waving the vid pick-up around, and reappeared over the vid-plate. Miles's exacerbated senses settled slightly. "So how's the weather up there?" Ivan peered at him more closely. "Are you wet? What have you been doing?"

"Forensic . . . plumbing," Miles offered after a pause.

"What?" Ivan's brow wrinkled.

"Never mind." Miles sneezed. "Look, I'm glad to see a familiar face and all that," he was, actually—a painful, strange gladness, "but I'm in the middle of my duty day, here."

"I got off-shift a couple of hours ago," Ivan remarked. "I'm taking Tatya out for dinner in a bit. You just caught me. So just tell me quick, how's life in the infantry?"

"Oh, great. Lazkowski Base is the real thing, y'know." Miles did not define what real thing. "Not a . . . warehouse for excess Vor lordlings like Imperial Headquarters."

"I do my job!" said Ivan, sounding slightly stung. "Actually, you'd like my job. We process information. It's amazing, all the stuff Ops accesses in a day's time. It's like being on top of the world. It would be just your speed."

"Funny. I've thought that Lazkowski Base would be just yours, Ivan. Suppose they could have got our orders reversed?"

Ivan tapped the side of his nose and sniggered. "I wouldn't tell." His humor sobered in a glint of real concern. "You, ah, take care of yourself up there, eh? You really don't look so good."

"I've had an unusual morning. If you'd sod off, I could go get a shower."

"Oh, right. Well, take care."

"Enjoy your dinner."

"Right-oh. 'Bye."

Voices from another universe. At that, Vorbarr Sultana was only a couple of hours away by sub-orbital flight. In theory. Miles was obscurely comforted, to be reminded that the whole planet hadn't shrunk to the lead-grey horizons of Kyril Island, even if his part of it seemed to have.

Miles found it difficult to concentrate on the weather, the rest of that day. Fortunately his superior didn't much notice. Since the scat-cat sinking Ahn had tended to maintain a guilty, nervous silence around Miles except when directly prodded for specific information. When his duty-day ended Miles headed straight for the infirmary.

The surgeon was still working, or at least sitting, at his desk console when Miles poked his head around the doorframe. "Good evening, sir."

The surgeon glanced up. "Yes, ensign? What is it?"

Miles took this as sufficient invitiation despite the unencouraging tone of voice, and slipped within. "I was wondering what you'd found out about that fellow we pulled from the culvert this morning."

The surgeon shrugged. "Not that much to find out. His ID checked. He died of drowning. All the physical and metabolic evidence—stress, hypothermia, the hematomas—are consistent with his being stuck in there for a bit less than half an hour before death. I've ruled it death by misadventure."

"Yes, but why?"

"Why?" The surgeon's eyebrows rose. "He slabbed himself, you'll have to ask him, eh?"

"Don't you want to find out?"

"To what purpose?"

"Well . . . to know, I guess. To be sure you're right."

The surgeon gave him a dry stare.

"I'm not questioning your medical findings, sir," Miles added hastily. "But it was just so damn weird. Aren't you curious?"

"Not any more," said the surgeon. "I'm satisfied it wasn't suicide or foul play, so whatever the details, it comes down to death from stupidity in the end, doesn't it?"

Miles wondered if that would have been the surgeon's final epitaph on him, if he'd sunk himself with the scat-cat. "I suppose so, sir."

Standing outside the infirmary afterward in the damp wind, Miles hesitated. The corpse, after all, was not Miles's personal property. Not a case of finders-keepers. He'd turned the situation over to the proper authority. It was out of his hands now. And yet . . .

There were still several hours of daylight left. Miles was having trouble sleeping anyway, in these almost-endless days. He returned to his quarters, pulled on sweat pants and shirt and running shoes, and went jogging.

The road was lonely, out by the empty practice fields. The sun crawled crabwise toward the horizon. Miles broke from a jog back to a walk, then to a slower walk. His leg-braces chafed, beneath his pants. One of these days very soon he would take the time to get the brittle long bones in his legs replaced with synthetics. At that, elective surgery might be a quasi-legitimate way to lever himself off Kyril Island, if things got too desperate before his six months were up. It seemed like cheating, though.

He looked around, trying to imagine his present surroundings in the dark and heavy rain. If he had been the private, slogging along this road about midnight, what would he have seen? What could possibly have attracted the man's attention to the ditch? Why the hell had he come out here in the middle of the night in the first place? This road wasn't on the way to anything but an obstacle course and a firing range.

There was the ditch . . . no, his ditch was the next one, a little farther on. Four culverts pierced the raised roadway along this half-kilometer straight stretch. Miles found the correct ditch and leaned on the railing, staring down at the now-sluggish trickle of drain water. There was nothing attractive about it now, that was certain. Why, why, why . . . ?

Miles sloped along up the high side of the road, examining the road surface, the railing, the sodden brown bracken beyond. He came to the curve and turned back, studying the opposite side. He arrived back at the first ditch, on the baseward end of the straight stretch, without discovering any view of charm or interest.

Miles perched on the railing and meditated. All right, time to try a little logic. What overwhelming emotion had led the private to wedge himself in the drain, despite the obvious danger? Rage? What had he been pursuing? Fear? What could have been pursuing him? Error? Miles knew all about error. What if the man had picked the wrong culvert . . . ?

Impulsively, Miles slithered down into the first ditch. Either the man had been methodically working his way through all the culverts—if so, had he been working from the base out, or from the practice fields back?—or else he had missed his intended target in the dark and rain and got into the wrong one. Miles would give them all a crawl-through if he had to, but he preferred to be right the first time. Even if there wasn't anybody watching. This culvert was slightly wider in diameter than the second, lethal one. Miles pulled his hand light from his belt, ducked within, and began examining it centimeter by centimeter.

"Ah," he breathed in satisfaction, midway beneath the road. There was his prize, stuck to the upper side of the culvert's arc with sagging tape. A package, wrapped in waterproof plastic. How *interesting*. He slithered out and sat in the mouth of the culvert, careless of the damp but carefully out of view from the road above.

He placed the packet on his lap and studied it with pleasurable anticipation, as if it had been a birthday present. Could it be drugs, contraband, classified documents, criminal cash? Personally, Miles hoped for classified documents, though it was hard to imagine anyone classifying anything on Kyril Island except maybe the efficiency reports. Drugs would be all right, but a spy ring would be just wonderful. He'd be a Security hero—his mind raced ahead, already plotting the next move in his covert investigation. Following the dead man's trail through subtle clues to some ringleader, who knew how high up? The dramatic arrests, maybe a commendation from Simon Illyan himself. . . . The package was lumpy, but crackled slightly—plastic flimsies?

Heart hammering, he eased it open—and slumped in stunned disappointment. A pained breath, half-laugh, half-moan, puffed from his lips.

Pastries. A couple of dozen lisettes, a kind of miniature popover glazed and stuffed with candied fruit, made, traditionally, for the midsummer day celebration. Month and a half old stale pastries. What a cause to die for. . . .

Miles' imagination, fueled by knowledge of barracks life, sketched in the rest readily enough. The private had received this package from some sweetheart/mother/sister, and sought to protect it from his ravenous mates, who would have wolfed it all down in seconds. Perhaps the man, starved for home, had been rationing them out to himself morsel by morsel in a lingering masochistic ritual, pleasure and pain mixed with each bite. Or maybe he'd just been saving them for some special occasion.

Then came the two days of unusual heavy rain, and the man had begun to fear for his secret treasure's, ah, liquidity margin. He'd come out to rescue his cache, missed the first ditch in the dark, gone at the second in desperate determination as the waters rose, realized his mistake too late. . . .

Sad. A little sickening. But not *useful*. Miles sighed, and bundled the lisettes back up, and trotted off with the package under his arm, back to the base to turn it over to the surgeon.

The surgeon's only comment, when Miles caught up with him and explained his findings, was "Yep. Death from stupidity, all right." Absently, he bit into a lisette and sniffed.

Miles's time on maintenance detail ended the next day without his finding anything in the sewers of greater interest than the drowned man. It was probably just as well. The following day Ahn's office corporal arrived back from his long leave. Miles discovered that the corporal, who'd been working the weather office for some two years, was a ready reservoir of the greater part of the information Miles had spent the last two weeks busting his brains to learn. He didn't have Ahn's nose, though.

Ahn actually left Camp Permafrost sober, walking up the transport's ramp under his own power. Miles went to the shuttle pad to see him off, not certain if he was glad or sorry to see the weatherman go. Ahn looked happy, though, his lugubrious face almost illuminated.

"So where are you headed, once you turn in your uniforms?" Miles asked him.

"The equator."

"Ah? Where on the equator?"

"*Anywhere* on the equator," Ahn replied with fervor.

Miles trusted he'd at least pick a spot with a suitable land mass under it.

Ahn hesitated on the ramp, looking down at Miles. "Watch out for Metzov," he advised at last.

This warning seemed remarkably late, not to mention maddeningly vague. Miles gave Ahn an exasperated look, up from under his raised eyebrows. "I doubt I'll be much featured on his social calendar."

Ahn shifted uncomfortably. "That's not what I meant."

"What do you mean?"

"Well . . . I don't know. I once saw . . ."

"What?"

Ahn shook his head. "Nothing. It was a long time ago. A lot of crazy things were happening, at the height of the Komarr revolt. But it's better that you should stay out of his way."

"I've had to deal with old martinets before."

"Oh, he's not exactly a martinet. But he's got a streak of . . . he can be a funny kind of dangerous. Don't ever really threaten him, huh?"

"Me, threaten Metzov?" Miles's face screwed up in bafflement. Maybe Ahn wasn't as sober as he smelled after all. "Come on, he can't be that bad, or they'd never put him in charge of trainees."

"He doesn't command the grubs. They have their own hierarchy comes in with 'em—the instructors report to their own commander. Metzov's just in charge of the base's permanent physical plant. You're a pushy little sod, Vorkosigan. Just don't . . . ever push him to the edge, or you'll be sorry. And that's all I'm going to say." Ahn shut his mouth determinedly, and headed up the ramp.

I'm already sorry, Miles thought of calling after him. Well, his punishment week was over now. Perhaps Metzov had meant the labor detail to humiliate Miles, but actually it had been quite interesting. Sinking his scat-cat, now, that had been humiliating. *That* he had done to himself. Miles waved one last time to Ahn as he disappeared into the transport shuttle, shrugged, and headed back across the tarmac toward the now-familiar admin building.

It took a full couple of minutes, after Miles's corporal had left the weather office for lunch, for Miles to yield to the temptation to scratch the itch Ahn had planted in his mind, and punch up Metzov's public record on the comconsole. The mere listing of the base commander's dates, assignments, and promotions was not terribly informative, though a little knowledge of history filled in between the lines.

Metzov had entered the Service some thirty-five years ago. His most rapid promotions had occurred, not surprisingly, during the conquest of the planet Komarr about twenty-five years ago. The wormhole-rich Komarr system was Barrayar's sole gate to the greater galactic wormhole route nexus. Komarr had proved its immense strategic importance to Barrayar earlier in the century, when its ruling oligarchy had accepted a bribe to let a Cetagandan invasion fleet pass through its wormholes and descend on Barrayar. Throwing the Cetagandans back out again had consumed a Barrayaran generation. Barrayar had turned its bloody lesson around in Miles's father's day. As an unavoidable side effect of securing Komarr's gates, Barrayar had been transformed from backwater cul-de-sac to a minor but significant galactic power, and was still wrestling with the consequences.

Metzov had somehow managed to end up on the correct side during Vordarian's Pretendership, a purely Barrayaran attempt to wrest power from then-five-year-old Emperor Gregor and his Regent, two decades past—picking the wrong side in that civil affray would have been Miles's first guess why such an apparently competent officer had ended up marking out his later years on ice on Kyril Island. But the dead halt to Metzov's career seemed to come during the Komarr Revolt, some sixteen years ago now. No hint in this file as to why, but for a cross-reference to another file. An Imperial Security code, Miles recognized. Dead end there.

Or maybe not. Lips compressed thoughtfully, Miles punched through another code on his comconsole.

"Operations, Commodore Jollif's office," Ivan began formally as his face materialized over the comconsole vid plate, then, "Oh, hello, Miles. What's up?"

"I'm doing a little research. Thought you might help me out."

"I should have known you wouldn't call me at HQ just to be sociable. So what d'you want?"

"Ah . . . do you have the office to yourself, just at present?"

"Yeah, the old man's stuck in committee. Nice little flap—a Barrayaran-registered freighter got itself impounded in the Hegen Hub—at Vervain Station—for suspicion of espionage."

"Can we get at it? Threaten rescue?"

"Not past Pol. No Barrayaran military vessels may jump through their wormholes, period."

"I thought we were sort of friends with Pol."

"Sort of. But the Vervani have been threatening to break off diplomatic relations with Pol, so the Polians are being extra-cautious. Funny thing about it, the freighter in question isn't even one of our real agents. Seems to be a completely manufactured accusation."

Wormhole route politics. Jumpship tactics. Just the sort of challenge his Imperial Academy courses had trained Miles to meet. Furthermore, it was probably warm on those spaceships and space stations. Miles sighed envy.

Ivan's eyes narrowed in belated suspicion. "Why do you ask if I'm alone?"

"I want you to pull a file for me. Ancient history, not current events," Miles reassured him, and reeled off the code-string.

"Ah." Ivan's hand started to tap it out, then stopped. "Are you crazy? That's an Imperial Security file. No can do!"

"Of course you can, you're right there, aren't you?"

Ivan shook his head smugly. "Not any more. The whole ImpSec file system's been made super-secure. You can't transfer data out of it except through a coded filter-cable, which you must physically attach. Which I would have to sign for. Which I would have to explain why I wanted it and produce authorization. You got an authorization for this? Ha. I thought not."

Miles frowned frustration. "Surely you can call it up on the internal system."

"On the internal system, yes. What I can't do is connect the internal system to any external system for a data dump. So you're out of luck."

"You got an internal system comconsole in that office?"

"Sure."

"So," said Miles impatiently, "call up the file, turn

your desk around, and let the two vids talk to each other. You can do that, can't you?"

Ivan scratched his head. "Would that work?"

"Try it!" Miles drummed his fingers while Ivan dragged his desk around and fiddled with focus. The signal was degraded but readable. "There, I thought so. Scroll it up for me, would you?"

Fascinating, utterly fascinating. The file was a collection of secret reports from an ImpSec investigation into the mysterious death of a prisoner in Metzov's charge, a Komarran rebel who had killed his guard and himself been killed while attempting to escape. When ImpSec had demanded the Komarran's body for an autopsy, Metzov had turned over cremated ashes and an apology; if only he had been told a few hours earlier the body was wanted, etc. The investigating officer hinted at charges of illegal torture—perhaps in revenge for the death of the guard?—but was unable to amass enough evidence to obtain authorization to fast-penta the Barrayaran witnesses, including a certain Tech-ensign Ahn. The investigating officer had lodged a formal protest of his superior officer's decision to close the case, and there it ended. Apparently. If there was any more to the story it existed only in Simon Illyan's remarkable head, a secret file Miles was not about to attempt to access. And yet Metzov's career had stopped, literally, cold.

"Miles," Ivan interrupted for the fourth time, "I really don't think we should be doing this. This is slit-your-throat-before-reading stuff, here."

"If we shouldn't do it, we shouldn't be *able* to do it. You'd still have to have the cable for flash-downloading. No real spy would be dumb enough to sit there inside Imperial HQ by the hour and scroll stuff through by hand, waiting to be caught and shot."

"That does it." Ivan killed the Security file with a swat of his hand. The vid image wavered wildly as

Ivan dragged his desk back around, followed by scrubbing noises as he frantically rubbed out the tracks in his carpet with his boot. "I didn't do this, you hear?"

"I didn't mean you. *We're* not spies." Miles subsided glumly. "Still . . . I suppose somebody ought to tell Illyan about the little hole they overlooked in his Security arrangements."

"Not me!"

"Why not you? Put it in as a brilliant theoretical suggestion. Maybe you'll earn a commendation. Don't tell 'em we actually did it, of course. Or maybe we were just testing your theory, eh?"

"You," said Ivan severely, "are career-poison. Never darken my vid-plate again. Except at home, of course."

Miles grinned, and permitted his cousin to escape. He sat awhile in the office, watching the colorful weather holos flicker and change, and thinking about his base commander, and the kinds of accidents that could happen to defiant prisoners.

Well, it had all been very long ago. Metzov himself would probably be retiring in another five years, with his status as a double-twenty-years-man and a pension, to merge into the population of unpleasant old men. Not so much a problem to be solved as to be outlived, at least by Miles. His ultimate purpose at Lazkowski Base, Miles reminded himself, was to escape Lazkowski Base, silently as smoke. Metzov would be left behind in time.

In the next weeks Miles settled into a tolerable routine. For one thing, the grubs arrived. All five thousand of them. Miles's status rose on their shoulders, to that of almost-human. Lazkowski Base suffered its first real snow of the season, as the days shortened, plus a mild wah-wah lasting half a day, both of which Miles managed to predict accurately in advance.

Even more happily, Miles was completely displaced as the most famous idiot on the island (an unwelcome notoriety earned by the scat-cat sinking) by a group of grubs who managed one night to set their barracks on fire while lighting fart-flares. Miles's strategic suggestion at the officers' fire-safety meeting next day that they tackle the problem with a logistical assault on the enemy's fuel supply, i.e., eliminate red-bean stew from the menu, was shot down with one icy glower from General Metzov. Though in the hallway later, an earnest captain from Ordnance stopped Miles to thank him for trying.

So much for the glamour of the Imperial Service. Miles took to spending long hours alone in the weather office, studying chaos theory, his readouts, and the walls. Three months down, three to go. It was getting darker.

CHAPTER FIVE

Miles was out of bed and half dressed before it penetrated his sleep-stunned brain that the galvanizing klaxon was not the wah-wah warning. He paused with a boot in his hand. Not fire or enemy attack, either. Not his department, then, whatever it was. The rhythmic blatting stopped. They were right, silence was golden.

He checked the glowing digital clock. It claimed midevening. He'd only been asleep about two hours, having fallen into bed exhausted after a long trip up-island in a snow storm to repair wind damage to Weather Station Eleven. The comm link by his bed was not blinking its red call light to inform him of any surprise duties he must carry out. He could go back to bed.

Silence was *baffling*.

He pulled on the second boot and stuck his head out his door. A couple of other officers had done the same, and were speculating to each other on the cause of the alarm. Lieutenant Bonn emerged from his quarters and strode down the hall, jerking on his parka. His face looked strained, half-worry, half-annoyance.

Miles grabbed his own parka and galloped after him. "You need a hand, Lieutenant?"

Bonn glanced down at him, and pursed his lips. "I might," he allowed.

Miles fell in beside him, secretly pleased by

65

Bonn's implicit judgment that he might in fact be useful. "So what's up?"

"Some sort of accident in a toxic stores bunker. If it's the one I think, we could have a real problem."

They exited the double-doored heat-retaining vestibule from the officers' quarters into a night gone crystal cold. Fine snow squeaked under Miles's boots and swept along the ground in a faint east wind. The brightest stars overhead held their own against the base's lights. The two men slid into Bonn's scat-cat, their breath smoking until the canopy-defrost cut in. Bonn headed west out of the base at high acceleration.

A few kilometers past the last practice fields, a row of turf-topped barrows hunched in the snow. A cluster of vehicles was parked at the end of one bunker—a couple of scat-cats, including the one belonging to the base fire marshall, and medical transport. Hand-lights moved among them. Bonn slewed in and pulled up, and popped his door. Miles followed him, crunching rapidly across the packed ice.

The surgeon was directing a pair of corpsmen, who were loading a foil-blanketed shape and a second coverall-clad soldier who shivered and coughed onto the med transport. "All of you, put everything you're wearing into the destruct bin when you hit the door," he called after them. "Blankets, bedding, splints, everything. Full decontamination showers for you all before you even start to worry about that broken leg of his. The pain-killer will hold him through it, and if it doesn't, ignore him and keep scrubbing. I'll be right behind you." The surgeon shuddered, turning away, whistling dismay through his teeth.

Bonn headed for the bunker door. "Don't open that!" the surgeon and the fire marshall called together. "There's nobody left inside," the surgeon added. "All evacuated now."

"What exactly happened?" Bonn scrubbed with a

gloved hand at the frosted window set in the door, in an effort to see inside.

"Couple of guys were moving stores, to make room for a new shipment coming in tomorrow," the fire marshall, a lieutenant named Yaski, filled him in rapidly. "They dumped their loader over, one got pinned underneath with a broken leg."

"That . . . took ingenuity," said Bonn, obviously picturing the mechanics of the loader in his mind.

"They had to have been horsing around," said the surgeon impatiently. "But that's not the worst of it. They took several barrels of fetaine over with them. And at least two broke open. The stuff's all over the place in there. We've sealed the bunker as best we could. Clean-up," the surgeon exhaled, "is your problem. I'm gone." He looked like he wanted to crawl out of his own skin, as well as his clothes. He waved, making quickly for his scat-cat to follow his corpsmen and their patients through medical decontamination.

"Fetaine!" Miles exclaimed in startlement. Bonn had retreated hastily from the door. Fetaine was a mutagenic poison invented as a terror weapon but never, so far as Miles knew, used in combat. "I thought that stuff was obsolete. Off the menu." His academy course in Chemicals and Biologicals had barely mentioned it.

"It is obsolete," said Bonn grimly. "They haven't made any in twenty years. For all I know this is the last stockpile on Barrayar. Dammit, those storage barrels shouldn't have broken open even if you'd dropped 'em out a shuttle."

"Those storage barrels are at least twenty years old, then," the marshall pointed out. "Corrosion?"

"In that case," Bonn craned his neck, "what about the rest of them?"

"Exactly," nodded Yaski.

"Isn't fetaine destroyed by heat?" Miles asked nervously, checking to make sure they were standing around discussing this upwind of the bunker. "Chemically dissociated into harmless components, I heard."

"Well, not exactly harmless," said Lieutenant Yaski. "But at least they don't unravel all the DNA in your balls."

"Are there any explosives stored in there, Lieutenant Bonn?" Miles asked.

"No, only the fetaine."

"If you tossed a couple of plasma mines through the door, would the fetaine all be chemically cracked before the roof melted in?"

"You wouldn't want the roof to melt in. Or the floor. If that stuff ever got loose in the permafrost . . . But if you set the mines on slow heat release, and threw a few kilos of neutral plas-seal in with 'em, the bunker might be self-sealing." Bonn's lips moved in silent calculation. ". . . Yeah, that'd work. In fact, that could be the safest way to deal with that crap. Particularly if the rest of the barrels are starting to lose integrity too."

"Depending on which way the wind is blowing," put in Lieutenant Yaski, looking back toward the base and then at Miles.

"We're expecting a light east wind with dropping temperatures till about 0700 tomorrow morning," Miles answered his look. "Then it'll shift around to the north and blow harder. Potential wah-wah conditions starting around 1800 tomorrow night."

"If we're going to do it that way, we'd better do it tonight, then," said Yaski.

"All right," said Bonn decisively. "I'll round up my crew, you round up yours. I'll pull the plans for the bunker, calculate the charges' release-rate, and meet you and the ordnance chief in Admin in an hour."

Bonn posted the fire marshall's sergeant as guard to keep everyone well away from the bunker. An unenviable duty, but not unbearable in present conditions, and the guard could retreat inside his scat-cat when the temperature dropped, toward midnight. Miles rode back with Bonn to the base Administration building to double-check his promises about wind direction at the weather office.

Miles ran the latest data through the weather computers, that he might present Bonn with the most refined possible update on predicted wind vectors over the next 26.7-hour Barrayaran day. But before he had the printout in his hand, he saw Bonn and Yaski out the window, down below, hurrying away from the Admin building into the dark. Perhaps they were meeting with the ordnance chief elsewhere? Miles considered chasing after them, but the new prediction was not significantly different from the older one. Did he really need to go watch them cauterize the poison dump? It could be interesting—educational—on the other hand, he had no real function there now. As his parents' only child—as the father, perhaps, of some future Count Vorkosigan—it was arguable if he even had the right to expose himself to such a vile mutagenic hazard for mere curiosity. There seemed no immediate danger to the base, till the wind shifted anyway. Or was cowardice masquerading as logic? Prudence was a virtue, he had heard.

Now thoroughly awake, and too rattled to even imagine recapturing sleep, he pottered around the weather office, and caught up on all the routine files he had set aside that morning in favor of the repairs junket. An hour of steady plugging finished off everything that even remotely looked like work. When he found himself compulsively dusting equipment and shelves, he decided it was time to go back to bed, sleep or no sleep. But a shifting light from the window caught his eye, a scat-cat pulling up out front.

Ah, Bonn and Yaski, back. Already? That had been fast, or hadn't they started yet? Miles tore off the plastic flimsy with the new wind readout and headed downstairs to the Base Engineering office at the end of the corridor.

Bonn's office was dark. But light spilled into the corridor from the Base Commander's office. Light, and angry voices rising and falling. Clutching the flimsy, Miles approached.

The door was open to the inner office. Metzov sat at his desk console, one clenched fist resting on the flickering colored surface. Bonn and Yaski stood tensely before him. Miles rattled the flimsy cautiously to announce his presence.

Yaski's head swivelled around, and his gaze caught Miles. "Send Vorkosigan, he's a mutant already, isn't he?"

Miles gave a vaguely-directed salute and said immediately, "Pardon me, sir, but no, I'm not. My last encounter with a military poison did teratogenic damage, not genetic. My future children should be as healthy as the next man's. Ah, send me where, sir?"

Metzov glowered across at Miles, but did not pursue Yaski's unsettling suggestion. Miles handed the flimsy wordlessly to Bonn, who glanced at it, grimaced, and stuffed it savagely into his trouser pocket.

"Of course I intended them to wear protective gear," continued Metzov to Bonn in irritation. "I'm not mad."

"I understood that, sir. But the men refuse to enter the bunker even with contamination gear," Bonn reported in a flat, steady voice. "I can't blame them. The standard precautions are inadequate for fetaine, in my estimation. The stuff has an incredibly high penetration value, for its molecular weight. Goes right through permeables."

"You can't *blame* them?" repeated Metzov in astonishment. "Lieutenant, you gave an order. Or you were supposed to."

"I did, sir, but—"

"But—you let them sense your own indecision. Your weakness. Dammit, when you give an order you have to give it, not dance around it."

"Why do we have to save this stuff?" said Yaski plaintively.

"We've been over that. It's our charge," Metzov grunted at him. "Our orders. You can't ask a man to give an obedience you don't give yourself."

What, blind? "Surely Research still has the recipe," Miles put in, feeling he was at last getting the alarming drift of this argument. "They can mix up more if they really want it. Fresh."

"Shut up, Vorkosigan," Bonn growled desperately out of the corner of his mouth, as General Metzov snapped, "Open your lip tonight with one more sample of your humor, Ensign, and I'll put you on charges."

Miles's lips closed over his teeth in a tight glassy smile. Subordination. The *Prince Serg*, he reminded himself. Metzov could go drink the fetaine, for all Miles cared, and it would be no skin off his nose. His clean nose, remember?

"Have you never heard of the fine old battlefield practice of shooting the man who disobeys your order, Lieutenant?" Metzov went on to Bonn.

"I . . . don't think I can make that threat, sir," said Bonn stiffly.

And besides, thought Miles, *we're not on a battlefield. Are we?*

"Techs!" said Metzov in a tone of disgust. "I didn't say threaten, I said shoot. Make one example, the rest will fall in line."

Miles decided he didn't much care for Metzov's brand of humor, either. Or was the general speaking literally?

"Sir, fetaine is a violent mutagen," said Bonn doggedly. "I'm not at all sure the rest would fall into line, no matter what the threat. It's a pretty unreasonable topic. I'm . . . a little unreasonable about it myself."

"So I see." Metzov stared at him coldly. His glare passed on to Yaski, who swallowed and stood straighter, his spine offering no concession. Miles tried to cultivate invisibility.

"If you're going to go on pretending to be military officers, you techs need a lesson in how to extract obedience from your men," Metzov decided. "Both of you go and assemble your crew in front of Admin in twenty minutes. We're going to have a little old-fashioned discipline parade."

"You're not—seriously thinking of shooting anyone, are you?" said Lieutenant Yaski in alarm.

Metzov smiled sourly. "I doubt I'll have to." He regarded Miles. "What's the outside temperature right now, Weather Officer?"

"Five degrees of frost, sir," replied Miles, careful now to speak only when spoken to.

"And the wind?"

"Winds from the east at nine kilometers per hour, sir."

"Very good." Metzov's eye gleamed wolfishly. "Dismissed, *gentlemen*. See if you can carry out your orders, this time."

General Metzov stood, heavily gloved and parka-bundled, beside the empty metal bannerpole in front of Admin, and stared down the half-lit road. Looking for what? Miles wondered. It was pushing midnight now. Yaski and Bonn were lining up their tech crews in parade array, some fifteen thermal-coveralled and parka-clad men.

Miles shivered, and not just from the cold. Metzov's seamed face looked angry. And tired. And old. And scary. He reminded Miles a bit of his grandfather on a bad day. Though Metzov was in fact younger than Miles's father; Miles had been a child of his father's middle age, some generational skew there. His grandfather, the old General Count Piotr himself, had sometimes seemed a refugee from another century. Now, the really old-fashioned discipline parades had involved lead-lined rubber hoses. How far back in Barrayaran history was Metzov's mind rooted?

Metzov smiled, a gloss over rage, and turned his head at a movement down the road. In a horribly cordial voice he confided to Miles, "You know, Ensign, there was a secret behind that carefully-cultivated interservice rivalry they had back on Old Earth. In the event of a mutiny you could always persuade the army to shoot the navy, or vice versa, when they could no longer discipline themselves. A hidden disadvantage to a combined Service like ours."

"Mutiny!" said Miles, startled out of his resolve to speak only when spoken to. "I thought the issue was poison exposure."

"It *was*. Unfortunately, due to Bonn's mishandling, it's now a matter of principle." A muscle jumped in Metzov's jaw. "It had to happen sometime, in the New Service. The Soft Service."

Typical Old Service talk, that, old men bullshitting each other about how tough they'd had it in the old days. "Principle, sir, what principle? It's *waste disposal*," Miles choked.

"It's a mass refusal to obey a direct order, Ensign. Mutiny by any barracks-lawyer's definition. Fortunately, this sort of thing is easy to dislocate, if you move quickly, while it's still small and confused."

The motion down the road resolved itself into a platoon of grubs in their winter-white camouflage gear, marching under the direction of a Base sergeant. Miles recognized the sergeant as part of Metzov's personal power-net, an old veteran who'd served under Metzov as far back as the Komarr Revolt, and who had moved on with his master.

The grubs, Miles saw, had been armed with lethal

nerve-disruptors, which were purely anti-personnel
hand weapons. For all the time they spent learning
about such things, the opportunity for even advanced
trainees such as these to lay hands on fully powered
deadly weapons was rare, and Miles could sense
their nervous excitement from here.

The sergeant lined the grubs up in a cross-fire
array around the stiff-standing techs, and barked an
order. They presented their weapons, and aimed
them, the silver bell-muzzles gleaming in the scattered light from the Admin building. A twitchy ripple ran through Bonn's men. Bonn's face was ghastly
white, his eyes glittering like jet.

"Strip," Metzov ordered through set teeth.

Disbelief, confusion; only one or two of the techs
grasped what was being demanded, and began to
undress. The others, with many uncertain glances
around, belatedly followed suit.

"When you are again ready to obey your orders,"
Metzov continued in a parade-pitched voice that carried to every man, "you may dress and go to work.
It's up to you." He stepped back, nodded to his
sergeant, and took up a pose of parade rest. "That'll
cool 'em off," he muttered to himself, barely loud
enough for Miles to catch. Metzov looked like he
fully expected to be out there no more than five
minutes; he looked like he was already thinking of
warm quarters and a hot drink.

Olney and Pattas were among the techs, Miles
noted, along with most of the rest of the Greek-
speaking cadre who had plagued Miles early on.
Others Miles had seen around, or talked to during
his private investigation into the background of the
drowned man, or barely knew. Fifteen naked men
starting to shiver violently as the dry snow whispered around their ankles. Fifteen bewildered faces
beginning to look terrified. Eyes shifted toward the
nerve-disruptors trained on them. *Give in*, Miles
urged silently. *It's not worth it*. But more than one

pair of eyes flickered at him, and squeezed shut in resolution.

Miles silently cursed the anonymous clever boffin who'd invented fetaine as a terror weapon, not for his chemistry, but for his insight into the Barraryaran psyche. Fetaine could surely never have been used, could never be used. Any faction trying to do so must rise up against itself and tear apart in moral convulsions.

Yaski, standing back from his men, looked thoroughly horrified. Bonn, his expression black and brittle as obsidian, began to strip off his gloves and parka.

No, no, no! Miles screamed inside his head. *If you join them they'll never back down. They'll know they're right.* Bad mistake, bad . . . Bonn dropped the rest of his clothes in a pile, marched forward, joined the line, wheeled, and locked eyes with Metzov. Metzov's eyes narrowed with new fury. "So," he hissed, "you convict yourself. Freeze, then."

How had things gone so bad, so fast? Now would be a good time to remember a duty in the weather office, and get the hell out of here. If only those shivering bastards would back down, Miles could get through this night without a ripple in his record. He had no duty, no function here. . . .

Metzov's eye fell on Miles. "Vorkosigan, you can either take up a weapon and be useful, or consider yourself dismissed."

He could leave. Could he leave? When he made no move, the sergeant walked over and thrust a nerve disruptor into Miles's hand. Miles took it up, still struggling to think with brains gone suddenly porridge. He did retain the wit to make sure the safety was "on" before pointing the disruptor vaguely in the direction of the freezing men.

This isn't going to be a mutiny. It's going to be a massacre.

One of the armed grubs giggled nervously. What

had they been told they were doing? What did they *believe* they were doing? Eighteen-, nineteen-year-olds—could they even recognize a criminal order? Or know what to do about it if they did?

Could Miles?

The situation was ambiguous, that was the problem. It didn't quite fit. Miles knew about criminal orders, every academy man did. His father came down personally and gave a one-day seminar on the topic to the seniors at midyear. He'd made it a requirement to graduate, by Imperial fiat back when he'd been Regent. What exactly constituted a criminal order, when and how to disobey it. With vid evidence from various historical test cases and bad examples, including the politically disastrous Solstice Massacre, that had taken place under the Admiral's own command. Invariably one or more cadets had to leave the room to throw up during that part.

The other instructors hated Vorkosigan's Day. Their classes were subtly disrupted for weeks afterward. One reason Admiral Vorkosigan didn't wait till any later in the year; he almost always had to make a return trip a few weeks after, to talk some disturbed cadet out of dropping out at almost the finale of his schooling. Only the academy cadets got this live lecture, as far as Miles knew, though his father talked of canning it on holovid and making it a part of basic training Service-wide. Parts of the seminar had been a revelation even to Miles.

But this . . . If the techs had been civilians, Metzov would clearly be in the wrong. If this had been in wartime, while being harried by some enemy, Metzov might be within his rights, even duty. This was somewhere between. Soldiers disobeying, but passively. Not an enemy in sight. Not even a physical situation threatening, necessarily, lives on the base (except theirs), though when the wind shifted that could change. *I'm not ready for this, not yet, not so soon.* What was right?

My career . . . Claustrophobic panic rose in Miles's chest, like a man with his head caught in a drain. The nerve disruptor wavered just slightly in his hand. Over the parabolic reflector he could see Bonn standing dumbly, too congealed now even to argue any more. Ears were turning white out there, and fingers and feet. One man crumpled into a shuddering ball, but made no move to surrender. Was there any softening of doubt yet, in Metzov's rigid neck?

For a lunatic moment Miles envisioned thumbing off the safety and shooting Metzov. And then what, shoot the grubs? He couldn't possibly get them all before they got him.

I could be the only soldier here under thirty who's ever killed an enemy before, in battle or out of it. The grubs might fire out of ignorance, or sheer curiosity. They didn't know enough *not* to. *What we do in the next half hour will replay in our heads as long as we breathe.*

He could try doing nothing. Only follow orders. How much trouble could he get into, only following orders? Every commander he'd ever had agreed, he needed to follow orders better. *Think you'll enjoy your ship duty, then, Ensign Vorkosigan, you and your pack of frozen ghosts? At least you'd never be lonely. . . .*

Miles, still holding up the nerve disruptor, faded backward, out of the grubs' line-of-sight, out of the corner of Metzov's eye. Tears stung and blurred his vision. From the cold, no doubt.

He sat on the ground. Pulled off his gloves and boots. Let his parka fall, and his shirts. Trousers and thermal underwear atop the pile, and the nerve-disruptor nested carefully on them. He stepped forward. His leg braces felt like icicles against his calves.

I hate passive resistance. I really, really hate it.

"What the hell do you think you're doing, Ensign?" Metzov snarled as Miles limped past him.

"Breaking this up, sir," Miles replied steadily. Even now some of the shivering techs flinched away from him, as if his deformities might be contagious. Pattas didn't draw away, though. Nor Bonn.

"Bonn tried that bluff. He's now regretting it. It won't work for you either, Vorkosigan." Metzov's voice shook too, though not from the cold.

You should have said "Ensign." What's in a name? Miles could see the ripple of dismay run through the grubs, that time. No, this hadn't worked for Bonn. Miles might be the only man here for whom this sort of individual intervention could work. Depending on how far gone Mad Metzov was by now.

Miles spoke now for both Metzov's benefit and the grubs'. "It's possible—barely—that Service Security wouldn't investigate the deaths of Lieutenant Bonn and his men, if you diddled the record, claimed some accident. I guarantee Imperial Security will investigate mine."

Metzov grinned strangely. "Suppose no witnesses survive to complain?"

Metzov's sergeant looked as rigid as his master. Miles thought of Ahn, drunken Ahn, silent Ahn. What had Ahn seen, once long ago, when crazy things were happening on Komarr? What kind of surviving witness had he been? A guilty one, perhaps? "S-s-sorry, sir, but I see at least ten witnesses, behind those nerve disruptors." Silver parabolas—they looked enormous, like serving dishes, from this new angle. The change in point of view was amazingly clarifying. No ambiguities now.

Miles continued, "Or do you propose to execute your firing squad and then shoot yourself? Imperial Security will fast-penta everyone in sight. You can't silence me. Living or dead, through my mouth or yours—or theirs—I will testify." Shivers racked Miles's body. Astonishing, the effect of just that little bit of east wind, at this temperature. He fought to keep the shakes out of his voice, lest cold be mistaken for fear.

"Small consolation, if you—ah—permit yourself to freeze, I'd say, Ensign." Metzov's heavy sarcasm grated on Miles's nerves. The man still thought he was winning. Insane.

Miles's bare feet felt strangely warm now. His eyelashes were crunchy with ice. He was catching up fast to the others, in terms of freezing to death, no doubt because of his smaller mass. His body was turning a blotchy purple-blue.

The snow-blanketed base was so silent. He could almost hear the individual snow grains skitter across the sheet ice. He could hear the vibrating bones of each man around him, pick out the hollow frightened breathing of the grubs. Time stretched.

He could threaten Metzov, break up his complacency with dark hints about Komarr, *the truth will out*. . . . He could call on his father's rank and position. He could . . . dammit, Metzov must realize he was overextended, no matter how mad he was. His discipline parade bluff hadn't worked and now he was stuck with it, stonily defending his authority unto death. *He can be a funny kind of dangerous, if you really threaten him*. . . . It was hard, to see through the sadism to the underlying fear. But it had to be there, underneath. . . . Pushing wasn't working. Metzov was practically petrified with resistance. What about pulling . . . ?

"But consider, sir," Miles's words stuttered out persuasively, "the advantages to yourself of stopping now. You now have clear evidence of a mutinous, er, conspiracy. You can arrest us all, throw us in the stockade. It's a better revenge, 'cause you get it all and lose nothing. I lose my career, get a dishonorable discharge or maybe prison—do you think I wouldn't rather die? Service Security punishes the rest of us for you. You get it all."

Miles's words had hooked him; Miles could see it, in the red glow fading from the narrowed eyes, in the slight bending of that stiff, stiff neck. Miles had only to let the line out, refrain from jerking on it and renewing Metzov's fighting frenzy, *wait*. . . .

Metzov stepped nearer, bulking in the half-light, haloed by his freezing breath. His voice dropped, pitched to Miles's ear alone. "A typical soft Vorkosigan answer. Your father was soft on Komarran scum. Cost us lives. A court-martial for the Admiral's little boy—that might bring down that holier-than-thou buggerer, eh?"

Miles swallowed icy spit. *Those who do not know their history*, his thought careened, *are doomed to keep stepping in it*. Alas, so were those who did, it seemed. "Thermo the damned fetaine spill," he whispered hoarsely, "and see."

"You're all under arrest," Metzov bellowed out suddenly, his shoulders hunching. "Get dressed."

The others looked stunned with relief then. After a last uncertain glance at the nerve disruptors they dove for their clothes, donning them with frantic cold-clumsy hands. But Miles had seen it complete in Metzov's eyes sixty seconds earlier. It reminded him of that definition of his father's. *A weapon is a device for making your enemy change his mind*. The mind was the first and final battleground, the stuff in between was just noise.

Lieutenant Yaski had taken the opportunity afforded by Miles's attention-arresting nude arrival on center stage to quietly disappear into the Admin building and make several frantic calls. As a result the trainee's commander, the base surgeon, and Metzov's second-in-command arrived, primed to persuade or perhaps sedate and confine Metzov. But by that time Miles, Bonn, and the techs were already dressed and being marched, stumbling, toward the stockade bunker under the argus-eyes of the nerve disruptors.

"Am I s-supposed to th-thank you for this?" Bonn

asked Miles through chattering teeth. Their hands and feet swung like paralyzed lumps; he leaned on Miles, Miles hung on him, hobbling down the road together.

"We got what we wanted, eh? He's going to plasma the fetaine on-site before the wind shifts in the morning. Nobody dies. Nobody gets their nuts curdled. We win. I think." Miles emitted a deathly cackle through numb lips.

"I never thought," wheezed Bonn, "that I'd ever meet anybody crazier than Metzov."

"I didn't do anything you didn't," protested Miles. "Except I made it work. Sort of. It'll all look different in the morning, anyway."

"Yeah. Worse," Bonn predicted glumly.

Miles jerked up out of an uneasy doze on his cell cot when the door hissed open. They were bringing Bonn back.

Miles rubbed his unshaven face. "What time is it out there, Lieutenant?"

"Dawn." Bonn looked as pale, stubbled, and criminally low as Miles felt. He eased himself down on his cot with a pained grunt.

"What's happening?"

"Service Security's all over the place. They flew in a captain from the mainland, just arrived, who seems to be in charge. Metzov's been filling his ear, I think. They're just taking depositions, so far."

"They get the fetaine taken care of?"

"Yep." Bonn vented a grim snicker. "They just had me out to check it, and sign the job off. The bunker made a neat little oven, all right."

"Ensign Vorkosigan, you're wanted," said the security guard who'd delivered Bonn. "Come with me now."

Miles creaked to his feet and limped toward the cell door. "See you later, Lieutenant."

"Right. If you spot anybody out there with breakfast, why don't you use your political influence to send 'em my way, eh?"

Miles grinned bleakly. "I'll try."

Miles followed the guard up the stockade's short corridor. Lazkowski Base's stockade was not exactly what one would call a high-security facility, being scarcely more than a living quarters bunker with doors that only locked from the outside and no windows. The weather usually made a better guard than any force screen, not to mention the 500-kilometer-wide icewater moat surrounding the island.

The Base security office was busy this morning. Two grim strangers stood waiting by the door, a lieutenant and a big sergeant with the Horus-eye insignia of Imperial Security on their sleek uniforms. *Imperial* Security, not Service Security. Miles's very own Security, who had guarded his family all his father's political life. Miles regarded them with possessive delight.

The Base security clerk looked harried, his desk console lit up and blinking. "Ensign Vorkosigan, sir, I need your palm print on this."

"All right. What am I signing?"

"Just the travel orders, sir."

"What? Ah . . ." Miles paused, holding up his plastic-mitted hands. "Which one?"

"The right, I guess would do, sir."

With difficulty, Miles peeled off the right mitten with his awkward left. His hand glistened with the medical gel that was supposed to be healing the frostbite. His hand was swollen, red-blotched and mangled-looking, but the stuff must be working. All his fingers now wriggled. It took three tries, pressing down on the ID pad, before the computer recognized him.

"Now yours, sir," the clerk nodded to the Imperial Security lieutenant. The ImpSec man laid his hand on the pad and the computer bleeped approval. He lifted it and glanced dubiously at the sticky sheen, looked around futilely for some towel, and wiped it surreptitiously on his trouser seam just behind his stunner holster. The clerk dabbed nervously at the pad with his uniform sleeve, and touched his intercom.

"Am I glad to see you fellows," Miles told the ImpSec officer. "Wish you'd been here last night."

The lieutenant did not smile in return. "I'm just a courier, Ensign. I'm not supposed to discuss your case."

General Metzov ducked through the door from the inner office, a sheaf of plastic flimsies in one hand and a Service Security captain at his elbow, who nodded warily to his counterpart on the Imperial side.

The general was almost smiling. "Good morning, Ensign Vorkosigan." His glance took in Imperial Security without dismay. Dammit, ImpSec should be making that near-murderer shake in his combat boots. "It seems there's a wrinkle in this case even I hadn't realized. When a Vor lord involves himself in a military mutiny, a charge of high treason follows automatically."

"What?" Miles swallowed, to bring his voice back down. "Lieutenant, I'm not under arrest by *Imperial* Security, am I?"

The lieutenant produced a set of handcuffs and proceeded to attach Miles to the big sergeant. *Overholt*, read the name on the man's badge, which Miles mentally redubbed Overkill. He had only to lift his arm to dangle Miles like a kitten.

"You are being detained, pending further investigation," said the lieutenant formally.

"How long?"

"Indefinitely."

The lieutenant headed for the door, the sergeant and perforce Miles following. "Where?" Miles asked frantically.

"Imperial Security Headquarters."

Vorbarr Sultana! "I need to get my things—"

"Your quarters have already been cleared."

"Will I be coming back here?"

"I don't know, Ensign."

Late dawn was streaking Camp Permafrost with grey and yellow when the scat-cat deposited them at the shuttlepad. The Imperial Security sub-orbital courier shuttle sat on the icy concrete like a bird of prey accidently placed in a pigeon cote. Slick and black and deadly, it seemed to break the sound barrier just resting there. Its pilot was at the ready, engines primed for takeoff.

Miles shuffled awkwardly up the ramp after Sergeant Overkill, the handcuff jerking coldly on his wrist. Tiny ice crystals danced in the northeasterly wind. The temperature would be stabilizing this morning, he could tell by the particular dry bite of the relative humidity in his sinuses. Dear God, it was past time to get off this island.

Miles took one last sharp breath, then the shuttle door sealed behind them with a snaky hiss. Within was a thick, upholstered silence that even the howl of the engines scarcely penetrated.

At least it was warm.

CHAPTER SIX

Autumn in the city of Vorbarr Sultana was a beautiful time of year, and today was exemplary. The air was high and blue, the temperature cool and perfect, and even the tang of industrial haze smelled good. The autumn flowers were not yet frosted off, but the Earth-import trees had turned their colors. As he was hustled out of the Security lift van and into a back entrance to the big blocky building that was Imperial Security Headquarters, Miles glimpsed one such tree. An Earth maple, with carnelian leaves and a silver-grey trunk, across the street. Then the door closed. Miles held that tree before his mind's eye, trying to memorize it, just in case he never saw it again.

The Security lieutenant produced passes that sped Miles and Overholt through the door guards, and led them into a maze of corridors to a pair of lift tubes. They entered the up tube, not the down one. So, Miles was not being taken directly to the ultra-secure cell block beneath the building. He woke to what this meant, and wished wistfully for the down tube.

They were ushered into an office on an upper level, past a Security captain, then into an inner office. A man, slight, bland, civilian-clothed, with brown hair greying at the temples, sat at his very large comconsole desk, studying a vid. He glanced up at Miles's escort. "Thank you, Lieutenant, Sergeant. You may go."

Overholt detached Miles from his wrist as the lieutenant asked, "Uh, will you be safe, sir?"

"I expect so," said the man dryly.

Yeah, but what about me? Miles wailed inwardly. The two soldiers exited, and left Miles alone, standing literally on the carpet. Unwashed, unshaven, still wearing the faintly reeking black fatigues he'd flung on—only last night? Face weather-raked, with his swollen hands and feet still encased in their plastic medical mittens—his toes now wriggled in their squishy matrix. No boots. He had dozed, in a jerky intermittent exhaustion, on the two-hour shuttle flight, without being noticeably refreshed. His throat was raw, his sinuses felt stuffed with packing fiber, and his chest hurt when he breathed.

Simon Illyan, Chief of Barrayaran Imperial Security, crossed his arms and looked Miles over slowly, from head to toe and back again. It gave Miles a skewed sense of *déja vù*.

Practically everyone on Barrayar feared this man's name, though few knew his face. This effect was carefully cultivated by Illyan, building in part—but only in part—on the legacy of his formidable predecessor, the legendary Security Chief Negri. Illyan and his department, in turn, had provided security for Miles's father for the twenty years of his political career, and had slipped up only once, during the night of the infamous soltoxin attack. Offhand, Miles knew of no one Illyan feared except Miles's mother. He'd once asked his father if this was guilt, about the soltoxin, but Count Vorkosigan had replied, No, it was only the lasting effect of vivid first impressions. Miles had called Illyan "Uncle Simon" all his life until he'd entered the Service, "Sir" after that.

Looking at Illyan's face now, Miles thought he finally grasped the distinction between exasperation, and utter exasperation.

Illyan finished his inspection, shook his head, and groaned, "Wonderful. Just wonderful."

Miles cleared his throat. "Am I . . . really under arrest, sir?"

"That is what this interview will determine," Illyan sighed, leaning back in his chair. "I have been up since two hours after midnight over this escapade. Rumors are flying all over the Service, as fast as the vid net can carry them. The facts appear to be mutating every forty minutes, like bacteria. I don't suppose you could have picked some more public way to self-destruct? Attempted to assassinate the Emperor with your pocket-knife during the Birthday Review, say, or raped a sheep in the Great Square during rush hour?" The sarcasm melted to genuine pain. "He had so much hope of you. How could you betray him so?"

No need to ask who "he" was. *The* Vorkosigan. "I . . . don't think I did, sir. I don't know."

A light blinked on Illyan's comconsole. He exhaled, with a sharp glance at Miles, and touched a control. The second door to his office, camouflaged in the wall to the right of his desk, slid open, and two men in dress greens ducked through.

Prime Minister Admiral Count Aral Vorkosigan wore the uniform as naturally as an animal wears its fur. He was a man of no more than middle height, stocky, grey-haired, heavy-jawed, scarred, almost a thug's body and yet with the most penetrating grey eyes Miles had ever encountered. He was flanked by his aide, a tall blond lieutenant named Jole. Miles had met Jole on his last home leave. Now, there was a perfect officer, brave and brilliant—he'd served in space, been decorated for some courage and quick thinking during a horrendous on-board accident, been rotated through HQ while recovering from his injuries, and promptly been snabbled up as his military secretary by the Prime Minister, who had a sharp eye for hot new talent. Jaw-dropping gorgeous, to boot, he ought to be making recruiting vids. Miles sighed in hopeless jealousy every time he ran across

him. Jole was even worse than Ivan, who while
darkly handsome had never been accused of brilliance.

"Thanks, Jole," Count Vorkosigan murmured to
his aide, as his eye found Miles. "I'll see you back
at the office."

"Yes, sir." So dismissed, Jole ducked back out,
glancing back at Miles and his superior with worried
eyes, and the door hissed closed again.

Illyan still had his hand pressed to a control on
his desk. "Are you officially here?" he asked Count
Vorkosigan.

"No."

Illyan keyed something off—recording equipment,
Miles realized. "Very well," he said, editorial doubt
injected into his tone.

Miles saluted his father. His father ignored the
salute and embraced him gravely, wordlessly, sat in
the room's only other chair, crossed his arms and
booted ankles, and said, "Continue, Simon."

Illyan, who had been cut off in the middle of what
had been shaping up, in Miles's estimation, to a
really classic reaming, chewed his lip in frustration.
"Rumors aside," Illyan said to Miles, "what really
happened last night out on that damned island?"

In the most neutral and succinct terms he could
muster, Miles described the previous night's events,
starting with the fetaine spill and ending with his
arrest/detainment/to-be-determined by Imperial Security. His father said nothing during the whole recita-
tion, but he had a light pen in his hand which he
kept turning absently around and over, *tap* against
his knee, around and over.

Silence fell when Miles finished. The light pen
was driving Miles to distraction. He wished his
father would put the damned thing away, or drop it,
or anything.

His father slipped the light pen back into his
breast pocket, thank God, leaned back, and steepled
his fingers, frowning. "Let me get this straight. You

say Metzov hopscotched the command chain and dragooned *trainees* for his firing squad?"

"Ten of them. I don't know if they were volunteers or not, I wasn't there for that part."

"Trainees." Count Vorkosigan's face was dark. "Boys."

"He was babbling something about it being like the army versus the navy, back on Old Earth."

"Huh?" said Illyan.

"I don't think Metzov was any too stable when he was exiled to Kyril Island after his troubles in the Komarr Revolt, and fifteen years of brooding about it didn't improve his grip." Miles hesitated. "Will . . . General Metzov be questioned about his actions at all, sir?"

"General Metzov, by your account," said Admiral Vorkosigan, "dragged a platoon of eighteen-year-olds into what came within a hair of being a mass torture-murder."

Miles nodded in memory. His body still twinged with assorted agonies.

"For that sin, there is no hole deep enough to hide him from my wrath. Metzov will be taken care of, all right." Count Vorkosigan was terrifyingly grim.

"What about Miles and the mutineers?" asked Illyan.

"Necessarily, I fear we will have to treat that as a separate matter."

"Or two separate matters," said Illyan suggestively.

"Mm. So, Miles, tell me about the men on the other end of the guns."

"Techs, sir, mostly. A lot of greekies."

Illyan winced. "Good God, had the man no political sense at all?"

"None that I ever saw. I thought it would be a problem." Well, later he'd thought of it, lying awake on his cell cot after the med squad left. The other political ramifications had spun through his mind.

Over half the slowly freezing techs had been of the Greek-speaking minority. The language separatists would have been rioting in the streets, had it become a massacre, sure to claim the general had ordered the greekies into the clean-up as racial sabotage. More deaths, chaos reverberating down the timeline like the consequences of the Solstice Massacre? "It . . . occurred to me, that if I died with them, at least it would be crystal clear that it hadn't been some plot of your government or the Vor oligarchy. So that if I lived, I won, and if I died, I won too. Or at least served. Strategy, of sorts."

Barrayar's greatest strategist of this century rubbed his temples, as if they ached. "Well . . . of sorts, yes."

"So," Miles swallowed, "what happens now, sirs? Will I be charged with high treason?"

"For the second time in four years?" said Illyan. "Hell, no. I'm not going through that again. I will simply disappear you, until this blows over. Where to, I haven't quite figured yet. Kyril Island is out."

"Glad to hear it." Miles eyes narrowed. "What about the others?"

"The trainees?" said Illyan.

"The techs. My . . . fellow mutineers."

Illyan twitched at the term.

"It would be seriously unjust if I were to slither up some Vor-privileged line and leave them standing charges alone," Miles added.

"The public scandal of your trial would damage your father's Centrist coalition. Your moral scruples may be admirable, Miles, but I'm not sure I can afford them."

Miles stared steadily at Prime Minister Count Vorkosigan. "Sir?"

Count Vorkosigan sucked thoughtfully on his lower lip. "Yes, I could have the charges against them quashed, by Imperial fiat. That would involve another price, though." He leaned forward intently, eyes peeling Miles. "You could never serve again. Rumors will travel even without a trial. No commander would have you, after. None could trust you, trust you to be a real officer, not an artifact protected by special privilege. I can't ask anyone to command you with his head cranked over his shoulder all the time."

Miles exhaled, a long breath. "In a weird sense, they were my men. Do it. Kill the charges."

"Will you resign your commission, then?" demanded Illyan. He looked sick.

Miles felt sick, nauseous and cold. "I will." His voice was thin.

Illyan looked up suddenly from a blank brooding stare at his comconsole. "Miles, how did you know about General Metzov's questionable actions during the Komarr Revolt? That case was Security-classified."

"Ah . . . didn't Ivan tell you about the little leak in the ImpSec files, sir?"

"*What?*"

Damn Ivan. "May I sit down, sir?" said Miles faintly. The room was wavering, his head thumping. Without waiting for permission, he sat cross-legged on the carpet, blinking. His father made a worried movement toward him, then restrained himself. "I'd been checking upon Metzov's background because of something Lieutenant Ahn said. By the way, when you go after Metzov, I strongly suggest you fast-penta Ahn first. He knows more than he's told. You'll find him somewhere on the equator, I expect."

"My *files*, Miles."

"Uh, yes, well, it turns out that if you face a secured console to an outgoing console, you can read off Security files from anywhere in the vid net. Of course, you have to have somebody inside HQ who can and will aim the consoles and call up the files for you. And you can't flash-download. But I, uh, thought you should know, sir."

"Perfect security," said Count Vorkosigan in a choked voice. Chortling, Miles realized in startlement.

Illyan looked like a man sucking on a lemon. "How did you," Illyan began, stopped to glare at the Count, started again, "how did you figure this out?"

"It was obvious."

"Airtight security, you said," murmured Count Vorkosigan, unsuccessfully suppressing a wheezing laugh. "The most expensive yet devised. Proof against the cleverest viruses, the most sophisticated eavesdropping equipment. And two ensigns waft right through it?"

Goaded, Illyan snapped, "I didn't promise it was idiot-proof!"

Count Vorkosigan wiped his eyes and sighed. "Ah, the human factor. We will correct the defect, Miles. Thank you."

"You're a bloody loose cannon, boy, firing in all directions," Illyan growled to Miles, craning his neck to see over his desk to where Miles sat in a slumping heap. "This, on top of your earlier escapade with those damned mercenaries, on top of it all—house arrest isn't enough. I won't sleep through the night till I have you locked in a cell with your hands tied behind your back."

Miles, who thought he might kill for a decent hour's sleep right now, could only shrug. Maybe Illyan could be persuaded to let him go to that nice quiet cell soon.

Count Vorkosigan had fallen silent, a strange thoughtful glow starting in his eye. Illyan noticed the expression too, and paused.

"Simon," said Count Vorkosigan, "there's no doubt ImpSec will have to go on watching Miles. For his sake, as well as mine."

"And the Emperor's" put in Illyan dourly. "And Barrayar's. And the innocent bystanders'."

"But what better, more direct and efficient way

for security to watch him than if he is assigned *to* Imperial Security?"

"What?" said Illyan and Miles together, in the same sharp horrified tone. "You're not serious," Illyan went on, as Miles added, "Security was never on my top-ten list of assignment choices."

"Not choice. Aptitude. Major Cecil discussed it with me at one time, as I recall. But as Miles says, he didn't put it on his list."

He hadn't put Arctic Weatherman on his list either, Miles recalled.

"You had it right the first time," said Illyan. "No commander in the Service will want him now. Not excepting myself."

"None that I could, in honor, lean on to take him. Excepting yourself. I have always," Count Vorkosigan flashed a peculiar grin, "leaned on you, Simon."

Illyan looked faintly stunned, as a top tactician beginning to see himself outmaneuvered.

"It works on several levels," Count Vorkosigan went on in that same mild persuasive voice. "We can put it about that it's an unofficial internal exile, demotion in disgrace. It will buy off my political enemies, who would otherwise try to stir profit from this mess. It will tone down the appearance of our condoning a mutiny, which no military service can afford."

"True exile," said Miles. "Even if unofficial and internal."

"Oh yes," Count Vorkosigan agreed softly. "But, ah—not true disgrace."

"Can he be trusted?" said Illyan doubtfully.

"Apparently." The count's smile was like the gleam off a knife blade. "Security can use his talents. Security more than any other department needs his talents."

"To see the ob**vious**?"

"And the less obvious. Many officers may be

trusted with the Emperor's life. Rather fewer with his honor."

Illyan, reluctantly, made a vague acquiescent gesture. Count Vorkosigan, perhaps prudently, did not troll for greater enthusiasm from his Security chief at this time, but turned to Miles and said, "You look like you need an infirmary."

"I need a bed."

"How about a bed in an infirmary?"

Miles coughed, and blinked blearily. "Yeah, that'd do."

"Come on, we'll find one."

He stood, and staggered out on his father's arm, his feet squishing in their plastic bags.

"Other than that, how was Kyril Island, Ensign Vorkosigan?" inquired the count. "You didn't vid home much, your mother noticed."

"I was busy. Lessee. The climate was ferocious, the terrain was lethal, a third of the population including my immediate superior was dead drunk most of the time. The average IQ equalled the mean temperature in degrees cee, there wasn't a woman for five hundred kilometers in any direction, and the base commander was a homicidal psychotic. Other than that, it was lovely."

"Doesn't sound like it's changed in the smallest detail in twenty-five years."

"You've been there?" Miles squinted. "And yet you let *me* get sent there?"

"I commanded Lazkowski Base for five months, once, while waiting for my captaincy of the cruiser *General Vorkraft*. During the period my career was, so to speak, in political eclipse."

So to speak. "How'd you like it?"

"I can't remember much. I was drunk most of the time. Everybody finds their own way of dealing with Camp Permafrost. I might say, you did rather better than I."

"I find your subsequent survival . . . encouraging, sir."

"I thought you might. That's why I mentioned it. It's not otherwise an experience I'd hold up as an example."

Miles looked up at his father. "Did . . . I do the right thing, sir? Last night?"

"Yes," said the count simply. "A right thing. Perhaps not the best of all possible right things. Three days from now you may think of a cleverer tactic, but you were the man on the ground at the time. I try not to second-guess my field commanders."

Miles's heart rose in his aching chest for the first time since he'd left Kyril Island.

Miles thought his father might take him to the great and familiar Imperial Military Hospital complex, a few kilometers away across town, but they found an infirmary closer than that, three floors down in ImpSec HQ. The facility was small but complete, with a couple of examining rooms, private rooms, cells for treating prisoners and guarded witnesses, a surgery, and a closed door labeled, chillingly, *Interrogation Chemistry Laboratory*. Illyan must have called down in advance, for a corpsman was hovering in attendance waiting to receive them. A Security surgeon arrived shortly, a little out of breath. He straighted his uniform and saluted Count Vorkosigan punctiliously before turning to Miles.

Miles fancied the surgeon was more used to making people nervous than being made nervous by them, and was awkward about the role reversal. Was it some aura of old violence, clinging to his father still after all these years? The power, the history? Some personal charsima, that made erstwhile forceful men flatten out like cowed dogs? Miles could sense that radiating heat perfectly clearly, and yet it didn't seem to affect him the same way.

Acclimatization, perhaps. The former Lord Regent

was the man who used to take a two-hour lunch every day, regardless of any crisis short of war, and disappear into his Residence. Only Miles knew the interior view of those hours, how the big man in the green uniform would bolt a sandwich in five minutes and then spend the next hour and a half down on the floor with his son who could not walk, playing, talking, reading aloud. Sometimes, when Miles was locked in hysterical resistance to some painful new physical therapy, daunting his mother and even Sergeant Bothari, his father had been the only one with the firmness to *insist* on those ten extra agonizing leg stretches, the polite submission to the hypospray, to another round of surgery, to the icy chemicals searing his veins. "You are Vor. You must not frighten your liege people with this show of uncontrol, Lord Miles." The pungent smell of this infirmary, the tense doctor, brought back a flood of memories. No wonder, Miles reflected, he had failed to be afraid enough of Metzov. When Count Vorkosigan left, the infirmary seemed altogether empty.

There did not appear to be much going on in ImpSec HQ this week. The infirmary was numbingly quiet, except for a trickle of headquarters staff coming down to cadge headache or cold remedies or hangover-killers from the pliant corpsman. A couple of techs spent three hours rattling around the lab one evening on a rush job, and rushed off. The doctor arrested Miles's incipient pneumonia just before it turned into galloping pneumonia. Miles brooded, and waited for the six-day antibiotic therapy to run its course, and plotted details of a home leave in Vorbarr Sultana that must surely be forthcoming when the medics released him.

"Why can't I go home?" Miles complained to his mother on her next visit. "Nobody's telling me anything. If I'm not under arrest, why can't I take home leave? If I am under arrest, why aren't the doors locked? I feel like I'm in limbo."

Countess Cordelia Vorkosigan vented an unlady-like snort. "You are in limbo, kiddo." Her flat Betan accent fell warmly on Miles's ears, despite her sardonic tone. She tossed her head—she wore her red-roan hair pinned back from her face and waving loose down her back today, gleaming against a rich autumn brown jacket picked out with silver embroidery, and the swinging skirts of a Vor-class woman. Grey-eyed, striking, her pale face seemed so alive with flickering thought one scarcely noticed she was not beautiful. For twenty-one years she'd passed as a Vor matron in the wake of her Great Man, yet still seemed as unimpressed by Barrayaran hierarchies as ever—though not, Miles thought, unmoved by Barrayaran wounds.

So why do I never think of my ambition as ship command like my mother *before me?* Captain Cordelia Naismith, Betan Astronomical Survey, had been in the risky business of expanding the wormhole nexus jump by blind jump, for humanity, for pure knowledge, for Beta Colony's economic advancement, for—what *had* driven her? She'd commanded a sixty-person survey vessel, far from home and help—there were certain enviable aspects to her former career, to be sure. Chain-of-command, for example, would have been a legal fiction out in the farbeyond, the wishes of Betan HQ a matter for speculation and side bets.

She moved now so wavelessly through Barrayaran society, only her most intimate observers realized how detached she was from it, fearing no one, not even the dread Illyan, controlled by no one, not even the Admiral himself. It was the casual fearlessness, Miles decided, that made his mother so unsettling. The Admiral's Captain. Following in her footsteps would be like firewalking.

"What's going on out there?" Miles asked. "This place is almost as much fun as solitary confinement, y'know? Have they decided I'm a mutineer after all?"

"I don't think so," said the Countess. "They're discharging the others—your Lieutenant Bonn and the rest—not precisely dishonorably, but without benefits or pensions or that Imperial Liegeman status that seems to mean so much to Barrayaran men—"

"Think of it as a funny sort of Reservist," Miles advised. "What about Metzov and the grubs?"

"He's being discharged the same way. He lost the most, I think."

"They're just turning him loose?" Miles frowned.

Countess Vorkosigan shrugged. "Because there were no deaths, Aral was persuaded he couldn't make a court martial with any harsher punishment stick. They decided not to involve the trainees with any charges."

"Hm. I'm glad, I think. And, ah . . . me?"

"You remain officially listed as detained by Imperial Security. Indefinitely."

"Limbo is supposed to be an indefinite sort of place." His hand picked at his sheet. His knuckles were still swollen. "How long?"

"However long it takes to have its calculated psychological effect."

"What, to drive me crazy? Another three days ought to do it."

Her lip quirked. "Long enough to convince the Barrayaran militarists that you are being properly punished for your, uh, crime. As long as you are confined in this rather sinister building, they can be encouraged to imagine you undergoing—whatever they imagine goes on in here. If you're allowed to run around town partying, it will be much harder to maintain the illusion that you've been hung upside down on the basement wall."

"It all seems so . . . unreal." He hunched back into his pillow. "I only wanted to serve."

A brief smile flicked her wide mouth up, and vanished. "Ready to reconsider another line of work, love?"

"Being Vor is more than just a job."

"Yes, it's a pathology. Obsessional delusion. It's a big galaxy out there, Miles. There are other ways to serve, larger . . . constituencies."

"So why do you stay here?" he shot back.

"Ah." She smiled bleakly at the touché. "Some people's needs are more compelling than guns."

"Speaking of Dad, is he coming back?"

"Hm. No. I'm to tell you, he's going to distance himself for a time. So as not to give the appearance of endorsing your mutiny, while in fact shuffling you out from under the avalanche. He's decided to be publicly angry with you."

"And is he?"

"Of course not. Yet . . . he was beginning to have some long-range plans for you, in his socio-political reform schemes, based on your completing a solid military career . . . he saw ways of making even your congenital injuries serve Barrayar."

"Yeah, I know."

"Well, don't worry. He'll doubtless think of some way to use this, too."

Miles sighed glumly. "I want something to *do*. I want my *clothes* back."

His mother pursed her lips, and shook her head.

He tried calling Ivan that evening.

"Where are you?" Ivan demanded suspiciously.

"Stuck in limbo."

"Well, I don't want any of it stuck to me," said Ivan roughly, and punched off-line.

CHAPTER SEVEN

The next morning Miles was moved to new quarters. His guide led him just one floor down, dashing Miles's hopes of seeing the sky again. The officer keyed open a door to one of the secured apartments usually used by protected witnesses. And, Miles reflected, certain political nonpersons. Was it possible life in limbo was having a chameleon effect, rendering him translucent?

"How long will I be staying here?" Miles asked the officer.

"I don't know, Ensign," the man replied, and left him.

His duffle, jammed with his clothes, and a hastily-packed box sat in the middle of the apartment's floor. All his worldly goods from Kyril Island, smelling moldy, a cold breath of arctic damp. Miles poked through them—everything seemed to be there, including his weather library—and prowled his new quarters. It was a one-room efficiency, shabbily furnished in the style of twenty years back, with a few comfortable chairs, a bed, a simple kitchenette, empty cupboards and shelves and closets. No abandoned garments or objects or leftovers to hint at the identity of any previous occupant.

There had to be bugs. Any shiny surface could conceal a vid pickup, and the ears were probably not even within the room. But were they switched on? Or, almost more of an insult, maybe Illyan wasn't even bothering to run them?

There was a guard in the outer corridor, and remote monitors, but Miles did not appear to have neighbors at present. He discovered he could leave the corridor, and walk about the few non-top-secured areas of the building, but the guards at the outside doors, briefed as to who he was, turned him back politely but firmly. He pictured himself attempting escape by rappelling down from the roof—he'd probably get himself shot, and ruin some poor guard's career.

A Security officer found him wandering aimlessly, conducted him back to his apartment, gave him a handful of chits for the building's cafeteria, and hinted strongly that it would be appreciated if he would stay in his quarters between meals. After he left Miles morbidly counted the chits, trying to guess the expected duration of his stay. There were an even hundred. Miles shuddered.

He unpacked his box and bag, ran everything that would go through the sonic laundry to eliminate the last lingering odor of Camp Permafrost, hung up his uniforms, cleaned his boots, arranged his possessions neatly on a few shelves, showered, and changed to fresh undress greens.

One hour down. How many to go?

He attempted to read, but could not concentrate, and ended sitting in the most comfortable chair with his eyes closed, pretending this windowless, hermetically-sealed chamber was a cabin aboard a spaceship. Outbound.

He was sitting in the same chair two nights later, digesting a leaden cafeteria dinner, when the door chimed.

Startled, Miles clambered up and limped to answer it personally. It was probably not a firing squad, though you never knew.

He almost changed his assumptions about the firing squad at the sight of the hard-faced Imperial

Security officers in dress greens who stood waiting.
"Excuse me, Ensign Vorkosigan," one muttered perfunctorily, and brushed past him to start running a
scan over Miles's quarters. Miles blinked, then saw
who stood behind them in the corridor, and breathed
an "Ah" of understanding. At a mere look from the
scanner man, Miles obediently held out his arms and
turned to be scanned.

"Clear, sir," the scanner man reported, and Miles
was sure it was. These fellows never, ever cut cor-
ners, not even in the heart of ImpSec itself.

"Thank you. Leave us, please. You may wait out
here," said the third man. The ImpSec men nodded
and took up parade rest flanking Miles's door.

Since they were both wearing officer's undress
greens, Miles exchanged salutes with the third man,
although the visitor's uniform bore neither rank nor
department insignia. He was thin, of middle height,
with dark hair and intense hazel eyes. A crooked
smile winked in a serious young face that lacked
laugh lines.

"Sire," Miles said formally.

Emperor Gregor Vorbarra jerked his head, and
Miles keyed his door closed on the Security duo.
The thin young man relaxed slightly. "Hi, Miles."

"Hello yourself. Uh . . ." Miles motioned toward
the armchairs. "Welcome to my humble abode. Are
the bugs running?"

"I asked not, but I wouldn't be surprised if Illyan
disobeys me, for my own good." Gregor grimaced,
and followed Miles. He swung a plastic bag from his
left hand, from which came a muted clank. He flung
himself into the larger chair, the one Miles had just
vacated, leaned back, hooked a leg over one chair
arm, and sighed wearily, as if all the air were being
let out of him. He held out the bag. "Here. Elegant
anesthesia."

Miles took it and peered in. Two bottles of wine,
by God, already chilled. "Bless you, my son. I've

been wishing I could get drunk for days, now. How did you guess? For that matter, how did you get in here? I thought I was in solitary confinement." Miles put the second bottle into the refrigerator, found two glasses, and blew the dust out of them.

Gregor shrugged. "They could scarcely keep me out. I'm getting better at insisting, you know. Though Illyan made sure my private visit was really private, you can wager. And I can only stay till 2500." Gregor's shoulders slumped, compressed by the minute-by-minute box of his schedule. "Besides, your mother's religion grants some kind of good karma for visiting the sick and prisoners, and I hear you've been the two in one."

Ah, so Mother had put Gregor up to this. He should have guessed by the Vorkosigan private label on the wine—heavens, she'd sent the *good* stuff. He stopped swinging the bottle by its neck and carried it with greater respect. Miles was lonely enough by now to be more grateful for than embarrassed by this maternal intervention. He opened the wine and poured, and by Barrayaran etiquette took the first sip. Ambrosia. He slung himself into another chair in a posture similar to Gregor's. "Glad to see you, anyway."

Miles contemplated his old playmate. If they'd been even a little closer in age, he and Gregor, they might have fallen more into the role of foster-brothers; Count and Countess Vorkosigan had been Gregor's official guardians ever since the chaos and bloodshed of Vordarian's Pretendership. The child-cohort had been thrown together anyway as "safe" companions, Miles and Ivan and Elena near-age-mates, Gregor, solemn even then, tolerating games a little younger than he might have preferred.

Gregor picked up his wine and sipped. "Sorry things didn't work out for you," he said gruffly.

Miles tilted his head. "A short soldier, a short

career." He took a bigger gulp. "I'd hoped to get off-planet. Ship duty."

Gregor had graduated from the Imperial Academy two years before Miles entered it. His brows rose in agreement. "Don't we all."

"You had a year on active space duty," Miles pointed out.

"Mostly in orbit. Pretend patrols, surrounded by Security shuttles. It got to be painful after a while, all the pretending. Pretending I was an officer, pretending I was doing a job instead of making everyone else's job harder just by being there . . . you at least were permitted real risk."

"Most of it was unplanned, I assure you."

"I'm increasingly convinced that's the trick of it," Gregor went on. "Your father, mine, both our grandfathers—all survived real military situations. That's how they became real officers, not this . . . study." His free hand made a downward chopping motion.

"Flung into situations," Miles disagreed. "My father's military career officially began the day Mad Yuri's death squad broke in and blew up most of his family—I think he was eleven, or something. I'd just as soon pass on that sort of initiation, thanks. It's not something anybody in their right mind would choose."

"Mm." Gregor subsided glumly. As oppressed tonight, Miles guessed, by his legendary father Prince Serg as Miles was by his live one Count Vorkosigan. Miles reflected briefly on what he had come to think of as "The Two Sergs." One—maybe the only version Gregor knew?—was the dead hero, bravely sacrificed on the field of battle or at least cleanly disintegrated in orbit. The other, the Suppressed Serg: the hysteriac commander and sadistic sodomite whose early death in the ill-fated Escobar invasion might have been the greatest stroke of political good fortune ever to befall Barrayar . . . had even a hint of this multi-faceted personality ever been permitted to filter back to Gregor? Nobody who knew Serg talked about him, Count Vorkosigan least of all. Miles had once met one of Serg's victims. Miles hoped Gregor never would.

Miles decided to change the subject. "So we all know what happened to me, what have you been up to for the last three months? I was sorry to miss your last birthday party. Up at Kyril Island they celebrated it by getting drunk, which made it virtually indistinguishable from any other day."

Gregor grinned, then sighed. "Too many ceremonies. Too much time standing up—I think I could be replaced at half my functions by a life-sized plastic model, and no one would notice. A lot of time spent ducking the broad marital hints of my assorted counsellors."

"Actually, they have a point," Miles had to allow. "If you got . . . run over by a teacart tomorrow, the succession question goes up for grabs in a big way. I can think offhand of at least six candidates with arguable stakes in the Imperium, and more would come out of the woodwork. Some without personal ambition would nevertheless kill to see that some of the others didn't get it, which is precisely why you still don't have a named heir."

Gregor cocked his head. "You're in that crowd yourself, you know."

"With this body?" Miles snorted. "They'd have to . . . really hate somebody, to tag me. At that point it really would be time to run away from home. Far and fast. Do me a favor. Get married, settle down, and have six little Vorbarras real quick."

Gregor looked even more depressed. "Now there's an idea. Running away from home. I wonder how far I'd get, before Illyan caught up with me?"

They both glanced involuntarily upward, though in fact Miles was still not certain where the room's bugs were located. "Better hope Illyan caught up with you before anybody else did." God, this conversation was getting morbid.

"I don't know, wasn't there an emperor of China who ended up pushing a broom somewhere? And a thousand lesser emigrees—countesses running restaurants—escape *is* possible."

"From being Vor? More like . . . trying to run away from your own shadow." There would be moments, in the dark, when success would seem achieved, but then—Miles shook his head, and checked out the still-lumpy bag. "Ah! You brought a tacti-go set." He didn't in the least want to play tacti-go, it had bored him by age fourteen, but anything was better than this. He pulled it out and set it up between them with determined good cheer. "Brings back old times." Hideous thought.

Gregor bestirred himself, and made an opening move. Pretending to be interested to amuse Miles, who was simulating interest to cheer Gregor, who was feigning . . . Miles, distracted, beat Gregor too fast on the first round, and began to pay more attention. On the next round he kept it closer, and was rewarded by a spark of genuine interest—blessed self-forgetfulness—on Gregor's part. They opened the second bottle of wine. At that point Miles began to feel the effects, going tongue-thick and sleepy and stupid; it took hardly any effort to let Gregor almost win the next round.

"I don't think I've beaten you at this since you were fourteen," sighed Gregor, concealing secret satisfaction at the low point-spread of that last round. "You should be an officer, dammit."

"This isn't a good war game, Dad says," commented Miles. "Not enough random factors and uncontrolled surprises to simulate reality. I like it that way." It was almost soothing, a mindless routine of logic, check and counter, multiple chained moves with, always, perfectly objective options.

"You should know." Gregor glanced up. "I still

don't understand why they sent you to Kyril Island. You've already commanded a real space fleet. Even if they were only a pack of grubby mercenaries."

"Shh. That episode is officially non-existent, in my military files. Fortunately. It wouldn't charm my superiors. I'd commanded, I hadn't obeyed. Anyway, I didn't so much command the Dendarii Mercenaries as hypnotize 'em. Without Captain Tung, who decided to prop up my pretensions for his own purposes, it would have all ended very unpleasantly. And much sooner."

"I always thought Illyan would do more with them, after," said Gregor. "However inadvertently, you brought a whole military organization secretly into the service of Barrayar."

"Yes, without them even knowing it themselves. Now, *that's* secret. Come on. Assigning them to Illyan's section was a legal fiction, everybody knew it." And would his own assignment to Illyan's section turn out to be a legal fiction too? "Illyan's too careful to get drawn into intergalactic military adventuring as a hobby. I'm afraid his main interest in the Dendarii Mercenaries is to keep them as far away from Barrayar as possible. Mercenaries thrive on other people's chaos.

"Plus, they're a funny size—less than a dozen ships, three or four thousand personnel—not your basic invisible six-man covert ops team, though they can field such, and yet they're too little to take on planetary situations. Space-based, not ground troops. Wormhole blockades were their specialty. Safe, easy on the equipment, mostly bullying unarmed civilians—which is how I first ran into them, when our freighter was stopped by their blockade, and the bullying went too far. I cringe to think of the risks I ran. Though I've often wondered if, knowing what I know now, I could have. . . ." Miles stopped, shook his head. "Or maybe it's like heights. Better not to look down. You freeze, and then you fall." Miles was not fond of heights.

"As a military experience, how did it compare with Lazkowski Base?" asked Gregor bemusedly.

"Oh, there were certain parallels," Miles admitted. "Both were jobs I wasn't trained for, both were potentially lethal, I got out of both by my skin—lost some skin. The Dendarii episode was . . . worse. I lost Sergeant Bothari. In a sense, I lost Elena. At least at Camp Permafrost I managed not to lose anyone."

"Maybe you're getting better," Gregor suggested.

Miles shook his head, and drank. He should have put on some music. The thick silence of this room was oppressive, when the conversation faltered. The ceiling was probably not hydraulically arranged to descend and crush him in his sleep; Security had far less messy ways of dealing with recalcitrant prisoners. It only seemed to lower at him. *Well, I'm short. Maybe it'd miss me.*

"I suppose it would be . . . improper," Miles began hesitantly, "to ask you to try and get me out of here. It's always seemed rather embarassing, to ask for Imperial favors. Like cheating, or something."

"What, are you asking one prisoner of ImpSec to rescue another?" Gregor's hazel eyes were ironic under black brows. "It's a little embarrassing to me to come up against the limits of my absolute Imperial Rule. Your father and Illyan, like two parentheses around me." His cupped hands closed in a squeezing motion.

It was a subliminal effect of this room, Miles decided. Gregor was feeling it too.

"I would if I could," Gregor added more apologetically. "But Illyan's made it crystal clear he wants you kept out of sight. For a time, anyway."

"Time." Miles swallowed the last of his wine, and decided he'd better not pour himself any more. Alcohol was a depressant, it was said. "How much time?

Dammit, if I don't get something to do soon, I'm going to be the first case of human spontaneous combustion recorded on vid." He jerked a rude finger at the ceiling. "I don't need to—don't even have to leave the building, but at least they could give me some *work*. Clerical, janitorial—I do terrific drains—anything. Dad talked with Illyan about assigning me to Security—as the only Section left that would take me—he must have had something more in mind than a m-, m-, mascot." He poured and drank again, to stop the spate of words. He'd said too much. Damn the wine. Damn the whine.

Gregor, who had built a little tower of tacti-go chips, toppled it with one finger. "Oh, being a mascot isn't bad work, if you can get it." He stirred the pile slowly. "I'll see what I can do. No promises."

Miles didn't know if it was the Emperor, the bugs, or wheels already in motion (grinding slowly), but two days afterwards he found himself assigned to the job of administrative assistant to the guard commander for the building. It was comconsole work; scheduling, payroll, updating computer files. The job was interesting for a week, while he was learning it, mind-numbing after that. By the end of a month, the boredom and banality were beginning to prey on his nerves. Was he loyal, or merely stupid? Guards, Miles now realized, had to stay in prison all day long too. Indeed, as a guard, one of his jobs was now to keep himself in. Damn clever of Illyan, nobody else could have held him, if he'd been determined on escape. He did find a window once, and looked out. It was sleeting.

Was he going to get out of this bloody box before Winterfair? How long did it take the world to forget him, anyway? If he committed suicide, could he be officially listed as shot by a guard while escaping? Was Illyan trying to drive him out of his mind, or just out of his Section?

Another month slipped by. As a spiritual exercise, he decided to fill his off-duty hours by watching every training vid in the military library, in strict alphabetical order. The assortment was truly astonishing. He was particularly bemused by the thirty-minute vid (under "H: Hygiene") explaining how to take a shower—well, yes, there probably were back-country recruits who really needed the instruction. After some weeks he had worked his way down to "L: Laser-rifle Model D-67; power-pack circuitry, maintenance, and repair," when he was interrupted by a call ordering him to report to Illyan's office.

Illyan's office was almost unchanged from Miles's last excruciating visit—same spartan windowless inner chamber occupied mainly by a comconsole desk that looked like it could be used to pilot a jump ship—but now there were two chairs. One was promisingly empty. Maybe Miles wouldn't end up so literally on the carpet this round? The other was occupied by a man in undress greens with captain's tabs and the Horus-eye insignia of Imperial Security on the collar.

Interesting fellow, that captain. Miles summed him out of the corner of his eye as he exchanged formal salutes with Illyan. Maybe thirty-five years old, he had something of Illyan's unmemorable bland look about the face, but was more heavily built. Pale. He might easily pass for some minor bureaucrat, a sedentary indoorsman. But that particular look could also be acquired by spending a great deal of time cooped up on spaceships.

"Ensign Vorkosigan, this is Captain Ungari. Captain Ungari is one of my galactic operatives. He has ten years experience gathering information for this department. His specialty is military evaluation."

Ungari favored Miles with a polite nod by way of acknowledging the introduction. His level gaze summed Miles right back. Miles wondered what the spy's evaluation of the dwarfish soldier standing before him might be, and tried to stand straighter. There was nothing obvious about Ungari's reaction to Miles.

Illyan leaned back in his swivel chair. "So tell me, Ensign, what have you heard lately from the Dendarii Mercenaries?"

"Sir?" Miles rocked back. *Not* the curve he was expecting . . . "I . . . lately, nothing. I had a message about a year ago from Elena Bothari—Bothari-Jesek, that is. But it was only private, uh, birthday greetings."

"That one I have," Illyan nodded.

Do you, you bastard.

"—Nothing since?"

"No, sir."

"Hm." Illyan waved a hand at the spare chair. "Sit down, Miles." His voice grew quicker and more businesslike. *Meat at last?* "Let's go over a little astrography. Geography is the mother of strategy, they say." Illyan fiddled with a control on his comconsole.

A wormhole nexus route map formed in three bright dimensions over the holovid plate. It looked rather like a ball-and-stick model of some weird organic molecule done in colored light, balls representing local-space crossings, sticks the wormhole-space jumps between; schematic, compressing information, rather than to scale. Illyan zoomed in on a portion, red and blue sparks in the center of an otherwise empty ball, with four sticks leading out at crazy angles to more complex balls like some skewed Celtic cross. "Look familiar?"

"That in the center is the Hegen Hub, isn't it, sir?"

"Good." Illyan handed him his controller. "Give me a strategic summation of the Hegen Hub, Ensign."

Miles cleared his throat. "It's a double star system with no habitable planets, a few stations and power-sats, and very little reason to linger in. Like many nexus connections, it's more route than place, taking its value by what's around it. In this case, four adjoining regions of local space with settled planets." Miles brightened each part of the image as he spoke, for emphasis.

"Aslund. Aslund is a cul-de-sac like Barrayar; the Hegen Hub is its sole gate to the greater galactic web. The Hegen Hub is as vital to Aslund as our gateway Komarr is to us.

"Jackson's Whole. The Hegen Hub is just one of five gates from Jacksonian local space; beyond Jackson's Whole lies half the explored galaxy.

"Vervain. Vervain has two exits; one to the Hub, the other into the nexus sectors controlled by the Cetagandan Empire.

"And fourth, of course, our, ah, good neighbor the Planet and Republic of Pol. Which in turn connects to our own multi-nexus Komarr. Also from Komarr is our one straight jump to the Cetagandan sector, which route has been either tightly controlled or outright barred to Cetagandan traffic ever since we conquered it." Miles glanced at Illyan for approval, hoping he was on the right track. Illyan glanced at Ungari, who allowed his brows to rise fractionally. Meaning what?

"Wormhole strategy. The devil's cat's cradle," Illyan muttered editorially. He squinted at his glowing schematic. "Four players, one game-board. It ought to be simple. . . .

"Anyway," Illyan stretched out his hand for the controller, and sat back with a sigh, "the Hegen Hub is more than a potential choke-point for the four adjoining systems. Twenty-five percent of our own commercial traffic passes through it, via Pol. And although Vervain is closed to Cetagandan military vessels just as Pol is closed to ours, the Cetas ship significant civilian exchange through the same slot and out past Jackson's Whole. Anything—like a war—that blocks the Hegen Hub would seem almost as damaging to Cetaganda as to us.

"And yet, after years of cooperative disinterest and dull neutrality, this empty region is suddenly alive with what I can only call an arms race. All four neighbors seem to be creating military interests. Pol has been beefing up the armament on all six of its jump point stations strung toward the Hub—even pulling forces from the side toward us, which I find a little startling, since Pol has been extremely wary of us ever since we took Komarr. The Jackson's Whole consortium is doing the same on its side. Vervain has hired a mercenary fleet called Randall's Rangers.

"All this activity is causing low-grade panic on Aslund, whose interest in the Hegen Hub is for obvious reasons most critical. They're throwing half this year's military budget into a major jumppoint station—hell, a floating fortress—and to cover the gap while they prepare, they too have hired guns. You may be familiar with them. They used to be called the Dendarii Free Mercenary Fleet." Illyan paused, and raised an eyebrow, watching for Miles's reaction.

Connections at last—or were there? Miles blew out his breath. "They were blockade specialists, at one time. Makes sense, I guess. Ah . . . used to be called the Dendarii? Have they changed lately?"

"They've recently reverted to their original title of Oseran Mercenaries, it seems."

"Strange. Why?"

"Why, indeed?" Illyan's lips compressed. "One of many questions, though hardly the most urgent. But it's the Cetagandan connection—or lack of it—that bothers me. General chaos in the region would be as damaging to Cetaganda as to us. But if, after the chaos passes, Cetaganda could somehow end up in control of the Hegen Hub—ah! Then they could block or control Barrayaran traffic as we do theirs through Komarr. Indeed, if you look at the other side of the Komarr-Cetaganda jump as being under their control, that would put them across two out of our four major galactic routes. Something labyrinthine, indirect—it smells of Cetaganda's methods. Or would, if I could spot their sticky hands pulling any of the strings. They must be there, even if I can't see them yet. . . ." Brooding, Illyan shook his head. "If the Jackson's Whole jump were cut, everyone would have to reroute through the Cetagadan Empire . . . profit, there. . . ."

"Or through us," Miles pointed out. "Why should Cetaganda do us that favor?"

"I have thought of one possibility. Actually, I've thought of nine, but this one's for you, Miles. What's the best way to capture a jump point?"

"From both ends at once," Miles recited automatically.

"Which is one reason Pol has been careful never to let us amass any military presence in the Hegen Hub. But let us suppose someone on Pol stumbles across that nasty rumor I had so much trouble scotching that the Dendarii Mercenaries are the private army of a certain Barrayaran Vor lordling? What will they think?"

"They'll think we're getting ready to jump them," said Miles. "They might go paranoid—panic—even seek a temporary alliance, with, say, Cetaganda?"

"Very good," nodded Illyan.

Captain Ungari, who had been listening with the attentive patience of a man who'd been over it all before, glanced at Miles as if faintly encouraged, and approved this hypothesis with a nod of his head.

"But even if perceived as an independent force," Illyan went on, "the Dendarii are one more destabilizing influence in the region. The whole situation is disturbing—growing tenser by the day, for no apparent reason. Only a little more force—one mistake, one lethal incident—could trigger turbulence, classic chaos, the real thing, unstoppable. Reasons, Miles! I want information."

Illyan, generally, wanted information with the same passion that a strung-out juba freak craved a spike. He turned now to Ungari. "So what do you think, Captain? Will he do?"

Ungari was slow to reply. "He's . . . more physically conspicuous than I'd realized."

"As camouflage, that's not necessarily a disadvantage. In his company you ought to be nearly invisible. The stalking goat and the hunter."

"Perhaps. But can he carry the load? I'm not going to have much time for babysitting." Ungari's voice was an urban baritone, evidently one of the modern educated officers, though he did not wear an Academy pin.

"The Admiral seems to think so. Am I to argue?"

Ungari glanced at Miles. "Are you sure the Admiral's judgment is not swayed by . . . personal hopes?"

You mean wishful thinking, Miles mentally translated that delicate hesitancy.

"If so, it's for the first time," Illyan shrugged. *And there's a first time for everything*, hung unspoken in the air. Illyan turned now to pin Miles with a gaze of grim intensity. "Miles, do you think you would—if required—be capable of playing the part of Admiral Naismith again, for a short time?"

He'd seen it coming, but the words spoken out loud were still a strange cold thrill. To activate that suppressed persona again. . . . *It wasn't just a part, Illyan.* "I could play Naismith again, sure. It's *stopping* playing Naismith that scares me."

Illyan allowed himself a wintry smile, taking this for a joke. Miles's smile was a little sicker. *You don't know, you don't know what it was like.* . . . Three parts fakery and flim-flam, and one part . . some-thing else. Zen, gestalt, delusion? Uncontrollable moments of alpha-state exaltation. . . . Could he do it again? Maybe he knew too much now. *First you freeze, and then you fall.* Perhaps it *would* only be play-acting, this time.

Illyan leaned back, held up his hands palm to palm, and let them fall in a releasing gesture. "Very well, Captain Ungari. He's all yours. Use him as you see fit. Your mission, then, is to gather information on the current crisis in the Hegen Hub; secondly, if possible, to use Ensign Vorkosigan to remove the Dendarii Mercenaries from the stage. If you decide to use a bogus contract to pull them out of the Hub, you can draw on the covert ops account for a convincing down-payment. You know the results I want. I'm sorry I can't make my orders more specific in advance of the intelligence you yourself must obtain."

"I don't mind, sir," said Ungari, smiling slightly.

"Hm. Enjoy your independence while it lasts. It ends with your first mistake." Illyan's tone was sardonic, but his eyes were confident, until he turned them toward Miles. "Miles, you'll be traveling as 'Admiral Naismith,' himself traveling incognito, returning, possibly, to the Dendarii fleet. Should Captain Ungari decide for you to activate the Naismith role, he'll pose as your bodyguard, so as to be always in position to control the situation. It's a little too much to ask Ungari to be responsible for his mission and also your safety, so you'll also have a real bodyguard. This setup will give Captain Ungari unusual freedom of movement, because it will account for your possession of a personal ship—we have a jump pilot and a fast courier we obtained from—never mind where, but it has no connection with Barrayar. It's under Jacksonian registration at present, which fits in nicely with Admiral Naismith's mysterious background. It's so obviously bogus, no one will look for a second layer of, er, bogusity." Illyan paused. "You will, of course, obey Captain Ungari's orders. *That* goes without saying." Illyan's direct stare was chill as a Kyril Island midnight.

Miles smiled dutifully, to show he took the hint. *I'll be good, sir—let me off planet!* From ghost to goat—was this a promotion?

at four of the six major Polar stations in the three-
between Pol and the Hegen Hub, with Ungari
counting, assessing, collecting computer-station...
...classified or... note was. Now they had arrived
at Pol's last far-flung depending of Hegen Hub, and
...onfront its... in the Hegen Hub, itself.
At one more... — then head-out, and the journal
...point to a more... at... and... computer
...at...

CHAPTER EIGHT

Victor Rotha, Procurement Agent. Sounded like a
pimp. Dubiously, Miles regarded his new persona
twinned over the vid plate in his cabin. What was
wrong with a simple spartan mirror, anyway? *Where*
had Illyan gotten this *ship?* Of Betan manufacture,
it was stuffed with Betan gimmickry of a luxurious
order. Miles entertained himself with a gruesome
vision of what could happen if the programming on
the elaborate sonic tooth-cleaner ever went awry.

"Rotha" was vaguely dressed, with respect to his
supposed point-of-origin. Miles had drawn the line
at a Betan sarong, Pol Station Six was not nearly
warm enough for it. He did wear his loose green
trousers held up with a Betan sarong rope, though,
and Betan style sandals. The green shirt was a cheap
synthetic silk from Escobar, the baggy cream jacket
an expensive one of like style. The eclectic wardrobe
of someone originally from Beta Colony, who'd been
knocking around the galaxy for a while, sometimes
up, sometimes down. Good. He muttered to himself
aloud, warming up his disused Betan accent, as he
pottered about the elaborate Owner's Cabin.

They had docked here at Pol Six a day ago without
incident. The whole three-week trip from Barrayar
had passed without incident. Ungari seemed to like
it that way. The ImpSec captain had spent most of
the journey counting things, taking pictures and
counting; ships, troops, security guards both civil
and military. They'd managed excuses to stop over

at four of the six jump point stations on the route between Pol and the Hegen Hub, with Ungari counting, measuring, sectioning, computer-stuffing, and calculating the whole way. Now they had arrived at Pol's last (or first, depending on your direction of travel) outpost, its toehold in the Hegen Hub itself.

At one time, Pol Six had merely marked the jump point, no more than an emergency stop and communications transfer link. No one had yet solved the problem of getting messages through a wormhole jump except by physically transporting them on a jump ship. In the most developed regions of the nexus, comm ships jumped hourly or even more often, to emit a tight-beam burst that traveled at the speed of light to the next jump point in that region of local space, where messages were picked up and relayed out in turn, the fastest possible flow of information. In the less developed regions, one simply had to wait, sometimes for weeks or months, for a ship to happen by, and hope they'd remember to drop off your mail.

Now Pol Six didn't just mark, it frankly guarded. Ungari had clicked his tongue in excitement, identifying and adding up Pol Navy ships clustered in the area around the new construction. They'd managed a spiral flight path into dock that revealed every side of the station, and all ships both moored and moving.

"Your main job here," Ungari had told Miles, "will be to give anyone watching us something more interesting to watch than me. Circulate. I doubt you'll need to expend any special effort to be conspicuous. Develop your cover identity—with luck, you may even pick up a contact or two who'll be worthy of further study. Though I doubt you'll run across anything of great value immediately, it doesn't work that way."

Now, Miles laid his samples case open on his bed and rechecked it. *Just a traveling salesman, that's me.* A dozen hand weapons, power-packs removed, gleamed wickedly back at him. A row of vid-disks described larger and more interesting weapons systems. An even more interesting—you might even say, "arresting"—collection of tiny disks nestled concealed in Miles's jacket. *Death. I can get it for you wholesale.*

Miles's bodyguard met him at the docking hatch. Why, oh God, had Illyan assigned Sergeant Overkill to this mission? Same reason he'd sent him to Kyril Island, because he was trusted, no doubt, but it embarrassed Miles to be working with a man who'd once arrested him. What did Overholt make of Miles, by now? Happily, the big man was the silent type.

Overholt was dressed as informally and eclectically as Miles himself, though with safety boots in place of sandals. He looked exactly like somebody's bodyguard trying to look like a tourist. Much the sort of man small-time arms dealer Victor Rotha would logically employ. *Both functional and decorative, he slices, dices, and chops.* . . . By themselves, either Miles or Overholt would be memorable. Together, well . . . Ungari was right. They needn't worry about being overlooked.

Miles led the way through the docking tube and into Pol Six. This docking spoke funneled into a Customs area, where Miles's sample case and person were carefully examined, and Overholt had to produce registration for his stunner. From there they had free run of the transfer station facilities, but for certain guarded corridors leading into the, as it were, militarized zones. Those areas, Ungari had made clear, were his business, not Miles's.

Miles, in good time for his first appointment, strolled slowly, enjoying the sensation of being on a space station. The place wasn't as free-wheeling as Beta Colony, but without question he moved in the midst of mainstream galactic technoculture. Not like poor half-backwards Barrayar. The brittle artificial

environment emitted its own whiff of danger, a whiff
that could balloon instantly into claustrophobic terror
in the event of a sudden depressurization emergency. A concourse lined with shops, hostels, and
eating facilities made a central meeting area.

A curious trio idled just across the busy concourse
from Miles. A big man dressed in loose clothing ideal
for concealing weapons scanned the area uneasily. A
professional counterpart of Sergeant Overkill's, no
doubt. He and Overholt spotted each other and
exchanged grim glances, carefully ignored each other
after that. The bland man he guarded faded into
near-invisibility beside his woman.

She was short, but astonishingly intense, slight
figure and white-blonde hair cropped close to her
head giving her an odd elfin look. Her black jumpsuit seemed shot with electric sparks, flowing over
her skin like water, evening-wear in the day-cycle.
Thin-heeled black shoes boosted her a few futile centimeters. Her lips were colored blood-carmine to
match the shimmering scarf that looped across ala-
baster collarbones to cascade from each shoulder,
framing the bare white skin of her back. She looked
. . . expensive.

Her eye caught Miles's fascinated stare. Her chin
lifted, and she stared back coldly.

"Victor Rotha?" The voice at Miles's elbow made
him jump.

"Ah . . . Mr. Liga?" Miles, wheeling, hazarded in
return. Rabbitlike pale features, protruding lip,
black hair; this was the man who claimed he wished
to improve the armament of his security guards at
his asteroid mining facility. Sure. How—and where—
had Ungari scraped Liga up? Miles was not sure he
wanted to know.

"I've arranged a private room for us to talk," Liga
smiled, tilting his head toward a nearby hostel
entrance. "Eh," Liga added, "looks like everybody's
doing business this morning." He nodded toward the

trio across the concourse, who were now a quartet and moving off. The scarves snapped along like banners, floating in the quick-stepping blonde's wake.

"Who was that woman?" asked Miles.

"I don't know," said Liga. "But the man they're following is your main competition here. The agent of House Fell, the Jacksonian armaments specialists."

He looked more like a middle-aged businessman type, at least from the back. "Pol lets the Jacksonians operate here?" Miles asked. "I thought tensions were high."

"Between Pol, Aslund, and Vervain, yes," said Liga. "The Jacksonian consortium is loudly claiming neutrality. They hope to profit from all sides. But this isn't the best place to talk politics. Let's go, eh?"

As Miles expected, Liga settled them in what was obviously an otherwise-unoccupied hostel room, rented for the purpose. Miles began his memorized pitch, working through the hand-weapons, baffle-gabbing about available inventory and delivery dates.

"I'd hoped," said Liga, "for something a little more . . . authoritative."

"I have another selection of samples aboard my ship," Miles explained. "I didn't want to trouble Pol customs with them. But I can give you an overview by vid."

Miles trotted out the heavy weapons manuals. "This vid is for educational purposes only, of course, as these weapons are of a grade illegal for a private person to own in Pol local space."

"In Pol space, yes," Liga agreed. "But Pol's law doesn't run in the Hegen Hub. Yet. All you have to do is cast off from Pol Six and take a little run out beyond the ten-thousand-kilometer traffic control limit to conduct any sort of business you want, perfectly legally. The problem comes in delivering the cargo back *in* to Pol local space."

"Difficult deliveries are one of my specialties," Miles assured him. "For a small surcharge, of course."

"Eh. Good . . ." Liga flicked fast-forward through the vid catalogue. "These heavy-duty plasma arcs, now . . . how do they compare with the cannon-grade nerve disruptors?"

Miles shrugged. "Depends entirely upon whether you want to blow away people alone, or people and property both. I can make you a very good price on the nerve disruptors." He named a figure in Pol credits.

"I got a better quote than that, on a device of the same kilowattage, lately," Liga mentioned disinterestedly.

"I'll bet you did," Miles grinned. "Poison, one credit. Antidote, one hundred credits."

"What's that supposed to mean, eh?" asked Liga suspiciously.

Miles unrolled his lapel and ran his thumb down the underside, and pulled out a tiny vid tab. "Take a look at this." He inserted it into the vid viewer. A figure sprang to life, and pirouetted. It was dressed from head to toe- and finger-tips in what appeared to be glittering skin-tight netting.

"A bit drafty for long underwear, eh?" said Liga sceptically.

Miles flashed him a pained smile. "What you're looking at is what every armed force in the galaxy would like to get their hands on. The perfected single-person nerve disruptor shield net. Beta Colony's latest technological card."

Liga's eyes widened. "First I'd heard they were on the market."

"The open market, no. These are, as it were, private advance sales." Beta Colony only advertised its second or third latest advantages; staying several steps ahead of everybody else in R&D had been the harsh world's stock-in-trade for a couple of generations. In time, Beta Colony would be marketing its new device galaxy-wide. In the meantime . . .

Liga licked his pouty lower lip. "We use nerve disruptors a lot."

For security guards? Right, sure. "I have a limited supply of shield nets. First come, first served."

"The price?"

Miles named a figure in Betan dollars.

"Outrageous!" Liga rocked back in his float chair.

Miles shrugged. "Think about it. It could put your . . . organization at a considerable disadvantage not to be the first to upgrade its defenses. I'm sure you can imagine."

"I'll . . . have to check it out. Eh . . . can I have that disk to show my, eh, supervisor?"

Miles pursed his lips. "Don't get caught with it."

"No way." Liga spun the demo vid through its paces one more time, staring in fascination at the sparkling soldier-figure, before pocketing the disk.

There. The hook was baited, and cast upon dark waters. It was going to be very interesting to see what nibbled, whether minnows or monstrous leviathans. Liga was a fish of the ramora underclass, Miles judged. Well, he had to start somewhere.

Back out on the concourse, Miles muttered worriedly to Overholt, "Did I do all right?"

"Very smooth, sir," Overholt reassured him.

Well, maybe. It had felt good, running by plan. He could almost feel himself submerging into the smarmy personality of Victor Rotha.

For lunch, Miles led Overholt to a cafeteria with seating open to the concourse, the better for anyone not-watching Ungari to observe them. He munched a sandwich of vat-produced protein, and let his tight nerves unwind a little. This act could be all right. Not nearly as overstimulating as—

"Admiral Naismith!"

Miles nearly choked on a half-chewed bite, his head swivelling frantically to identify the source of the surprised voice. Overholt jerked to full-alert, though he managed to keep his hand from flying prematurely to his concealed stunner.

Two men had paused beside his table. One Miles did not recognize. The other . . . damn! He knew that face. Square-jawed, brown-skinned, too neat and fit for his age to pass as anything but a soldier despite his Polian civilian clothes. The name, the name . . . ! One of Tung's commandos, a combat-drop-shuttle squad commander. The last time Miles had seen him they'd been suiting up together in the *Triumph*'s armory, preparing for a boarding battle. Clive Chodak, that was his name.

"I'm sorry, you're mistaken," Miles's denial was pure spinal reflex. "My name is Victor Rotha."

Chodak blinked. "What? Oh! Sorry. That is—you look a lot like somebody I used to know." He took in Overholt. His eyes queried Miles urgently. "Uh, can we join you?"

"No!" said Miles sharply, panicked. No, wait. He shouldn't throw away a possible contact. This was a complication for which he should have been prepared. But to activate Naismith prematurely, without Ungari's orders. . . . "Anyway, not here," he amended hastily.

"I . . . see, sir." With a short nod, Chodak immediately withdrew, drawing his reluctant companion with him. He managed to glance back over his shoulder only once. Miles restrained the impulse to bite his napkin in half. The two men faded into the concourse. By their urgent gestures, they appeared to be arguing.

"Was that smooth?" Miles asked plaintively.

Overholt looked mildly dismayed. "Not very." He frowned down the concourse in the direction the two men had disappeared.

It didn't take Chodak more than an hour to track Miles down aboard his Betan ship in dock. Ungari was still out.

"He says he wants to talk to you," said Overholt. He and Miles studied the vid monitor of the hatchway, where Chodak shifted impatiently from foot to foot. "What do you think he really wants?"

"Probably, to talk to me," said Miles. "Damn me if I don't want to talk to him, too."

"How well did you know him?" asked Overholt suspiciously, staring at Chodak's image.

"Not well," Miles admitted. "He seemed a competent non-com. Knew his equipment, kept his people moving, stood his ground under fire." In truth, thinking back, Miles's actual contacts with the man had been brief, all in the course of business . . . but some of those minutes had been critical, in the wild uncertainty of shipboard combat. Was Miles's gut-feel really adequate security clearance for a man he hadn't seen for almost four years? "Scan him, sure. But let's let him in and see what he has to say."

"If you so order it, sir," said Overholt neutrally.

"I do."

Chodak did not seem to resent being scanned. He carried only a registered stunner. Though he had also been an expert at hand-to-hand combat, Miles recalled, a weapon no one could confiscate. Overholt escorted him to the small ship's wardroom/mess—the Betans would have called it the rec room.

"Mr. Rotha," Chodak nodded. "I, uh . . . hoped we could talk here privately." He looked doubtfully at Overholt. "Or have you replaced Sergeant Bothari?"

"Never." Miles motioned Overholt to follow him into the corridor, didn't speak till the doors sighed shut. "I think you are an inhibiting presence, Sergeant. Would you mind waiting outside?" Miles didn't specify whom Overholt inhibited. "You can monitor, of course."

"Bad idea," Overholt frowned. "Suppose he jumps you?"

Miles's fingers tapped nervously on his trouser seam. "It's a possibility. But we're heading for

Aslund next, where the Dendarii are stationed, Ungari says. He may bear useful information."

"If he tells the truth."

"Even lies can be revealing." With this doubtful argument Miles squeezed back into the wardroom, shedding Overholt.

He nodded to his visitor, now seated at a table. "Corporal Chodak."

Chodak brightened. "You do remember."

"Oh, yes. And, ah . . . are you still with the Dendarii?"

"Yes, sir. It's Sergeant Chodak, now."

"Very good. I'm not surprised."

"And, um . . . the Oseran Mercenaries."

"So I understand. Whether it's good or not remains to be seen."

"What are you posing as, sir?"

"Victor Rotha is an arms dealer."

"That's a good cover," Chodak nodded, judiciously.

Miles tried to put a casual mask on his next words by punching up two coffees. "So what are you doing on Pol Six? I thought the Den—the fleet was hired out on Aslund."

"At Aslund Station, here in the Hub," Chodak corrected. "It's just a couple days' flight across-system. What there is of it, so far. Government contractors." He shook his head.

"Behind schedule and over cost?"

"You got it." He accepted the coffee without hesitation, holding it between lean hands, and took a preliminary slurp. "I can't stay long." He turned the cup, set it on the table. "Sir, I think I may have accidently done you a bad turn. I was so startled to see you there. . . . Anyway, I wanted to . . . to warn you, I guess. Are you on the way back to the fleet?"

"I'm afraid I can't discuss my plans. Not even with you."

Chodak gave him a penetrating stare from black almond eyes. "You always were tricky."

"As an experienced combat soldier, do you prefer frontal assaults?"

"No, sir!" Chodak smiled slightly.

"Suppose you tell me. I take it you are—or are one—of the fleet intelligence agents scattered around the Hub. There had better be more than one of you, or the organization's fallen apart sadly in my absence." In fact, half the inhabitants of Pol Six at the moment were probably spies of some stripe, considering the number of potential players in this game. Not to mention double agents—ought they to be counted twice?

"Why have you been gone so *long*, sir?" Chodak's tone was almost accusative.

"It wasn't my intention," Miles temporized. "For a portion of the time I was a prisoner in a . . . place I'd rather not describe. I only escaped about three months back." Well, that was one way of describing Kyril Island.

"You, sir! We could have rescued—"

"No, you couldn't have," Miles said sharply. "The situation was one of extreme delicacy. It was resolved to my satisfaction. But I was then faced with . . . considerable clean-up in areas of my operations other than the Dendarii fleet. Far-flung areas. Sorry, but you people are not my only concern. Nevertheless, I'm worried. I should have heard more from Commodore Jesek." Indeed, he should have.

"Commodore Jesek no longer commands. There was a financial reorganization and command restructuring, about a year ago, through the committee of captain-owners and Admiral Oser. Spearheaded by Admiral Oser."

"Where is Jesek?"

"He was demoted to fleet engineer."

Disturbing, but Miles could see it. "Not necessarily a bad thing. Jesek was never as aggressive as, say, Tung. And Tung?"

Chodak shook his head. "He was demoted from chief-of-staff to personnel officer. A nothing-job."

"That seems . . . wasteful."

"Oser doesn't trust Tung. And Tung doesn't love Oser, either. Oser's been trying to force him out for a year, but he hangs on, despite the humiliation of . . . um. It's not easy to get rid of him. Oser can't afford—yet—to decimate his staff, and too many key people are personally loyal to Tung."

Miles's eyebrow rose. "Including yourself?"

Chodak said distantly, "He got things done. I considered him a superior officer."

"So did I."

Chodak nodded shortly. "Sir . . . the thing is . . . the man who was with me in the cafeteria is my senior here. And he's one of Oser's. I can't think of any way short of killing him to stop him reporting our encounter."

"I have no desire to start a civil war in my own command structure," said Miles mildly. *Yet.* "I think it's more important that he not suspect you spoke to me privately. Let him report. I've struck deals with Admiral Oser before, to our mutual benefit."

"I'm not sure Oser thinks so, sir. I think he thinks he was screwed."

Miles barked a realistic laugh. "What, I doubled the size of the fleet during the Tau Verde war. Even as third officer, he ended up commanding more than he had before, a smaller slice of a bigger pie."

"But the side he originally contracted us to lost."

"Not so. Both sides gained from that truce we forced. It was a win-win result, except for a little lost face. What, can't Oser feel he's won unless somebody else loses?"

Chodak looked grim. "I think that may be the case, sir. He says—I've heard him say—you ran a scam on us. You were never an admiral, never an officer of any kind. If Tung hadn't double-crossed him, he'd have kicked your ass to hell." Chodak's gaze on Miles was broodingly thoughtful. "What were you really?"

Miles smiled gently. "I was the winner. Remember?"

Chodak snorted, half-amused. "Yee-ah."

"Don't let poor Oser's revisionist history fog your mind. You were there."

Chodak shook his head ruefully. "You didn't really need my warning, did you." He moved to stand up.

"Never assume anything. And, ah . . . take care of yourself. That means, cover your ass. I'll remember you, later."

"Sir." Chodak nodded. Overholt, waiting in the corridor in a quasi-Imperial Guardsman pose, escorted him firmly to the shuttle hatch.

Miles sat in the wardroom, and nibbled gently on the rim of his coffee cup, considering certain surprising parallels between command restructuring in a free mercenary fleet and the internecine wars of the Barrayaran Vor. Might the mercenaries be thought of as a miniature, simplified, or laboratory version of the real thing? *Oser should have been around during the Vordarian's Pretendership, and seen how the big boys operate.* Still, Miles had best not underestimate the potential dangers and complexities of the situation. His death in a miniature conflict would be just as absolute as his death in a large one.

Hell, what death? What had he to do with the Dendarii, or the Oserans, after all? Oser was right, it had been a scam, and the only wonder was how long it had taken the man to wake to the fact. Miles could see no immediate need to reinvolve himself with the Dendarii at all. In fact, he could be well-rid of a dangerous political embarrassment. Let Oser have them, they'd been his in the first place anyway.

I have three sworn liege-people in that fleet. My own personal body politic.

How *easy* it had been to slip back into being Naismith. . . .

Anyway, activating Naismith wasn't Miles's decision. It was Captain Ungari's.

Ungari was the first to point this out, when he returned later and Overholt briefed him. A controlled man, his fury showed by subtle signs, a sharpening of the voice, deeper lines of tension around the eyes and mouth. "You violated your cover. You *never* break cover. It's the first rule of survival in this business."

"Sir, may I respectfully submit, I didn't blow it," Miles replied steadily. "Chodak did. He seemed to realize it, too, he's not stupid. He apologized as best he could." Chodak indeed might be subtler than first glance would indicate, for at this point, he had an in with both sides in the putative Dendarii command schism, whoever came out on top. Calculation or chance? Chodak was either smart or lucky, in either case he could be a useful addition to Miles's side. . . . *What side, huh? Ungari isn't going to let me near the Dendarii after this.*

Ungari frowned at the vidplate, which had just replayed the recording of Miles's interview with the mercenary. "It sounds more and more like the Naismith cover may be too dangerous to activate at all. If your Oser's little palace coup is anything like what this fellow indicates, Illyan's fantasy of you simply ordering the Dendarii to get lost is straight out the airlock. I thought it sounded too easy." Ungari paced the wardroom, tapping his right fist into his left palm. "Well, we may still get some use out of Victor Rotha. Much as I'd like to confine you to quarters—"

Strange, how many of his superiors said that.

"—Liga wants to see Rotha again this evening. Maybe to place an order for some of our fictitious cargo. String it out—I want you to get past him to the next level of his organization. His boss, or his boss's boss."

"Who owns Liga, do you suspect?"

Ungari stopped pacing, and turned his hands palm-out. "The Cetagandans? Jackson's Whole? Any one of half-a-dozen others? ImpSec is spread thin out here. But if it were proved Liga's criminal organization are Cetagandan puppets, it could be worth sending a full-time agent to penetrate their ranks. So find out! Hint at more goodies in your bag. Take bribes. Blend in. And move it along. I'm almost finished here, and Illyan particularly wants to know when Aslund Station will be fully operational as a defensive base."

Miles punched the door chime of the hostel room. His chin tic'd up. He cleared his throat and straightened his shoulders. Overholt glanced up and down the empty corridor.

The door hissed open. Miles blinked in astonishment.

"Ah, Mr. Rotha." The light cool voice belonged to the brief blonde he'd seen in the concourse that morning. Her jumpsuit was now skin-fitting red silk with a downcurving neckline, a glittering red ruff rising from the back of the neck to frame her sculptured head, and high-heeled red suede boots. She favored him with a high-voltage smile.

"I'm sorry," said Miles automatically. "I must be in the wrong place."

"Not at all." A slim hand opened in an expansive, welcoming gesture. "You're right on time."

"I had an appointment with a Mr. Liga, here."

"Yes, and I've taken over the appointment. Do come in. My name is Livia Nu."

Well, she couldn't possibly be carrying any concealed weapons. Miles stepped within, and was unsurprised to see her bodyguard, idling in one corner of the hostel room. The man nodded to Overholt, who nodded back, both wary as two cats. And where was the third man? Not here, evidently.

She drifted to a liquid-filled settee, and arranged herself upon it.

"Are you, uh, Mr. Liga's supervisor?" Miles asked. No, Liga had denied knowing who she was. . . .

She hesitated fractionally. "In a sense, yes."

One of them was lying—no, not necessarily. If she were indeed high in Liga's organization, he would not have identified her to Rotha. Damn.

"—but you may think of me as a procurement agent."

God. Pol Six really was hip-deep in spies. "For whom?"

"Ah," she smiled. "One of the advantages of dealing with small suppliers is always their no-questions-asked policy. One of the few advantages."

"No-questions-asked is House Fell's slogan, I believe. They have the advantage of a fixed and secure base. I've learned to be cautious about selling arms to people who might be shooting at me in the near future."

Her blue eyes widened. "Who would want to shoot at you?"

"Misguided folk," Miles tossed off. Ye gods. He was not in control of this conversation. He exchanged a harried look with Overholt, who was being out-blanded by his counterpart.

"We must chat." She patted the cushion beside her invitingly. "Do sit down, Victor. Ah," she nodded to her bodyguard, "why don't you wait outside."

Miles seated himself on the edge of the settee, trying to guess the woman's age. Her complexion was smooth and white. Only the skin of her eyelids was soft and faintly puckered. Miles thought of Ungari's orders—take bribes, blend in. . . . "Perhaps you should wait outside also," he said to Overholt.

Overholt looked torn, but of the two, he clearly wanted more to keep an eye on the large armed man. He nodded, apparently in acquiescence, actually in approval, and followed her man out.

Miles smiled in what he hoped was a friendly way. She looked positively seductive. Miles eased cautiously back in the cushions, and tried to look seduceable. A veritable espionage fantasy encounter, of the sort Ungari had told him never happened. Maybe they just never happened to Ungari, eh? *My, what sharp teeth you have, Miss.*

Her hand went to her cleavage—a riveting gesture—and withdrew a tiny, familiar vid disk. She leaned over to insert it in the vid player on the low table before them, and it took Miles a moment to shift his attention to the vid. The little glittering soldier-figure went through its stylized gestures once again. Ha. So, she really was Liga's supervisor. Very good, he was getting somewhere now.

"This is really remarkable, Victor. How did you come by it?"

"A happy accident."

"How many can you supply?"

"A strictly limited number. Say, fifty. I'm not a manufacturer. Liga did mention the price?"

"I thought it high."

"If you can find another supplier who offers these for less, I will be happy to match his price and knock off ten percent." Miles managed to bow sitting down.

She made a faint amused sound, down in her throat. "The volume offered is too low."

"There are several ways you could profit from even a small number of these, if you got into the trade early enough. Such as selling working models to interested governments. I mean to have a share of that profit, before the market is saturated and the price drops. You could too."

"Why don't you? Sell them directly to governments, that is."

"What makes you think I haven't?" Miles smiled.

"But—consider my routes out of this area. I came in past Barrayar and Pol. I must exit via either Jackson's Whole or the Cetagandan Empire. Unfortunately, through either route I run a high risk of being relieved of this particular cargo without any compensation whatsoever." For that matter, where had Barrayar obtained its working model of the shield-suit? Was there a real Victor Rotha, and where was he now? Where *had* Illyan gotten their ship?

"So, you carry them with you?"

"I didn't say that."

"Hm." She smiled. "Can you deliver one tonight?"

"What size?"

"Small." One long-nailed finger traced a line down her body, from breast to thigh, to indicate exactly how small.

Miles sighed mournfully. "Unfortunately, these were sized for the average-to-large combat soldier. Cutting one down is a considerable technical challenge—one which I am in fact still working on myself."

"How thoughtless of the manufacturer."

"I entirely agree, Citizen Nu."

She looked at him more carefully. Did her smile grow slightly more genuine?

"Anyway, I prefer to sell them in wholesale lots. If your organization isn't financially up to it—"

"An arrangement might yet be made."

"Promptly, I trust. I'll be moving on soon."

She murmured absently, "Perhaps not . . ." then looked up with a quick frown. "What's your next stop?"

Ungari had to file a public flight plan anyway. "Aslund."

"Hm . . . yes, we must come to some arrangement. Absolutely."

Were those blue flickers what were called bedroom eyes? The effect was lulling, almost hypnotic. *I finally meet a woman who's barely taller than I am, and I don't even know which side she's on.* He of all men ought not to mistake short for weak or helpless.

"Can I meet your boss?"

"Who?" Her brows lowered.

"The man I saw you both with this morning."

". . . oh. So, you've already seen him."

"Set me up a meeting. Let's do serious business. Betan dollars, remember."

"Pleasure before business, surely." Her breath puffed against his ear, a faint spicy fog.

Was she trying to soften him up? What *for?* Ungari had said, don't break cover. Surely it would be in character for Victor Rotha to take all he could get. Plus ten percent. "You don't have to do this," he managed to choke out. His heart was beating entirely too fast.

"I don't do *everything* for business reasons," she purred.

Why, indeed, should she bother to seduce a sleazy little gun runner? What pleasure was in it for her? What was in it *besides* pleasure for her? *Maybe she likes me.* Miles winced, picturing himself offering that explanation to Ungari. Her arm circled his neck. His hand, unwilled, rose to stroke the fine pelt of her hair. A highly aesthetic tactile experience, just as he'd imagined. . . .

Her hand tightened. In pure nervous reflex, Miles leapt to his feet.

And stood there feeling like an idiot. It had been a caress, not incipient strangulation. The angle was all wrong for attack leverage.

She flung herself back in the seat, slim arm stretching along the top of the cushions. "Victor!" Her voice was amused, her brow arched. "I wasn't going to bite your neck."

His face was hot. "I-have-to-go-now." He cleared his throat to bring his voice back down to its lower register. His hand swooped to pluck the vid disk from the player. Her hand leapt toward it, then fell back languidly, pretending disinterest. Miles hit the door comm.

Overholt was there at once, in the sliding door aperture. Miles's gut eased. If his bodyguard had been gone, Miles would have known this at once for some kind of set-up. Too late, of course.

"Maybe later," Miles gabbled. "After you've taken delivery. We could get together." Delivery of a non-existent cargo? What was he saying?

She shook her head in disbelief. Her laugh followed him down the corridor. It had a brittle edge.

Miles lurched awake when the lights snapped on in his cabin. Ungari, fully dressed, was in the doorway. Behind him their jump pilot, wearing only his underwear and a sleep-stunned expression, jittered uncertainly.

"Dress later," Ungari snarled to the pilot. "Just get us free of the dock and run us out beyond the ten-thousand-kilometer limit. I'll be up to help set course in a few minutes." He added half to himself, "As soon as I know where the devil we're going. *Move.*"

The pilot fled. Ungari strode to Miles's bedside. "Vorkosigan, what the hell happened in that hostel room?"

Miles squeezed his eyes against the glares of both the lights and Ungari, and suppressed an impulse to hide under the covers from both. "Ha?" His mouth was dry with sleep.

"I've just gotten an advance warning—bare minutes advance warning—of an arrest order being put out by Pol Six civil security for Victor Rotha."

"But I never touched the lady!" Miles protested, dizzied.

"Liga's body was found murdered in your meeting room."

"What!"

"The security lab has just finished timing it—to about when you met. Were to meet. The arrest order will be on the net in minutes, and we'll be locked in here."

"But I didn't. I never even saw Liga, only his boss, Livia Nu. I mean—if I'd done any such thing, I'd have reported it to you immediately, sir!"

"Thank you," said Ungari dryly. "I'm glad to know that." His voice harshened. "You're being framed, of course."

"Who—" Yes. There could have been another, grimmer way for Livia Nu to have relieved Liga of that top secret vid disk. But if she wasn't Liga's superior, or even a member of his Polian criminal organization at all, who was she? "We need to know more, sir! This could be the start of something."

"This could be the *end* of our mission. Damn! And now we can't retreat back through Pol to Barrayar. Cut off. Where next?" Ungari paced, evidently thinking aloud. "I want to go to Aslund. Its extradition treaty with Pol has broken down at present, but . . . then there are your mercenary complications. Now that they've connected Rotha to Naismith. Thanks to your carelessness."

"From what Chodak said, I don't think Admiral Naismith would exactly be welcomed back with open arms," Miles agreed reluctantly.

"Jackson's Whole's consortium station has no extradition treaty with anyone. This cover's gone completely sour. Rotha and Naismith, both useless. It has to be the Consortium. I'll ditch this ship there, go underground, and double back to Aslund on my own."

"What about me, sir?"

"You and Overholt will have to split off and take the long way home."

Home. Home in disgrace. "Sir . . . running away looks bad. Suppose we sat tight, and cleared Rotha of the charges? We wouldn't be cut off any more, and Rotha would still be a viable cover. It's possible we're being hustled into doing just this, cutting and running."

"I don't see how anyone could have anticipated my information source in Polian civil security. I think we're meant to be locked up here in dock." Ungari tapped his right fist into his palm once, a gesture of decision this time. "The Consortium it is." He wheeled and exited, boots tromping down the deck. A change of vibration and air pressure, and a few muted clanks, told Miles their ship was now breaking from Pol Six.

Miles said aloud to the empty cabin, "But what if they have plans for both contingencies? *I* would." He shook his head doubtfully, and rose to dress and follow Ungari.

CHAPTER NINE

The Jacksonian Consortium's jump point station, Miles decided, differed from Pol's mainly in the assortment of things its merchants offered for sale. He stood before the book-disk dispenser in a concourse very like Pol Six's and flicked the vid fast-forward through a huge catalogue of pornography. Well, mostly fast-forward, his search was punctuated by a few pauses, from bemused to stunned. Nobly resisting curiosity, he reached the military history section only to find a disappointingly thin collection of titles.

He inserted his credit card and the machine dispensed three wafers. Not that he was all that interested in *The Adumbration of Trigonial Strategy in the Wars of Minos IV*, but it was going to be a long, dull ride home, and Sergeant Overholt did not promise to be the most sparkling of traveling companions. Miles pocketed the disks and sighed. What a waste of time, effort, and anticipation this mission had been.

Ungari had arranged for the "sale" of Victor Rotha's ship, pilot, and engineer to a front man who would deliver it, eventually, back to Barrayaran Imperial Security. Miles's pleading suggestions to his superior on how to make more use of Rotha, Naismith, or even Ensign Vorkosigan had then been interrupted by an ultra-coded message from ImpSec HQ, for Ungari's eyes only. Ungari had withdrawn to decode it, and emerged half an hour later, dead-white around the lips.

He had then moved his timetable up and departed within the hour on a commercial ship to Aslund Station. Alone. Refusing to impart the contents of the message to Miles, or even to Sergeant Overholt. Refusing to take Miles along. Refusing Miles permission to at least continue military observations independently on the Consortium.

Ungari left Overholt to Miles, or vice versa. It was a little hard to tell who had been left in charge of whom. Overholt seemed to be acting less like a subordinate and more like a nanny all the time, discouraging Miles's attempted explorations of the Consortium, insisting he keep safely to his hostel room. They waited now to board an Escobaran commercial liner slated for a nonstop run to Escobar, where they would report to the Barrayaran Embassy which would no doubt ship them home. Home, and with nothing to show for it.

Miles checked his chrono. Another twenty minutes to kill before boarding. They might as well go sit. With an irritable glance at his shadow Overholt, Miles trudged wearily down the concourse. Overholt followed, frowning general disapproval.

Miles brooded on Livia Nu. In fleeing from her erotic invitation he'd surely missed the adventure of his short lifetime. Yet that hadn't been the look of love on her face. Anyway, he'd worry about a woman who could fall madly in love at first sight with Victor Rotha. The light in her eyes had been more on the order of a gourmet contemplating an unusual hors d'oeuvre just presented by the waiter. He'd felt like he'd had parsley sticking out of his ears.

She might have been dressed like a courtesan, moved like a courtesan, but there'd been none of the courtesan's eagerness to please about her, nothing servile. The gestures of power in the garments of powerlessness. Unsettling.

So beautiful.

Courtesan, criminal, spy, what was she? Above all, who did she belong to? Was she Liga's boss, or Liga's opponent? Or Liga's fate? Had she killed the rabbity man herself? Whatever else she was, Miles was increasingly convinced, she was a key piece in the puzzle of the Hegen Hub. They should have followed her up, not fled from her. Sex wasn't the only opportunity he'd missed. The meeting with Livia Nu was going to bother him for a long time.

Miles looked up to find his way blocked by a pair of Consortium goons—civil security officers, he corrected his thought ironically. He stood, feet planted, and lifted his chin. What now? "Yes, gentlemen?"

The big one looked to the enormous one, who cleared his throat. "Mr. Victor Rotha?"

"If I am, then what?"

"An arrest order has been purchased for you. It charges you with the murder of one Sydney Liga. Do you wish to outbid?"

"Probably." Miles's lip curled in exasperation. What a development. "Who's bidding for my arrest?"

"The name is Cavilo."

Miles shook his head. "Don't even know him. Is he with Polian Civil Security, by chance?"

The officer checked his report panel. "No." He added chattily, "The Polians almost never do business with us. They think we ought to trade them criminals for free. As if we wanted any back!"

"Huh. That's supply and demand for you." Miles blew out his breath. Illyan was not going to be thrilled about *this* charge on his expense account. "How much did this Cavilo offer for me?"

The officer checked his panel again. His brows rose. "Twenty thousand Betan dollars. He must want you a lot."

Miles made a small leaky noise. "I don't have that much *on* me."

The officer pulled out his come-along stick. "Well, then."

"I'll have to make arrangements."

"You'll have to make arrangements from Detention, sir."

"But I'll miss my ship!"

"That's probably the idea," the officer agreed. "Considering the timing and all."

"Suppose—if that's all this Cavilo wants—he then withdraws his bid?"

"He'll lose a substantial deposit."

Jacksonian justice was truly blind. They'd sell it to anyone. "Uh, may I have a word with my assistant?"

The officer pursed his lips, and studied Overholt suspiciously. "Make it fast."

"What d'you think, Sergeant?" Miles turned to Overholt and asked lowly. "They don't seem to have an order for you. . . ."

Overholt looked tense, tight mouth annoyed and eyes almost panicked. "If we could make it to the ship. . . ."

The rest hung unspoken. The Escobarans shared the Polian disapproval of Jacksonian Consortium "law." Once aboard the liner, Miles would be on Escobaran "soil"; the captain would not voluntarily yield him up. Could, would, this Cavilo be able to bid enough to intern the whole Escobaran liner? The sum involved would be astronomical. "Try."

Miles turned back toward the Consortium officers, smiling, wrists held out in surrender. Overholt exploded into action.

The sergeant's first kick sent the enormous goon's come-along stick flying. Overholt's momentum flowed into a whirl that brought his double hands up against the second goon's head with great force. Miles was already in motion. He dodged a wild grab, and sprinted as best he could up the concourse. At this point he spotted the third goon, in plainclothes. Miles could tell who he was by the glitter of the tangle-field he tossed in front of Miles's pistoning legs. The man snorted with laughter as Miles pitched forward, trying to roll and save his brittle bones. Miles hit the concourse floor with a whump that knocked the air from his lungs. He inhaled through clenched teeth, not crying out, as the pain in his chest competed with the burn of the tangle-net around his ankles. He wrenched himself around on the floor, looking back the way he had come.

The less enormous goon was standing bent over, hands to his head, dizzied. The other was retrieving his come-along stick from where it had skittered to a stop. By elimination, the stunned heap on the pavement must be Sergeant Overholt.

The goon with the stick stared at Overholt and shook his head, and stepped over him toward Miles. The dizzied goon pulled out his own stick and gave the downed man a shock to the head, and followed without a backward glance. Nobody, apparently, wanted to buy Overholt.

"There will be a ten percent surcharge for resisting arrest," the spokesman-goon remarked coldly down to Miles. Miles squinted up the shiny columns of his boots. The shock-stick came down like a club. On the third blazing blow he began screaming. On the seventh, he passed out.

He came to consciousness altogether too soon, while still being dragged along between the two uniformed men. He was shivering uncontrollably. His breathing was messed up somehow, irregular shallow gasps that didn't give him enough air. Waves of pins-and-needles pulsed through his nervous system. He had a kaleidoscopic impression of lift tubes and corridors, and more bare functional corridors. They jerked to a halt at last. When the goons let his arms go he fell to hands and knees, then the cold floor.

Another civil security officer peered over a com-console desk at him. A hand grasped Miles's head by the hair, and yanked it back; the red flicker of a retinal scan blinded him momentarily. His eyes seemed extraordinarily sensitive to light. His shaking hands were pressed hard against some sort of identification pad; released, he fell back into his huddle. His pockets were stripped out, stunner, IDs, tickets, cash, all dumped pell-mell into a plastic bag. Miles emitted a muffled squeak of dismay as they bundled the white jacket, with all its useful secrets, into the bag as well. The lock was keyed closed with his thumbprint, pinched against it.

The Detention officer craned his neck. "Does he want to outbid?"

"Unh . . ." Miles managed to respond, when his head was pulled back again.

"He said he did," the arresting goon said helpfully.

The Detention officer shook his head. "We're going to have to wait till the shock wears off. You guys overdid it, I think. He's only a little runt."

"Yeah, but he had a big guy with him who gave us trouble. The little mutant seemed to be in charge, so we let him take payment for both."

"That's fair," the Detention officer conceded. "Well, it'll be a while. Throw him in the cooler till he stops shaking enough to talk."

"Sure that's a good idea? Funny-looking as he is, the boy-oh might want to play games. He might still ransom himself."

"Mm." The Detention officer looked Miles over judiciously. "Throw him in the waiting room with Marda's techies, then. They're a quiet bunch, they'll leave him alone. And they'll be gone soon."

Miles was dragged again—his legs didn't respond at all to his will, only jerking spasmodically. The leg braces seemed to have had some amplifying effect on the shocks administered there, or maybe it was the combination with the tangle-field. A long room like a barracks, with a row of cots down each wall, swam past his vision. The goons heaved him, not unkindly, onto an empty cot in the less-populated end of the room. The senior one made a dim sort of effort to straighten him out, tossed a light blanket across his still uncontrollably-twitching form, and they left him.

A little time passed, with nothing to distract him from the full enjoyment and appreciation of his new array of physical sensations. He'd thought he'd sampled every sort of agony in the catalogue, but the goons' shock-sticks had found out nerves and synapses and ganglial knots he'd never known he possessed. Nothing like pain, to concentrate the attention upon the self. Practically solipsistic, it was. But it seemed to be easing—if only his body would stop these quasi-epileptic seizures, which were exhausting him. . . .

A face wavered into view. A familiar face.

"Gregor! Am I glad to see you," Miles burbled inanely. He felt his burning eyes widen. His hands shot out to clench Gregor's shirt, a pale blue prisoner's smock. "*What the hell are you doing here?*"

"It's a long story."

"Ah! Ah!" Miles struggled up onto his elbow and stared around wildly for assassins, hallucinations, he knew not what. "God! Where's—"

Gregor pushed him back down with a hand on his chest. "Calm down." And under his breath, "And shut up! . . . You better rest a bit. You don't look very good right now."

Actually, Gregor didn't look so good himself, sitting on the edge of Miles's cot. His face was pale and tired, peppered with beard stubble. His normally military-cut and combed black hair was a tangle. His hazel eyes looked nervous. Miles choked back panic.

"My name is Greg Bleakman," the emperor informed Miles urgently.

"I can't remember what my name is right now," Miles stuttered. "Oh—yeah. Victor Rotha. I think. But how did you get from—"

Gregor looked around vaguely. "The walls have ears, I think?"

"Yes, maybe." Miles subsided slightly. The man on the next cot shook his head with a God-save-me-from-these-assholes look, turned over and put his pillow over his head. "But, uh . . . did you get here, like, under your own power?"

"Unfortunately, all my own doing. You remember that time we were joking about running away from home?"

"Yeah?"

"Well," Gregor took a breath, "it turned out to be a really bad idea."

"Couldn't you have figured that out in advance?"

"I—" Gregor broke off, to stare up the long room as a guard stuck his head in the door to bawl, "Five minutes!"

"Oh, hell."

"What? What?"

"They're coming for us."

"Who's coming for who, what the hell is going on, *Gregor*—Greg—"

"I had a berth on a freighter, I thought, but they dumped me off here. Without pay," Gregor explained rapidly. "Stiffed me. I didn't have so much as a half-mark on me. I tried to get something on an out-bound ship, but before I could, I got arrested for vagrancy. Jacksonian law is insane," he added reflectively.

"I know. Then what?"

"They were apparently making a deliberate sweep, press-gang style. Seems some enterpreneur is selling tech-trained work gangs to the Aslunders, to work on their Hub station, which is running behind schedule."

Miles blinked. "Slave labor?"

"Of a sort. The carrot is, when the sentence is up, we're to be discharged on Aslund Station. Most of these techs don't seem to mind too much. No pay, but we—they—will be fed and housed, and escape Jacksonian security, so in the end they'll be no worse off than when they started, broke and unemployed. Most of them seem to think they'll find berths outbound from Aslund eventually. Being without funds is not such a heinous crime, there."

Miles's head pounded. "They're taking you away?"

Tension pooled in Gregor's eyes, contained, not permitted to seep over into the rest of his stiff face. "Right now, I think."

"God! I can't let—"

"But how did you find me here—" Gregor began in turn, then looked in frustration up the room, where blue-smocked men and women were grumbling to their feet. "Are you here to—"

Miles stared around frantically. The blue-clad man on the cot next to his now lay on his side, watching them with a bored glower. He wasn't over-tall. . . .

"You!" Miles scrambled overboard, and crouched at the man's side. "You want to get out of this trip?"

The man looked slightly less bored. "How?"

"Trade clothes. Trade ID's. You take my place, I take yours."

The man looked suspicious. "What's the catch?"

"No catch. I got a lot of credit. I was going to buy my way out of here in a while." Miles paused. "There's going to be a surcharge for my resisting arrest, though."

"Ah." A catch identified, the man looked slightly more interested.

"Please! I have to go with—with my friend. Right now." The babble was rising, as the techs assembled in the room's far end by the exit. Gregor wandered around behind the man's cot.

The man pursed his lips. "Naw," he decided. "If whatever you're in for is worse than this, I don't want anything to do with it." He swung to a sitting position, preparing to rise and join the line.

Miles, still crouched on the floor, raised his hands in supplication. "Please—"

Gregor, perfectly placed, pounced. He grabbed the man around the neck in a neat choke and flipped him over the side of his cot, out of sight. Thank God the Barrayaran aristocracy still insisted on military training for its scions. Miles staggered to his feet, the better to obscure the view from up the room. Some small thumping noises came from the floor. In a few moments, a prisoner's blue smock skidded under the cot to fetch up at Miles's sandaled feet. Miles squatted and pulled it on over his green silks—fortunately, it was a bit oversized—then struggled into the loose trousers that followed. Some shoving sounds, as the man's unconscious body was pushed out of sight under the cot, and Gregor stood, panting slightly, very white.

"I can't get these damn belt strings," Miles said. They skittered from his trembling hands.

Gregor tied up Miles's pants, and rolled up his overlong trouser legs. "You need his ID, or you can't get food or register your work-credits," Gregor hissed out of the corner of his mouth, and leaned artistically against the end of the cot in an idle pose.

Miles checked his pocket and found the standard computer card. "All right." He stood next to Gregor, teeth bared in a weird grin. "I'm about to pass out."

Gregor's hand locked his elbow. "Don't. It'll draw attention."

They walked up the room and slipped into the end of the shuffling, complaining, blue-clad line. A sleepy-looking guard at the door checked them out, running a scanner over the IDs.

". . . twenty-three, twenty-four, twenty-five. That's it. Take 'em away."

They were turned over to another set of guards, not in the uniform of the Consortium but some minor Jacksonian House livery, gold and black. Miles kept his face down as they were herded out of Detention. Only Gregor's hand kept him on his feet. They passed through a corridor, another corridor, down a lift tube—Miles nearly threw up during the drop—another corridor. *What if this damned ID has a locator?* Miles thought suddenly. At the next drop tube he shed it; the little card twinkled away into the dim distance, silent and unnoticed. A docking bay, a hatchway, the brief weightlessness of the flexible docking tube, and they boarded a ship. *Sergeant Overholt, where are you now?*

It was clearly an intra-system carrier, not a jump ship, and not very large. The men were separated from the women and directed down opposite ends of a corridor lined with cabin doors leading to four-bunk cubicles. The prisoners spread out, selecting their quarters without apparent interference from the guards.

Miles made a quick count and multiplication. "We can get one to ourselves, if we try," he whispered urgently to Gregor. He ducked into the nearest, and they hit the door control quickly. Another prisoner made to follow them in, to be met with a united snarl of "Back off!" He withdrew hastily. The door did not slide open again.

The cabin was dirty, and lacked such amenities as bedding for the mattresses, but the plumbing worked. As Miles got a drink of lukewarm water he heard and felt the hatch close, and the ship undock. They were safe for the moment. How long?

"When do you think that guy you choked is going to wake up?" Miles asked Gregor, who sat on the edge of one bunk.

"I'm not sure. I've never choked a man before." Gregor looked sick. "I . . . felt something strange, under my hand. I'm afraid I might have broken his neck."

"He was still breathing," Miles said. He walked to the opposite lower bunk and prodded it. No sign of vermin. He seated himself gingerly. The severe shakes were passing off, leaving only a tremula, but he still felt weak in the knees. "When he wakes up— as soon as they find him, whether he wakes up or not—it's not going to take them long to figure out where I went. I should have just waited, and followed you, and bought you back. Assuming I could bid myself free. This was a *stupid* idea. Why didn't you stop me?"

Gregor stared. "I thought you knew what you were doing. Isn't Illyan right behind you?"

"Not as far as I know."

"I thought you were in Illyan's department now. I thought you were sent to find me. This . . . isn't some kind of bizarre rescue?"

"No!" Miles shook his head, and immediately regretted the motion. "Maybe you'd better begin at the beginning."

"I'd been on Komarr for a week. Under the domes. High-level talks on wormhole route treaties—we're still trying to get the Escobarans to permit passage of our military vessels. There's some idea of letting their inspection teams seal our weapons during passage. Our general staff thinks it's too much, theirs thinks it's too little. I signed a couple of agreements—whatever the Council of Ministers shoved in front of me—"

"Dad makes you *read* them, surely."

"Oh, yes. Anyway, there was a military review that afternoon. And a state dinner in the evening, which broke up early, a couple of the negotiators had to catch ships. I went back to my quarters, some oligarch's old town house. Big place at the edge of the dome, near the shuttleport. My suite was high in this building. I went out on the balcony—it didn't help much. Still felt claustrophobic, under the dome."

"Komarrans don't like open air, either," Miles noted in fairness. "I knew one who had breathing problems—like asthma—whenever he had to go outside. Strictly psychosomatic."

Gregor shrugged, gazing at his shoes. "Anyway, I noticed . . . there were no guards in sight. For a change. I don't know why the hole, there'd been a man there earlier. They thought I was asleep, I guess. It was after midnight. I couldn't sleep. I was leaning over the balcony, and thinking, if I toppled off . . ." Gregor hesitated.

"It would be quick," Miles supplied dryly. He knew that state of mind, oh yes.

Gregor glanced up at him, and smiled ironically. "Yes. I was a little drunk."

You were a lot drunk.

"Quick, yes. Smash my skull. It would hurt a lot, but not for long. Maybe even not a lot. Maybe just a flash of heat."

Miles shuddered, concealed in his shock-stick tremula.

"I went over—I caught these plants. Then I realized, I could climb down as easily as up. More easily. I felt free, as if I *had* died. I started walking. Nobody stopped me. All the time, I expected someone to stop me.

"I ended up in the freightyard end of the shuttleport. At a bar. I told this fellow, this free trader, I was a norm-space navigator. I'd done that, on my ship duty. I'd lost my ID, and was afraid Barrayaran Security would rough me up. He believed me—or believed something. Anyway, he gave me a berth. We probably broke orbit before my batman went in to wake me that morning."

Miles chewed his knuckles. "So from Imp Sec's point of view, you evaporated from a fully guarded room. No note, no trace—and on *Komarr*."

"The ship made a straight run through to Pol—I stayed aboard—and then nonstop to the Consortium. I didn't get along too well at first, on the freighter. I thought I was doing better. Guess not. But I thought, Illyan was probably right behind me anyway."

"Komarr." Miles rubbed his temples. "Do you realize what has to be happening back there? Illyan will be convinced it's some sort of political kidnapping. I bet he's got every Security operative and half the army tearing those domes apart bolt by bolt, looking for you. You're way out ahead of them. They won't look beyond Komarr till . . ." Miles counted out days on his fingers. "Still, Illyan should have alerted all his outlying agents . . . almost a week ago. Ha! I bet that was the message that put Ungari up in the air, just before he left in such a hurry. Sent to Ungari, not to me." *Not to me. Nobody's even counting me.* "But it should have been all over the news—"

"It was, sort of," Gregor offered. "There was a sententious announcement that I'd been ill and retired to rest in seclusion at Vorkosigan Surleau. They're suppressing."

Miles could just picture it. "Gregor, how could you do this! They'll be going insane back home!"

"I'm sorry," said Gregor stiffly. "I knew it was a mistake . . . almost immediately. Even before the hangover cut in."

"Why didn't you get off at Pol, then, and go to the Barrayaran embassy?"

"I thought I might still . . . dammit," he broke off, "why should these people *own* me?"

"Childish, stunt," Miles gritted through his teeth.

Gregor's head jerked up in anger, but he said nothing.

The full realization of his position was just beginning to sink in to Miles, like lead in his belly. *I'm the only man in the universe who knows where the Emperor of Barrayar is right now. If anything happens to Gregor, I could be his heir. In fact, if anything happens to Gregor, quite a lot of people will think I . . .*

And if the Hegen Hub found out who Gregor really was, a free-for-all of epic proportions could follow. The Jacksonians would take him for simple ransom. Aslund, Pol, Vervain, any or all might seek some power play. The Cetagandans most of all—if they could gain possession of Gregor in secret, who knew what subtle psychological programming they might attempt; if openly, what threats? And Miles and Gregor were both trapped on a ship they didn't control—Miles might be snatched away at any moment by Consortium goons or worse—

Miles was an ImpSec officer, now, however junior or disgraced. And ImpSec's sworn duty was the Emperor's safety. The Emperor, Barrayar's unifying icon. Gregor, unwilling flesh pressed into that mold. Icon, flesh, which claimed Miles's allegiance? *Both. He's mine. A prisoner, on the run, trailed by God-knows-what enemies, suicidally depressed, and all mine.*

Miles choked down a lunatic cackle.

CHAPTER TEN

With a little reflection, possible now that the shock-stick reverberations were wearing off, Miles realized that he needed to hide. Gregor, by his place as a contract slave, would be warm, fed, and safe all the way to Aslund Station if Miles did not endanger him. Maybe. Miles added it to his life's lessons list. Call it Rule 27B. Never make key tactical decisions while having electro-convulsive seizures.

Miles began by examining the bunk cubicle. The vessel was not a prison ship; the cabin had originally been designed as cheap transport, not a secured cell. Empty storage cupboards beneath the two bunk-stacks were too large and obvious. A floor panel lifted for access to between-decks control, coolant and power lines, and the grav grid—long, narrow, flat. . . . Rough voices in the corridor propelled Miles's decision. He squeezed himself into the slice of space, face up, arms tight to his sides, and exhaled.

"You always were good at hide-and-seek," said Gregor admiringly, and pressed the panel down.

"I was smaller then," Miles mumbled through squashed cheeks. Pipes and circuit boxes sank into his back and buttocks. Gregor refastened the catches, and all was dark and silent for a few minutes. Like a coffin. Like a pressed flower. Some kind of biological specimen, anyway. Canned ensign.

The door hissed open; footsteps passed over

Miles's body, compressing him still further. Would they notice the muffled echo from this strip of floor?

"On your feet, Techie." A guard's voice, directed to Gregor. Thumpings and bangings, as the mattresses were flipped and the cupboard doors flung open. Yes, he'd figured the cupboards for useless.

"Where is he, Techie?" From the directions of the shufflings, Miles placed Gregor as now near the wall, probably with an arm twisted up behind his back.

"Where is who?" said Gregor in a smeary tone. Face against the wall, all right.

"Your little mutant buddy."

"The weird little guy who followed me in? He's no buddy of mine. He left."

More shuffling—"Ow!" The Emperor's arm had just been lifted another five centimeters, Miles gauged.

"Where'd he go?"

"I don't know! He didn't look so good. Somebody'd worked him over with a shock stick. Recently. I wasn't about to get involved. He took off again a few minutes before we undocked."

Good Gregor; depressed maybe, stupid no. Miles's lips drew back. His head was turned, with one cheek against the floor above and the other pressing against something that resembled a cheese grater.

More thumps. "All right! He left! Don't hit me!"

Unintelligible guard growls, the crackle of a shock stick, a sharp intake of breath, a thump as of a body curling up on a lower bunk.

A second guard's voice, edged with uncertainty, "He must have doubled back onto the Consortium before we cast off."

"Their problem, good. But we'd better search the whole ship to be sure. Detention sounded ready to chew ass on this one."

"Chew or be chewed?"

"Hah. *I'm* taking no bets."

The booted feet—four of them, Miles estimated—stalked toward the cabin door. The door hissed closed. Silence.

He was going to have a truly remarkable collection of bruises on his backside, Miles decided, by the time Gregor got around to popping the lid. He could get about half a breath with each pulse of his lungs. He needed to pee. Come on, Gregor. . . .

He must certainly free Gregor from his slave labor contract as soon as possible after their arrival at Aslund Station. Contract laborers of this order were bound to be stuck with the dirtiest and most dangerous jobs, the most exposure to radiation, to dubious life-support systems, to long, exhausting, accident-prone hours. Though—true—it was also an incognito no enemy would quickly penetrate. Once free to move they must find Ungari, the man with the credit cards and the contacts; after that—well, after that Gregor would be Ungari's problem, eh? Yes, all simple, right and tight. No need to panic at all.

Had they taken Gregor away? Dare he release himself, and risk—

Shuffling footsteps; a widening line of light, as his lid was raised. "They're gone," Gregor whispered. Miles unmolded himself, centimeter by painful centimeter, and climbed onto the floor, a suitable staging area. He would attempt to stand up very soon now.

Gregor had one hand pressed to a red mark on his cheek. Self-consciously, he lowered his hand to his side. "They tapped me with a shock stick. It . . . wasn't as bad as I'd imagined." If anything, he looked faintly proud of himself.

"They were using low power," Miles growled up at him. Gregor's face grew more masked. He offered Miles a hand up. Miles took it and grunted to his feet, and sat heavily on a bunk. He told Gregor about his plans for finding Ungari.

Gregor shrugged, dully acquiescent. "Very well. It will be quicker than my plan."

"Your plan?"

"I was going to contact the Barrayaran Consul on Aslund."

"Oh. Good." Miles subsided. "Guess you . . . didn't really need my rescue, at that."

"I could have made it on my own. I got this far. But . . . then there was my other plan."

"Oh?"

"*Not* to contact the Barrayaran Consul. . . . Maybe it's just as well you came along when you did." Gregor lay back on his bunk, staring blindly upward. "One thing is certain, an opportunity like this will never come again."

"To escape? And just how many would die, back home, to buy your freedom?"

Gregor pursed his lips. "Taking Vordarian's Pretendership as a benchmark for palace coups—say, seven or eight thousand."

"You're not counting in Komarr."

"Ah. Yes. Adding in Komarr would inflate the figure," Gregor conceded. His mouth twitched in an irony altogether devoid of humor. "Don't worry, I'm not serious. I just . . . wanted to know. I could have made it on my own, don't you think?"

"Of course! That's not the question."

"It was for me."

"Gregor," Miles's fingers tapped in frustration, against his knee. "You're doing this to yourself. You *have* real power. Dad fought through the whole Regency to preserve it. Just be more assertive!"

"And, Ensign, if I, your supreme commander, ordered you to leave this ship at Aslund Station and forget you ever saw me, would you?"

Miles swallowed. "Major Cecil said I had a problem with subordination."

Gregor almost grinned. "Good old Cecil. I remember him." His grin faded to nothing. He rolled up onto one elbow. "But if I can't even control one rather short ensign, how much less an army or a government? Power isn't the question. I've had all your Dad's lectures on power, its illusions and uses. It will come to me in time, whether I want it or not. But do I have the strength to handle it? Think about the bad showing I made during Vordrozda and Hessman's plot, four years ago."

"Will you make that mistake again? Trust a flatterer?"

"Not that one, no."

"Well, then."

"But I must do better, or I might be as bad for Barrayar as no emperor at all."

Just how unintentional had that topple off the balcony been? Miles gritted his teeth. "I didn't answer your question—about orders—as an ensign. I answered it as Lord Vorkosigan. And as a friend."

"Ah."

"Look, you don't need my rescue. Such as it is. Illyan's maybe, not mine. But it makes *me* feel better."

"It's always nice to feel useful," Gregor agreed. They mirrored edged smiles. Gregor's smile lost its bitter bite. "And . . . it's nice to have company."

Miles nodded. "That, truly."

Miles spent quite a lot of time over the next two days squashed under the deck or crouched in the cupboards, but their cabin was searched only once and that very early on. Twice other prisoners wandered in to chat with Gregor, and once, on Miles's suggestion, Gregor returned the visit. Gregor really was doing quite well, Miles thought. Gregor divided his rations with Miles automatically, without complaint or even comment, and would not accept a larger portion although Miles urged it on him.

Gregor was herded out with the rest of the labor crew soon after the ship docked at Aslund Station.

Miles waited nervously, trying to give as long as possible for the ship to quiet down, for the crew to go off-guard, yet not so long as to risk the ship undocking and thrusting off with him still aboard.

The corridor, when Miles cautiously poked his head out, was dark and deserted. The docking hatch was unguarded, on this side. Miles still wore the blue smock and pants over his other clothes, on the calculated risk the work gangs were treated as trustys, with the run of the station, and he would at least blend in at a distance.

He stepped out firmly, and nearly panicked when he found a man in the gold and black House livery idling around the hatch's exit. His stunner was holstered; his hands cradled a steaming plastic cup. His squinting red eyes regarded Miles incuriously. Miles favored him with a brief smile, not breaking stride. The guard returned a sour grimace. Evidently his charge was to prevent strange people from entering, not leaving, the ship.

The station-side loading bay beyond the hatch proved to contain half a dozen coveralled maintenance personnel, working quietly down on one end. Miles took a deep breath, and walked casually across the bay without looking around, as if he knew just where he was going. Just an errand boy. No one hailed him.

Reassured, Miles marched off purposefully at random. A wide ramp led to a great chamber, raucous with new construction and busy work crews in all sorts of dress—a fighter-shuttle refueling and repairs bay, judging by the half-assembled equipment. Just the sort of thing to interest Ungari. Miles didn't suppose he'd be so lucky as to . . . no. No sign of Ungari camouflaged among these crews. There were a number of men and women in dark blue Aslunder military uniforms, but they appeared to be overworked and absorbed engineer-types, not suspicious guards.

Miles kept walking briskly nonetheless, out another corridor.

He found a portal, its transparent plexi bellied out to offer passers-by a wide-angle view. He put one foot on the lower edge and leaned out—casually— and bit back a few choice swear words. Glittering a few kilometers off was the commercial transfer station. A tiny glint of a ship was docking even now. The military station was apparently being designed as a separate facility, or at least not connected yet. No wonder blue-smocks could wander at will. Miles stared across the gap in mild frustration. Well, he'd search this place first for Ungari, the other later. Somehow. He turned and started—

"Hey, you! Little techie!"

Miles froze, controlling a reflexive urge to sprint— that tactic hadn't worked last time—and turned, trying for an expression of polite inquiry. The man who'd hailed him was big but unarmed, wearing tan supervisor's coveralls. He looked harried. "Yes, sir?" said Miles.

"You're just what I need." The man's hand fell heavily on Miles's shoulder. "Come with me."

Miles perforce followed, trying to stay calm, maybe project a little bored annoyance.

"What's your specialization?" the man asked.

"Drains," Miles intoned.

"Perfect!"

Dismayed, Miles followed the man to where two half-finished corridors intersected. An archway gaped raw and uncapped by molding, though the molding lay ready to install.

The super pointed to a narrow space between walls. "See this pipe?"

Sewage, by the grey color-coding, air and grav pumped. It disappeared in darkness. "Yeah?"

"There's a leak somewhere behind this corridor wall. Crawl in and find it, so's we don't have to tear out all the damn paneling we just put up."

"Got a light?"

The man fished in his pocketed coverall and produced a hand light.

"Right," sighed Miles. "Is it hooked up yet?"

"About to be. Damn thing failed the final pressure test."

Only air would be spewing out. Miles brightened slightly. Maybe his luck was changing.

He slid in and inched along the smooth round surface, listening and feeling. About seven meters in he found it, a rush of cool air from a crack under his hands, quite marked. He shook his head, attempted to turn in the constricted space, and put his foot through the paneling.

He stuck his head out the hole in astonishment, and glanced up and down the corridor. He wriggled a chunk of paneling from the edge and stared at it, turning it in his hands.

Two men putting up light fixtures, their tools sparking, turned to stare. "What the hell are you doing?" said the one in tan coveralls, sounding outraged.

"Quality control inspection," said Miles glibly, "and boy, do you have a problem."

Miles considered kicking the hole wider and just walking back to his starting point, but turned and inched instead. He emerged by the anxiously waiting super.

"Your leak's in section six," Miles reported. He handed the man his panel chunk. "If those corridor panels are supposed to be made of flammable fiberboard instead of spun silica on a military installation planned to withstand enemy fire, somebody's hired a real poor designer. If they're not—I suggest you take a couple of those big goons with the shock sticks and go pay a visit to your supplier."

The super swore. Lips compressed, he grasped the nearest panel edge fronting the wall and twisted hard. A fist-sized segment cracked and tore off.

"Bitchen. How much of this stuff's been installed already?"

"Lots," Miles suggested cheerfully. He turned to escape before the super, worrying off fragments and muttering under his breath, thought of another chore. Flushed and sweating, Miles skittered off and didn't relax till he'd rounded the second corner.

He passed a pair of armed men in grey-and-white uniforms. One turned to stare. Miles kept walking, teeth clenching his lower lip, and did not look back.

Dendarii! or, Oserans! Here, aboard this station— how many, where? Those two were the first he'd seen. Shouldn't they be out on patrol somewhere? He wished he were back in the walls, like a rat in the wainscotting.

But if most of the mercenaries here were a danger to him, there was one—Dendarii truly, not Oseran— who might be a help. If he could make contact. If he dared make contact. Elena . . . he could seek out Elena. . . . His imagination outraced him.

Miles had left Elena four years ago as Baz Jesek's wife, as Tung's military apprentice, as much protection as he could get her at the time. But he hadn't had any messages from Baz since Oser's command coup—could Oser be intercepting them? Now Baz was demoted, Tung apparently disgraced—what position in the mercenary fleet did Elena hold now?

What position in his heart? He paused in grave doubt. He'd loved her passionately, once. Once, she'd known him better than any other human being. Yet her daily hold on his mind had passed, like his grief for her dead father Sergeant Bothari, fading in the rush of his new life. But for an occasional twinge, like an old bonebreak. He wanted/did not want/ to see her again. To talk to her again. To touch her again. . . .

But more to the practical point, she would recognize Gregor; they'd all been playmates in their youth. A second line of defense for the Emperor?

Reopening contact with Elena might be emotionally awkward—all right, emotionally searing. But it was better than this ineffectual and dangerous wandering around. Now that he'd scouted the layout, he must somehow get into position to bring his resources to bear. How much human credit did Admiral Naismith still have? Interesting question.

He needed to find a place to watch without being seen. There were all sorts of ways to be invisible while in plain sight, as his blue smock was presently demonstrating. But his unusual height—well, short-ness—made him reluctant to rely on clothes alone. He needed—ha!—tools, such as the case a tan-cover-alled man had just set down in the corridor while he ducked into a lavatory. Miles had the case in hand and was around the corner in a blink.

A couple of levels away he found a corridor leading to a cafeteria. Hm. Everyone must eat; therefore, everyone must pass this way in time. The food smells excited his stomach, which protested half-rations or less for the past three days by gurgling. He ignored it. He pulled a panel off the wall, donned a pair of protective goggles from the tool case by way of a modest facial disguise, climbed into the wall to half-conceal his height, and began pretending to work on a control box and some pipes, diagnostic scanners placed decoratively to hand. His view up the corri-dor was excellent.

From the wafting odors, he judged they were serving an unusually good grade of vat-grown beef in there, though they were also doing something nasty to vegetables. He tried not to salivate into the beam of the tiny laser-solderer he manipulated while he studied passers-by. Very few were civilian-clothed, Rotha's wear would clearly have been more conspic-uous than the blue smock. Lots of color-coded cover-alls, blue smocks, some similar green smocks; not a few Aslunder military blues, mostly lower ranks. Did the Dendarii—Oserans—mercenaries—aboard eat elsewhere? He was considering abandoning his out-post—he'd about repaired the control boxes to death by now—when a duo of grey-and-whites passed. Not faces he knew, he let them go by unhailed.

He contemplated the odds reluctantly. Of all the couple thousand mercenaries now present around the Aslunders' wormhole jump, he might know a few hundred by sight, fewer by name. Only some of the mercenary fleet's ships were now docked at this half-built military station. And of the portion of a portion, how many people could he trust absolutely? Five? He let another quartet of grey-and-whites pass, though he was certain that older blonde woman was an engineering tech from the *Triumph*, once loyal to Tung. Once. He was getting ravenous.

But the leather-colored face topping the next set of grey-and-whites to pass down the corridor made Miles forget his stomach. It was Sergeant Chodak. His luck had turned—maybe. For himself, he'd take the chance, but to risk Gregor . . . ? Too late to waffle now, Chodak had spotted Miles in turn. The Sergeant's eyes widened in astonishment before his face grew swiftly blank.

"Oh, Sergeant," Miles caroled, tapping a control box, "would you take a look at this, please?"

"I'll be along in a minute," Chodak waved on his companion, a man in the uniform of an Aslunder ranker.

When their heads were together and their backs to the corridor, Chodak hissed, "Are you insane? What are you *doing* here?" It was a mark of his agitation that he omitted his habitual "sir."

"It's a long story. For now, I need your help."

"But how did you get in here? Admiral Oser has guards all over the transfer station, on the lookout for you. You couldn't smuggle in a sand-flea."

Miles smirked convincingly. "I have my methods." And his next plan had been to scheme his way across to that very transfer station . . . Truly, God protected fools and madmen. "For now, I need to make contact with Commander Elena Bothari-Jesek. Urgently. Or, failing her, Engineering Commodore Jesek. Is she here?"

"She should be. The *Triumph*'s in dock. Commodore Jesek is out with the repairs tender, I know."

"Well, if not Elena, Tung. Or Arde Mayhew. Or Lieutenant Elli Quinn. But I prefer Elena. Tell her—but no one else—that I have our old friend Greg with me. Tell her to meet me in an hour in the contract-laborers quarters, Greg Bleakman's cubicle. Can do?"

"Can do, sir." Chodak hurried off, looking worried. Miles patched up his poor battered wall, replaced the panel, picked up his tool box, and marched casually away, trying not to feel like he had a flashing red light atop his head. He kept his goggles on and his face down, and chose the least-populated corridors he could find. His stomach growled. *Elena will feed you*, he told it firmly. *Later*. A rising population of blue and green smocks told Miles he was nearing the contract laborer's quarters.

There was a directory. He hesitated, then punched up "Bleakman, G." Module B, Cubicle 8. He found the module, checked his chrono—Gregor should be off-shift by now—and knocked. The door sighed open and Miles slipped within. Gregor was there, sitting up sleepily on his bunk. It was a one-man cubicle, offering privacy, though barely room to turn around. Privacy was a greater psychological luxury than space. Even slave-techs must be kept minimally happy, they had too much power for potential sabotage to risk driving them over the edge.

"We're saved," Miles announced. "I've just made contact with Elena." He sat down heavily on the end of the bunk, weak with the sudden release of tension in this safe pocket.

"Elena's here?" Gregor scrubbed a hand through his hair. "I thought you wanted your Captain Ungari."

"Elena's the first step to Ungari. Or, failing Ungari, to smuggling us out of here. If Ungari hadn't been so damn insistent on the left hand not knowing what the right was doing, it would be a lot easier. But this will do." He studied Gregor in worry. "Have you been all right?"

"A few hours putting up light fixtures isn't going to break my health, I assure you," said Gregor dryly.

"Is that what they had you doing? Not what I'd pictured, somehow . . ."

Gregor seemed all right, anyway. Indeed, the Emperor was acting almost cheerful about his stint as a slave laborer, as Gregor's morose standards of cheer went. *Maybe we ought to send him to the salt mines for two weeks every year, to keep him happy and content with his regular job.* Miles relaxed a little.

"It's hard to imagine Elena Bothari as a mercenary," Gregor added reflectively.

"Don't underestimate her." Miles concealed a moment of raw doubt. Almost four years. He knew how much he had changed in four years. What of Elena? Her years could have been hardly less hectic. *Times change. People change with them. . .* No. As well doubt himself as Elena.

The half-hour wait for his chrono to creep to the appointed moment was a bad interval, enough to loosen Miles's driving tension and wash him in weariness but not enough to rest or refresh him. He was miserably conscious of losing his edge, of a crying need for alertness when alertness and straight-thinking escaped like sand between his fingers. He rechecked his chrono. *An hour* had been too vague. He should have named the minute. But who knew what difficulties or delays Elena must overcome from her end?

Miles blinked hard, realizing from his wavering and disconnected thoughts that he was falling asleep sitting up. The door hissed open without Gregor's having released the lock.

"Here he is, men!"

A half-squad of grey-and-white clad mercenaries filled the aperture and the corridor beyond. It hardly needed the stunners and shock-sticks in their hands, the purposive descent on his person, to tell Miles this hairy crew was not Elena's. The surge of adrenalin scarcely cleared the fatigue-fog from his head. *And what do I pretend to be now? A moving target?* He sagged against the wall, not even bothering, though Gregor lurched to his feet and made a valiant try in the constricted space, an accurate karate-kick sending a stunner flying from the hand of a closing mercenary. Two men smashed Gregor against the wall for his effort. Miles winced.

Then Miles himself was jerked from the bunk to be coiled, triple-coiled, in a tangle-net. The field burned against him. They were using enough power to immobilize a plunging horse. *What do you think I am, boys?*

The excited squad leader cried into his wrist comm, "I got him, sir!"

Miles raised an ironic brow. The squad leader flushed and straightened, his hand twitching in the effort not to salute. Miles smiled slightly. The squad leader's lips tightened. *Ha. Almost got you going, didn't I?*

"Take them away," ordered the squad leader.

Miles was carried out the door between two men, his bound feet dangling ridiculous inches from the floor. A groaning Gregor was dragged in his wake. As they passed a cross-corridor, Miles saw Chodak's strained face from the corner of his eye, floating in the shadows.

He damned his own judgment then. *You thought you could read people. Your one demonstrable talent. Right. Sure. Should have, should have, should have,* mocked his mind, like the caw of some vile scavenging bird surprised at a carcass.

When they were dragged across a large docking bay and through a small personnel hatch, Miles knew at once where he was. The *Triumph,* the pocket dreadnought that had occasionally served as the fleet's flagship, was doing that duty again now. Tung of the dubious current status had been captain-owner of the *Triumph,* once, before Tau Verde. Oser had used to favor his own *Peregrine* as flag—was this some deliberate political statement? The corridors of the ship had a strange, painful, powerful familiarity. The odors of men, metal, and machinery. That crooked archway, legacy of the lunatic ramming that had captured her on Miles's first encounter, still not properly straightened out . . . *I thought I had forgotten more.*

They were hustled along swiftly and secretly, a pair of squadmen going ahead to clear the corridor of witnesses before them. This was going to be a very private chat, then. Fine, that suited Miles. He would have preferred to avoid Oser altogether, but if they must meet again, he would simply have to find some way of turning it to use. He ordered his persona as if adjusting his cuffs—Miles Naismith, space mercenary and mystery entrepreneur, come to the Hegen Hub for . . . what? And his glum if faithful sidekick Greg, of course—he would have to think of some particularly benign explanation for Gregor.

They clattered down the corridor past the tactics room, the *Triumph*'s combat nerve center, and fetched up at the smaller of the two briefing rooms across from it. The holovid plate in the center of the gleaming conference table was dark and silent. Admiral Oser sat equally dark and silent at the table's head, flanked by a pale blond man Miles presumed to be a loyal lieutenant; not anyone Miles knew from before. Miles and Gregor were forcibly seated in two chairs pulled back and distanced from the table, that their hands and feet might be unconcealed. Oser dismissed all but one guard to the corridor outside.

Oser's appearance hadn't changed much in four years, Miles decided. Still lean and hawk-faced, dark hair maybe a little greyer at the temples. Miles had remembered him as taller, but he was actually shorter than Metzov. Oser reminded Miles somehow of the general. Was it the age, the build? The hostile glower, the murderous pinpricks of red light in the eye?

"Miles," Gregor muttered out of the corner of his mouth, "what did you do to piss this guy off?"

"Nothing!" Miles protested back, sotto voce. "Nothing on purpose, anyway."

Gregor looked less than reassured.

Oser placed his palms flat on the table before him and leaned forward, staring at Miles with predatory intensity. If Oser'd had a tail, Miles fancied, its end would be flicking back and forth. "What are you doing here?" Oser opened bluntly, without preamble.

You brought me, don't you know? Not the time to get cute, no. Miles was highly conscious of the fact that he did not precisely look his best. But Admiral Naismith wouldn't care, he was too goal-directed; Naismith would carry on painted blue, if he had to. He answered equally bluntly. "I was hired to do a military evaluation of the Hegen Hub for an interested non-combatant who ships through here." There, the truth up front, where it was sure to be disbelieved. "Since they don't care for mounting rescue expeditions, they wanted enough warning to clear the Hub of their citizens before hostilities break out. I'm doing a little arms dealing on the side. A cover that pays for itself."

Oser's eyes narrowed. "Not Barrayar . . ."

"Barrayar has its own operatives."

"So does Cetaganda . . . Aslund fears Cetagandan ambitions."

"As well they should."

"Barrayar is equidistant."

"In my professional opinion," fighting the tangle-field, Miles favored Oser with a small bow, sitting down—Oser almost nodded back, but caught himself—"Barrayar is no threat to Aslund in this generation. To control the Hegen Hub, Barrayar must control Pol. With the terraforming of their own second continent plus the opening of the planet Sergyar, Barrayar is rather oversupplied with frontiers at present. And then there is the problem of holding restive Komarr. A military adventure toward Pol would be a serious overextension of Barrayar's human resources just now. Cheaper to be friends, or at least neutral."

"Aslund also fears Pol."

"They are unlikely to fight unless attacked first. Keeping peace with Pol is cheap and easy. Just do nothing."

"And Vervain?"

"I haven't evaluated Vervain yet. It's next on my list."

"Is it?" Oser leaned back in his chair, crossing his arms. It was not a relaxed gesture. "As a spy, I could have you executed."

"But I'm not an *enemy* spy," Miles answered, simulating easiness. "A friendly neutral or—who knows?—potential ally."

"And what is your interest in my fleet?"

"My interest in the Denda—in the mercenaries is purely academic, I assure you. You are simply part of the picture. Tell me, what's your contract with Aslund like?" Miles cocked his head, talking shop.

Oser almost answered, then his lips thinned in annoyance. If Miles had been a ticking bomb he could not have more thoroughly commanded the mercenary's attention.

"Oh, come on," Miles scoffed in the lengthening silence. "What could I do, by myself with one man?"

"I remember the last time. You entered Tau Verde local space with a staff of four. Four months later you were dictating terms. So what are you planning now?"

"You overestimate my impact. I merely helped people along in the direction they wished to go. An expediter, so to speak."

"Not for me. I spent three years recovering the ground I lost. In my own fleet!"

"It's hard to please everyone." Miles intercepted Gregor's look of mute horror, and toned himself down. Come to think, Gregor had never met Admiral Naismith, had he? "Even you were not seriously damaged."

Oser's jaw compressed further. "And who's he?" He jerked a thumb at Gregor.

"Greg? He's just my batman," Miles cut across Gregor's opening mouth.

"He doesn't look like a batman. He looks like an officer."

Gregor looked insensibly cheered at this unbiased encomium.

"You can't go by looks. Commodore Tung looks like a wrestler."

Oser's eyes were suddenly freezing. "Indeed. And how long have you been in correspondence with *Captain* Tung?"

By the sick lurch in his belly, Miles realized mentioning Tung had been a major mistake. He tried to keep his features cooly ironic, not reflecting his unease. "If I'd been in correspondence with Tung, I should not have been troubled with making this personal evaluation of Aslund Station."

Oser, elbows on table, hands clasped, studied Miles in silence for a full minute. At last one hand fell open, to point at the guard, who straightened attentively. "Space them," Oser ordered.

"What?!" yelped Miles.

"You," the pointing finger collected Oser's silent lieutenant, "go with them. See that it's done. Use the portside access lock, it's closest. If *he*," pointing to Miles, "starts to talk, stop his tongue. It's his most dangerous organ."

The guard released the tangle field from Miles's legs and pulled him to his feet.

"Aren't you even going to have me chemically interrogated?" asked Miles, dizzied by this sudden downturn.

"And contaminate my interrogators? The last thing I want is to give you rein to talk, to anyone. I can think of nothing more fatal than for the rot of disloyalty to start in my own Intelligence section. Whatever your planned speech, removing your air will neutralize it. You nearly convince *me*." Oser almost shuddered.

We were getting on so well, yes. . . . "But I—" they were hoisting Gregor to his feet too. "But you don't need to—"

Two waiting members of the half-squad fell in as they were bundled out the door, frog-marching Miles and Gregor rapidly down the corridor. "But—!" The conference room door hissed closed.

"This is not going well, Miles," Gregor observed, his pale face a weird compound of detachment, exasperation, and dismay. "Any more bright ideas?"

"You're the man who was experimenting with wingless flight. Is this any worse than, say, plummeting?"

"At my own hand," Gregor began to drag his feet, to struggle, as the airlock chamber heaved into view, "not at the whim of a bunch of . . ." it took three guards to wrestle him now, "bloody *peasants!*"

Miles was getting seriously frantic. Screw the damn cover. "You know," he called out loudly, "you fellows are about to throw a fortune in ransom out the airlock!"

Two guards kept wrestling with Gregor, but the third paused. "How big a fortune?"

"Huge," Miles promised. "Buy your own fleet."

The lieutenant abandoned Gregor and closed on Miles, drawing a vibra-knife. The lieutenant was interpreting his orders with horrific literality, Miles realized when the man went for a grip on his tongue. He almost got it—the evil insect whine of the knife dopplered centimeters from Miles's nose—Miles bit the thick thrusting fingers, and twisted against the grip of the guard holding him. The tangle field binding Miles's arms to his torso whined and crackled, unbreakable. Miles jammed backward against the crotch of the man behind, who yipped at the field's bite. His grip slipped and Miles dropped, rolling and banging into the lieutenant's knees. It wasn't exactly a judo throw; the lieutenant more-or-less tripped over him.

Gregor's two opponents were distracted, as much by the bloody barbaric promise of the vibra-knife show as by Miles's ultimately futile struggles. They did not see the leather-faced man step out from a cross-corridor, aim his stunner, and spray. They arched convulsively as the buzzing charges struck their backs, and dropped heap-fashion to the deck. The man who'd been holding Miles, and was now trying to grab him again as he flopped around evasively as a fish, whirled just in time to intersect a beam square in the face.

Miles flung himself across the blond lieutenant's head, pinning him—only momentarily, alas—to the deck. Miles wriggled, to press the tangle-field into the man's face, then was heaved off with a curse. The lieutenant had one knee under himself, preparing to launch an attack and wobbling around in search of his target, when Gregor hopped over and kicked him in the jaw. A stunner charge hit the lieutenant in the back of the head and he went down.

"Damn fine soldiering," Miles panted to Sergeant

Chodak in the sudden silence. "I don't think they even saw what hit them." *So, I called him straight the first time. Haven't lost my touch after all. Bless you, Sergeant.*

"You two aren't so bad yourselves, for men with both hands tied behind their backs." Chodak shook his head in harried amusement, and trod forward to release the tangle-fields.

"What a team," said Miles.

CHAPTER ELEVEN

A quick ring of boots from further up the corridor drew Miles's eye. He exhaled, a long-held breath, and stood. *Elena.*

She wore a mercenary officer's undress uniform, grey-and-white pocketed jacket, trousers, ankle-topping boots gleaming on her long, long legs. Still tall, still slim, still with pale pure skin, ember-brown eyes, arched aristocratic nose and long sculptured jaw. *She's cut her hair,* Miles thought, stupid-stunned. Gone was the straight-shining black cascade to her waist. Now it was clipped out over her ears, only little dark points grace-noting her high cheekbones and forehead, a similar point echoed at the nape of her neck; severe, practical, very smart. Soldierly.

She strode up, eyes taking in Miles, Gregor, the four Oserans. "Good work, Chodak." She dropped to one knee beside the nearest body and probed its neck for a pulse. "Are they dead?"

"No, just stunned," Miles explained.

She regarded the open inner airlock door with some regret. "I don't suppose we can space them."

"They were going to space us, but no. But we probably ought to get them out of sight while we run," said Miles.

"Right." She rose and nodded to Chodak, who began helping Gregor drag the stunned bodies into the airlock. She frowned at the blond lieutenant, going past feet-first. "Not that spacing wouldn't *improve* some personalities."

"Can you give us a bolt-hole?"

"That's what we came for." She turned to the three soldiers who had followed her cautiously into view. A fourth stood guard at the nearest cross-corridor. "It seems we just got lucky," she told them. "Scout ahead and clear the aisles on our escape route—subtly. Then disappear. You weren't here and didn't see this."

They nodded and withdrew. Miles heard a retreating mutter, "Was that *him*?" "Yeah . . ."

Miles, Gregor, and Elena, with the bodies, piled cozily into the lock and closed the inner door temporarily. Chodak stood guard outside. Elena helped Gregor pull the boots from the Oseran nearest his size while Miles stripped off his blue prisoner's outfit and stood, revealing Victor Rotha's wrinkled clothing, much the worse for four days wear, sleep, and sweat. Miles wished for boots to replace the vulnerable sandals, but none here came close to his size.

Gregor and Elena exchanged looks, each warily amazed at the other, as Gregor yanked on grey-and-whites and plunged his feet into the boots.

"It's really you." Elena shook her head in dismay. "What are you doing here?"

"It was by mistake," said Gregor.

"No lie. Whose?"

"Mine, I'm afraid," said Miles. Somewhat to his annoyance, Gregor did not gainsay this.

A peculiar smile, her first, quirked Elena's lips. Miles decided not to ask her to explain it. This hurried practical exchange did not in the least resemble any of the dozens of conversations he had rehearsed in his head for this first, poignant meeting with her.

"The search will be up in minutes, when these guys don't report back," Miles jittered. He collected two stunners, the tangle-field, and the vibra-knife, and stuck them in his waistband. On second thought, he swiftly relieved the four Oserans of credit cards, pass chits, IDs, and odd cash, stuffing his pockets and Gregor's, and made sure Gregor ditched his prisoner's traceable ID. To his secret delight, he also found a half-eaten ration bar, and bit into it there and then. He chewed as Elena led the way back out the lock. He conscientiously offered a bite to Gregor, who shook his head. Gregor'd probably had dinner in that cafeteria.

Chodak hastily straightened Gregor's uniform, and they all marched off, Miles to the center, half-concealed, half-guarded. Before he could go half-paranoid at his conspicuousness they took to a drop-tube, emerged several decks down, and found themselves at a large cargo-lock, engaged to a shuttle. One of Elena's scout squad, leaning as if idle against the wall, nodded. With a half-salute to Elena, Chodak split off and they hurried away. Miles and Gregor followed Elena across the flex-seal of the shuttle hatch and into the empty cargo hold of one of the *Triumph*'s shuttles, stepping from the artificial gravity field of the mother ship abruptly into the vertigo of free fall. They floated forward to the pilot's compartment. Elena sealed the compartment hatch behind them, and anxiously gestured Gregor to the vacant seat at the engineering/comm station.

The pilot's and co-pilot's seats were filled. Arde Mayhew grinned cheerfully over his shoulder at Miles, and waved/saluted hello. Miles recognized the shaved bullet-head of the second man even before he turned.

"Hello, son." Ky Tung's smile was far more ironic than cheerful. "Welcome back. You took your sweet time." Tung, arms folded, did not salute.

"Hello, Ky," Miles nodded to the Eurasian. Tung had not changed, anyway. Still looked any age between forty and sixty. Still built like an ancient tank. Still seemed to see more than he spoke, most uncomfortable for the guilty of conscience.

Mayhew the pilot spoke into his comm. "Traffic control, I've traced that red light on my panel now. Defective pressure reading. All fixed. We're ready to break away."

"About time, C-2," a disembodied voice returned. "You're clear."

The pilot's swift hands activated hatch seal controls, aimed attitude jets. Some hissing and clanks, and the shuttle popped away from its mothership and started on its trajectory. Mayhew killed the comm and breathed a long sigh of relief. "Safe. For now."

Elena wedged herself across the aisle behind Miles, long legs locking. Miles hooked an arm around a handhold to anchor against Mayhew's current mild accelerations. "I hope you're right," said Miles, "but what makes you think so?"

"He means, safe to talk," said Elena. "Not safe in any cosmic sense. This is a routine scheduled run, except for us unlisted passengers. We know you haven't been missed yet, or traffic control would have stopped us. Oser will search the *Triumph* and the military station for you first. We may even be able to slip you back aboard the *Triumph* after the search has passed to wider areas."

"This is Plan B," Tung explained, swiveling around to half-face Miles. "Or maybe Plan C. Plan A, on the assumption that your rescue was going to be a lot noisier, was to flee at once to the *Ariel*, now on picket-station, and declare the revolution. I'm grateful for the chance to bring things off a little, er, less spontaneously."

Miles choked. "God! That would have been worse than the first time." Pitched into an interlocking chain of events he did not control, drafted gonfalonier' to some mercenary military mutiny, thrust to the lead of its parade with all the free will of a head on a pike. . . . "No. No spontaneity, thanks. Definitely not."

"So," Tung steepled his thick fingers, "what *is* your plan?"

"My what?"

"Plan," Tung pronounced the word with sardonic care. "In other words, why are you here?"

"Oser asked me that same question," sighed Miles. "Would you believe, I'm here by accident? Oser wouldn't. You wouldn't happen to know *why* he wouldn't, would you?"

Tung pursed his lips. "Accident? Maybe. . . . Your 'accidents,' I once noticed, have ways of entangling your enemies that are the green envy of mature and careful strategists. Far too consistent for chance, I concluded it had to be unconscious will. If only you'd stuck with me, son, between us we could've . . . or maybe you are simply a supreme opportunist. In which case I direct your attention to the opportunity now before you to retake the Dendarii Mercenaries."

"You didn't answer my question," Miles noted.

"You didn't answer mine," Tung countered.

"I don't want the Dendarii Mercenaries."

"I do."

"Oh." Miles paused. "Why don't you split off with the personnel who are loyal to you and start your own, then? It's been done."

"Shall we swim through space?" Tung imitated fish fins with his waving fingers, and puffed his cheeks. "Oser controls the equipment. Including my ship. The *Triumph* is everything I've accumulated in a thirty-year career. Which I lost through your machinations. Somebody owes me another. If not Oser, then . . ." Tung glowered significantly at Miles.

"I tried to give you a fleet in trade," said Miles, harried. "How'd you lose control of it—old strategist?"

Tung tapped a finger to his left breast, to indicate a touché. "Things went well at first, for a year, year and a half after we departed Tau Verde. Got two sweet little contracts in a row out toward the East-net—small-scale commando operations, sure things. Well, not too sure—kept us on our toes. But we brought them off."

Miles glanced at Elena. "I'd heard about those, yes."

"On the third, we got into troubles. Baz Jesek had gotten more and more involved with equipment and maintenance—he is a good engineer, I'll give him that—I was tactical commander, and Oser—I thought by default, but now I think design—took up the administrative slack. Could have been good, each doing what he did best, if Oser'd been working with and not against us. In the same situation, I'd have sent assassins. Oser employed guerilla accountants.

"We took a bit of a beating on that third contract. Baz was up to his ears in engineering and repairs, and by the time I got out of sickbay, Oser'd lined up one of his no-combat specials—wormhole guard duty work. Long-term contract. Seemed like a good idea at the time. But it gave him a wedge. With no actual combat going on, I . . ." Tung cleared his throat, "got bored, didn't pay attention. Oser'd out-flanked me before I realized there was a war on. He sprang the financial reorganization on us—"

"I told you not to trust him, six months before that," Elena put in with a frown, "after he tried to seduce me."

Tung shrugged uncomfortably. "It seemed like an understandable temptation."

"To bang his commander's wife?" Elena's eyes sparked. "Anyone's wife? I knew then he wasn't level. If my oaths meant nothing to him, how little did his own?"

"He did take no for an answer, you said," Tung excused himself. "If he'd kept leaning on you, I'd have been willing to step in. I thought you ought to be flattered, ignore it, and go on."

"Overtures of that sort contain a judgment of my

character that I find anything but flattering, thank you," Elena snapped.

Miles bit his knuckles, hard and secretly, remembering his own longings. "It might just have been an early move in his power-play," he put in. "Probing for weaknesses in his enemies' defenses. And in this case, not finding them."

"Hm." Elena seemed faintly comforted by this view. "Anyway, Ky was no help, and I got tired of playing Cassandra. Naturally, I couldn't tell Baz. But Oser's double-dealing didn't come as a complete surprise to *all* of us."

Tung frowned, frustrated. "Given the nucleus of his own surviving ships, all he had to do was swing the votes of half the other captain-owners. Auson voted with him. I could have strangled the bastard."

"You lost Auson yourself, with your moaning about the *Triumph*," Elena put in, still acerb. "He thought you threatened his captaincy of it."

Tung shrugged. "As long as I was Chief-of-Staff/Tactical, in charge during actual combat, I didn't think he could really hurt my ship. I was content to let the *Triumph* ride along as if owned by the fleet corporation. I could wait—till *you* got back," his dark eyes glinted at Miles, "and we found out what was going on. And then you never came back."

"The king will return, eh?" murmured Gregor, who had been listening with fascination. He raised an eyebrow at Miles.

"Let it be a lesson to you," Miles murmured back through set teeth. Gregor subsided, less humorous.

Miles turned to Tung. "Surely Elena disabused you of any such immediate expectation."

"I tried," muttered Elena. "Although . . . I suppose, I couldn't help hoping a bit myself. Maybe you'd . . . quit your other project, come back to us."

If I flunked out of the Academy, eh? "It wasn't a project I could quit, short of death."

"I know that now."

"In five minutes, max," put in Arde Mayhew, "I've either got to lock into the transfer station traffic control for docking, or else cut for the *Ariel*. Which is it going to be, folks?"

"I can put over a hundred loyal officers and non-coms at your back at a word," said Tung to Miles. "Four ships."

"Why not at your own back?"

"If I could, I would have already. But I'm not going to tear the fleet apart unless I can be certain of putting it back together again. All of it. But with you as leader, with your reputation—which has grown in the retelling—"

"Leader? Or figurehead?" The image of that pike bobbed in Miles's mind's eye again.

Tung's hands opened noncommittally. "As you wish. The bulk of the officer cadre will go for the winning side. That means we must appear to be winning quickly, if we move at all. Oser has about another hundred personally loyal to himself, which we're going to have to physically overpower if he insists on holding out—which suggests to my mind that a well-timed assassination could save a lot of lives."

"Jolly. I think you and Oser have been working together too long, Ky. You're starting to think alike. Again. I did not come here to seize command of a mercenary fleet. I have other priorities." He schooled himself not to glance at Gregor.

"What higher priorities?"

"How about, preventing a planetary civil war? Maybe an interstellar one?"

"I have no professional interest in that." It almost succeeded in being a joke.

Indeed, what were Barrayar's agonies to Tung? "You do if you're on the doomed side. You only get paid for winning, and only get to spend your pay if you live, mercenary."

Tung's narrow eyes narrowed further. "What do you know that I don't? *Are* we on the doomed side?"

I am, if I don't get Gregor back. Miles shook his head. "Sorry. I can't talk about that. I've got to get to—" Pol closed to him, the Consortium station blocked, and now Aslund become even more dangerous, "Vervain." He glanced at Elena. "Get us both to Vervain."

"You working for the Vervani?" Tung asked.

"No."

"Who, then?" Tung's hands twitched, so tense with his curiosity they seemed to want to squeeze out information by main force.

Elena noticed the unconscious gesture too. "Ky, back off," she said sharply. "If Miles wants Vervain, Vervain he shall have."

Tung looked at Elena, at Mayhew. "Do you back him, or me?"

Elena's chin lifted. "We're both oath-sworn to Miles. Baz too."

"And you have to ask why I need you?" said Tung in exasperation to Miles, gesturing at the pair. "What is this larger game, that you all seem to know all about, and I, nothing?"

"I don't know anything," chirped Mayhew. "I'm just going by Elena."

"Is this a chain of command, or a chain of credulity?"

"There's a difference?" Miles grinned.

"You've exposed us, by coming here," Tung argued. "Think! We help you, you leave, we're left naked to Oser's wrath. There's too many witnesses already. There might be safety in victory, none in half-measures."

Miles looked with anguish at Elena, picturing her, quite vividly in light of his recent experiences, being shoved out an airlock by evil, witless goons. Tung noted with satisfaction the effect of his plea on Miles and sat smugly back. Elena glared at Tung.

Gregor stirred uneasily. "I think . . . should you become refugees on Our behalf," (Elena, Miles saw, heard that official capital O too, as Tung and Mayhew of course could not) "We can see that you do not suffer. Financially, at least."

Elena nodded understanding and acceptance. Tung leaned toward Elena, jerking his thumb at Gregor. "All right, who is this guy?" Elena shook her head mutely.

Tung vented a small hiss. "You've no means of support visible to me, son. What if we become corpses on your behalf?"

Elena remarked, "We've risked becoming corpses for much less."

"Less than what?" snapped Tung.

Mayhew, his eyes going briefly distant, touched the communications plug in his ear. "Decision time, folks."

"Can this ship go across-system?" asked Miles.

"No. Not fueled up for it," Mayhew shrugged apology.

"Not fast enough or armored for it, either," said Tung.

"You'll have to smuggle us out on commercial transport, past Aslunder security," Miles said unhappily.

Tung stared around at his recalcitrant little committee, and sighed. "Security's tighter for incoming than outgoing. I think it can be done. Take us in, Arde."

After Mayhew had docked the cargo shuttle at its assigned loading niche at the Aslunders' transfer station, Miles, Gregor, and Elena lay low, locked in the pilot's compartment. Tung and Mayhew went off "to see what we can do," as Tung put it, rather airily to Miles's mind. Miles sat and nibbled his knuckles nervously, and tried not to jump with each thump, clink, or hiss of the robotic loaders placing supplies for the mercenaries on the other side of the bulk-head. Elena's steady profile did not twitch at every little noise, Miles noticed enviously. *I loved her once. Who is she now?*

Could one choose *not* to fall in love all over again with this new person? A chance to choose. She seemed tougher, more willing to speak her mind—this was good—yet her thoughts had a bitter tang. Not good. That bitterness made him ache.

"Have you been all right?" he asked her hesi-tantly. "Apart from this command structure mess, that is. Tung treating you right? He was supposed to be your mentor. On-the-job, for you, the training I was getting in the classroom . . ."

"Oh, he's a good mentor. He stuffs me with mili-tary information, tactics, history . . . I can run every phase of a combat drop patrol now, logistics, map-ping, assault, withdrawal, even emergency shuttle take-offs and landings, if you don't mind a few bumps. I'm almost up to really handling my fictional rank, at least on fleet equipment. He likes teaching."

"It seemed to me you were a little . . . tense, with him."

She tossed her head. "Everything is tense, just now. It's not possible to be 'apart from' this com-mand structure mess, thank you. Although . . . I suppose I haven't quite forgiven Tung for not being infallible about it. I thought he was, at first."

"Yeah, well, there'a a lot of fallibility going around these days," Miles said uncomfortably. "Uh . . . how's Baz?" *Is your husband treating you right?* he wanted to demand, but didn't.

"He's well," she replied, not looking happy, "but discouraged. This power struggle was alien to him, repugnant, I think. He's a tech at heart, he sees a job that needs doing, he does it . . . Tung hints that if Baz hadn't buried himself in Engineering he might have forseen—prevented—fought the takeover, but I think it was the other way around. He couldn't lower himself to fight on Oser's back-stabbing level, so he withdrew to where he could keep his own standards of honesty . . . for a little while longer. This schism's affected morale all up and down the line."

"I'm sorry," said Miles.

"You should be." Her voice cracked, steadied, harshened. "Baz felt he'd failed you, but you failed us first, when you never came back. You couldn't expect us to keep up the illusion forever."

"Illusion?" said Miles. "I knew . . . it would be difficult, but I thought you might . . . grow into your roles. Make the mercenaries your own."

"The mercenaries may be enough for Tung. I thought they might be for me, too, till we came to the killing. . . . I hate Barrayar, but better to serve Barrayar than nothing, or your own ego."

"What does Oser serve?" Gregor asked curiously, brows raised at this mixed declamation about their homeworld.

"Oser serves Oser. 'The fleet,' he says, but the fleet serves Oser, so it's just a short circuit," said Elena. "The fleet is no home-country. No building, no children . . . sterile. I don't mind helping out the Aslunders, though, they need it. A poor planet, and scared."

"You and Baz—and Arde—could have left, gone off on your own," began Miles.

"How?" said Elena. "You gave us the Dendarii in *charge*. Baz was a deserter once. Never again."

All my fault, right, thought Miles. *Great.*

Elena turned to Gregor, who had acquired a strange guarded expression on his face while listening to her charges of abandonment. "You still haven't said what you're doing here in the first place, besides putting your feet in things. Was this supposed to be some sort of secret diplomatic mission?"

"You explain it," said Miles to Gregor, trying not to grit his teeth. *Tell her about the balcony, eh?*

Gregor shrugged, eyes sliding aside from Elena's level look. "Like Baz, I deserted. Like Baz, I found it was not the improvement I'd hoped for."

"You can see why it's urgent to get Gregor back home as quickly as possible," Miles put in. "They think he's missing. Maybe kidnapped." Miles gave Elena a quick edited version of their chance meeting in Consortium Detention.

"God." Elena's lips pursed. "I see why it's urgent to you to get him off your hands, anyway. If anything happened to him in your company, fifteen factions would cry 'Treason plot!'"

"That thought has occurred to me, yes," growled Miles.

"Your father's Centrist coalition government would be the first thing to fall," Elena continued. "The military right would get behind Count Vorinnis, I suppose, and square off with the anti-centralization liberals. The French speakers would want Vorville, the Russian Vortugalov—or has he died yet?"

"The far-right blow-up-the-wormhole isolationist loonie faction would field Count Vortrifrani against the anti-Vor pro-galactic faction who want a written constitution," put in Miles glumly. "And I do mean field."

"Count Vortrifrani scares me," Elena shivered. "I've heard him speak."

"It's the suave way he mops the foam from his lips," said Miles. "The Greek minorists would seize the moment to attempt secession—"

"Stop it!" Gregor, who had propped his forehead on his hands, said from behind the barrier of his arms.

"I thought that was *your* job," said Elena tartly. At his bleak look, raising his head, she softened, her mouth twisting up. "Too bad I can't offer you a job with the fleet. We can always use formally-trained officers, to train the rest if nothing else."

"A mercenary?" said Gregor. "There's a thought. . . ."

"Oh, sure. A lot of our people are former regular military folk. Some are even legitimately discharged."

Fantasy lit Gregor's eye with brief amusement. He sighted down his grey-and-white jacket sleeve. "If only you were in charge here, aye, Miles?"

"No!" Miles cried in a suffused voice.

The light died. "It was a joke."

"Not funny." Miles breathed carefully, praying it would not occur to Gregor to make that an *order*. . . . "Anyway, we're now trying to make it to the Barrayaran Consul on Vervain Station. It's still there, I hope. I haven't heard news for days—what's going on with the Vervani?"

"As far as I know, it's business as usual, except for the heightened paranoia," said Elena. "Vervain's putting its resources into ships, not stations—"

"Makes sense, when you've got more than one wormlike to guard," Miles conceded.

"But it makes Aslund perceive the Vervani as potential aggressors. There's an Aslunder faction that's actually urging a first strike before the new Vervani fleet comes on-line. Fortunately, the defensive strategists have prevailed so far. Oser has set the price for a strike by us prohibitively high. He's not stupid. He knows the Aslunders couldn't back us up. Vervain hired a mercenary fleet as a stopgap too—in fact, that's what gave the Aslunders the idea to hire us. They're called Randall's Rangers, though I understand Randall is no more."

"We shall avoid them," Miles asserted fervently.

"I hear their new second officer is a Barrayaran. You might be able to swing some help, there."

Gregor's brows rose in speculation. "One of Illyan's plants? Sounds like his work."

Was that where Ungari had gone? "Approach with caution, anyway," Miles allowed.

"About time," Gregor commented under his breath.

"The Ranger's commander's name is Cavilo—"

"What?" yelped Miles.

Elena's winged brows rose. "Just Cavilo. Nobody seems to know if it's the given or surname—"

"Cavilo is the person who tried to buy me—or Victor Rotha—at the Consortium Station. For twenty thousand Betan dollars."

Elena's brows stayed up. "Why?"

"I don't know why." Miles rethought their goal. Pol, the Consortium, Aslund . . . no, it still came up Vervain. "But we definitely avoid the Vervani's mercs. We step off the ship and go straight to the Consul, go to ground, and don't even squeak till Illyan's men arrive to take us home, Momma. Right."

Gregor sighed. "Right."

No more playing secret agent. His best efforts had only served to get Gregor nearly murdered. It was time to try less hard, Miles decided.

"Strange," said Gregor, looking at Elena—at the new Elena, Miles guessed—"to think you've had more combat experience than either of us."

"Than both of you," Elena corrected dryly. "Yes, well . . . actual combat . . . is a lot stupider than I'd imagined. If two groups can cooperate to the incredible extent it takes to meet in battle, why not put in a tenth that effort to talk? That's not true of guerilla wars, though," Elena went on thoughtfully. "A guerilla is an enemy who won't play the game. Makes more sense to me. If you're going to be vile, why not be totally vile? That third contract—if I ever get involved in another guerilla war, I want to be on the side of the guerillas."

"Harder to make peace, between totally vile enemies," Miles reflected. "War is not its own end, except in some catastrophic slide into absolute damnation. It's peace that's wanted. Some better peace than the one you started with."

"Whoever can be the most vile longest, wins?" Gregor posited.

"Not . . . historically true, I don't think. If what you do during the war so degrades you that the next peace is worse. . . ." Human noises from the cargo bay froze Miles in midsentence, but it was Tung and Mayhew returning.

"Come on," Tung urged. "If Arde doesn't keep to schedule, he'll draw attention."

They filed into the cargo hold, where Mayhew held the control leash of a float pallet with a couple of plastic packing crates attached. "Your friend can pass as a fleet soldier," Tung told Miles. "For you, I found a box. It would have been classier to roll you up in a carpet, but since the freighter captain is male, I'm afraid the historical reference would be wasted."

Dubiously, Miles regarded the box. It seemed to lack air holes. "Where are you taking me?"

"We have a regular irregular arrangement, for getting fleet intelligence officers in and out quietly. Got this inner-system freighter captain, an independent owner—he's Vervani, but he's been on the payroll three times before. He'll take you across, get you through Vervani customs. After that you're on your own."

"How much danger is this arrangement to you all?" Miles worried.

"Not a lot," said Tung, "all things considered. He'll think he's delivering more mercenary agents, for a price, and naturally keep his mouth shut. It'll be days before he gets back to even be questioned. I arranged it all myself, Elena and Arde didn't appear, so he can't give them away."

"Thank you," Miles said quietly.

Tung nodded, and sighed. "If only you'd stayed on with us. What a soldier I could've made of you, these last three years."

"If you do find yourselves out of a job as a consequence of helping us," Gregor added, "Elena will know how to put you in touch."

Tung grimaced. "In touch with what, eh?"

"Better not to know," said Elena, helping Miles position himself in the packing crate.

"All right," grumbled Tung, "but . . . all right."

Miles found himself face to face with Elena, for the last time till—when? She hugged him, but then gave Gregor an identical, sisterly embrace. "Give my love to your mother," she told Miles. "I often think of her."

"Right. Uh . . . give my best to Baz. Tell him, it's all right. Your personal safety comes first, yours and his. The Dendarii are, are, were . . ." he could not quite bring himself to say, *not important*, or, a *naive dream*, or, *an illusion*, though that last came closest. "A good try," he finished lamely.

The look she gave him was cool, edged, indecipherable—no, readily decodable, he feared. *Idiot*, or stronger words to that effect. He sat down, his head to his knees, and let Mayhew affix the lid, feeling like a zoological specimen being crated for shipment to the lab.

The transfer went smoothly. Miles and Gregor found themselves installed in a small but decent cabin designed for the freighter's occasional supercargo. The ship undocked, free of Aslund Station and danger of discovery, some three hours after they boarded. No Oseran search parties, no uproars . . . Tung, Miles had to admit, still did good work.

Miles was intensely grateful for a wash, a chance to clean his remaining clothes, a real meal, and sleep in safety. The ship's tiny crew seemed allergic to their corridor; he and Gregor were left strictly alone. Safe for three days, as he chugged across the Hegen Hub yet again, in yet another identity. Next stop, the Barrayaran consulate on Vervain Station.

Oh, God, he was going to have to write a report

on all this when they got there. True confessions, in the approved ImpSec official style (dry as dust, judging from samples he'd read). Ungari, now, given the same tour, would have produced columns of concrete, objective data, all ready to be reanalyzed six different ways. What had Miles counted? *Nothing, I was in a box.* He had little to offer but gut feel based on a limited view snatched while dodging what seemed like every security goon in the system. Maybe he should center his report on the security forces, eh? One ensign's opinion. The general staff would be so impressed.

So what was his opinion, by now? Well, Pol didn't seem to be the source of the troubles in the Hegen Hub; they were reacting, not acting. The Consortium seemed supremely uninterested in military adventures, the only party weak enough for the eclectic Jacksonians to take on and beat was Aslund, and there would be little profit in conquering Aslund, a barely terraformed agricultural world. Aslund was paranoid enough to be dangerous, but only half-prepared, and shielded by a mercenary force waiting only the right spark to itself split into warring factions. No sustained threat there. The action, the energy for this destabilization, by elimination must be coming from or via Vervain. How could one find out . . . no. He'd sworn off secret agenting. Vervain was somebody else's problem.

Miles wondered wanly if he could persuade Gregor to give him an Imperial pardon from writing a report, and if Illyan would accept it. Probably not.

Gregor was very quiet. Miles, stretched out on his bunk, tucked his hands behind his head and smiled to conceal worry, as Gregor—somewhat regretfully, it seemed to Miles—put aside his stolen Dendarii uniform and donned civilian clothes contributed by Arde Mayhew. The shabby trousers, shirt, and jacket hung a little short and loose on Gregor's spare frame; so dressed he seemed a down-on-his-luck drifter,

with hollow eyes. Miles secretly resolved to keep
him away from high places.

Gregor regarded him back. "You were weird, as
Admiral Naismith, you know? Almost like a different
person."

Miles shrugged himself up onto one elbow. "I
guess Naismith is me with no brakes. No constraints.
He doesn't have to be a good little Vor, or any kind
of a Vor. He doesn't have a problem with subordination, he isn't subordinate to anyone."

"I noticed." Gregor ordered the Dendarii uniform
in Barrayaran regulation folds. "Do you regret having to duck out on the Dendarii?"

"Yes . . . no . . . I don't know." *Deeply.* The chain
of command, it seemed, pulled both ways on a middle link. Pull hard enough, and that link must twist
and snap. . . . "I trust you don't regret escaping contract slavery."

"No . . . it wasn't what I'd pictured. It was peculiar, that fight at the airlock, though. Total strangers
wanting to kill me without even knowing who I was.
Total strangers trying to kill the emperor of Barrayar,
I can understand. This . . . I'm going to have to
think about this one."

Miles allowed himself a brief crooked grin. "Like
being loved for yourself, only different."

Gregor gave him a sharp glance. "It was strange
to see Elena again, too. Bothari's dutiful daughter
. . . she's changed."

"I'd meant her to," Miles avowed.

"She seems quite attached to her deserter husband."

"Yes," Miles said shortly.

"Had you meant that too?"

"Not mine to choose. It . . . follows logically, from
the integrity of her character. I might have forseen
it. Since her convictions about loyalty just saved both
our lives, I can hardly . . . hardly regret them, eh?"

Gregor's brow rose, an oblique gloss.

Miles bit down irritation. "Anyway, I hope she'll

be all right. Oser's proved himself dangerous. She
and Baz seem to be protected only by Tung's admittedly eroding power base."

"I'm surprised you didn't take up Tung's offer."
Gregor grinned as briefly as Miles had. "Instant
admiralty. Skip all those tedious Barrayaran inter-
vening steps."

"Tung's offer?" Miles snorted. "Didn't you hear
him? I thought you said Dad made you read all those
treaties. Tung didn't offer command, he offered a
fight, at five to one odds against. He sought an ally,
front-man, or cannon-fodder, not a boss."

"Oh. Hm." Gregor settled back on his bunk.
"That's so. Yet I still wonder if you'd have chosen
something other than this prudent retreat if I hadn't
been along." His lids were hooded over a sharp glance.

Miles choked on visions. A sufficiently liberal
interpretation of Illyan's vague "use Ensign Vorkosigan to clear the Dendarii Mercenaries from the
Hub" might be stretched to include . . . no. "No. If
I hadn't run into you, I'd be on my way to Escobar
with Sergeant-nanny Overholt. You, I suppose, would
still be installing lights." Depending, of course, on
what the mysterious Cavilo—Commander Cavilo?—
had planned for Miles once he'd caught up with him
in Consortium Detention.

So where was Overholt, by now? Had he reported
to HQ, tried to contact Ungari, been picked off by
Cavilo? Or followed Miles? Too bad Miles couldn't
have followed Overholt to Ungari—no, that was cir-
cular reasoning. It was all very weird, and they were
well out of it.

"We're well out of it," Miles opined to Gregor.

Gregor rubbed the pale grey mark on his face,
fading shadow of his shock-stick encounter. "Yeah,
probably. I was getting good at the lights, though."

Almost over, Miles thought as he and Gregor followed the freighter captain through the hatch tube

into the Vervain Station docking bay. Well, maybe
not quite. The Vervani captain was nervous, obse-
quious, clearly tense. Still, if the man had managed
this spy transfer three times before, he should know
what he was doing by now.

The docking bay with its harsh lighting was the
usual chilly echoing cavern, arranged to the rigid
grid-pattern taste of robots, not human curves. It
was in fact empty of humans, its machinery silent.
Their path had been cleared before them, Miles supposed, though if he'd been doing it he'd have picked
the busiest chaotic period of loading or unloading to
slip something past.

The captain's eyes darted from corner to corner.
Miles could not help following his glance. They
stopped near a deserted control booth.

"We wait here," the freighter captain said. "There
are some men coming who will take you the rest of
the way." He leaned against the booth wall and
kicked it gently with one heel in an idle compulsive
rhythm for several minutes. then he stopped kicking
and straightened, head turning.

Footsteps. Half a dozen men emerged from a
nearby corridor. Miles stiffened. Uniformed men,
with an officer, judging by their posture, but they
weren't wearing the garb of either Vervani civil or
military security. Unfamiliar short-sleeved tan fatigues
with black tabs and trim, and short black boots. They
carried stunners, drawn and ready. *But if it walks
like an arrest squad, and talks like an arrest squad,
and quacks like an arrest squad . . .*

"Miles," muttered Gregor doubtfully, taking in
the same cues, "is this in the script?" The stunners
were pointed their way, now.

"He's pulled this off three times," Miles offered
in unfelt reassurance. "Why not a fourth?"

The freighter captain smiled thinly, and stepped
away from the wall, out of the line of fire. "I pulled

it off twice," he informed them. "The third time, I got caught."

Miles's hands twitched. He held them carefully away from his sides, biting back swear words. Slowly, Gregor raised his hands as well, face wonderfully blank. Score one for Gregor's self-control, as always, the one virtue his constrained life had surely inculcated.

Tung had set this up. All by himself. Had Tung known? Sold by *Tung? No . . .!* "Tung said you were reliable," Miles grated to the freighter captain.

"What's Tung to me?" the man snarled back. "I have a family, mister."

Under the stunners' aim, two—God, goons again!—soldiers stepped forward to lean Miles and Gregor, hands to the wall, and shake them down, relieving them of all their hard-won Oseran weapons, equipment, and multiple IDs. The officer examined the cache. "Yeah, these are Oser's men, all right." He spoke into his wrist comm. "We have them."

"Carry on," a thin voice returned. "We'll be right down. Cavilo out."

Randall's Rangers, evidently, hence the unfamiliar uniforms. But why no Vervani in sight? "Pardon me," Miles said mildly to the officer, "but are you people acting under the misapprehension we are Aslunder agents?"

The officer stared down at him and snorted.

"I wonder if it might not be time to establish our real identity," Gregor murmured tentatively to Miles.

"Interesting dilemma," Miles returned out of the corner of his mouth. "We better find out if they shoot spies."

A brisk tapping of boots heralded a new arrival. The squad braced as the sound rounded the corner. Gregor came to attention too, in automatic military courtesy, his straightness looking very strange hung about with Arde Mayhew's clothes. Miles no doubt looked least military of all, with his mouth gaping open in shock. He closed it before something flew in, such as his foot.

Five feet tall and a bit added by black boots with higher-than-regulation heels. Cropped blonde hair like a dandelion aureole on that sculptured head. Crisp tan-and-black rank-gilded uniform that fit her body language in perfect complement. *Livia Nu.*

The officer saluted. "Commander Cavilo, ma'am."

"Very good, Lieutenant. . . ." her blue eyes, falling on Miles, widened in unfeigned surprise, instantly covered. "Why, *Victor,* darling," her voice went syrupy with exaggerated amusement and delight, *"fancy* meeting you here. Still selling miracle suits to the unwitting?"

Miles spread his empty hands. "This is the totality of my luggage, ma'am. You should have bought when you could."

"I wonder." Her smile was tight and speculative. Miles found the glitter in her eyes disturbing. Gregor, silent, looked frantically bewildered.

So, your name wasn't Livia Nu, and you weren't a procurement agent. So why the devil was the commandant of Vervain's mercenary force meeting incognito on Pol Station with a representative of the most powerful House of the Jacksonian Consortium? *That was no mere arms deal, darling.*

Cavilo/Livia Nu raised her wrist comm to her lips. "Sickbay, *Kurin's Hand.* Cavilo here. I'm sending you up a couple of prisoners for questioning. I may sit in on this one myself." She keyed off.

The freighter captain stepped forward, half-fearful, half-pugnacious. "My wife and son. Now you prove they're safe."

Judiciously, she looked him over. "You may be good for another run. All right." She gestured to a soldier. "Take this man to the *Kurin's* brig and let him have a look at the monitors. Then bring him back to me. You're a fortunate traitor, captain. I have another job for you by which you may earn them—"

"Their freedom?" the freighter captain demanded.

She frowned slightly at the interruption. "Why should I inflate your salary? Another week of life."

He trailed off after the soldier, hands clenched angrily, teeth clenched prudently.

What the hell? Miles thought. He didn't know much about Vervain, but he was pretty sure not even their martial law made provisions for holding innocent relatives hostage against the good behavior of unconvicted traitors.

The freighter captain gone, Cavilo keyed her wristcom again. "*Kurin's Hand* Security? Ah, good. I'm sending you my pet double agent. Run the recording we made last week of Cell Six for his motivation, ai? Don't let him know it's not real-time . . . right. Cavilo out."

So, was the man's family free? Already dead? Being held elsewhere? What were they getting into here?

More boots rounded the corner, a heavy regulation tread. Cavilo smiled sourly, but smoothed the expression into something sweeter as she turned to greet the newcomer.

"Stanis, darling. Look what we netted this time. It's that little renegade Betan who was trying to deal stolen arms on Pol Station. It appears he isn't an independent after all."

The tan and black Rangers' uniform looked just fine on General Metzov, too, Miles noted crazily. Now would be a wonderful time to roll up his eyes and pass out, if only he had the trick of it.

General Metzov stood equally riveted, his iron-grey eyes ablaze with sudden unholy joy. "He's no Betan, Cavie."

CHAPTER TWELVE

"He's a Barrayaran. And not just any Barrayaran. We've got to get him out of sight, quickly," Metzov went on.

"Who sent him, then?" Cavilo stared anew at Miles, her lip in a dubious curl.

"God," Metzov avowed fervently. "God has delivered him into my hand." Metzov, that cheerful, was an unusual and alarming sight. Even Cavilo raised her brow.

Metzov glanced at Gregor for the first time. "We'll take him and his—bodyguard, I suppose . . ." Metzov slowed.

The pictures on the mark-notes didn't look much like Gregor, being several years out of date, but the emperor had appeared in enough vid-casts—not dressed like this, of course. . . . Miles could almost see Metzov thinking, *The face is familiar, I just can't place the name.* . . . Maybe he wouldn't recognize Gregor. Maybe he wouldn't *believe* it.

Gregor, drawn up in a dignity concealing dismay, spoke for the first time. "Is this yet another of your old friends, Miles?"

It was the measured, cultured voice that triggered the connection. Metzov's face, reddened with excitement, drained white. He looked around involuntarily—for Illyan, Miles guessed.

"Uh, this is General Stanis Metzov," Miles explained.

"The Kyril Island Metzov?"

"Yeah."

"Oh." Gregor maintained his closed reserve, nearly expressionless.

"Where is your security, sir?" Metzov demanded of Gregor, his voice harsh with unacknowledged fear.

You're looking at it, Miles mourned.

"Not far behind, I imagine," Gregor essayed, cool. "Let Us go Our way, and they will not trouble you."

"Who is this fellow?" Cavilo tapped a boot impatiently.

"What," Miles couldn't help asking Metzov, "what are you doing here?"

Metzov went grim. "How shall a man my age, stripped of his Imperial Pension—his life savings— live? Did you hope I would sit down and quietly starve? Not I."

Inopportune, to remind Metzov of his grudge, Miles realized. "This . . . looks like an improvement over Kyril Island," Miles suggested hopefully. His mind still boggled. Metzov, working under a woman? The internal dynamics of this command chain must be fascinating. Stanis *darling?*

Metzov did not look amused.

"*Who are they?*" Cavilo demanded again.

"Power. Money. Strategic leverage. More than you can imagine," Metzov answered.

"Trouble," Miles put in. "More than you can imagine."

"You are a separate matter, mutant," Metzov said.

"I beg to differ, General," said Gregor in his best Imperial tones. Feeling for footing in this floating conversation, though concealing his confusion well.

"We must take them to the *Kurin's Hand* at once. Out of sight," said Metzov to Cavilo. He glanced at the arrest squad. "Out of hearing. We'll continue this in private."

They marched off, escorted by the patrol. Metzov's gaze felt like a knife blade in Miles's back, prodding and probing. They passed through several deserted docking bays till they arrived at a major one actively servicing a ship. The command ship, judging by the number and formality of duty guards.

"Take them to Medical for questioning," Cavilo ordered the squad as they were saluted through a personnel hatch by the officer in charge.

"Hold on that," said Metzov. He stared around the cross-corridors, almost jittering. "Do you have a guard who's deaf and mute?"

"Hardly!" Cavilo stared indignantly at her mysteriously agitated subordinate. "To the brig, then."

"No," said Metzov sharply. Hesitating to throw the Emperor into a cell, Miles realized. Metzov turned to Gregor and said with perfect seriousness, "May I have your parole, sire—sir?"

"What?" cried Cavilo. "Have you stripped a gear, Stanis?"

"A parole," Gregor noted gravely, "is a promise given between honorable enemies. Your honor I am willing to assume. But are you thus declaring yourself Our enemy?"

Excellent bit of weaseling, Miles approved.

Metzov's eye fell on Miles. His lips thinned. "Perhaps not yours. But you have a poor choice of favorites. Not to mention advisors."

Gregor was now very hard to read. "Some acquaintances are imposed on me. Also some advisors."

"To my cabin," Metzov held up his hand as Cavilo opened her mouth to object, "for now. For our initial conversation. Without witnesses, or Security recordings. After that, we decide, Cavie."

Cavilo, eyes narrowing, closed her mouth. "All right, Stanis. Lead off." Her hand curved open ironically, and gestured them onward.

Metzov posted two guards outside his cabin door, and dismissed the rest. When the door had sealed behind them, he tied Miles with a tangle-cord and sat him on the floor. With helplessly ingrained deference, he then seated Gregor in the padded station chair at his comconsole desk, the best the spartan chamber had to offer.

Cavilo, seated cross-legged on the bed watching the play, objected to the logic of this. "Why tie up the little one and leave the big one loose?"

"Keep your stunner drawn, then, if he worries you," Metzov advised. Breathing heavily, he stood hands on hips and studied Gregor. He shook his head, as if still not believing his eyes.

"Why not your stunner?"

"I have not yet decided whether to draw a weapon in his presence."

"We're *alone* now, Stanis," Cavilo said in a sarcastic lilt. "Would you kindly explain this insanity? And it had better be good."

"Oh yes. That—" he pointed to Miles, "is Lord Miles Vorkosigan, the son of the Prime Minister of Barrayar. Admiral Aral Vorkosigan—I trust you've heard of *him*."

Cavilo's brows lowered. "What was he doing on Pol Six in the guise of a Betan gunrunner, then?"

"I'm not sure. The last I'd heard he was under arrest by Imperial Security, though of course no one believed they were serious about it."

"Detainment," Miles corrected. "Technically."

"And he—" Metzov swung to point to Gregor, "is the Emperor of Barrayar. Gregor Vorbarra. What *he's* doing here, I cannot imagine."

"Are you sure?" Even Cavilo was taken aback. At Metzov's stern nod, her eye lit with speculation. She looked at Gregor as if for the first time. "*Really*. How *interesting*."

"But where is his security? We must tread very cautiously, Cavie."

"What's he worth to them? Or for that matter, to the highest bidder?"

Gregor smiled at her. "I'm Vor, ma'am. In a sense, *the* Vor. Risk in service is the Vorish trade.

I wouldn't assume my value was infinite, if I were you."

Gregor's complaint had some truth to it, Miles thought; when he wasn't being emperor he seemed hardly anyone at all. But he sure did the *role* well.

"An opportunity, yes," said Metzov, "but if we create an enemy we can't handle—"

"If we hold *him* hostage, we ought to be able to handle them with ease," Cavilo commented thoughtfully.

"An alternate and more prudent course," Miles interjected, "would be to help us swiftly and safely on our way, and collect a lucrative and honorable thank-you. An, as it were, win-win strategy."

"Honorable?" Metzov's eyes burned. He fell into a brooding silence, then muttered. "But what are they doing here? And where's the snake Illyan? I want the mutant, in any case. Damn! It must be played boldly, or not at all." He stared malignantly at Miles. "Vorkosigan . . . so. And what is Barrayar to me now, a Service that stabbed me in the back after thirty-five years. . . ." He straightened decisively, but still did not, Miles noticed, draw a weapon in the emperor's presence. "Yes, take them to the brig, Cavie."

"Not so fast," said Cavilo, looking newly pensive. "Send the little one to the brig, if you like. He's nothing, you say?"

The only son of the most powerful military leader on Barrayar kept his mouth shut for a change. If, if, if . . .

"By comparison," Metzov temporized, looking suddenly fearful of being cheated of his prey.

"Very well." Cavilo slid her stunner, which she had stopped aiming and started playing with some time back, soundlessly into her holster. She moved to unseal the door and beckon to the guards. "Put him," she gestured to Gregor, "in Cabin Nine, G Deck. Cut the outgoing comm, lock the door, and post a guard with a stunner. But supply him with any reasonable comfort he may request." She added aside to Gregor, "It's the most comfortable visiting officer's quarters the *Kurin's Hand* can supply, ah—"

"Call me Greg," Gregor sighed.

"Greg. Nice name. Cabin Nine is next to my own. We will continue this conversation shortly, after you, ah, freshen up. Perhaps over dinner. Oversee his arrival there, will you, Stanis?" She favored both men with an impartial, glittering smile, and wafted out, a neat trick in boots. She stuck her head back in and indicated Miles. "Bring *him* along to the brig."

Miles was removed by the second guard with a wave of a stunner and the prod of a blessedly inactivated shock-stick, to follow in her wake.

The *Kurin's Hand,* judging from his passing glimpses, was a much larger command ship than the *Triumph,* able to field bigger and punchier combat drop or boarding forces, but correspondingly sluggish in maneuver. Its brig was larger too, Miles discovered shortly, and more formidably secured. A single entrance opened onto an elaborate guard monitor station, from which led two dead-end cell bays.

The freighter captain was just leaving the guard station, under the watchful eye of the squadman detailed to escort him. He exchanged a hostile look with Cavilo.

"As you see, they remain in good health," Cavilo said to him. "My half of the bargain, Captain. See that you continue to complete your own part."

Let's see what happens. . . . "You saw a recording," Miles piped up. "Demand to see 'em in the flesh."

Cavilo's white teeth clenched rigidly, but her annoyed grimace melted seamlessly into a vulpine smile as the freighter captain jerked around. "What? You . . ." he planted himself mulishly. "All right, which of you is lying?"

"Captain, that's all the guarantee you get," said

Cavilo, gesturing to the monitors. "You chose to gamble, gamble you shall."

"Then that—" he pointed to Miles, "is the last result you get."

A subtle hand motion down by her trouser seam brought the guards to the alert, stunners drawn. "Take him out," she ordered.

"No!"

"Very well," her eyes widened in exasperation, "take him to Cell Six. And lock him in."

As the freighter captain turned, torn between resistance and eagerness, Cavilo motioned the guard to open distance from his prisoner. He fell away, brows rising in question. Cavilo glanced at Miles and smiled very sourly, as if to say, *All right, Smartass, watch me.* In a cold smooth motion Cavilo flipped open her left side holster seal, brought up a nerve disruptor, took careful aim, and fried the back of the captain's head. He convulsed once and dropped, dead before he hit the deck.

She walked over and pensively prodded the body with the pointed toe of her boot, then glanced up at Miles, whose jaw was gaping open. "You *will* keep your mouth shut next time, won't you, little man?"

Miles's mouth shut with a snap. *You had to experiment. . . .* At least now he knew who'd killed Liga. The rabbity Polian's reported death seemed suddenly real and vivid. The exalted look flashing over Cavilo's face as she blew the freighter captain away fascinated even as it horrified Miles. *Who did you really see in your gunsights, darling?* "Yes, ma'am," he choked, trying to conceal his shakes, delayed reaction to this shocking turn. *Damn* his tongue. . . .

She stepped down to the security monitoring station and spoke to the tech at—frozen at—her post. "Unload the recording of General Metzov's cabin that includes the last half-hour, and give it to me. Start a fresh one. No, don't play it back!" She placed the disk in a breast pocket and carefully sealed the flap. "Put this one in Cell Fourteen," she nodded toward Miles. "Or, ah—if it's empty, make that Cell Thirteen." Her teeth bared briefly.

The guards re-searched Miles, and took ID scans. Cavilo blandly informed them that his name should be entered as Victor Rotha.

As he was pulled to his feet, two men with medical insignia arrived with a float-pallet to remove the body. Cavilo, watching without expression now, remarked tiredly to Miles, "You chose to damage my double-agent's utility. A vandal's prank. He had better uses than as an object-lesson for a fool. I do not warehouse non-useful items. I suggest you start thinking of how you can make yourself more useful to me than as merely General Metzov's catnip toy." She smiled faintly into some invisible distance. "Though he does jump for you, doesn't he? I shall have to explore that motivation."

"What is the use of Stanis-darling to you?" Miles dared, pig-headed-defiant in his wash of angry guilt. Metzov as her paramour? Revolting thought.

"He's an experienced ground combat commander."

"What's a fleet on all-space wormhole guard duty want with a ground commander?"

"Well, then," she smiled sweetly, "he amuses me."

That was supposed to have been the first answer. "No accounting for taste," Miles muttered inanely, careful not to be heard. Should he warn her about Metzov? On second thought, should he warn Metzov about *her*?

His head was still spinning with this new dilemma when the blank door of his solitary cell sealed him in.

It didn't take long for Miles to exhaust the novelties of his new quarters, a space a little larger than two by two meters, furnished only with two padded benches and a fold-out lavatory. No library viewer, no relief from the wheel of his thoughts mired in the quag of his self-recriminations.

A Ranger field-ration bar, inserted some time later through a force-shielded aperture in the door, proved even more repellent than the Barrayaran Imperial version, resembling a rawhide dog chew. Wetted with spit, it softened slightly, enough to tear off gummy shreds if your teeth were in good health. More than a temporary distraction, it promised to last till the next issue. Probably nutritious as hell. Miles wondered what Cavilo was serving Gregor for dinner. Was it as scientifically vitamin-balanced?

They'd been so close to their goal. Even now, the Barrayaran consulate was only a few locks and levels away, less than a kilometer. If only he could get there from here. If a chance came . . . On the other hand, how long would Cavilo hesitate to disregard diplomatic custom and violate the consulate, if she saw some utility in it? About as long as she'd hesitated to shoot the freighter captain in the back, Miles gauged. She would surely have ordered the consulate, and all known Barrayaran agents on Vervain Station, watched by now. Miles unstuck his teeth from a fragment of ration-leather, and hissed.

A beeping from the code-lock warned Miles he was about to have a visitor. Interrogation, so soon? He'd expected Cavilo to wine, dine, and evaluate Gregor first, then get back to him. Or was he to be a mere project for underlings? He swallowed, throat tight on a ration blob, and sat up, trying to look stern and not scared.

The door slid back to reveal General Metzov, still looking highly military and efficient in the tan and black Ranger fatigues.

"Sure you don't need me, sir?" the guard at his elbow asked as Metzov shouldered through the opening.

Metzov glanced contemptuously at Miles, looking

low and unmilitary in Victor Rotha's now limp and grimy green silk shirt, baggy trousers, and bare feet—the processing guards had taken his sandals. "Hardly. *He's* not going to jump me."

Damn straight, Miles agreed with regret.

Metzov tapped his wrist comm. "I'll call you when I'm done."

"Very well, sir." The door sighed closed. The cell seemed suddenly very tiny indeed. Miles drew his legs up, sitting in a small defensive ball on his pallet. Metzov stood at ease, contemplating Miles for a long, satisfied moment, then settled himself comfortably on the bench opposite.

"Well, well," said Metzov, his mouth twisting. "What a turn of fate."

"I thought you'd be dining with the Emperor," said Miles.

"Commander Cavilo, being female, can get a little scattered under stress. When she calms down again, she'll see the need for my expertise in Barrayaran matters," said Metzov in measured tones.

In other words, you weren't invited. "You left the Emperor *alone* with her?" *Gregor, watch your step!*

"Gregor's no threat. I fear his upbringing has made him altogether weak."

Miles choked.

Metzov sat back, allowed his fingers to tap gently on his knee. "So tell me, Ensign Vorkosigan—if it is still Ensign Vorkosigan. There being no justice in the world, I suppose you've retained your rank and pay. What are you doing here? With *him*?"

Miles was tempted to confine himself to name, rank, and serial number, except Metzov knew all those already. Was Metzov an enemy, exactly? Of Barrayar, that is, not of Miles personally. Did Metzov divide the two in his own mind? "The Emperor became separated from his security. We hoped to regain contact with them via the Barrayaran consulate here." There, nothing in that that wasn't perfectly obvious.

"And where did you come from?"

"Aslund."

"Don't bother playing the idiot, Vorkosigan. I know Aslund. Who sent you there in the first place? And don't bother lying, I can cross-question the freighter captain."

"No, you can't. Cavilo killed him."

"Oh?" A flicker of surprise, suppressed. "Clever of her. He was the only witness to know where you went."

Had that been part of Cavilo's calculation, when she'd raised her nerve disruptor? Probably. And yet . . . the freighter captain was also the only corroborating witness who knew where they'd come *from*. Maybe Cavilo was not so formidable as she seemed at first glance.

"Again," Metzov said patiently—Miles could see he felt he had all the time in the world—"how did you come to be in the Emperor's company?"

"How do you think?" Miles countered, buying time.

"Some plot, of course," Metzov shrugged.

Miles groaned. "Oh, of course!" He uncurled in his indignation. "And what sane—or insane, for that matter—chain of conspiracy do you imagine accounts for our arrival here, alone, from Aslund? I mean, I know what it really was, I lived it, but what does it look like?" *To a professional paranoid, that is.* "I'd just love to hear it."

"Well . . ." Metzov was drawn out in spite of himself. "You have somehow separated the Emperor from his security. You must either be setting up an elaborate assassination, or planning to implement some form of personality-control."

"That's what just *springs* to mind, huh?" Miles thumped his back against the wall with a frustrated growl, and slumped.

"Or perhaps you're on some secret—and therefore dishonorable—diplomatic mission. Some sellout."

"If so, where's Gregor's security?" Miles sang. "Better watch out."

"So, my first hypothesis is proved."

"In that case, where's *my* security?" Miles snarled. Where, indeed?

"A Vorkosigan plot—no, perhaps not the Admiral's. He controls Gregor at home—"

"Thank you, I was about to point that out."

"A twisted plot from a twisted mind. Do you dream of making yourself emperor of Barrayar, mutant?"

"A nightmare, I assure you. Ask Gregor."

"It scarcely matters. The medical staff will squeeze out your secrets as soon as Cavilo gives the go-ahead. In a way, it's a shame fast-penta was ever invented. I'd enjoy breaking every bone in your body till you talked. Or screamed. You won't be able to hide behind your father's," he grinned briefly, "skirts, out here, Vorkosigan." He grew thoughtful. "Maybe I will anyway. One bone a day, for as long as they last."

206 bones in the human body. 206 days. Illyan ought to be able to catch up with us in 206 days. Miles smiled bleakly.

Metzov looked too comfortable to arise and initiate this plan immediately, though. This speculative conversation scarcely constituted a serious interrogation. But if not for interrogation, nor revenge-tortures, why was the man here?

His lover threw him out, he felt lonely and strange and wanted someone familiar to talk to. Even a familiar enemy. It was weirdly understandable. But for the Komarr invasion, Metzov had probably never set foot off Barrayar in his life. A life spent mostly in the constrained, ordered, predictable world-within-in-a-world of the Imperial military. Now the rigid man was adrift, and faced with more free-will choices

than he'd ever imagined. *God. The maniac's home-
sick.* Chilling insight.

"I'm beginning to think I may have accidentally
done you a good turn," Miles began. If Metzov was
in a talking mood, why not encourage him? "Cavilo's
certainly better-looking than your last commander."

"She is that."

"Is the pay higher?"

"Everyone pays more than the Imperial Service,"
Metzov snorted.

"Not boring, either. On Kyril Island, every day
was like every other day. Here, you don't know
what's going to happen next. Or does she confide in
you?"

"I'm essential to her plans." Metzov practically
smirked.

"As a bedroom warrior? Thought you were infantry. Switching specialties, at your age?"

Metzov merely smiled. "Now you're getting obvious, Vorkosigan."

Miles shrugged. *If so, I'm the only obvious thing
here.* "As I recall, you didn't think much of women
soldiers. Cavilo seems to have made you change your
tune."

"Not at all." Metzov sat back smugly. "I expect to
be in command of Randall's Rangers in six months."

"Isn't this cell monitored?" Miles asked, startled.
Not that he cared how much trouble Metzov's mouth
bought him, but still. . . .

"Not at present."

"Cavilo planning to retire, is she?"

"There are a number of ways her retirement might
be expedited. The fatal accident Cavilo arranged for
Randall might easily be repeated. Or I might even
work out a way to charge her with it, since she was
stupid enough to brag about murder in bed."

*That was no boast, that was a warning, dunder-
head.* Miles's eyes nearly crossed, imagining pillow-
talk between Metzov and Cavilo. "You two must

have a lot in common. No wonder you get on so well."

Metzov's amusement thinned. "I have nothing in common with that mercenary slut. I was an Imperial officer." Metzov glowered. "Thirty-five years. And they wasted me. Well, they'll discover their mistake."

Metzov glanced at his chrono. "I still don't understand your presence here. Are you sure there isn't something else you want to say to me now, privately, before you say everything tomorrow to Cavilo under fast-penta?"

Cavilo and Metzov, Miles decided, had set up the old interrogation game of good-guy-bad-guy. Except they'd gotten their signals mixed, and both accidentally taken the part of bad-guy. "If you really want to be helpful, get Gregor to the Barrayaran Consul. Or even just get out a message that he's here."

"In good time, we may. Given suitable terms." Metzov's eyes were narrowed, studying Miles. As puzzled by Miles as Miles by him? After a stretched silence, Metzov called the guard on his wristcom, and withdrew, with no more violent parting threat than "See you tomorrow, Vorkosigan." Sinister enough.

I don't understand your presence here either, Miles thought as the door hissed closed and the lock beeped. Clearly, some kind of planetary ground-attack was in the planning stage. Were Randall's Rangers to spearhead a Vervani invasion force? Cavilo had met secretly with a high-ranking Jackson's Consortium representative. Why? To guarantee Consortium neutrality during the coming attack? That made excellent sense, but why hadn't the Vervani dealt directly? So they could disavow Cavilo's arrangements if the balloon went up too early?

And who, or what, was the target? Not the Consortium Station, obviously, nor its distant parent Jackson's Whole. That left Aslund and Pol. Aslund, a cul-de-sac, was not strategically tempting. Better to take Pol first, cut Aslund off from the Hub (with Consortium cooperation) and mop up the weak planet at leisure. But Pol had Barrayar behind it, who would like nothing better than an alliance with its nervous neighbor that would give the imperium a toehold in the Hegen Hub. An open attack must drive Pol into Barrayar's waiting arms. That left Aslund, but . . .

This makes no sense. It was almost more disturbing than the thought of Gregor supping unguarded with Cavilo, or the fear of the promised chemical interrogation. *I'm not seeing something. This makes no sense.*

The Hegen Hub turned in his head, in all its strategic complexity, all the light-dimmed night cycle. The Hub, and pictures of Gregor. Was Cavilo feeding him mind-altering drugs? Doggie chews, like Miles's? Steak and champagne? Was Gregor being tortured? Being seduced? Visions of Cavilo/Livia Nu's dramatic red evening-wear undulated in Miles's mind's eye. Was Gregor having a wonderful time? Miles thought Gregor'd had little more experience with women than he had, but he'd been out of touch with the Emperor these last few years; for all he knew Gregor was keeping a harem now. No, that couldn't be, or Ivan would have picked up the scent, and commented. At length. How susceptible was Gregor to a very old-fashioned form of mind-control?

The day-cycle crept by with Miles anticipating every moment being taken out for his very first experience of fast-penta interrogation from the wrong end of the hypospray. What would Cavilo and Metzov make of the bizarre truth of his and Gregor's odyssey? Three ration-chews arrived at interminable intervals, and the lights dimmed again, marking another ship-night. Three meals, and no interrogation. What was keeping them out there? No noises or subtle gravitic vibrations suggested the ship had left dock, they were still locked to Vervain Station. Miles tried to exercise himself weary, pacing, two steps, turn, two steps, turn, two steps . . . but merely succeeded in increasing his personal stink and making himself dizzy.

Another day writhed by, and another light-dimmed "night." Another breakfast chew fell through onto the floor. Were they artificially stretching or compressing time, confusing his biological clock to soften him up for interrogation? Why bother?

He bit his fingernails. He bit his toenails. He pulled tiny green threads from his shirt and tried flossing his teeth. Then he tried making little green designs with tiny, tiny knots. Then he hit on the idea of weaving messages. Could he macramé "Help, I am a prisoner . . ." and plant it on the back of someone's jacket by static charge? If someone ever came back, that is? He got as far as a delicate gossamer H, E, L, caught the thread on a hangnail while rubbing his stubbled chin, and reduced his plea to an illegible green wad. He pulled another thread and started over.

The lock twinkled and beeped. Miles snapped alert, realizing only then that he had fallen into an almost hypnotic fugue in his mumbling isolation. How much time had passed?

His visitor was Cavilo, crisp and businesslike in her Ranger's fatigues. A guard took up station just outside the cell door, which closed behind her. Another private chat, it seemed. Miles struggled to pull his thoughts together, to remember what he was about.

Cavilo settled herself opposite Miles in the same spot Metzov had chosen, in somewhat the same leisurely posture, leaning forward, hands clasped loosely on her knees, attentive, assured. Miles sat cross-legged, back to the wall, feeling distinctly at the disadvantage.

"Lord Vorkosigan, ah . . ." she cocked her head,

interrupting herself aside, "you don't look at all well."

"Solitary confinement doesn't suit me." His disused voice came out raspy, and he had to stop and clear his throat. "Perhaps a library viewer," his brain grated into gear, "—or better, an exercise period." Which would get him out of this cell, and in contact with subornable humans. "My medical problems compel me to a self-disciplined life-style, if they're not to flare up and impede me. I definitely need an exercise period, or I'm going to get really stick."

"Hm. We'll see." She ran a hand through her short hair, and refocused. "So, Lord Vorkosigan. Tell me about your mother."

"Huh?" A most dizzying sharp left turn, for a military interrogation. "Why?"

She smiled ingratiatingly. "Greg's tales have interested me."

Greg's tales? Had the Emperor been fast-penta'd? "What . . . do you want to know?"

"Well . . . I understand Countess Vorkosigan is an off-worlder, a Betan who married into your aristocracy."

"The Vor are a military caste, but yes."

"How was she received, by the power-class—whatever they choose to call themselves? I'd thought Barrayarans were totally provincial, prejudiced against off-worlders."

"We are," Miles admitted cheerfully. "The first contact most Barrayarans—of all classes—had with off-worlders, after the end of the Time of Isolation when Barrayar was rediscovered, was with the Cetagandan invasion forces. They left a bad impression that lingers even now, three, four generations after we threw them off."

"Yet no one questioned your father's choice?"

Miles jerked up his chin in bafflement. "He was in his forties. And . . . and he was *Lord Vorkosi-*

gan." *So am I, now. Why doesn't it work for me like that?*

"Her background made no difference?"

"She was Betan. Is Betan. In the Astronomical Survey first, but then a combat officer. Beta Colony had just helped beat us soundly in that stupid attempt we made to invade Escobar."

"So despite being an enemy, her military background actually helped gain her respect and acceptance among the Vor?"

"I guess so. Plus, she established quite a local military reputation in the fighting of Vordarian's Pretendership, the year I was born, twice. Led loyal troops, oh, several times, when my father couldn't be two places at once." And had been personally responsible for the five-year-old emperor-in-hiding's safety. More successfully than her son was doing so far for the twenty-five-year-old Gregor. *Total screwup* was the phrase that sprang to mind, actually. "Nobody's messed with her since."

"Hm." Cavilo sat back, murmuring half to herself, "so, it has been done. Therefore, it can be done."

What, what can be done? Miles rubbed a hand over his face, trying to wake up and concentrate. "How is Gregor?"

"Quite amusing."

Gregor the Lugubrious, amusing? But then, if it matched the rest of her personality, Cavilo's sense of humor was probably vile. "I meant his health."

"Rather better than yours, from the look of you."

"I trust he's been better fed."

"What, a taste of real military life too strong for you, Lord Vorkosigan? You've been fed the same as my troops."

"Can't be." Miles held up a ragged half-gnawed breakfast chew. "They'd have mutinied by now."

"Oh, dear." She regarded the repellent morsel with a sympathetic frown. "Those. I thought they'd been condemned. How did they end up here? Someone must be economizing. Shall I order you a regular menu?"

"Yes, thank you," said Miles immediately, and paused. She had neatly misdirected his attention from Gregor to himself. He must keep his mind on the Emperor. How much *useful* information had Gregor spilled, by now?

"You realize," Miles said carefully, "you are creating a massive interplanetary incident between Vervain and Barrayar."

"Not at all," said Cavilo reasonably. "I'm Greg's friend. I've rescued him from falling into the hands of the Vervani secret police. He's now under my protection, until the opportunity arises to restore him to his rightful place."

Miles blinked. "Do the Vervani have a secret police, as such?"

"Close enough," Cavilo shrugged. "Barrayar, of course, definitely does. Stanis seems quite worried about them. They must be very embarrassed, back in ImpSec, to have so thoroughly mislaid their charge. I fear their reputation is exaggerated."

Not quite. I'm ImpSec, and I know where Gregor is. So technically, ImpSec is right on top of the situation. Miles wasn't sure whether to laugh or cry. *Or right under it.*

"If we're all such good friends," said Miles, "why am I locked in this cell?"

"For your protection too, of course. After all, General Metzov has openly threatened to, ah—what was it—break every bone in your body." She sighed. "I'm afraid dear Stanis is about to lose his utility."

Miles blanched, remembering what else Metzov had said in that conversation. "For . . . disloyalty?"

"Not at all. Disloyalty can be very useful at times, under proper management. But the overall strategic situation may be about to change drastically. Unimaginably. And after all the time I wasted cultivating him, too. I hope all Barrayarans are not so tedious as Stanis." She smiled briefly. "I very much hope it."

She leaned forward, growing more intent. "Is it true that Gregor, ah, ran away from home to evade pressure from his advisors to marry a woman he loathed?"

"He hadn't mentioned it to me," said Miles, startled. Wait—what was Gregor about, out there? He'd better be careful not to step on his lines. "Though there is . . . concern. If he were to die without an heir any time soon, many fear a factional struggle would follow."

"He has no heir?"

"The factions can't agree. Except on Gregor."

"So his advisors would be glad to see him marry."

"Overjoyed, I expect. Uh . . ." Miles's unease at this turn of the conversation bloomed into sudden light, like the flash before the shock-wave. "Commander Cavilo—you're *not* imagining you could make yourself Empress of Barrayar, are you?"

Her smile grew sharp. "Of course I couldn't. But Greg could." She straightened, evidently annoyed by Miles's stunned expression. "Why not? I'm the right sex. And, apparently, of the right military background."

"How old are you?"

"Lord Vorkosigan, really, what a rude question." Her blue eyes glinted. "If we were on the same side, we could work together."

"Commander Cavilo, I don't think you understand Barrayar. Or Barrayarans." Actually, there'd been eras in Barrayaran history where Cavilo's command style would have fit right in. Mad Emperor Yuri's reign of terror, for example. But they'd spent the last twenty years trying to get *away* from all that.

"I need your cooperation," Cavilo said. "Or at any rate, it could be very useful. To both of us. Your neutrality would be . . . tolerable. Your active opposition, however, would be a problem. For you. But we should avoid getting caught in negative attitude traps at this early stage, I think?"

"Whatever did happen to that freighter captain's wife and child? Widow and orphan, rather?" Miles inquired through his teeth.

Cavilo hesitated fractionally. "The man was a traitor. Of the worst sort. Sold out his planet for money. He was caught in an act of espionage. There is no moral difference between ordering an execution, and carrying it out."

"I agree. So do a lot of legal codes. How about a difference between execution and murder? Vervain is not at war. His actions may have been illegal, warranting arrest, trial, jail or sociopath therapy—where did the trial part drop out?"

"A Barrayaran, arguing legalities? How strange."

"And what happened to his family?"

She'd had a moment to think, blast it. "The tedious Vervani demanded their release. Naturally, I didn't want him to know they were out of my hands, or I'd lose my only hold on his actions at a distance."

Lie or truth? No way to tell. *But she backpedals from her mistake. She let establishing her dominance through terror rule her reactions, before she was sure of her ground. Because she was unsure of her ground. I know the look that was on her face. Homicidal paranoids are as familiar as breakfast, I had one for a bodyguard for seventeen years.* Cavilo, for a brief instant, seemed homey and routine, if no less dangerous. But he should strive to appear convinced, non-threatening, even if it made him gag.

"It's true," he conceded, "it's rank cowardice to give an order you're not willing to carry out yourself. And you're no coward, Commander, I'll grant you that." There, that was the right tone, persuadable but not changing his stance too suspiciously fast.

Her brow rose sardonically, as if to say, *Who are you to judge?* But her tension eased slightly. She glanced at her chrono and rose. "I'll leave you now, to think about the advantages of cooperation. You're theoretically familiar with the mathematics of the Prisoner's Dilemma, I hope. It will be an interesting test of your wits, to see if you can connect theory with practice."

Miles managed a weird return smile. Her beauty, her energy, even her flaring ego, did exert a real fascination. Had Gregor indeed been . . . activated, by Cavilo? Gregor, after all, hadn't watched her raise her nerve disruptor and . . . What weapon was a good ImpSec man to use, in the face of this personal assault on Gregor? Try and seduce her back? To sacrifice himself for the Emperor by flinging himself on Cavilo had about as much appeal as belly-smothering a live sonic grenade.

Besides, he doubted he could work it. The door slid closed, eclipsing her scimitar smile. Too late, he raised a hand to remind her of her promise to change his rations.

But she remembered anyway. Lunch arrived on a trolley, with an experienced, if expressionless, batman to serve it in five elegant courses with two wines and expresso coffee for an antidote. Miles didn't think Cavilo's troops ate like this, either. He envisioned a platoon of smiling, replete, obese gourmets strolling happily into battle . . . the dog chews would be much more effective for raising aggression levels.

A chance remark to his waiter brought a package along with the next meal-trolley, which proved to contain clean underwear, a set of insignialess Ranger fatigues cut down to his fit, and a pair of soft felt slippers; also a tube of depilatory and assorted toiletries. Miles was inspired to wash, by sections, in the fold-out lavatory basin, and shave before dressing. He felt almost human. Ah, the virtues of cooperation. Cavilo was not exactly subtle.

God, where had she come from? A mercenary veteran, she had to have been around for a while to have risen this far, even with shortcuts. Tung might know. *I think she must have lost bad at least once.* He wished Tung were here now. Hell, he wished *Illyan* were here now.

Her flamboyance, Miles increasingly felt, was an effective act, meant to be viewed at a distance like stage makeup, to dazzle her troops. At the right range, it might work rather well, like the popular Barrayaran general of his grandfather's generation who'd gained visibility by carrying a plasma rifle like a swagger stick. Usually uncharged, Miles had heard privately—the man wasn't stupid. Or a Vorish ensign who wore a certain antique dagger at every opportunity. A trademark, a banner. A calculated bit of mass psychology. Cavilo's public persona pushed the envelope of that strategy, surely. Was she scared inside, knowing herself for overextended? *You wish.*

Alas, after a dose of Cavilo, one thought of Cavilo, fogging one's tactical calculations. Focus, ensign. Had she forgotten Victor Rotha? Had Gregor concocted some bullshit explanation to account for their Pol Station encounter? Gregor seemed to be feeding Cavilo skewed facts—or were they? Maybe there really was a loathed proposed bride, and Gregor had not trusted Miles enough to mention it. Miles began to regret being quite so acerbic to Gregor.

His thoughts were still running like a hyped-up rat on an exercise wheel, spinning to nowhere, when the door code-lock beeped again. Yes, he would fake cooperation, promise anything, if only she'd give him a chance to check on Gregor.

Cavilo appeared with a soldier in tow. The man looked vaguely familiar—one of the arresting goons? No. . . .

The man ducked his head through the cell door, stared at Miles a moment in bemusement, and turned to Cavilo.

"Yeah, that's him, all right. Admiral Naismith, of the Tau Verde Ring war. I'd recognize the little runt anywhere." He added aside to Miles, "What are you doing here, sir?"

Miles mentally transmuted the man's tan and blacks to grey and white. Yeah. There'd been several thousand mercenaries involved in the Tau Verde war. They all had to have gone somewhere.

"Thank you, that will be all, Sergeant." Cavilo took the man by the arm and firmly pulled him away. The non-com's fading advice drifted back down the cell bay, "You ought to try and hire him, ma'am, he's a military genius. . . ."

Cavilo reappeared after a moment, to stand in the aperture with her hands on her hips and her chin outthrust in exasperated disbelief. "How many people *are* you, anyway?"

Miles opened his hands and smiled weakly. Just as he'd been about to talk his way out of this hole . . .

"Huh." She spun on her heel, the closing door cutting off her sputter.

Now what? He'd slam his fist into the wall in frustration, but the wall was sure to slam back with greater devastation.

CHAPTER THIRTEEN

However, all three of his identities were granted an exercise period that afternoon. A small on-board gymnasium was cleared for his exclusive use. He studied the setup sharply for the hour as he tried out various pieces of equipment, checking distances and trajectories to guarded exits. He could see a couple of ways Ivan might succeed in jumping a guard and making a break for it. Not fragile, short-legged Miles. For a moment, he found himself actually wishing he had Ivan along.

On the way back to Cell 13 with his escort, Miles passed another prisoner being checked in at the guard station. He was a shambling, wild-eyed man, his blond hair damped to brown with sweat. Miles's shock of recognition was the greater for the changes it had to encompass. *Oser's lieutenant.* The bland-faced killer was transformed.

He wore only grey trousers, his torso was bare. Livid shock-stick marks dappled his skin. Recent hypospray injection points marched like little pink paw prints up his arm. He mumbled continuously through wet lips, shivered and giggled. Just coming back from interrogation, it seemed.

Miles was so startled he reached over to grasp the man's left hand, to check—yes, there were his own scabbed-over teeth marks across the knuckles, souvenir of last week's fight at the *Triumph*'s airlock, across the system. The silent lieutenant wasn't silent any more.

Miles's guards motioned him sternly along. Miles almost tripped, staring back over his shoulder till the door of Cell 13 sighed shut, imprisoning him once more.

What are you doing here? That had to be the most-asked, least-answered question in the Hegen Hub, Miles decided. Though he bet the Oseran lieutenant had answered it—Cavilo must command one of the sharpest counter-intelligence departments in the Hub. How fast had the Oseran mercenary traced Miles and Gregor here? How soon had Cavilo's people spotted him and picked him up? The marks on his body were not over a day old. . . .

Most important question of all, had the Oseran come to Vervain Station as part of a general, systematic sweep, or had he followed specific clues—was Tung compromised? Elena arrested? Miles shuddered, and paced frenetically, helplessly. *Have I just killed my friends?*

So, what Oser knew, Cavilo now knew, the whole silly mix of truth, lies, rumors and mistakes. So the identification of Miles as "Admiral Naismith" hadn't necessarily come from Gregor as Miles had first assumed. (The Tau Verde veteran had clearly been scrounged up as an unbiased cross-check.) If Gregor was systematically withholding information from her, Cavilo would now realize it. If he was withholding anything. Maybe he was in love by now. Miles's head throbbed, feeling on the verge of exploding.

The guards came for him in the middle of the night-cycle, and made him dress. Interrogation at last, eh? He thought of the drooling Oseran, and cringed. He insisted on washing up, and adjusted every burr-seam and cuff of his Ranger fatigues with slow deliberation, till the guards began to shift impatiently and tap fingers suggestively on shock sticks. He too would shortly be a drooling fool. On the other hand, what could he possibly say under fast-penta at this point that could make things worse? Cavilo had it all, as far as he could tell. He shrugged off the guards' grasps, and marched out of the brig between them with all the forlorn dignity he could muster.

They led him through the night-dimmed ship and exited a lift-tube at something marked "G-Deck." Miles snapped alert. Gregor was supposed to be around here somewhere. . . . They arrived at an otherwise-blank cabin door marked 10A, where the guards beeped the code-lock for permission to enter. The door slid aside.

Cavilo sat at a comconsole desk, a pool of light in the somber room making her blond-white hair gleam and glow. They had arrived at the Commander's personal office, apparently, adjoining her quarters. Miles strained his eyes and ears for signs of the Emperor. Cavilo was fully-dressed in her neat fatigues. At least Miles wasn't the only one going short on sleep these days; he fancied optimistically that she looked a little tired. She placed a stunner out on her desk, ominously ready to her right hand, and dismissed the guards. Miles craned his neck, looking for the hypospray. She stretched, and sat back. The scent of her perfume, a greener, sharper, less musky scent than she'd worn as Livia Nu, sublimated from her white skin and tickled Miles's nose. He swallowed.

"Sit down, Lord Vorkosigan."

He took the indicated chair, and waited. She watched him with calculating eyes. The insides of his nostrils began to itch abominably. He kept his hands down, and still. The first question of this interview would not catch him with his fingers shoved up his nose.

"Your Emperor is in terrible trouble, little Vor lord. To save him, you must return to the Oseran Mercenaries, and retake them. When you are back in command, we will communicate further instructions."

Miles boggled. "Danger from what?" he choked. "You?"

"Not at all! Greg is my best friend. The love of my life, at last. I'd do anything for him. I'd even give up my career." She smirked piously. Miles's lip curled in repelled response; she grinned. "If any other course of action occurs to you besides following your instructions to the letter, well . . . it could land Greg in unimaginable troubles. At the hands of worse enemies."

Worse than you? Not possible . . . is it? "Why do you want me in charge of the Dendarii Mercenaries?"

"I can't tell you." Her eyes widened, positively sparkling at her private, ironic joke. "It's a surprise."

"What would you give me to support this enterprise?"

"Transportation to Aslund Station."

"What else? Troops, guns, ships, money?"

"I'm told you could do it with your wits alone. This I wish to see."

"Oser will kill me. He's already tried once."

"That's a chance I must take."

I really like that "I," lady. "You mean me to be killed," Miles deduced. "What if I succeed instead?" His eyes were starting to water; he sniffed. He would have to rub his madly-itching nose soon.

"The key of strategy, little Vor," she explained kindly, "is not to choose *a* path to victory, but to choose so that *all* paths lead to a victory. Ideally. Your death has one use; your success, another. I will emphasize that any premature attempt to contact Barrayar could be very counterproductive. Very."

A nice aphorism on strategy; he'd have to remember that one. "Let me hear my marching orders from my own supreme commander, then. Let me talk to Gregor."

"Ah. *That* will be your reward for success."

"The last guy who bought that line got shot in the back of his head for his credulity. What say we save steps, and you just shoot me now?" He blinked and sniffed, tears now running down the side of his nose.

"*I* don't wish to shoot you." She actually batted her eyelashes at him, then straightened, frowning. "Really, Lord Vorkosigan, I hardly expected you to dissolve into tears."

He inhaled; his hands made a helpless pleading gesture. Startled, she tossed him a handkerchief from her breast pocket. A green-scented handkerchief. Without other recourse, he pressed it to his face.

"Stop crying, you cowar—" Her sharp order was interrupted by his first, mighty sneeze, followed by a rapid volley of repeats.

"I'm not crying, you bitch, I'm allergic to your goddamn perfume!" Miles managed to choke out between paroxysms.

She held her hand to her forehead and broke into giggles; real ones, not mannered ploys for a change. The real, spontaneous Cavilo at last; he'd been right, her sense of humor was vile. "Oh, dear," she gasped. "This gives me the most marvelous idea for a gas grenade. A pity I'll never . . . ah, well."

His sinuses throbbed like kettle drums. She shook her head helplessly, and tapped out something on her comconsole.

"I think I had best speed you on your way, before you explode," she told him.

Bent over in his seat wheezing, his water-clouded gaze fell on his brown felt slippers. "Can I at least have a pair of boots for this trip?"

She pursed her lips in a moment of thought. ". . . No," she decided. "It will be more interesting to see you carry on just as you are."

"In this uniform, on Aslund, I'll be like a cat in a dog suit," he protested. "Shot on sight by mistake."

"By mistake . . . on purpose . . . goodness, you're

going to have an exciting time." She keyed the door lock open.

He was still sneezing and gasping as the guards came in to take him away. Cavilo was still laughing.

The effects of her poisonous perfume took half an hour to wear off, by which time he was locked in a tiny cabin aboard an inner-system ship. They had boarded via a lock on the *Kurin's Hand;* he hadn't even set foot on Vervain Station again. Not a chance of a break for it.

He checked out the cabin. Its bed and lavatory arrangements were highly reminiscent of his last cell. Space duty, hah. The vast vistas of the wide universe, hah. The glory of the Imperial Service— un-hah. He'd lost Gregor. . . . *I may be small, but I screw up big because I'm standing on the shoulders of GIANTS.* He tried pounding on the door and screaming into the intercom. No one came.

It's a surprise.

He could surprise them all by hanging himself, a briefly attractive notion. But there was nothing up high to hook his belt on.

All right. This courier-type ship was swifter than the lumbering freighter in which he and Gregor had taken three days to cross the system last time, but it wasn't instantaneous. He had at least a day and a half to do some serious thinking, he and Admiral Naismith.

It's a surprise. God.

An officer and a guard came for him, very close to the time Miles estimated they would arrive back at Aslund Station's defense perimeter. *But we haven't docked yet. This seems premature.* His nervous exhaustion still responded to a shot of adrenalin; he inhaled, trying to clear his frenzy-fogged brain back to alertness again. Much more of this, though, and no amount of adrenalin would do him any good. The officer led him through the short corridors of the little ship to Nav and Com.

The Ranger captain was present, leaning over the communication console manned by his second officer. The pilot and flight engineer were busy at their stations.

"If they board, they'll arrest him, and he'll be automatically delivered as ordered," the second officer was saying.

"If they arrest him, they could arrest us too. She said to plant him, and she didn't care if it was head or feet first. She didn't order us to get ourselves interned," said the captain.

A voice from the comm; "This is the picket ship *Ariel*, Aslund Navy Contract Auxiliary, calling the *C6-WG* out of Vervain Hubside Station. Cease accelerating, and clear your portside lock for boarding for pre-docking inspection. Aslund Station reserves the right to deny you docking privileges if you fail to cooperate in pre-docking inspection." The voice took on a cheery tone, "I reserve the right to open fire if you don't stand and deliver in one minute. That's enough stalling, boys." The voice, once gone ironic, was suddenly intensely familiar. *Bel?*

"Cease accelerating," the captain ordered, and motioned the second to close the comm channel. "Hey you, Rotha," he called to Miles. "Come over here."

So I'm "Rotha" again. Miles mustered a smarmy smile, and sidled closer. He eyed the viewer, striving to conceal his hungry interest. The *Ariel*? Yes, there it was in the vid display, the sleek Illyrican-built cruiser . . . did Bel Thorne still command her? *How can I get myself onto that ship?*

"Don't throw me out there!" Miles protested urgently. "The Oserans are after my hide. I swear, I didn't know the plasma arcs were defective!"

"What plasma arcs?" asked the captain.

"I'm an arms dealer. I sold them some plasma

arcs. Cheap. Turns out they had a tendency to lock
on overload and blow their user's hand off. I didn't
know, I got them wholesale."

The Ranger captain's right hand opened and
closed in sympathetic identification. He rubbed his
palm unconsciously on his trousers, back of his
plasma arc holster. He studied Miles, frowning
sourly. "Headfirst it is," he said after a moment.
"Lieutenant, you and the corporal take this little
mutant to the portside personnel lock, pack him in
a bod-pod, and eject him. We're going home."

"No," said Miles weakly, as they each took an arm.
Yes! He dragged his feet, careful not to offer enough
resistance to risk his bones. "You're not going to
space me . . . !" The *Ariel*, my God. . . .

"Oh, the Aslunder merc'll pick you up," said the
captain. "Maybe. If they don't decide you're a bomb,
and try to set you off in space with plasma fire from
their ship or something." Smiling slightly at this
vision, he turned back to the comm, and intoned in
a bored traffic-control sing-song, "*Ariel*, ah, this is
the *C6-WG*. We chose to, ah, change our filed flight
plan and return to Vervain Station. We therefore
have no need for pre-docking inspection. We are
going to leave you a, ah, small parting gift, though.
Quite small. What you choose to do with it is your
problem. . . ."

The door to Nav and Com closed behind them. A
few meters of corridor and a sharp turn brought
Miles and his handlers to a personnel hatch. The
corporal held Miles, who struggled; the lieutenant
opened a locker and shook out a bod-pod.

The bod-pod was a cheap inflatable life-support
unit designed to be entered in seconds by endan-
gered passengers, suitable either for pressurization
emergencies or abandoning ship. They were also
dubbed idiot-balloons. They required no knowledge
to operate because they had no controls, merely a
few hours of recycleable air and a locator-beeper.

Passive, foolproof, and not recommended for claustrophobes, they were very cost-effective in saving lives—when adequate pick-up ships arrived in time.

Miles emitted a realistic wail as he was stuffed into the bod-pod's dank, plastic-smelling interior. A jerk of the rip cord, and it sealed and inflated automatically. He had a brief, horrible flashback to the mud-sunken bubble-shelter on Kyril Island, and choked back a real scream. He was tumbled as his captors rolled the pod into the airlock. A whoosh, a thump, a lurch, and he was free-falling in pitch darkness.

The spherical pod was little more than a meter in diameter. Miles, half-doubled-up, felt around, his stomach and inner ear protesting the spin imparted by the ejecting kick outward, till his shaking fingers found what he hoped was a cold-light tube. He squeezed it, and was rewarded with a nauseous greenish glow.

The silence was profound, broken only by the tiny hiss of the air recycler and his ragged breathing. *Well . . . it's better than the last time somebody tried to shove me out an airlock.* He had several minutes in which to imagine all the possible courses of action the *Ariel* might take instead of picking him up. He had just discarded skin-crawling anticipation of the ship opening fire on him in favor of abandonment to cold dark asphyxiation, when he and his pod were wrenched by a tractor beam.

The tractor beam's operator, clearly, had ham hands and palsy, but after a few minutes of juggling the return of gravity and outside sound reassured Miles he'd been safely stowed in a working airlock. The swish of the inner door, garbled human voices. Another moment, and the idiot balloon began to roll. He yelped loudly, and curled up into a protective ball to roll with the flow till the motion stopped. He sat up, and took a deep breath, and tried to straighten his uniform.

Muffled thumps against the bod-pod's fabric. "Somebody in there?"

"Yeah!" Miles called back.

"Just a minute. . . ."

Squeaks, clinks, and a rending grind, as the seals were broken. The bod-pod began to collapse as the air sighed out. Miles fought his way clear of its folds, and stood, shakily, with all the gracelessness and indignity of a newly-hatched chick.

He was in a small cargo bay. Three grey-and-white uniformed soldiers stood in a circle around him, aiming stunners and nerve-disruptors at his head. A slim officer with captain's insignia leaned with one foot on a canister, watching Miles emerge.

The officer's neat uniform and soft brown hair gave no clue whether one was looking at a delicate man or an unusually determined woman. This ambiguity was deliberately cultivated; Bel Thorne was a Betan hermaphrodite, minority descendant of a century-past social/genetic experiment that had not caught on. Thorne's expression melted from scepticism to astonishment as Miles rose into view.

Miles grinned back. "Hello, Pandora. The gods send you a gift. But there's a catch."

"Isn't there always?" Face lighting with delight, Thorne strode forward to grasp Miles's waist with bubbling enthusiasm. "Miles!" Thorne held Miles away again, and gazed avidly down into his face. "What are you doing here?"

"Somehow, I figured that might be your first question," Miles sighed.

"—and what are you doing in the Ranger-suit?"

"*Goodness*, I'm glad you're not of the shoot-first-and-ask-questions-later school." Miles kicked his slippered feet clear of the deflated bod-pod. The soldiers, somewhat uncertainly, held their aim. "Ah—" Miles gestured toward them.

"Stand down, men," Thorne ordered. "It's all right."

"I wish that were true," Miles said. "Bel, we've got to talk."

Thorne's cabin aboard the *Ariel* was the same wrenching mix of familiarity and change Miles had encountered in all the mercenary matters. The shapes, the sounds, the smells of the *Ariel*'s interior triggered cascades of memory. The captain's cabin was now overlaid with Bel's personal possessions; vid library, weapons, campaign souvenirs including a half-melted space-armor helmet that had been slagged saving Thorne's life, now made into a lamp; a small cage housing an exotic pet from Earth Thorne called a *hamster*.

Between sips of a cup of Thorne's private stock of non-synthetic tea, Miles gave Thorne the Admiral-Naismith version of reality, closely related to the one he'd given Oser and Tung; the Hub evaluation assignment, the mystery employer, etc. Gregor, of course, was edited out, together with any mention of Barrayar; Miles Naismith spoke with a pure Betan accent. Otherwise Miles stuck as close as he could to the facts of his sojourn with Randall's Rangers.

"So Lieutenant Lake's been captured by our competitors," Thorne mused upon Miles's description of the blond lieutenant he'd passed in the *Kurin's Hand*'s brig. "Couldn't happen to a nicer fellow, but—we'd better change our codes again."

"Quite." Miles set down his cup, and leaned forward. "I was authorized by my employer not only to observe but to prevent war in the Hegen Hub, if possible." Well, sort of. "I'm afraid it may no longer be possible. What does it look like from your end?"

Thorne frowned. "We were last in-dock five days ago. That's when the Aslunders concocted this pre-docking inspection routine. All the smaller ships were pressed into round-the-clock service on it. With their military station nearing completion, our employers are getting jumpier about sabotage—bombs, biologicals . . ."

"I won't argue with that. What about, ah, Fleet internal matters?"

"You mean rumors of your death, life, and/or resurrection? They're all over, fourteen garbled versions. I'd have discounted 'em—you've been sighted before, y'know—but then suddenly Oser arrested Tung."

"What?" Miles bit his lip. "Only Tung? Not Elena, Mayhew, Chodak?"

"Only Tung."

"That makes no sense. If he'd arrested Tung, he'd have fast-penta'd him, and he'd have to have spilled on Elena. Unless she's been left free as bait."

"Things got real tense, when Tung was taken. Ready to explode. I think if Oser'd moved on Elena and Baz it would have sparked the war right then. Yet he hasn't backed down and reinstated Tung. Very unstable. Oser's taking care to keep the old inner circle separated, that's why I've been out here for nearly a bloody week. But last time I saw Baz he was damn near edgy enough to commit to fight. And that was the last thing he'd wanted to do."

Miles exhaled slowly. "A fight . . . is exactly what Commander Cavilo wants. It's why she shipped me back gift-wrapped in that . . . undignified package. The Bod-pod of Discord. She doesn't care if I win or lose, as long as her enemy's forces are thrown into chaos just as she springs her *surprise*."

"Have you figured out what her surprise is, yet?"

"No. The Rangers were setting up for some sort of ground-attack, at one point. Sending me here suggests they're aiming for Aslund, against all strategic logic. Or something else? The woman's mind is incredibly twisted. Gah!" He slapped his fist gently into his palm in nervous rhythm. "I've got to talk to Oser. And he's got to listen this time. I've thought it over. Cooperation between us may be the one and only course of action Cavilo doesn't expect, doesn't have a half-sawn-through branch of her strategy-tree ready and waiting for me. . . . Are you willing to put it all on the line for me, Bel?"

Thorne pursed lips judiciously. "From here, yeah. The *Ariel's* the fleet's fastest ship. I can outrun retribution if I have to." Thorne grinned.

Should we run to Barrayar? No—Cavilo still held Gregor. Better appear to be following instructions. For a time yet.

Miles took a long breath, and settled himself firmly in the station chair in the *Ariel's* Nav and Com room. He'd cleaned up, and borrowed a mercenary's grey-and-white uniform from the smallest woman on the ship. The rolled-up pant cuffs were stuffed neatly out of sight down boots that almost fit. A belt covered the fastener gaping open at the too-narrow waistband. The loose jacket looked all right, sitting down. Permanent alterations later. He nodded to Thorne. "All right. Open your channel."

A buzz, a glitter, and Admiral Oser's hawk face materialized over the vid plate. "Yes, what is it— you!" His teeth shut with a beak's snap; his hand, a vague unfocused blur to the side, tapped on intercom keys and vid controls.

He can't throw me out the airlock this time, but he can cut me off. Time to talk fast.

Miles leaned forward and smiled. "Hello, Admiral Oser. I've completed my evaluation of Vervani forces in the Hegan Hub. And my conclusion is, you are in deep trouble."

"How did you get on this secured channel?" snarled Oser. "Tight-beam, double-encode—comm officer, trace this!"

"How, you will be able to determine in a few minutes. You'll have to keep me on-line till you do," said Miles. "But your enemy is at Vervain Station, not here. Not Pol, not Jackson's Whole. And most certainly not me. Note I said Vervain Station, not Vervain. You know Cavilo? Your opposite number, across-system?"

"I've encountered her once or twice." Oser's face was guarded now, waiting for his scrambling tech team to report.

"Face like an angel, mind like a rabid mongoose?"

Oser's lips twitched very slightly. "You've met her."

"Oh, yes. She and I had several heart-to-heart talks. They were . . . educational. Information is the most valuable trade-good in the Hub right now. At any rate, mine is. I want to deal."

Oser held up his hand for a pause, and keyed off-line briefly. When his face returned, its expression was black. "Captain Thorne, this is mutiny!"

Thorne leaned into the range of the vid pick-up, and said brightly, "No, sir, it's not. We are trying to save your ungrateful neck, if you will permit it. Listen to the man. He has lines we don't."

"He has lines, all right," and under his breath, "Damn Betans, sticking together. . . ."

"Whether you fight me, or I fight you, Admiral Oser, we both lose," said Miles rapidly.

"You can't win," said Oser. "You cannot take my fleet. Not with the *Ariel*."

"The *Ariel*'s just a starter-set, if it comes to that. But no, I probably can't win. What I can do is make an unholy mess. Divide your forces—screw you with your employer—every weapon-charge you expend, every piece of equipment that's damaged, every soldier hurt or killed is *pure loss* in an in-fight like this. Nobody wins but Cavilo, who expends nothing. Which is precisely what she sent me back here for. How much profit do you forsee in doing precisely what your enemy wishes you to, eh?"

Miles waited, breathless. Oser's jaw worked, chewing over this impassioned argument. "What's your profit?" he asked at last.

"Ah. I'm afraid I'm the dangerous variable in that calculation, Admiral. I'm not in it for profit." Miles grinned. "So I don't care what I wreck."

"Any information you had from Cavilo is worth shit," said Oser.

He begins to barter—he's hooked, he's hooked. . . . Miles tamped down exultation, cultivated a serious expression. "Anything Cavilo says must certainly be sifted with great care. But, ah . . . beauty is as beauty does. And I've found her vulnerable side."

"Cavilo has no vulnerable side."

"Yes, she does. Her passion for utility. Her self-interest."

"I fail to see how that makes her vulnerable."

"Precisely why you need to add *me* to your Staff at once. You need my vision."

"Hire you!" Oser recoiled in astonishment.

Well, he'd achieved surprise, anyway. A military objective of sorts. "I understand the post of Chief-of-Staff/Tactical is now empty."

Oser's expression flowed from astonished to stunned to a kind of amused fury. "You're insane."

"No, just in a tearing hurry. Admiral, there's nothing irrevocable gone wrong between us. Yet. You attacked me—not the other way around—and now you expect me to attack you back. But I'm not on holiday, and I don't have time to waste on personal amusements like revenge."

Oser's eyes narrowed. "What about Tung?"

Miles shrugged. "Keep him locked up, for now, if you insist. Unharmed, of course." *Just don't tell him I said so.*

"Suppose I hang him."

"Ah . . . *that* would be irrevocable." Miles paused. "I will point out, jailing Tung is like cutting off your right hand before heading into battle."

"What battle? With whom?"

"It's a surprise. Cavilo's surprise. Though I've

developed an idea or two on the problem, that I'd
be willing to share."

"Would you?" Oser had that same man-sucking-a-
lemon expression Miles had now and then surprised
on Illyan's face. It seemed almost homey.

Miles continued, "As an alternative to my becoming your employee, I'm willing to become your
employer. I'm authorized to offer a bona fide contract, all the usual perqs, equipment replacement,
insurance, from my . . . sponsor." *Illyan, hear my
plea.* "Not in conflict with Aslund's interests. You
can collect twice for the same fight, and you don't
even have to switch sides. A mercenary's dream."

"What guarantees can you offer up front?"

"It seems to me that I'm the one who's owed a
guarantee, sir. Let us begin with small steps. I won't
start a mutiny; you stop trying to thrust me out air-
locks. I will join you openly—everyone to know I've
arrived—I will make my information available to
you." How thin his "information" seemed, in the
breeze of these airy promises. No numbers, no troop
movements; all *intentions*, shifting mental topo-
graphies of loyalty, ambition, and betrayal. "We will
confer. You may even have an angle I lack. Then we
go on from there."

Oser thinned his lips, bemused, half-persuaded,
deeply suspicious.

"The risk, I would point out," said Miles, "the
personal risk, is more mine than yours."

"I think—"

Miles hung suspended on the mercenary's words.

"I think I'm going to regret this," Oser sighed.

The detailed negotiations just to bring the *Ariel*
into dock took another half day. As the initial excitement wore off, Thorne became more thoughtful. As
the *Ariel* actually maneuvered into its clamps, Thorne
grew positively meditative.

"I'm still not exactly sure what's supposed to keep

Oser from bringing us in, stunning us, and hanging us at leisure," Thorne said, buckling on a sidearm. Thorne kept the complaint to an undertone, in care for the tender ears of the escort squad kitting up nearby in the *Ariel's* shuttle hatch corridor.

"Curiosity," said Miles firmly.

"All right, stun, fast-penta, and hang, then."

"If he fast-penta's me, I'll tell him exactly the facts I was going to tell him anyway." *And a few more besides, alas.* "And he'll have fewer doubts. So much the better."

Miles was rescued from further hollow flummery by the clank and hiss of the flex-tubes sealing. Thorne's sergeant undogged the hatch without hesitation, though he was also careful not to stand silhouetted in the aperture, Miles noted.

"Squad, form up!" the sergeant ordered. His six people checked their stunners. Thorne and the sergeant in addition bore nerve disruptors, a nicely-calculated mix of weapons; stunners to allow for human error, the nerve disruptors to encourage the other side not to risk mistakes. Miles went unarmed. With a mental salute to Cavilo—well, a rude gesture, actually—he'd put his felt slippers back on. Thorne at his side, he took the lead of the little procession and marched through the flex tube into one of the Aslunder military station's almost-finished docking bays.

True to his word, Oser had a party of witnesses lined up and waiting. The squad of twenty or so bore a mix of weapons almost identical to the *Ariel's* group. "We're outnumbered," muttered Thorne.

"It's all in the mind," Miles muttered in return. "March like you had an empire at your back." *And don't look over your shoulder, they may be gaining on us. They'd better be gaining on us.* "The more people who see me, the better."

Oser himself stood waiting in parade rest, looking highly dyspeptic. Elena—*Elena!*—stood at his side, unarmed, face frozen. Her tight-lipped stare at Miles was tense with suspicion, not of his motives, perhaps, but certainly of his methods. *Now what foolishness?* her eyes asked. Miles gave her the briefest of ironic nods before saluting Oser.

Reluctantly, Oser returned the military courtesy. "Now—'Admiral'—let us return to the *Triumph* and get down to business," he grated.

"Indeed, yes. But let's have a little tour of this Station on the way, eh? The non-top-secured areas, of course. My last view was so . . . rudely cut short, after all. After you, Admiral?"

Oser gritted his teeth. "Oh, after you, Admiral."

It became a parade. Miles led them around for a good forty-five minutes, including a march through the cafeteria during the dinner rush with several noisy stops to greet by name the few old Dendarii he recognized, and favor the others with blinding smiles. He left babble in his wake, those in the dark demanding explanation from those in the know.

An Aslunder work crew was busy tearing out fiberboard paneling, and he paused to compliment them on their labors. Elena seized an opportunity of Oser's distraction to bend down and breathe fiercely in Miles's ear, *"Where's Gregor?"*

"Thereby hangs—me, if I fail to get him back," Miles whispered. "Too complicated, tell you later."

"Oh, God." She rolled her eyes.

When he had, judging from the admiral's darkening complexion, just about reached the limits of Oser's strained tolerance, Miles suffered himself to be led *Triumph*-ward again. There. Obedient to Cavilo's orders, Miles had made no attempt to contact Barrayar. But if Ungari couldn't find him after this, it was time to fire the man. A prairie bird thrumming out a mad mating dance could scarcely have put on a more conspicuous display.

Finishing touches on construction were still in progress around the *Triumph*'s docking bay as Miles marched his parade across it. A few Aslunder workers in tan, light blue, and green leaned over to goggle down from catwalks. Military techs in their dark blue uniforms paused in mid-installation to stare, then had to re-sort connections and realign bolts. Miles refrained from smiling and waving, lest Oser's set jaw crack. No more baiting, time to get serious. The thirty or so mercenaries could change from honor guard to prison guard with his next roll of the dice.

Thorne's tall sergeant, marching beside Miles, gazed around the bay, noting new construction. "The robotic loaders should be fully automated by this time tomorrow," he noted. "That'll be an improvement—*crap!*" His hand descended abruptly on Miles's head, shoving him downward. The sergeant half-spun, clawed hand arcing toward his holster, when the crackling blue bolt of a nerve disruptor charge struck him square in the chest at the level Miles's head had been. He spasmed, his breath stopping. The smell of ozone, hot plastic, and blistered meat slapped Miles's nose. Miles kept on diving, hitting the deck, rolling. A second bolt splattered on the deck, its outwashing field stinging like twenty wasps up Miles's outstretched arm. He jerked his hand back.

As the sergeant's corpse collapsed, Miles grabbed at the man's jacket and jerked himself underneath, burrowing his head and spine under where the meat was thickest, the sergeant's torso. He drew his arms and legs in as tight as he could. Another bolt crackled into the deck nearby, then two struck the body in close succession. Even with the absorbing mass between it was worse than the blow of a shock-stick on high power.

Miles's ringing ears heard screaming, thumping, yelling, running, chaos. The chirping buzz of stunner fire. A voice. "He's up there! Go get him!", and another voice, high and hoarse. "You spotted him—

he's yours. *You* go get him!" Another bolt hit the decking.

The weight of the big man, the stench of his fatal injury, pressed into Miles's face. He wished the fellow'd massed another fifty kilos. No wonder Cavilo had been willing to front twenty thousand Betan dollars toward a line on a shield-suit. Of all the loathesome weapons Miles had ever faced, this had to be the most personally terrifying. A head injury that didn't quite kill him, but stole his humanity and left him animal or vegetable was the worst nightmare. His intellect was surely his sole justification for existence. Without it . . .

The crackle of a nerve disruptor *not* aimed his way penetrated his hearing. Miles turned his head to scream, cloth- and meat-muffled, "Stunners! Stunners! We want him alive for questioning!" *He's yours, you go get him. . . .* He should shove out from under this body and join the fight. But if he was the assassin's special target, and why else pump charges into a corpse . . . perhaps he ought to stay right here. He squirmed, trying to draw his hands and legs in tighter.

The shouting died down; the firing stopped. Someone kneeling beside him tried to roll the sergeant's body off Miles. It took Miles a moment to realize he had to unclutch the dead man's uniform jacket before he could be rescued. He straightened his fingers with difficulty.

Thorne's face wavered over him, white and breathing open-mouthed, urgent. "Are you all right, Admiral?"

"I think," Miles panted.

"He was aiming at you," Thorne reported. "Only."

"I noticed," Miles stuttered. "I'm only lightly fried." Thorne helped him sit up. He was shaking as badly as after the shock-stick beating. He regarded his spasming hands, lowered one to touch the corpse beside him in morbid wonder. *Every day of the rest of my life will be your gift. And I don't even know your name.* "Your sergeant—what was his name?"

"Collins."

"Collins. Thanks."

"Good man."

"I saw."

Oser came up, looking strained. "Admiral Naismith, this was *not* my doing."

"Oh?" Miles blinked. "Help me up, Bel. . . ." That might have been a mistake, Thorne then had to help him keep standing as his muscles twitched. He felt weak, washed-out as a sick man. *Elena—where? She had no weapon. . . .*

There she was, with another female mercenary. They were dragging a man in the dark blue uniform of an Aslunder ranker toward Miles and Oser. Each woman held a booted foot; the man's arms trailed nervelessly across the deck. Stunned? Dead? They dropped the feet with a thump beside Miles, with the matter-of-fact air of lionesses delivering prey to their cubs. Miles stared down at a very familiar face indeed. *General Metzov. What are you doing here?*

"Do you recognize this man?" Oser asked an Aslunder officer who had hurried up to join them. "Is he one of yours?"

"I don't know him—" The Aslunder knelt to check for IDs. "He has a valid pass. . . ."

"He could have had me, and gotten away," said Elena to Miles, "but he kept firing at you. You were bright to stay put."

A triumph of wit, or a failure of nerve? "Yes. Quite." Miles made another attempt to stand on his own, gave up, and leaned on Thorne. "I hope you didn't kill him."

"Just stunned," said Elena, holding up the weapon as evidence. Some intelligent person must have tossed it to her when the melee began. "He probably has a broken wrist."

"Who *is* he?" asked Oser. Quite sincerely, Miles judged.

"Why, Admiral," Miles bared his teeth, "I told you I was going to deliver you more intelligence data than your Section could collect in a month. May I present," rather like an entree at that—he made a gesture designed to evoke a waiter lifting a domed cover from a silver platter, but which probably looked like another muscle spasm, "General Stanis Metzov. Second-in-command, Randall's Rangers."

"Since when do senior staff officers undertake field assassinations?"

"Excuse me, second-in-command as of three days ago. That may have changed. He was up to his stringy neck in Cavilo's schemes. You, I, and he have an appointment with a hypospray."

Oser stared. "You planned this?"

"Why do you think I spent the last hour flitting around the Station, if not to smoke him out?" Miles said brightly. *He must have been stalking me this whole time. I think I'm going to throw up. Have I just claimed to be brilliant, or incredibly stupid?* Oser looked like he was trying to figure out the answer to that same question.

Miles stared down at Metzov's unconscious form, trying to think. Had Metzov been sent by Cavilo, or was this murder attempt entirely on his own time? If sent by Cavilo—had she planned him to fall alive into her enemies' hands? If not, was there a back-up assassin around here somewhere, and if so was his target Metzov, if Metzov succeeded, or Miles, if Metzov failed? Or both? *I need to sit down and draw a flow-chart.*

Medical squads had arrived. "Yes, sickbay," said Miles faintly. "Till my old friend here wakes up."

"I'll agree to that," said Oser, shaking his head in something akin to dismay.

"Better put a protective as well as holding guard on our prisoner. I'm not sure if he was meant to survive capture."

"Right," Oser agreed bemusedly.

Thorne supporting one arm and Elena the other, Miles staggered home into the *Triumphs'* hatchway.

CHAPTER FOURTEEN

Miles sat trembling on a bench in a glassed-in cubicle normally used for bio-isolation in the *Triumph*'s sickbay, and watched Elena tie General Metzov to a chair with a tangle-cord. It would have given Miles a smug sense of turn-about, if the interrogation upon which they were about to embark was not so fraught with dangerous complications. Elena was disarmed again. Two stunner-armed men stood guard beyond the soundproof transparent door, glancing in occasionally. It had taken all Miles's eloquence to keep the audience for this initial questioning limited to himself, Oser, and Elena.

"How hot can this man's information be?" Oser had inquired irritably. "They let him go out in the field."

"Hot enough that I think you should have a chance to think about it before broadcasting it to a committee," Miles had argued. "You'll still have the recording."

Metzov looked sick and silent, tight-mouthed and unresponsive. His right wrist was neatly bandaged. Awakening from stun accounted for the sick; the silence was futile, and everyone knew it. It was a kind of strange courtesy, not to badger him with questions before the fast-penta cut in.

Now Oser frowned at Miles. "Are you up to this yet?"

Miles glanced down at his still-shaking hands. "As long as no one asks me to do brain surgery, yes.

Proceed. I have reason to suspect that time is of the essence."

Oser nodded to Elena, who held up a hypospray to calibrate the dose, and pressed it to Metzov's neck. Metzov's eyes shut briefly in despair. After a moment his clenched hands relaxed. The muscles of his face unlocked to sag into a loose, idiotic smile. The transformation was most unpleasant to watch. Without the tension his face looked aged.

Elena checked Metzov's pulse and pupils. "All right. He's all yours, gentlemen." She stepped back to lean against the doorframe with folded arms, her expression almost as closed as Metzov's had been.

Miles opened his hand. "After you, Admiral."

Oser's mouth twisted. "Thank you. Admiral." He walked over to stare speculatively into Metzov's face. "General Metzov. Is your name Stanis Metzov?"

Metzov grinned. "Yeah, that's me."

"Presently second-in-command, Randall's Rangers?"

"Yeah."

"Who sent you to assassinate Admiral Naismith?"

Metzov's face took on an expression of sunny bewilderment. "Who?"

"Call me Miles," Miles suggested. "He knows me under a . . . pseudonym." His chance of getting through this interview with his identity undisclosed equalled that of a snowball surviving a wormhole jump to the center of a sun, but why rush the complications?

"Who sent you to kill Miles?"

"Cavie did. Of course. He escaped, you see. I was the only one she could trust . . . trust . . . the bitch. . . ."

Miles's brow twitched. "In fact, Cavilo shipped me back here herself," he informed Oser. "General Metzov was therefore set up. But to what end? My turn, now, I think."

Oser made the after-you gesture and stepped back. Miles tottered off his bench and into Metzov's line-of-sight. Metzov breathed rage even through the fast-penta euphoria, then grinned vilely.

Miles decided to start with the question that had driven him most nuts the longest. "Who—what target—was your ground-attack planned to be upon?"

"Vervain," said Metzov.

Even Oser's jaw dropped. The blood thudded in Miles's ears in the stunned silence.

"Vervain is your *employer*," Oser choked.

"God—God!—finally it adds up!" Miles almost capered; it came out a stagger, which Elena lurched away from the wall to catch. "Yes, yes, *yes.* . . ."

"It's *insane*," said Oser. "So that's Cavilo's surprise."

"That's not the end of it, I'll bet. Cavilo's drop forces are bigger than ours by far, but no way are they big enough to take on a fully-settled planet like Vervain on the ground. They can only raid and run."

"Raid and run, right," smiled Metzov equably.

"What was your particular target, then?" asked Miles urgently.

"Banks . . . art museums . . . gene banks . . . hostages. . . ."

"That's a *pirate* raid," said Oser. "What the hell were you going to do with the loot?"

"Drop it off on Jackson's Whole, on the way out; they fence it."

"How did you figure to escape the irate Vervani Navy, then?" asked Miles.

"Hit them just before the new fleet comes on-line. Cetagandan invasion fleet'll catch 'em in orbital dock. Sitting targets. Easy."

The silence this time was utter.

"*That's* Cavilo's surprise," Miles whispered at last. "Yeah. that one's *worthy* of her."

"Cetagandan . . . invasion?" Oser unconsciously began to chew a fingernail.

"God, it fits, it fits." Miles began to pace the cubicle with uneven steps. "What's the only way to take a wormhole jump? From both sides at once. The

Vervani aren't Cavilo's employers—the *Cetagandans* are." He turned to point at the slack-lipped, nodding general. "And now I see Metzov's place, clear as day."

"Pirate," shrugged Oser.

"No—goat."

"What?"

"This man—you apparently don't know—was cashiered from the Barrayaran Imperial Service for brutality."

Oser blinked. "From the Barrayaran Service? That must have taken some doing."

Miles bit down a twinge of irritation. "Well, yes. He, ah . . . took on the wrong victim. But anyway, don't you see it? The Cetagandan invasion fleet jumps through into Vervani local space on Cavilo's invitation—probably on Cavilo's signal. The Rangers raid, do a fast trash of Vervain. The Cetagandans, out of the kindness of their hearts, 'rescue' the planet from the treacherous mercenaries. The Rangers run. Metzov is left behind as goat—just like throwing the guy out of the troika to the wolves," oops, that wasn't a very Betan metaphor, "to be publicly hung by the Cetagandans to demonstrate their 'good faith.' See, this evil Barrayaran harmed you, you need our Imperial protection from the Barrayaran Imperial threat, and here we are.

"And Cavilo gets paid *three* times. Once by the Vervani, once by the Cetagandans, and the third time by Jackson's Whole when she fences her loot on the way out. Everybody profits. Except the Vervani, of course." He paused to catch his breath.

Oser was beginning to look convinced, and worried. "Do you think the Cetagandans plan to punch through into the Hub? Or will they stop at Vervain?"

"Of course they'll punch through. The Hub is the strategic target; Vervain is just a stepping stone to it. Hence the 'bad mercenary' setup. The Cetagandans want to expend as little energy as possible pacifying Vervani. They'll probably label them an 'allied satrapy,' hold the space routes, and barely touch down on the planet. Absorb them economically over a generation. The question is, will the Cetagandans stop at Pol? Will they try to take it on this one move, or leave it as a buffer between them and Barrayar? Conquest or wooing? If they can bait the Barrayarans into attacking through Pol without permission, it might even drive the Polians into a Cetagandan alliance—agh!" He paced again.

Oser looked like he'd bitten into something nasty. With half a worm in it. "I wasn't hired to take on the Cetagandan Empire. I expected to be fighting the Vervani's mercenaries, at most, if the whole thing didn't just fizzle out. If the Cetagandans arrive here, in force in the Hub, we'll be . . . trapped. Penned up with a cul-de-sac at our backs." And in a trailing mutter, "Maybe we ought to think about getting out while the getting's good. . . ."

"But Admiral Oser, don't you realize," Miles pointed to Metzov, *"she'd* never have let him out of her sight with all this in his head if it was still an active plan. She may have meant him to die trying to kill me, but there was always the chance he might not—that just this sort of interrogation might result. All this is the *old* plan. There must be a *new* plan." *And I think I know what it is.* "There is . . . another factor. A new X in the equation." *Gregor.* "Unless I miss my guess, the Cetagandan invasion is now a considerable embarrassment to Cavilo."

"Admiral Naismith, I would believe that Cavilo would double-cross anyone you care to name— except the Cetagandans. They'd spend a generation, pursuing their revenge. She couldn't run far enough. She wouldn't live to spend her profits. Incidently, what conceivable profit outweighs triple pay?"

But if she expects to have the Barrayaran Empire to defend her from retribution—all our Security resources. . . . "I see one way she could expect to get away with it," said Miles. "If it works out like she wants, she'll have all the protection she wants. And all the profits."

It could work, it really could. If Gregor were indeed under her spell. And if two embarrassingly hostile character witnesses, Miles and General Metzov, conveniently killed each other. Abandoning her fleet, she could take Gregor and flee before the oncoming Cetagandans, presenting herself to Barrayar as Gregor's "rescuer" at great personal cost; if in addition a smitten Gregor urged her as his fiancee, worthy mother to a future scion of the military caste—the romantic appeal of the drama could swing popular support enough to overwhelm cooler advisors' judgments. God knew Miles's own mother had laid the groundwork for that scenario. *She could really bring this off. Empress Cavilo of Barrayar. It even scans.* And she could cap her career by betraying absolutely *everybody*, even her own forces. . . .

"Miles, the look on your face . . ." said Elena in worry.

"When?" said Oser. "When will the Cetagandans attack?" He got Metzov's wandering attention, and repeated the question.

"Only Cavie knows." Metzov snickered. "Cavie knows everything."

"It has to be imminent," Miles argued. "It may even be starting now. Guessing from Cavilo's timing of my return here. She meant the De—the Fleet to be paralyzed with our infighting right now."

"If that's true," murmured Oser, "what to do . . . ?"

"We're too far away. A day and a half from the action. Which will be at the Vervain Station wormhole. And beyond, in Vervani local space. We have to get closer. We have to move the Fleet across-system—pin Cavilo up against the Cetagandans. Blockade her—"

"Whoa! I'm not mounting a headlong attack against the Cetagandan Empire!" interrupted Oser sharply.

"You must. You'll have to fight them sooner or later. You pick the time, or they will. The only chance of stopping them is at the wormhole. Once they're through, it will be impossible."

"If I moved my fleet away from Aslund, the Vervani would think we were attacking them."

"And mobilize, go on the alert. Good. But in the wrong direction—not good. We would end up being a feint for Cavilo. Damn! No doubt another branch of her strategy-tree."

"Suppose—if the Cetagandans are now such an embarrassment to Cavilo as you claim—she doesn't send her code?"

"Oh, she still needs them. But for a different purpose. She needs them to flee from. And to mass-murder her witnesses for her. But she doesn't need them to succeed. In fact, she now needs their invasion to bog down. If she's really thinking as long-term as she should be, in her new plan."

Oser shook his head, as if to clear it. "Why?"

"Our only hope—Aslund's only hope—is to capture Cavilo, and fight the Cetagandans to a standstill at the Vervain Station wormhole. No, wait—we have to hold both sides of the Hub-Vervain jump. Until reinforcements arrive."

"What reinforcements?"

"Aslund, Pol—once the Cetagandans actually materialize in force, they'll see their threat. And if Pol comes in on Barrayar's side instead of Cetaganda's, Barrayar can pour forces through via them. The Cetagandans can be stopped, if everything occurs in the right order." But could Gregor be rescued alive? Not a path to victory, but all paths. . . .

"Would the Barrayarans come in?"

"Oh, I think so. Your counter-intelligence must keep track of these things—haven't they noticed a sudden increase in Barrayaran Intelligence activity here in the Hub the last few days?"

"Now that you mention it, yes. Their coded traffic has quadrupled."

Thank God. Maybe relief was closer than he'd dared hope. "Have you broken any of their codes?" Miles asked brightly, while he was at it.

"Only the least sensitive one, so far."

"Ah. Good. That is, too bad."

Oser stood with his arms folded, gnawing at his lip, intensely inward for a full minute. It reminded Miles uncomfortably of the meditative expression the admiral'd had just before ordering him shoved out the nearest airlock, barely more than a week back. "No," Oser said at last. "Thanks for the information. In return, I suppose I will spare your life. But we're pulling out. It's not a fight we can possibly win. Only some propaganda-blinded planetary force, with a planet's resources behind it, can afford that sort of insane self-sacrifice. I designed my fleet to be a fine tactical tool, not a, a damn doorstop made of dead bodies. I'm not a—as you say—goat."

"Not a goat, a spearhead."

"Your 'spearhead' has no spear behind it. No."

"Is that your last word, sir?" asked Miles in a thin voice.

"Yes." Oser reached to key his wristcom, to call in the waiting guards. "Corporal, this party's going to the brig. Call down and notify them."

The guard saluted through the glass as Oser keyed off.

"But sir," Elena approached him, her arms raised in pleading. With a snake-strike sideways flick of her wrist, she jabbed the hypospray against the side of Oser's neck. His eyes widened, his pulse beat once, twice, three times, as his lips drew back in rage. He tensed to strike her. His blow sagged in mid-arc.

The guards beyond the glass snapped alert at Oser's sudden movement, drawing their stunners.

Elena caught Oser's hand and kissed it, smiling gratefully. The guards relaxed; one nudged the other and said something pretty nasty, judging from their grins, but Miles's wits were too momentarily scattered to try and read lips.

Oser swayed and panted, fighting the drug. Elena sidled up the captured arm and slipped a hand cozily around his waist, half-turning him so they stood with their backs to the door. The stereotypical stupid fast-penta smile slipped across and receded from Oser's face, then fixed itself at last.

"He acted like I was unarmed." Elena shook her head in exasperation, and slipped the hypospray into her jacket pocket.

"Now what?" Miles hissed frantically as the guard-corporal bent over the door's code-lock.

"We all go to the brig, I guess. Tung's there," said Elena.

"Ah . . ." Oh-hell-we'll-never-bring-this-off. Had to try. Miles smiled cheerily at the entering guards, and helped them release Metzov, largely getting in their way and keeping their attention off the peculiarly happy-looking Oser. At a moment when their eyes were elsewhere, he tripped Metzov, who staggered.

"You'd better each take one of his arms, he's not too steady," Miles told the guards. He was none too steady himself, but he managed to block the doorway so the guards and Metzov led the way, himself second, and Elena, arm-in-arm with Oser, followed last. "Come, love, come," he heard Elena intone behind him, like a woman coaxing a cat to her lap.

It was the longest short walk he'd ever taken. He dropped back to growl out of the corner of his mouth to Elena, "All right, we get to the brig, it will be stocked with Oser's finest. What then?"

She bit her lip. "Don't know."

"That's what I was afraid of. Turn right here." They swung around the next corner.

A guard looked back over his shoulder. "Sir?"

"Carry on, boys," Miles called. "When you've got that spy locked up, report back to us at the Admiral's cabin."

"Very good, sir."

"Keep walking," breathed Miles. "Keep smiling. . . ."

The guards' footsteps faded. "Where now?" asked Elena. Oser stumbled. "This is untenable."

"Admiral's cabin, why not?" Miles decided. His grin was fixed and fey. Elena's inspired mutinous gesture had given him the best break of the day. He had the momentum now. He wouldn't stop till he was brought down bodily. His head spun with the unutterable relief of at last getting the shifting, writhing, chittering *might-be-might-be-might-be* nailed to a fixed *is. The time is now. The word is go.*

Maybe. If.

They passed a few Oseran techs. Oser was sort of nodding. Miles hoped it would pass as casual acknowledgment of their salutes. Nobody turned and cried Hey!, anyway. Two levels and another turn brought them to the well-remembered corridors of officer's country. They passed the Captain's cabin (God, he'd have to deal with Auson, and soon); Oser's palm, pressed by Elena against the lock, admitted them to the quarters Oser had made his flag office. When the door slipped shut behind them Miles realized he'd been holding his breath.

"We're in it now," said Elena, sagging for a moment with her back to the door. "You going to run out on us again?"

"Not this time," Miles replied grimly. "You may have noticed one item I didn't bring up for discussion, down in sickbay."

"Gregor."

"Just so. Cavilo holds him hostage aboard her flagship right now."

Elena's neck bent in dismay. "She means to sell him to the Cetagandans for a bonus, then?"

"No. Weirder than that. She means to marry him."

Elena's lip curled in astonishment. "What? Miles, there's no way she could have got such an impossible notion in her head, unless—"

"Unless Gregor planted it. Which, I believe, he did. Watered and fertilized it, too. What I don't know is whether he was serious, or playing for time. She was very careful to keep us separated. You knew Gregor almost as well as I do. What do you think?"

"It's hard to imagine Gregor love-struck to idiocy. He was always . . . rather quiet. Almost, well, undersexed. Compared to, say, Ivan."

"I'm not sure that's a fair comparison."

"No, you're right. Well, compared to you, then."

Miles wondered just how to take that. "Gregor never had much in the way of opportunities, when we were younger. I mean, no privacy. Security always in his back pocket. That . . . that can inhibit a man, unless he's a bit of an exhibitionist."

Her hand turned, as if measuring out Gregor's smooth gripless surface. "He was not that."

"Certainly Cavilo must be taking care to present only her most attractive side."

Elena licked her lips in thought. "Is she pretty?"

"Yeah, if you happen to like blonde power-mad homicidal maniacs, I suppose she could be quite overwhelming." His hand closed, the texture of Cavilo's pelted hair remembered like an itch on his palm. He rubbed it on his trouser seam.

Elena brightened slightly. "Ah. You don't like her."

Miles gazed up at Elena's Valkyrie face. "She's too short for my taste."

Elena grinned. "That, I believe." She guided the shambling Oser to a chair and sat him down. "We're going to have to tie him up soon. Or something."

The comm buzzed. Miles went to Oser's desk console to answer it. "Yes?" he said in his calmest bored voice.

"Corporal Meddis here, sir. We've put the Vervani agent in Cell Nine."

"Thank you, Corporal. Ah . . ." It was worth a try, "We still have some fast-penta left. Would you two please bring Captain Tung up here for questioning?"

Beyond range of the vid pick-up, Elena's dark brows rose in hope.

"Tung, sir?" The guard's voice was doubtful. "Uh, may I add a couple of reinforcements to my squad, then?"

"Sure . . . see if Sergeant Chodak's around, he may have some people up for extra duties. In fact, isn't he on the extra-duty roster himself?" He glanced up to see Elena hold up her thumb and forefinger in an O.

"I think so, sir."

"Fine, whatever. Carry on. Naismith out." He keyed off the comm and stared at it, as if it had transmuted into Aladdin's lamp. "I don't think I'm destined to die today. I must be being saved for day after tomorrow."

"You think?"

"Oh, yes. I'll have a much bigger, more public and spectacular chance to blow it all away then. Be able to take thousands more lives down with me."

"Don't you fall into one of your stupid funks now, you haven't got time for it." She rapped the hypospray smartly across his knuckles. "You've got to think us out of this hole."

"Yes, ma'am," Miles said meekly, rubbing his hand. *Whatever happened to "my lord"? No respect, none.* . . . But he was strangely comforted. "By the way, when Oser arrested Tung for arranging my getaway, why didn't he go on to take you and Arde and Chodak, and the rest of your cadre?"

"He didn't arrest Tung for that. At least, I don't think so. He was baiting Tung, which is his habit, they were both on the bridge at the same time—that was unusual—and Tung finally lost his temper and tried to deck him. Did deck him, I heard, and was part way to strangling him when security pulled him off."

"It had nothing to do with us, then?" That was a relief.

"I'm . . . not sure. I wasn't there. It might have been an emergency diversion, to get Oser's attention away from making just that connection." Elena nodded to the still-blandly-smiling Oser. "And now?"

"Leave him loose, till Tung is delivered. We're all just happy allies here." Miles grimaced. "But for the love of God don't let anybody try to talk to him."

The door comm buzzed. Elena went to stand behind Oser's chair with one hand on his shoulder, trying to look as allied as possible. Miles went to the door and keyed the lock. The door slid open.

Six nervous squadmen surrounded a hostile-looking Ky Tung. Tung wore prisoner's bright yellow pajamas, and radiated malice like a small pre-nova sun. His teeth clenched in utter confusion when he saw Miles.

"Ah, thank you, Corporal," said Miles. "We will be having a little informal staff conference after this interrogation. I'd appreciate it if you and your squad would stand guard out here. And in case Captain Tung gets violent again, we'd better have—oh, Sergeant Chodak and a couple of your people inside." He emphasized the *your* with no change of voice, but only a direct look into Chodak's eyes.

Chodak made the catch. "Yes, sir. You, Private, come with me."

I'm promoting you to lieutenant, Miles thought, and stood aside to let the sergeant and his chosen man guide Tung within. Oser, looking cheerful, was quite clearly visible to the squad for a moment before the door hissed closed again.

Oser was clearly visible to Tung, too. Tung shrugged off his guards and stalked toward the admiral. "What now, you son-of-a-bitch, do you think you—" Tung paused, as Oser continued to smile dimly up at him. "What's wrong with him?"

"Nothing," shrugged Elena. "I think that dose of fast-penta made a real improvement in his personality. Too bad it's only temporary."

Tung threw back his head and barked a laugh, and whirled to shake Miles by the shoulders. "You did it, you little—you came back! We're in business!"

Chodak's man twitched, as if uncertain which way, or whom, to jump. Chodak caught him by the arm, shook his head silently, and indicated the wall by the door. Chodak holstered his stunner and leaned against the doorframe with his arms folded; after a startled moment, his man followed suit, flanking the other side. "Fly on the wall," Chodak grinned out of the corner of his mouth to him. "Consider it a gift."

"It wasn't exactly voluntary," said Miles through his teeth to Tung, only in part to keep from biting his tongue in the blast of the Eurasian's enthusiasm. "And we're not in business yet." *Sorry, Ky. I can't be your front man this time. You've got to follow me.* Miles kept his face stern, and removed Tung's hands from his shoulders with icy deliberation. "That Vervani freighter captain you found delivered me straight to Commander Cavilo. And I've been wondering ever since if it was an accident."

"Ah!" Tung fell back, looking as if Miles had just hit him in the stomach.

Miles felt like he had. No, Tung was no traitor. But Miles dared not give up the only edge he had. "Betrayal, or botchery, Ky?" *And have you stopped beating your wife?*

"Botchery," whispered Tung, gone sallow-pale. "Dammit, I'm going to kill the triple-crossing—"

"That's already been done," said Miles coldly. Tung's brows rose in surprised respect.

"I came to the Hegen Hub on a contract," continued Miles, "which is now in disarray almost beyond repair. I haven't come back here to put you in operational combat command of the Dendarii—" a beat, as Tung's worried features attempted to settle on an expression, "unless you are prepared to serve *my* ends. Priorities and targets are to be my choice. Only the *how* is yours." And just who was going to put whom in command of the Dendarii? As long as that question didn't occur to Tung.

"As my ally," began Tung.

"Not ally. Your commander. Or nothing," said Miles.

Tung stood stockily, his brows struggling to find their level. In a mild tone he finally said, "Daddy Ky's little boy is growing up, it seems."

"That's not the half of it. Are you in, or out?"

"The other half of this is something I've got to hear." Tung sucked on his lower lip. "In."

Miles stuck out his hand. "Done."

Tung took it. "Done." His grip was determined.

Miles let out a long breath. "All right. I gave you some half-truths, last time. Here's what's really going on." He began to pace, his shaking not all from the nerve disruptor nimbus. "I do have a contract with an interested outsider, but it wasn't for 'military evaluation,' which is the smoke screen I gave Oser. The part I told you about preventing a planetary civil war was not smoke. I was hired by the Barrayarans."

"They don't normally hire mercenaries," said Tung.

"I'm not a normal mercenary. I'm being paid by Barrayaran Imperial Security," God, at least one whole-truth, "to find and rescue a hostage. On the side I hope to stop a now-imminent Cetagandan invasion fleet from taking over the Hub. Our second strategic priority will be to hold both sides of the

Vervain wormhole jump and as much else as we can till Barrayaran reinforcements arrive."

Tung cleared his throat. "Second priority? What if they don't arrive? There's Pol to cross. . . . And, ah, hostage-rescue does not normally take precedence over fleetwide strat-tac ops, eh?"

"Given the identity of this hostage, I guarantee their arrival. The Barrayaran emperor, Gregor Vorbarra, was kidnapped. I found him, lost him, and now I've got to get him back. As you can imagine, I expect the reward for his safe return to be substantial."

Tung's face was a study in appalled enlightenment. "That skinny neurasthenic git you had in tow before—that wasn't *him*, was it?"

"Yes, it was. And between us, you and I managed to deliver him straight to Commander Cavilo."

"Oh. Shit." Tung rubbed his burr-haired skull. "She'll sell him straight to the Cetagandans."

"No. She means to collect her reward from Barrayar."

Tung opened his mouth, closed it, held up a finger. "Wait a minute. . . ."

"It's *complicated*," Miles conceded helplessly. "That's why I'm going to delegate the simple part, holding the wormhole, to you. The hostage-rescue part will be my responsibility."

"Simple. The Dendarii mercenaries. All five thousand of us. Singlehanded. Against the Cetagandan Empire. Have you forgotten how to count in the last four years?"

"Think of the glory. Think of your reputation. Think how great it'll look on your next resume."

"On my cenotaph, you mean. Nobody will be able to collect enough of my scattered atoms to bury. You going to cover my funeral expenses, son?"

"Splendidly. Banners, dancing girls, and enough beer to float your coffin to Valhalla."

Tung sighed. "Make it plum wine to float the boat,

eh? Drink the beer. Well." He stood silent a moment, rubbing his lips. "The first step is to put the fleet on one-hour-alert status instead of twenty-four."

"They're not already?" Miles frowned.

"We were defensive. We figured we had at least thirty-six hours to study anything coming at us across the Hub. Or, so Oser figured it. It'll take about six hours to bring us up to one-hour readiness."

"Right . . . that's the second step, then. Your first step will be to kiss and make up with Captain Auson."

"Kiss my ass!" cried Tung. "That vacuumhead—"

"Is needed to command the *Triumph* while you run Fleet Tac. You can't do both. I can't reorganize the fleet this close to the action. If I had a week to weed out—well, I don't. Oser's people must be persuaded to stay on their jobs. If I have Auson," Miles's upheld hand closed cage-like, "I can run the rest. One way or another."

Turng growled frustrated acquesience. "All right." His glower faded to a slow grin. "I'd pay money to watch you make him kiss Thorne, though."

"One miracle at a time."

Captain Auson, a big man four years ago, had put on a little more weight but seemed otherwise unchanged. He stepped into Oser's cabin, took in the stunners aimed his way, and stood, hands clenching. When he saw Miles, sitting on the edge of Oser's comconsole desk (a psychological ploy to put his head level with everyone else's; in the station chair Miles feared he looked like a child in need of a booster seat at the dinner table), Auson's expression melted from anger to horror. "Oh, hell! Not you again!"

"But of course," shrugged Miles. The stunner-armed flies on the wall, Chodak and his man, suppressed grins of happy anticipation. "The action's about to start."

"You can't take this—" Auson broke off to peer at Oser. "What did you do to him?"

"Let's just say, we adjusted his attitude. As for the fleet, it's already mine." Well, he was working on it, anyway. "The question is, will you choose to be on the winning side? Pocket a combat bonus? Or shall I give command of the *Triumph* to—"

Auson bared his teeth to Tung in a silent snarl.

"—Bel Thorne?"

"What?" Auson yelped. Tung flinched, wincing. "You can't—"

Miles cut over him, "Do you happen to recall how you graduated from command of the *Ariel* to command of the *Triumph*? Yes?"

Auson pointed to Tung. "What about him?"

"My contractor will contribute value equal to the *Triumph*, which will become Tung's vested share in the fleet corporation. In return Commodore Tung will relinquish all claim on the ship itself. I will confirm Tung's rank as Chief of Staff/Tactical, and yours as captain of the flagship *Triumph*. Your original contribution, equal to the value of the *Ariel* less liens, will be confirmed as your vested share in the fleet corporation. Both ships will be listed as owned by the fleet."

"Do you go along with this?" Auson demanded of Tung.

Miles prodded Tung with a steely look. "Yeah," said Tung grudgingly.

Auson frowned over this. "It isn't just the money . . ." he paused, brow wrinkling. "What combat bonus? What combat?"

He who hesitates, is had. "Are you in or out?"

Auson's moon face took on a cunning look. "I'm in—if he apologizes."

"What? This meatmind thinks—"

"Apologize to the man, Tung dear," Miles sang

through his teeth, "and let's get on. Or the *Triumph* gets a captain who can be its own first mate. Who, among other manifold virtues, doesn't *argue* with me."

"Of course not, the little Betan flipsider's in love," snapped Auson. "I've never been able to figure out if it wants to get screwed or bugger you—"

Miles smiled and held up a restraining hand. "Now, now." He nodded toward Elena, who had holstered her stunner in favor of a nerve disruptor. Pointed steadily at Auson's head.

Her smile reminded Miles unsettlingly of one of Sergeant Bothari's. Or worse, of Cavilo's. "Have I ever mentioned, Auson, how much the sound of your voice *irritates* me?" she inquired.

"You wouldn't fire," said Auson uncertainly.

"I wouldn't stop her," Miles lied. "I need your ship. It would be convenient—but not necessary—if you would command her for me." His gaze flicked like a knife toward his putative Chief of Staff/Tac. "*Tung?*"

With ill-grace, Tung mouthed a nobly-worded, if vague, apology to Auson for past slurs on his character, intelligence, ancestory, appearance—as Auson's face darkened Miles stopped Tung's catalogue in mid-list and made him start over. "Keep it simpler."

Tung took a breath. "Auson, you can be a real shithead sometimes, but dammit, you can fight when you have to. I've seen you. In the tight and the bad and the crazy, I'll take you at my back before any other captain in the fleet."

One side of Auson's mouth curled up. "Now, *that's* sincere. Thank you so much. I really appreciate your concern for my safety. How tight and bad and crazy do you think this is going to get?"

Tung, Miles decided, had a most unsavory chuckle.

The captain-owners were brought in one by one, to be persuaded, bribed, blackmailed and bedazzled till Miles's mouth was dry, throat raw, voice hoarse. Only the *Peregrine*'s captain tried to physically fight. He was stunned and bound, and his second-in-command given the immediate choice between brevet promotion and a long walk out a short airlock. He chose promotion, though his eyes said, *Another day*. As long as that other day came after the Cetagandans, Miles was satisfied.

They moved to the larger conference chamber across from the Tactics Room for the strangest Staff conference Miles had ever attended. Oser was fortified with a booster shot of fast-penta and propped up at the head of the table like a stuffed and smiling corpse. At least two others were tied to their chairs gagged. Tung traded his yellow pajamas for undress greys, commodore's insignia pinned hastily over his captain's tags. The reaction of the audience to Tung's initial tactical presentation ranged from dubious to appalled, overcome (almost) by the pelting headlong pace of the actions demanded of them. Tung's most compelling argument was the sinister suggestion that if they didn't set themselves up as the wormhole's defenders, they might be required to attack through it later against a prepared Cetagandan defense, a vision that generated shudders all around the table. *It could be worse* was always an unassailable assertion.

Partway through, Miles massaged his temples and leaned over to whisper to Elena, "Was it always this bad, or have I just forgotten?"

She pursed her lips thoughtfully and murmured back, "No, the insults were better in the old days."

Miles muffled a grin.

Miles made a hundred unauthorized claims and unsupported promises, and at last things broke up, each to their duty stations. Oser and the *Peregrine*'s captain were marched away under guard to the brig. Tung paused only to frown down at the brown felt slippers. "If you're going to command my outfit, son, would you please do an old soldier a favor and get a pair of regulation boots?" At last only Elena remained.

"I want you to re-interrogate General Metzov," Miles told her. "Pull out all the Ranger tactical disposition data you can—codes, ships on-line, off-line, last known positions, personnel oddities, plus whatever he may know about the Vervani. Edit out any unfortunate references he may make to my real identity, and pass it on to Ops, with the warning that not everything Metzov thinks is true, necessarily is. It may help."

"Right."

Miles sighed, slumping wearily on his elbows at the empty conference table. "You know, the planetary patriots like the Barrayarans—us Barrayarans—have it wrong. Our officer cadre thinks that mercenaries have no honor, because they can be bought and sold. But honor is a luxury only a free man can afford. A good Imperial officer like me isn't honorbound, he's just *bound*. How many of these honest people have I just lied to their deaths? It's a strange game."

"Would you change anything, today?"

"Everything. Nothing. I'd have lied twice as fast if I'd had to."

"You do talk faster in your Betan accent," she allowed.

"You understand. Am I doing the right thing? If I can bring it off. Failure being automatically wrong." *Not a path to disaster, but all paths. . . .*

Her brows rose. "Certainly."

His lips twisted up. "So you," *whom I love*, "my Barrayaran lady who hates Barrayar, are the only person in the Hub I can honestly sacrifice."

She tilted her head in consideration of this. "Thank you, my lord." She touched her hand to the top of his head, passing out of the chamber.

Miles shivered.

CHAPTER FIFTEEN

Miles returned to Oser's cabin for a fast perusal of the admiral's comconsole files, trying to get a handle on all the changes in equipment and personnel that had occurred since he'd last commanded, and to assimilate the Dendarii/Aslunder intelligence picture of events in the Hub. Somebody brought him a sandwich and coffee, which he consumed without tasting. The coffee was no longer working to keep him alert, though he was still keyed to an almost unbearable tension.

As soon as we undock, I'll crash in Oser's bed. He'd better spend at least some of the thirty-six hours transit time sleeping, or he'd be more liability than asset upon arrival. When he would have to deal with Cavilo, who made him feel like the proverbial unarmed man in the battle of wits even when he was at his best.

Not to mention the Cetagandans. Miles considered the historical three-legged-race between weapons development and tactics.

Projectile weapons for ship-to-ship combat in space had early been made obsolete by mass shielding and laser weapons. Mass shielding, designed to protect moving ships from space debris encountered at normal-space speeds up to half-cee, shrugged off missiles without even trying. Laser weapons in turn had been rendered useless by the arrival of the Sword-swallower, a Betan-developed defense that actually used the enemy fire as its own power source; a similar principle in the plasma mirror, developed in Miles's parents' generation, promised to do the same to the shorter-range plasma weapons. Another decade might see plasma all phased out.

The up-and-coming weapon for ship-to-ship fighting in the last couple of years seemed to be the gravitic imploder lance, a modification of tractor-beam technology; variously-designed artificial-gravity shields were still lagging behind in protection from it. The imploder beam made ugly twisty wreckage where it hit mass. What it did to a human body was a horror.

But the energy-sucking imploder lance's range was insanely short, in terms of space speeds and distances, barely a dozen kilometers. Now, ships had to cooperate to grapple, to slow and close up and manuever. Given also the small scale of wormhole volumes, fighting looked like it might suddenly become tight and intimate once again, except that too-tight formations invited "sun wall" attacks of massed nuclears. Round and round. It was hinted that ramming and boarding could actually become practical popular tactics once again. Till the next surprise arrived from the devil's workshops, anyway. Miles longed briefly for the good old days of his grandfather's generation, when people could kill each other from a clean fifty thousand kilometers. Just bright sparks.

The effect of the new imploders on concentration of firepower promised to be curious, especially where a wormhole was involved. It was now possible that a small force in a small area could apply as much power per cubic whatever as a large force, which could not squeeze its largeness down to the effective range; although the difference in reserves still held good, of course. A large force willing to make sacrifices could keep beating away till sheer numbers overcame the smaller concentration. The Cetagandan ghem-lords were not allergic to sacrifice, though generally preferring to start with subordinates, or better still, allies. Miles rubbed his knotted neck muscles.

The cabin buzzer blatted; Miles reached across the comconsole desk to key the door open.

A lean, dark-haired man in his early thirties wearing mercenary grey-and-whites with tech insignia stood uncertainly in the aperture. "My lord?" he said in a soft voice.

Baz Jesek, Fleet Engineering Officer. Once, Barrayaran Imperial Service deserter on the run; subsequently liege-sworn as a private Armsman to Miles in his identity as Lord Vorkosigan. And finally, husband to the woman Miles loved. Once loved. Still loved. Baz. Damn. Miles cleared his throat uncomfortably. "Come in, Commodore Jesek."

Baz trod soundlessly across the deck matting, looking defensive and guilty. "I just got in off the repairs tender, and heard the word that you were back." His Barrayaran accent was polished thin and smooth by his years of galactic exile, significantly less pronounced than four years ago.

"Temporarily, anyway."

"I'm . . . sorry you didn't find things as you'd left them, my lord. I feel like I've squandered Elena's dowry that you bestowed. I didn't realize the implications of Oser's economic maneuvers until . . . well . . . no excuses."

"The man finessed Tung, too," Miles pointed out. He cringed inwardly, to hear Baz apologize to him. "I gather it wasn't exactly a fair fight."

"It wasn't a fight at all, my lord," Baz said slowly. "That was the problem." Baz stood to parade rest. "I've come to offer you my resignation, my lord."

"Offer rejected," said Miles promptly. "In the first place, liege-sworn Armsmen can't resign, in the second place, where am I going to get a competent fleet engineer on," he glanced at his chrono, "two hour's notice, and in the third place, in the third place . . . I need a witness to clear my name if things go wrong. Wronger. You've got to fill me in on Fleet equipment capabilities, then help get it all in motion. And I've got to fill you in on what's really going on. You're the only one besides Elena I can trust with the secret half of this."

With difficulty, Miles persuaded the hesitant engineer to sit down. Miles poured out a speed-edited precis of his adventures in the Hegen Hub, leaving out only mention of Gregor's half-hearted suicide attempt; that was Gregor's private shame. Miles was not altogether surprised to learn Elena had not confided his earlier, brief and ignominious return, rescue, and departure from the Dendarii; Baz seemed to think the presence of the incognito Emperor obvious and sufficient reason for her silence. By the time Miles finished, Baz's inner guilt was quite thoroughly displaced by outer alarm.

"If the Emperor is killed—if he doesn't return— the mess at home could go on for years," Baz said. "Maybe you should let Cavilo rescue him, rather than risk—"

"Up to a point, that's just what I intend to do," said Miles. "If only I knew Gregor's *mind*." He paused. "If we lose both Gregor and the wormhole battle, the Cetagandans will arrive on our doorstep just at the point we will be in maximum internal disarray. What a temptation to them—what a lure— they've always wanted Komarr—we could be looking down the throat of the second Cetagandan invasion, almost as much a surprise to them as to us. They may prefer deep-laid plans, but they're not above a little opportunism—not an opportunity this overwhelming—"

Determinedly, driven by this vision, they turned to the tech specs, Miles reminding himself about the ancient saying about the want of a nail. They had nearly completed an overview when the comm officer on duty paged Miles through his comconsole.

"Admiral Naismith, sir?" The comm officer stared with interest at Miles's face, then went on, "There's a man in the docking bay who wants to see you. He claims to have important information."

Miles bethought himself of the theorized backup assassin. "What's his ID?"

"He says to tell you his name's Ungari. That's all he'll say."

Miles caught his breath. The cavalry at last! Or a clever ploy to gain admittance. "Can you give me a look at him, without letting him know he's being scanned?"

"Right, sir." The comm officer's face was replaced on the vid by a view of the *Triumph*'s docking bay. The vid zoomed down to focus on a pair of men in Aslunder tech coveralls. Miles melted with relief. Captain Ungari. And blessed Sergeant Overholt.

"Thank you, comm officer. Have a squad escort the two men to my cabin." He glanced at Baz. "In, uh, about ten minutes." He keyed off and explained, "It's my ImpSec boss. Thank God! But—I'm not sure I'd be able to explain to him the peculiar status of your desertion charges. I mean, he's ImpSec, not Service Security, and I don't imagine your old arrest order is exactly at the top of his list of concerns right now, but it might be . . . simpler, if you avoid him, eh?"

"Mm." Baz grimaced in agreement. "I believe I have duties to attend to?"

"No lie. Baz . . ." for a wild moment he longed to tell Baz to take Elena and run, safe away from the coming danger, "It's going to get real crazy soon."

"With Mad Miles back in charge, how could it be otherwise?" Baz shrugged, smiling. He started for the door.

"I'm not as crazy as Tung—Good God, nobody calls me that, do they?"

"Ah—it's an old joke. Only among a few old Dendarii." Baz's step quickened.

And there are very few old Dendarii. That, unfortunately, was not a funny joke. The door hissed closed behind the engineer.

Ungari. Ungari. Somebody in charge at last. *If only I had Gregor with me, I could be done right now. But at least I can find out what Our Side has been up to all this time.* Exhausted, he laid his head down on his arms on Oser's comconsole desk, and smiled. Help. Finally.

Some wriggling dream was fogging his mind; he snatched himself back from too-long-delayed sleep as the cabin buzzer blatted again. He rubbed his numb face and hit the lock control on the desk. "Enter." He glanced at the chrono; he'd lost only four minutes, on that downward slide of consciousness. It was definitely time for a break.

Chodak and two Dendarii guards escorted Captain Ungari and Sergeant Overholt into the room. Ungari and Overholt were both dressed in tan Aslunder supervisor's coveralls, no doubt with IDs and passes to match. Miles smiled happily at them.

"Sergeant Chodak, you and your men wait outside." Chodak looked sadly disappointed at this exclusion. "And if she's finished with her current task, ask Commander Elena Bothari-Jesek to attend on us here. Thanks."

Ungari waited impatiently till the door had hissed closed behind Chodak to stride forward. Miles stood up and saluted him smartly. "Glad to see y—"

To Miles's surprise, Ungari did not return the salute; instead his hands clenched on Miles's uniform jacket and lifted. Miles sensed that it was only with the greatest restraint that Ungari's grip had closed on his lapels and not his neck. "Vorkosigan, you idiot! What the hell kind of game have you been up to?"

"I found Gregor, sir. I—" don't say *lost him.* "I'm mounting an expedition to recover him right now. I'm so glad you made contact with me, another hour and you'd have missed the boat. If we pool our information and resources—"

Ungari's clutch did not loosen, nor did his peeled-back lips relax. "We know you found the Emperor, we traced you both here from Consortium Detention. Then you both vanished utterly."

"Didn't you ask Elena? I thought you would—look sir, sit down, please," *and put me down, dammit*— Ungari seemed not to notice that Miles's toes were stretched to the floor, "and tell me what all this looked like from your point of view. It's very important."

Ungari, breathing heavily, released Miles and sat in the indicated station chair, or at least on its edge. At a hand signal, Overholt took up a pose of parade rest at his shoulder. Miles gazed with some relief at Overholt, whom he'd last seen face-down unconscious on the Consortium Station concourse; the sergeant appeared fully recovered, if tired and strained.

Ungari said, "When he finally woke up, Sergeant Overholt followed you to Consortium Detention, but by then you'd disappeared. He thought *they'd* done it, they thought *he'd* done it. He spent bribe-money like water, finally got the story from the contract-slave you'd beaten up—a day later, when the man could finally talk—"

"He lived, then," said Miles. "Good, Gre—we were worried about that."

"Yes, but Overholt didn't recognize the emperor at first, in the contract-slave records—the sergeant hadn't been on the need-to-know list about his disappearance."

A faint irate look passed over the sergeant's face, as if in memory of great injustices.

"—it wasn't until he'd made contact with me here, we dead-ended, and we retraced all the steps in hopes of finding some clue about you we'd overlooked, that I identified the missing contract-slave as Emperor Gregor. *Days* lost."

"I was sure you'd make contact with Elena Bothari-Jesek, sir. She knew where we'd gone. You knew she was my sworn liegewoman, it's in my files."

Ungari shot him a flat-lipped glare, but did not otherwise offer explanation for this gaffe. "When the first wave of Barrayaran agents hit the Hub, we finally had enough reinforcements to mount a serious search—"

"Good! So they know Gregor's in the Hub, back home. I was afraid Illyan would still be squandering all his resources on Komarr, or worse, towards Escobar."

Ungari's fingers clenched again. "Vorkosigan, *what did you do with the emperor?*"

"He's safe, but in great danger." Miles thought that one over a second. "That is, he's all right for the moment, I think, but that will change with the tactical—"

"We know *where* he is, he was spotted three days ago by an agent in Randall's Rangers."

"Must have been just after I left," Miles calculated. "Not that he could have spotted me, I was in the brig—what are we doing about it?"

"Rescue forces are being scrambled; I don't know how large a fleet."

"What about permission to cross Pol?"

"I doubt they'll wait for it."

"We've got to alert them, not to offend Pol! The—"

"Ensign, Vervain holds the emperor!" Ungari snarled in exasperation. "I'm not going to tell the—"

"Vervain doesn't hold Gregor, Commander Cavilo does," Miles interrupted urgently. "It's strictly nonpolitical, a plot for her personal gain. I think—in fact, I'm dead certain—the Vervani government doesn't know the first thing about her 'guest'. Our rescue forces must be warned to commit no hostile act until the Cetagandan invasion shows up."

"*The what?*"

Miles faltered, and said in a smaller voice, "You mean you don't know anything about the Cetagandan invasion?" He paused. "Well, just because you don't have the word yet, doesn't mean Illyan hasn't figured it out. Even if we haven't spotted where they're massing, inside the Empire, as soon as ImpSec adds up how many Cetagandan warships have disappeared from their home bases, they'll realize something must be up. Somebody must still be keeping track of such things, even in the current flap over Gregor." Ungari was still sitting there looking stunned, so Miles kept explaining. "I expect a Cetagandan force to invade Vervani local space and continue on to secure the Hegen Hub, with Commander Cavilo's connivance. Very shortly. I plan to take the Dendarii fleet across-system and fight them at the Vervani wormhole, hold it till Gregor's rescue fleet arrives. I hope they're sending more than a diplomatic negotiation team. . . . By the way, do you still have that blank mercenary contract credit chit Illyan gave you? I need it."

"You, mister," Ungari began when he had mastered his voice again, "are going *nowhere* but to our safe-house on Aslund Station. Where you will wait quietly—very quietly—until Illyan's reinforcements arrive to take you *off my hands*."

Miles politely ignored this impractical outburst. "You have to have been collecting data for your report to Illyan. Got anything I can use?"

"I have a complete report on Aslund Station, its naval and mercenary dispositions and strengths, but—"

"*I* have all that, now." Miles tapped his fingers impatiently on Oser's comconsole. "Damn. I wish you'd spent the last two weeks on Vervain Station instead."

Ungari gritted, "Vorkosigan, you will stand up now, and come with Sergeant Overholt and me. Or so help me I will have Overholt carry you bodily."

Overholt was eyeing him with cool calculation, Miles realized. "That could be a serious mistake, sir. Worse than your failure to contact Elena. If you will just let me explain the over-all strategic situation—"

Goaded beyond endurance, Ungari snapped, "Overholt, grab him."

Miles hit the alarm on his comconsole desk as Overholt swooped down on him. He dodged around his station chair, knocking it loose from its clamps, as Overholt missed his first grab. The cabin door hissed open. Chodak and his two guards pelted through, followed by Elena. Overholt, chasing Miles around the end of the comconsole desk, skidded straight into Chodak's stunner fire. Overholt dropped with a massive thud; Miles winced. Ungari lurched to his feet and stopped, bracketed by the aim of four Dendarii stunners. Miles felt like bursting into tears, or possibly cackles. Neither would be useful. He got control of his breath and voice.

"Sergeant Chodak, take these two men to the *Triumph*'s brig. Put them . . . put them next to Metzov and Oser, I guess."

"Yes, Admiral."

Ungari went bravely silent, as befit a captured spy, and suffered himself to be led out, though the veins in his neck pulsed with suppressed fury as he glared back at Miles.

And I can't even fast-penta him, Miles thought mournfully. An agent on Ungari's level was certain to have been implanted with an induced allergic reaction to fast-penta; not euphoria, but anaphylactic shock and death, would result from such a dose. In a moment two more Dendarii appeared with a float pallet and removed the inert Overholt.

As the door closed behind them, Elena asked, "All right, what was all that about?"

Miles sighed deeply. "That, unfortunately, was my ImpSec superior, Captain Ungari. He was not in a listening mood."

Elena's eye lit with a skewed enthusiasm. "Dear God, Miles. Metzov—Oser—Ungari—all in a row— you sure are hard on your commanding officers. What are you going to do when the time comes to let them all out?"

Miles shook his head mutely. "I don't know."

The fleet disengaged from Aslund Station within the hour, maintaining strict comm silence; the Aslunders, naturally, were thrown into a panic. Miles sat in the *Triumph*'s comm center and monitored their frantic queries, resolved not to interfere with the natural course of events unless the Aslunders opened fire. Until he again laid hands on Gregor, he must at all costs present the correct profile to Cavilo. Let her think she was getting what she wanted, or at least what she'd asked for.

In fact, the natural course of events promised to deliver more of the results Miles wanted than he could have gained through planning and persuasion. The Aslunders had three main theories, Miles deduced from their comm chatter; the mercenaries were flee-ing from the Hub altogether at secret word of some impending attack, the mercenaries were off to join one or more of Aslund's enemies, or worst of all, the mercenaries were opening an unprovoked attack on said enemies, with subsequent retribution to recoil on the Aslunder's heads. Aslunder forces went to maximum alert status. Reinforcements were called for, mobile forces shifted into the Hub, reserves brought on-line as the sudden departure of their faithless mercenaries stripped them of assumed defenses.

Miles breathed relief as the last of the Dendarii fleet cleared the Aslunders' region and headed into open space. Delayed by the confusion, no Aslunder naval pursuit force could catch them now till they decelerated near the Vervain wormhole. Where, with the arrival of the Cetagandans, it should not be hard to persuade the Aslunders to reclassify themselves as Dendarii reserves.

Timing was, if not everything, a lot. Suppose Cavilo hadn't already transmitted her go-code to the Cetagandans. The sudden movement of the Dendarii fleet might well spook her into aborting the plot. Fine, Miles decided. In that case he would have stopped the Cetagandan invasion without a shot being fired. A perfect war of maneuver, by Admiral Aral Vorkosigan's own definition. *Of course, I'll have political egg on my face and a lynch mob after me from three sides, but Dad will understand. I hope.* That would leave staying alive and rescuing Gregor as his only tactical goals, which in present contrast seemed absurdly, delightfully simple. Unless, of course, Gregor didn't want to be rescued. . . .

Further, finer branches of the strategy-tree must await events, Miles decided blearily. He staggered off to Oser's cabin to fall into bed and sleep for twelve solid, sodden hours.

The *Triumph's* comm officer woke Miles, paging him on the vid. Miles, in his underwear, padded across to the comconsole and slung himself into the station chair. "Yes?"

"You asked to be apprised of messages from Vervain Station, sir."

"Yes, thank you." Miles rubbed amber grains of sleep from his eyes, and checked the time. Twelve hours flight-time left till their arrival at target. "Any signs of abnormal activity levels at Vervain Station or their wormhole yet?"

"Not yet, sir."

"All right. Continue to monitor, record, and track any outbound traffic. What's the transmission time lag from us to them at present?"

"Thirty-six minutes, sir."

"Mm. Very well. Pipe the message down here." Yawning, he leaned his elbows on Oser's comconsole and studied the vid. A high-ranking Vervani officer appeared over the plate, and demanded explanation for the Oseran/Dendarii Fleet's movements. He sounded a lot like the Aslunders. No sign of Cavilo. Miles keyed the comm officer. "Transmit back that their important message was hopelessly garbled by static and a malfunction in our de-scrambler. Urgently request a repeat, with amplification."

"Yes, sir."

In the ensuing seventy minutes Miles took a leisurely shower, dressed in a properly fitting uniform (and boots) that had been provided while he slept, and ate a balanced breakfast. He strolled into the *Triumph*'s Nav and Com just in time for the second transmission. This time, Commander Cavilo stood, arms crossed, at the Vervani officer's shoulder. The Vervani repeated himself, literally with amplification, his voice was louder and sharper this time around. Cavilo added, "Explain yourselves at once, or we will regard you as a hostile force and respond accordingly."

That was the amplification he'd wanted. Miles settled himself in the comm station chair and adjusted his Dendarii uniform as neatly as possible. He made sure the admiral's rank insignia was clearly visible in the vid. "Ready to transmit," he nodded to the comm officer. He smoothed his features into as straight-faced and dead-serious an expression as he could manage.

"Admiral Miles Naismith, Commanding, Dendarii Free Mercenary Fleet, speaking. To Commander Cavilo, Randall's Rangers, eyes only. Ma'am. I have accomplished my mission precisely as you ordered. I remind you of the reward you promised me for my success. What are your next instructions? Naismith out."

The comm officer logged the recording into the tight-beam scrambler. "Sir," she said uncertainly, "if that's for Commander Cavilo's eyes only, should we be sending it on the Vervain command channel? The Vervani will have to de-process it before sending it on. It will be seen by a lot of eyes besides hers."

"Just so, Lieutenant," said Miles. "Go ahead and transmit."

"Oh. And when—if—they respond, what do you want me to do?"

Miles checked his chrono. "By the time of their next response, our line of travel should take us behind the twin suns' interference corona. We should be out of communications for a good, oh, three hours."

"I can boost the gain, sir, and cut through—"

"No, no, Lieutenant. The interference is going to be something terrible. In fact, if you can stretch that to four hours, so much the better. But make it look real. Until we're in range for a tight-beam conference between myself and Cavilo in near-real-time, I want you to think of yourself as a non-communications officer."

"Yes, sir," she grinned. "Now I understand."

"Carry on. Remember, I want maximum inefficiency, incompetence, and error. On the Vervani channels, that is. You've worked with trainees, surely. Be creative."

"Yes, *sir*."

Miles went off to find Tung.

He and Tung were deeply engrossed in the tactical computer display in the *Triumph*'s tactics room, running projected wormhole scenarios, when the comm officer paged again.

"Changes at Vervain Station, sir. All outgoing commercial ship traffic has been halted. Incoming are being denied permission to dock. Encoded transmissions on all military channels have just about tripled. And four large warships just jumped."

"Into the Hub, or out to Vervain?"

"Out to Vervain, sir."

Tung leaned forward. "Dump data into the tactics display as you confirm it, Lieutenant."

"Yes, sir."

"Thank you," said Miles. "Continue to keep us advised. And monitor civilian clear-code messages, too, any you can pick up. I want to keep tabs on the rumors as they start to fly."

"Right, sir. Out."

Tung keyed up what was laughingly called the "real-time" tactics display, a colorful schematic, as the comm officer shunted the new data. He studied the identity of the four departing warships. "It's starting," he said grimly. "You called it."

"You don't think it's something we're causing?"

"Not those four ships. They wouldn't have moved off-station if they weren't badly wanted elsewhere. Better get your ass over to—that is, transfer your flag to the *Ariel*, son."

Miles rubbed his lips nervously, and eyed what he'd mentally dubbed his "Little Fleet" in the schematic display in the *Ariel*'s tactics room. The equipment was now displaying the *Ariel* itself plus the two next-fastest ships in the Dendarii forces. His own personal attack-group; fast, maneuverable, amenable to violent course-changes, requiring less turning-room than any other possible combination. Admittedly, they were low in firepower. But if things went as Miles projected, firing was not going to be a desirable option anyway.

The *Ariel*'s tac room was manned now by a mere skeleton crew; Miles, Elena as his personal communications officer, Arde Mayhew for all other systems. Inner Circle all, in anticipation of this next most-private conversation. If it came to actual combat, he'd turn the chamber over to Thorne, presently exiled to Nav and Com. And then, perhaps, retire to his cabin and slit his belly open.

"Let's see Vervain Station now," he told Elena in

her comm station chair. The main holovid display in the center of the room whirled dizzyingly at her touch on the controls. The schematic representation of their target area seemed to boil with shifting lines and colors, representing ship movements, power shunts to various weapons systems and shieldings, and communications transmissions. The Dendarii were now barely a million kilometers out, a little more than three light-seconds. The rate of closure was slowing as the Little Fleet, fully two hours ahead of the slower ships of the main Dendarii fleet, decelerated.

"They're sure stirred up now," Elena commented. Her hand went to her ear-bug. "They're reiterating their demands that we communicate."

"But still not launching a counter-attack," Miles observed, studying the schematic. "I'm glad they realize where the true danger lies. All right. Tell them that we've got our comm problems straightened out—finally—but say again that I will speak first only to Commander Cavilo."

"They—ah—I think they're finally putting her through. I've got a tight-beam coming in on the dedicated channel."

"Trace it." Miles hung over her shoulder as she coaxed this information from the comm net.

"The source is moving. . . ."

Miles closed his eyes in prayer, snapped them open again at Elena's triumphant, "Got it! There. That little ship."

"Give me its course and energy profile. Is she heading toward the wormhole?"

"No, away."

"Ha!"

"It's a fast ship—small—it's a *Falcon*-class courier," Elena reported. "If her goal is Pol—and Barrayar—she must intersect our triangle."

Miles exhaled. "Right. Right. She waited to speak on a line her Vervani bosses couldn't monitor. I thought she might. Wonder what lies she's told them? She's past the point of no return, does she know it?" He opened his arms to the new short vector line in the schematic. "Come, love. Come to me."

Elena raised her brow sardonically at him. "Coming through. Your sweetheart is about to appear on Monitor Three."

Miles swung into the indicated Station chair, settling himself before the holovid plate, which began to sparkle. Now was the time to muster every bit of self-control he'd ever owned. He smoothed his face to an expression of cool ironic interest, as Cavilo's fine features formed before him. Out of range of the vid pick-up, he rubbed his sweating palms on his trouser knees.

Cavilo's blue eyes were alight with triumph, constrained by her tight mouth and tense brows as if in echo of Miles's ships constraining her flight-path. "Lord Vorkosigan. What are you doing here?"

"Following your orders, ma'am. You told me to go get the Dendarii. And I've transmitted nothing to Barrayar."

A six-second time-lag, as the tight-beam flew from ship to ship and returned her answer. Alas that it gave her as much time to think as it did him.

"I didn't order you to cross the Hub."

Miles wrinkled his brow in puzzlement. "But where else would you need my fleet except at the point of action? I'm not dense."

Cavilo's pause this time was longer than accounted for by the transmission lag. "You mean you didn't get Metzov's message?" she asked.

Damn near. What a fabulous array of double meanings there. "Why, did you send him as a courier?"

Lag. "Yes!"

A palpable lie for a palpable lie. "I never saw him. Maybe he deserted. He must have realized he'd lost your love to another. Perhaps he's holed up in some spaceport bar right now, drowning his sorrows." Miles sighed deeply at this sad scenario.

Cavilo's concerned attentive expression melted to rage when this one arrived. "Idiot! I know you took him prisoner!"

"Yes, and I've been wondering ever since why you allowed that to happen. If that accident was undesired, you should have taken precautions against it."

Cavilo's eyes narrowed; she shifted her ground. "I feared Stanis's emotions made him unreliable. I wanted to give him one more chance to prove himself. I gave my backup man orders to kill him if he tried to kill you, but when Metzov missed, the dolt waited."

Substitute *as soon as/succeeded* for that *if/tried*, and the statement was probably near-truth. Miles wished he had a recording of that Ranger agent's field report, and Cavilo's blistering reply. "There, you see? You *do* want subordinates who can think for themselves. Like me."

Cavilo's head jerked back. "You, for a subordinate? I'd sooner sleep with a snake!"

Interesting image, that. "You'd better get used to me. You're seeking entry into a world strange to you, familiar to me. The Vorkosigans are an integral part of Barrayar's power-class. You could use a native guide."

Lag. "Exactly. I'm trying—I must—get your emperor to safety. You're blocking his flight path. Out of my way!"

Miles spared a glance for the tactics display. Yes, just so. *Good, come to me.* "Commander Cavilo, I feel certain you are missing an important datum in your calculations about me."

Lag. "Let me clarify my position, little Barrayaran. I hold your emperor. I control him absolutely."

"Fine, let me hear those orders from him, then."

Lag . . . fractionally briefer, yes. "I can have his throat cut before your eyes. Let me pass!"

"Go ahead," Miles shrugged. "It'll make an awful mess on your deck, though."

She grinned sourly, after the lag. "You bluff badly."

"I bluff not at all. Gregor is far more valuable alive to you than to me. You can do nothing, where you're going, except through him. He's your meal ticket. But has anyone mentioned to you yet that if Gregor dies, I could become the next emperor of Barrayar?" Well, arguably, but this was hardly time to go into the finer details of the six competing Barrayaran succession theories.

Cavilo's face froze. "He said . . . he had no heir. You said so too."

"None *named*. Because my father refuses to be named, not because he lacks the bloodlines. But ignoring the bloodlines doesn't erase them. And I am my father's only child. And he can't live forever. Ergo . . . So, resist my boarding parties, by all means. Threaten away. Carry out your threats. Give me the Imperium. I shall thank you prettily, before I have you summarily executed. Emperor Miles the First. How does it sound? As good as Empress Cavilo?" Miles gave it an intense beat, "*Or*, we could work together. The Vorkosigans have traditionally felt that the substance was better than the name. The power behind the throne, as my father before me—who has held just that power, as Gregor has doubtless told you, for far too long—you're not going to dislodge *him* by batting your eyelashes. He's immune to women. But I know his every weakness. I've thought it through. This could be my big chance, one way or another. By the way—milady— do you care which emperor you wed?"

The time lag allowed him to fully savor her changes of expression, as his plausible calumnies thudded home. Alarm; revulsion; finally, reluctant respect.

"I underestimated you, it seems. Very well . . . Your ships may escort us to safety. Where—clearly— we must confer further."

"I will *transport* you to safety, aboard the *Ariel*. Where we will confer immediately."

Cavilo straightened, nostrils flaring. "No way."

"All right, let's compromise. I will abide by Gregor's orders, and Gregor's orders only. As I said, milady, you'd better get used to this. No Barrayaran will take orders from you directly at first, till you've established yourself. If that's the game you're choosing to play, you'd better start practicing. It only gets more complicated after this. Or, you can choose to resist, in which case I get it all." *Play for time, Cavilo! Bite!*

"I'll get Gregor." The vid went to the grey haze of a holding-signal.

Miles flung himself back in his station chair, rubbed his neck and rolled his head, trying to relieve his screaming nerves. He was shaking. Mayhew was staring at him in alarm.

"Damn," said Elena in a hushed voice. "If I didn't know you, I'd think you were Mad Yuri's understudy. The look on your face . . . am I reading too much into all that innuendo, or did you in fact just connive to assassinate Gregor in one breath, offer to cuckold him in the next, accuse your father of homosexuality, suggest a patricidal plot against him, and league yourself with Cavilo—what are you going to do for an encore?"

"Depends on the straight lines. I can hardly wait to find out," Miles panted. "Was I convincing?"

"You were *scary*."

"Good." He wiped his palms on his trousers again. "It's mind-to-mind, between Cavilo and me, before it ever becomes ship-to-ship . . . She's a compulsive plotter. If I can smoke her, wind her in with words, with what-ifs, with all the bifurcations of her strategy-tree, just long enough to get her eye off the one real *now* . . ."

"Signal," Elena warned.

Miles straightened, waited. The next face to form over the vid plate was Gregor's. Gregor, alive and well. Gregor's eyes widened, then his face went very still.

Cavilo hovered behind his shoulder, just slightly out of focus. "Tell him what we want, love."

Miles bowed sitting down, as profoundly as physically possible. "Sire. I present you with the Emperor's Own Dendarii Free Mercenary Fleet. Do with us as You will."

Gregor glanced aside, evidently at some tactical readout analogous to the *Ariel's* own. "By God, you've even got them *with* you. Miles, you are supernatural." The flash of humor was instantly muffled in sere formality. "Thank you, Lord Vorkosigan. I accept your vassal-offering of troops."

"If you would care to step aboard the *Ariel*, sire, you can take personal command of your forces."

Cavilo leaned forward, interrupting. "And *now* his treachery is made plain. Let me play a portion of his last words for you, Greg." Cavilo reached past Gregor to touch a control, and Miles was treated to an instant replay of his breathless sedition, beginning with—naturally—the flim-flam about the named heir, and ending with his offer of himself as a substitute Imperial groom. Very nicely selected, clearly unedited.

Gregor listened with his head in a thoughtful tilt, his face perfectly controlled, as the Miles-image stammered to its damning conclusion. "But does this surprise you, Cavie?" asked Gregor in an innocent tone, taking her hand and looking over his shoulder at her. From the expression on her face, *something* was surprising her. "Lord Vorkosigan's mutations have driven him mad, everyone knows that! He's been sulking around muttering like that for years. Of course, I trust him no further than I can throw him—"

Thanks, Gregor. I'll remember that line.

"—but as long as he feels he can further his interests by furthering ours, he'll be a valuable ally. House Vorkosigan has always been powerful in Barrayaran affairs. His grandfather Count Piotr put my grandfather Emperor Ezar on the throne. They'd make an equally powerful enemy. I should prefer us to rule Barrayar with their cooperation."

"Their extermination would do as well, surely," Cavilo glared at Miles.

"Time is on our side, love. His father is an old man. He, is a mutant. His bloodline-threat is empty, Barrayar would never accept a mutant as emperor, as Count Aral well knows and as even Miles realizes in his saner moments. But he can trouble us, if he chooses. An interesting balance of power, eh, Lord Vorkosigan?"

Miles bowed again. "I think much on it." *So have you, apparently.* He spared a quelling glance at Elena, who had fallen off her station chair somewhere around Gregor's word-picture of Miles's mad soliloquies, aside at state banquets no doubt, and was now sitting on the floor with her sleeve jammed in her mouth to muffle the shrieks of laughter. Her eyes blazed, over the grey cloth. She got control of her stifled giggles and scrambled back into her seat. *Close your mouth, Arde.*

"Then, Cavie, let's join my would-be Grand Vizier. At that point, I will control his ships. And your wish," he turned his head to kiss her hand, still resting in his grasp on his shoulder, "will be my command."

"Do you really think it's safe? If he's as psycho as you say."

"Brilliant—nervous—skittish—but he's all right as long as his medications are adjusted properly, I promise you. I expect his dose is a little off at the moment, due to our irregular travels."

The transmission time-lag was much reduced, now. "Twenty minutes to rendezvous, sir," Elena reported, off-sides.

"Will you transfer in your shuttle, or ours, sire?" Miles inquired politely.

Gregor shrugged carelessly. "Commander Cavilo's choice."

"Ours," said Cavilo immediately.

"I will be waiting." *And ready*.

Cavilo broke transmission.

CHAPTER SIXTEEN

Miles watched through the vid link as the first
space-armored Ranger stepped into the *Ariel*'s shuttle hatch corridor. The wary point-man was followed
immediately by four more, who scanned the empty
passageway, converted into a chamber by the closed
blast doors sealing each end. No enemies, no targets,
not even automatic weapons threatened them. An
utterly deserted chamber. Bewildered, the Rangers
took up a defensive stance around the shuttle hatch.

Gregor stepped through. Miles was unsurprised to
see that Cavilo had not provided the Emperor with
space armor. Gregor wore a neatly-pressed set of
Ranger fatigues, minus insignia; his only protection
was his boots. Even they would be quite inadequate,
if one of those heavy-armored monsters stepped on
his toe. Battle armor was lovely stuff, proof against
stunners and nerve disruptors, most poisons and biologicals; resistant (to a degree) to plasma fire and
radioactivity, stuffed with clever built-in weaponry,
tac comps, and telemetry. Very suitable for a boarding expedition. Though in fact, Miles had once captured the *Ariel* himself with fewer personnel, less
formidably armed and totally unarmored. He'd had
surprise on his side, then.

Cavilo came through behind Gregor. She wore
space armor, though for the moment she carried her
helmet tucked under her arm like a decapitated
head. She stared around the empty corridor, and

frowned. "All right, what's the trick?" she demanded loudly.

To answer your question. . . . Miles pressed the button on the remote-control box in his hand.

A muffled explosion made the corridor reverberate. The flex-tube tore violently away from the shuttle hatch. The automatic doors, sensing the pressure drop, clapped shut instantly. A bare breath of air escaped. Good system. Miles had made the techs make sure it was working properly, before they'd inserted the directional mines in the shuttle clamps. He checked his monitors. Cavilo's combat shuttle was tumbling away from the side of the *Ariel* now, thrusters and sensors damaged in the same blast that propelled it outward, its weapons and reserve Rangers useless until the no-doubt-frantic pilot regained attitude control. If he could.

"Keep an eye on him, Bel, I don't want him coming back to haunt us," Miles spoke into his comm link to Thorne, on deck in the *Ariel's* tactics room.

"I can blow him up now, if you like."

"Wait a little. We're a long way from sorted out, down here." *God help us now.*

Cavilo was snapping her helmet on, her startled troops in defensive formation around her. All dressed up, and nothing to shoot. Let them settle down for just a moment, enough to prevent spinal-reflexive fusilades, but not enough to think. . . .

Miles glanced around at his own space-armored troops, six in number, and closed his own helmet. Not that numbers mattered. A million troops with nuclears, one guy with a club; either would suffice when the target was one unarmed hostage. Miniaturizing the situation, Miles realized sadly, had made no qualitative difference. He could still screw up just as big. The main difference was his plasma cannon, sighted down the corridor. He nodded to Elena, manning the big weapon. Not normally an indoor toy, it would stop charging space armor. And blow out the hull beyond. Miles figured that, theoretically, they could blow away, oh, one out of Cavilo's five at this range, if they came on at a dead run, before all became hand-to-hand, or glove-to-glove.

"Here we go," Miles warned through his command channel. "Remember the drill." He pressed another control; the blast doors between his group and Cavilo's began to draw back. Slowly, not suddenly, at a rate carefully calculated to inspire dread without startling.

Full broadcast on all channels plus loudspeaker. It was absolutely essential to Miles's plan that he get in the first word.

"Cavilo!" he shouted. "Deactivate your weapons and freeze, or I'll blow Gregor to atoms!"

Body language was a wonderful thing. It was amazing, how much expression could come through the blank shining surface of space armor. The littlest armored figure stood openhanded, stunned. Bereft of words; bereft, for precious seconds, of reactions. Because, of course, Miles had just stolen her opening line. *Now what do you have to say for yourself, love?* It was a desperate ploy. Miles had judged the hostage-problem logically insoluable; therefore, clearly the only thing to do was make it Cavilo's problem instead of his own.

Well, he'd obtained as much as the *freeze* part, anyway. But he dared not let the standoff stand. "Drop it, Cavilo! It only takes one nervous twitch to convert you from Imperial fiancee to no one of importance at all. And then to no one at all. And you're making me *real tense.*"

"You said he was safe," Cavilo hissed to Gregor.

"His meds must be further off-dose than I thought," Gregor replied, looking anxious. "No, watch—he's bluffing. I'll prove it."

Hands held out open to his sides, Gregor walked straight toward the plasma cannon. Miles's jaw fell open, behind his faceplate. *Gregor, Gregor, Gregor . . . !*

Gregor gazed steadily into Elena's faceplate. His step never quickened or faltered. He stopped only when his chest touched the beaded tip of the cannon. It was an enormously dramatic and arresting moment. Miles was so lost in appreciation, it took him that long to move his finger an imperceptible few centimeters and hit the button on his control box that closed the blast doors.

The shield hadn't been programmed for slow-closure; it banged shut faster than the eye could follow. Brief noises, from the other side, of plasma fire, shouts; Cavilo screaming at one of her men just in time to stop him from the fatal error of firing a mine at the wall of a closed chamber he himself occupied. Then silence.

Miles dropped his plasma rifle, tore off his helmet. "God almighty, I wasn't expecting *that*. Gregor, you're a genius."

Gently, Gregor raised a finger and moved the tip of the plasma cannon aside.

"Don't worry," said Miles. "None of our weapons are charged. I didn't want to risk any accidents."

"I was almost certain that was the case," Gregor murmured. He stared back over his shoulder at the blast doors. "What would you have done if I'd been asleep on my feet?"

"Kept talking. Tried for various compromises. I had a trick or two yet . . . behind the other blast door, there's a squad with live weapons. In the end, if she didn't bite, I was prepared to surrender."

"That's what I was afraid of."

Some peculiar muffled noises penetrated the blast doors.

"Elena, take over," said Miles. "Mop up. Take Cavilo alive if possible, but I don't want any Dendarii to die trying. Take no chances, trust nothing she says."

"I have the picture." Elena waved a salute, and motioned to her squad, which broke up to insert weapons-charges. Elena began to confer over the command-channel headset with the leader of the twin squad waiting on Cavilo's other side and with the commander of the *Ariel's* combat shuttle, closing in from space.

Miles motioned Gregor along the corridor, removing him as swiftly as possible from the region of potential messiness. "To the tactics room, and I'll fill you in. You have some decisions to make."

They entered a lift-tube, and rose. Miles breathed easier with every meter he increased the range between Gregor and Cavilo.

"My biggest worry," Miles said, "till we spoke face-to-face, was that Cavilo really had done what she thought she had, fogged your mind. I didn't see where she could be getting her ideas except from you. Wasn't sure what I could do in that case, except play along till I could hand you over to higher experts on Barrayar. If I survived. I didn't know how fast you'd see through her."

"Oh, at once," shrugged Gregor. "She had the same hungry smile Vordrozda used to get. And a dozen lesser cannibals, since. I can smell a power-hungry flatterer at a thousand meters, now."

"I yield to my master in strategy," Miles's armored hand made a genuflecting motion. "Do you know you rescued yourself? She'd have taken you all the way home, even if I hadn't come along."

"It was easy." Gregor frowned. "All that was required was that I have no personal honor at all." Gregor's eyes, Miles realized, were deathly, devoid of triumph.

"You can't cheat an honest man," said Miles uncertainly. "Or woman. What would you have done, if she'd got you home?"

"Depends." Gregor stared into the middle distance. "If she'd managed to get you killed, I suppose

I'd have had her executed." Gregor glanced back, as they stepped out of the tube. "This is better. Maybe . . . maybe there's some way to give her a fair chance."

Miles blinked. "I'd be very careful about giving Cavilo any kind of a chance at all, if I were you. Even with tongs. Does she deserve it? Do you realize what's going on, how many she's betrayed?"

"In part. And yet . . ."

"Yet, what?"

Gregor's tone was so low as to be nearly inaudible. "I wish she had been real."

". . . and that's the present tactical situation in the Hub and Vervain local space, as far as my information goes," Miles concluded his presentation to Gregor. They had the *Ariel's* briefing room all to themselves; Arde Mayhew stood guard in the corridor. Miles had begun his speed-precis as soon as Elena reported that the hostile boarders had been successfully secured. He'd paused only to peel out of his ill-fitting armor and back into his Dendarii greys. The armor had been hastily borrowed from the same female soldier who'd lent him kit before, and the plumbing perforce left unconnected.

Miles froze the holovid display in the center of the table. Would that he could freeze real time and events the same way, at the touch of a keypad, that he might halt their terrible rush. "You'll notice our biggest intelligence holes are in precise information about the Cetagandan forces. I'm hoping the Vervani will plug some of those gaps, if we can persuade them we're their allies, and the Rangers may yield more. One way or another.

"Now—sire—the decision lands on you. Fight or flight? I can detach the *Ariel* from the Dendarii right now, to run you home, with little loss to this hot and dirty wormhole fight. Firepower and armor, not speed, are going to be at a premium there. There's not much doubt which course my father and Illyan would vote for."

"No." Gregor stirred. "On the other hand, they aren't here."

"True. Alternately, going to the opposite extreme, do you wish to be commander-in-chief of this mess? In fact, as well as name?"

Gregor smiled softly. "What a temptation. But don't you think there's a certain . . . hubris, in undertaking field leadership without a prior apprenticing in field followership?"

Miles reddened slightly. "I—hem!—face a similar dilemma. You've met the solution, his name's Ky Tung. We'll be conferring with him when we transfer back to the *Triumph*, later." Miles paused. "There are a couple of other things you might do for us. If you choose. Real things."

Gregor rubbed his chin, watching Miles as he might a play. "Trot them out. Lord Vorkosigan."

"Legitimatize the Dendarii. Present them to the Vervani as the Barrayaran pickup force. I can only bluff. Your breath is law. You can conclude a legally binding defensive treaty between Barrayar and Vervain—Aslund too, if we can bring them in. Your greatest value is—sorry—diplomatic, not military. Go to Vervain Station, and deal with these people. And I do mean deal."

"Safely behind the lines," Gregor noted dryly.

"Only if we win, on the other side of the jump. If we lose, the lines will come to you."

"I would I could be a soldier. Some lowly lieutenant, with only a handful of men to care for."

"There's no moral difference between one and ten thousand, I assure you. You're just as thoroughly damned however many you get killed."

"I want to be in on the fight. Probably the only chance I'll have in my life for real risk."

"What, the risk you run every day from lunatic

assassins isn't enough thrill for you? You want more?"

"Active. Not passive. Real service."

"If—in your judgment—the best and most vital service you can give everyone else risking their lives here is as a minor field officer, I will of course support you to the best of my ability," said Miles bleakly.

"Ouch," murmured Gregor. "You can turn a phrase like a knife, you know?" He paused. "Treaties, eh?"

"If you would be so kind, sire."

"Oh, stop it," Gregor sighed. "I will play my assigned part. As always."

"Thank you." Miles thought of offering some apology, some solace, then thought better of it. "The other wild card is Randall's Rangers. Who are now, unless I miss my guess, in considerable disarray. Their second-in-command has vanished, their commander has deserted at the start of the action—how was it the Vervani let her make an exit, by the way?"

"She told them she was going out to confer with you—implied she'd somehow added you to her forces. She was going to jump her fast courier to the hot side immediately thereafter, supposedly."

"Hm. She may have inadvertantly paved our way—is she denying involvement with the Cetagandans?"

"I don't think the Vervani have caught on yet about the Rangers opening the door to the Cetagandans. At the time we left Vervain Station they were still putting the Rangers' failures to defend the Cetagandan-side jump down to incompetence."

"Probably with considerable supporting evidence. I doubt the bulk of the Rangers knew about the betrayal, or it couldn't have stayed secret this long. And whatever inner cadre that was working with the Cetas, were left in the dark when Cavilo took off on her Imperial tangent. You realize, Gregor, you did this? Sabotaged the Cetagandan invasion single-handedly?"

"Oh," breathed Gregor, "it took both hands."

Miles decided not to touch that one. "Anyway—if we can—we need to lock the Rangers down. Get them under control, or at least out from behind everyone's backs."

"Very well."

"I suggest a round of good-guy-bad-guy. I'll be happy to take the part of bad guy."

Cavilo was brought in between two men with hand tractors. She still wore her space armor, now marred and scarred. Her helmet was gone. The armor's weapons packs had been removed, control systems disconnected, and joints locked, turning it into a hundred-kilo prison, tight as a sarcophagus. The two Dendarii soldiers set her upright near the end of the conference table and stepped back with a flourish. A statue with a live head, some Pygmalion-like metamorphosis interrupted and horribly incomplete.

"Thank you, gentlemen, dismissed," said Miles. "Commander Bothari-Jesek, please stay."

Cavilo rolled her short-cropped blonde head in futile resistance, the limit of physically possible motion. She glared furiously at Gregor as the soldiers exited. "You snake," she snarled. "You *bastard*."

Gregor sat with his elbows on the conference table, chin resting in his hands. He raised his head to say tiredly, "Commander Cavilo, both my parents died violently in political intrigue before I was six years old. A fact you might have researched. Did you think you were dealing with an *amateur*?"

"You were out of your league from the beginning, Cavilo," said Miles, walking slowly around her as if inspecting his prize. Her head turned to follow him, then had to swivel to pick up his orbit on the other side. "You should have stuck to your original contract. Or your second plan. Or your third. You should, in fact, have stuck to *something*. Anything. Your total self-interest didn't make you strong, it made you a rag in the wind, anybody's to pick up. Now, Gregor—though not I—thinks you should be given a chance to earn your worthless life."

"You haven't got the balls to shove me out the airlock." Her eyes were slitted with her rage.

"I wasn't planning to." Since it clearly made her skin crawl, Miles circled her again. "No. Looking ahead—when this is over—I thought I might give you to the Cetagandans. A treaty tidbit that will cost us nothing, and help turn them up sweet. I imagine they'll be looking for you, don't you?" He fetched up before her and smiled.

Her face drained. The tendons stood out on her slender neck.

Gregor spoke. "But if you do as we ask, I will grant you safe passage out of the Hegen Hub, via Barrayar, when this is over. Together with any surviving remnant of your forces that will still follow you. It will give you a two-month head start on the Cetagandan vengeance for this debacle."

"In fact," put in Miles, "if you play your part, you could even come out of this a heroine. What fun!"

Gregor's glower at him was not entirely feigned.

"I'll get you," Cavilo breathed to Miles.

"It's the best deal you'll get today. Life. Salvage. A new start, far from here—very far from here. That, Simon Illyan will assure. Far away, but not unwatched."

Calculation began to edge out the rage in her eyes. "What do you want me to do?"

"Not much. Yield up what control you still have of your forces to an officer of our choice. Probably a Vervani liaison, they're paying for you, after all. You will introduce your replacement to your chain of command, and retire to the safety of the *Triumph*'s brig for the duration."

"There won't be any surviving remnant of the Rangers when this is done!"

"There is that chance," Miles conceded. "You were going to throw them all away. Note, please, I'm not offering a choice between this and some better deal. It's this or the Cetagandans. Whose approval of treason is strictly limited to those who deal in their favor."

Cavilo looked like she wanted to spit, but said, "Very well. I yield. You have your deal."

"Thank you."

"But you . . ." her eyes were chips of blue ice, her voice low and venomous, "you will learn, little man. You're riding high today, but time will bring you down. I'd say, just wait twenty years, but I doubt you're going to live that long. Time will teach you how much *nothing* your loyalties will buy you. The day they finally grind you up and spit you out, I'm just sorry I won't be there to watch, 'cause you're gonna be *hamburger*."

Miles called the soldiers back in. "Take her away." It was almost a plea. As the door closed behind the prisoner and her porters, he turned to find Elena's eyes upon him.

"God, that woman makes me cold," he shivered.

"Ah?" Gregor remarked, elbows still planted. "Yet in a weird way, you seem to get along with each other. You think alike."

"Gregor!" Miles protested. "Elena?" he called for a counter-vote.

"You're both very twisty," said Elena doubtfully. "And, er, short." At Miles's tight-lipped look of outrage she explained, "It's more a matter of pattern than content. If you were power-crazy, instead of, of . . ."

"Some other kind of crazy, yes, go on."

"—you could plot like that. You seemed to kind of enjoy figuring her out."

"Thank-you-I-think." He hunched his shoulders.

Was it true? Could that be himself in twenty years? Sick with cynicism and unvented rage, a shelled self thrilled only by mastery, power games, control, armor-plate with a wounded beast inside?

"Let's get back to the *Triumph*," he said shortly. "We've all got work to do."

Miles paced impatiently across the short breadth of Admiral Oser's cabin aboard the *Triumph*. Gregor leaned hip-slung on the edge of the comconsole desk, watching him oscillate.

". . . naturally the Vervani will be suspicious, but with the Cetagandans breathing down their necks they'll have a real will to believe. And deal. You'll want to make it as attractive as possible, to close things up quickly, but of course don't give away any more than you have to—"

Gregor said dryly, "Perhaps you'd like to come along and operate my holoprompter?"

Miles stopped, cleared his throat. "Sorry. I know you know more about treaties than I do. I . . . babble when I'm nervous, sometimes."

"Yes, I know."

Miles managed to keep his mouth shut, though not his feet still, until the cabin buzzer blatted.

"Prisoners as ordered, sir," came Sergeant Chodak's voice over the intercom.

"Thank you, enter." Miles leaned across the desk and hit the door control.

Chodak and a squad marched Captain Ungari and Sergeant Overholt into the cabin. The prisoners were indeed just as Miles had ordered; washed, shaved, combed, and provided with fresh pressed Dendarii greys with equivalent rank insignia. They also looked palpably surly and hostile about it.

"Thank you, Sergeant, you and your squad are dismissed."

"Dismissed?" Chodak's eyebrows questioned the wisdom of this. "Sure you don't want us to at least stand-to in the corridor, sir? Remember the last time."

"It won't be necessary this time."

Ungari's glare denied that airy assertion. Chodak withdrew doubtfully, keeping his stunner-aim steady on the pair until the doors closed across his view.

Ungari inhaled deeply. "Vorkosigan! You mutinous little mutant, I'm going to have you court-martialed, skinned, stuffed, and mounted for this—"

They had not yet noticed quiet Gregor, still leaning on the comconsole and also wearing courtesy Dendarii greys, though without insignia, there being no Dendarii equivalent for emperor.

"Uh, sir—" Miles motioned the dark-faced captain's eye toward Gregor.

"Those are such widely shared sentiments, Captain Ungari, that I'm afraid you might have to stand in line and wait your turn," Gregor remarked, smiling slightly.

The remaining air went out of Ungari unvoiced. He braced to attention; to his credit, the uppermost of the wildly mixed emotions on his face was profound relief. "*Sire.*"

"My apologies, Captain," said Miles, "for my high-handed treatment of you and Sergeant Overholt, but I judged my plan for retrieving Gregor too, uh, delicate for, for . . ." *your nerves,* "I thought I'd better take personal responsibility." *You were happier not watching, really. And I was happier not having my elbow jogged.*

"Ensigns don't have personal responsibility for operations of this magnitude, their commanders do," Ungari snarled. "As Simon Illyan would have been the first to point out to me if your plan—however delicate—had failed. . . ."

"Well, then, congratulations, sir; you have just rescued the emperor," snapped Miles. "Who, as your commander-in-chief, has a few orders for you, if you will permit him to get a word in edgewise."

Ungari's teeth closed. With visible effort, he dismissed Miles from his attention and focused on Gregor. "Sire?"

Gregor spoke. "As the only members of ImpSec within a couple million kilometers—except for Ensign Vorkosigan, who has other chores—I'm attaching you and Sergeant Overholt to my person, until we make contact with our reinforcements. I may also require courier duties of you. Before we leave the *Triumph*, please share any pertinent intelligence you may possess with Dendarii Ops; they're now my Imperial, uh . . ."

"Most obedient servants," suggested Miles under his breath.

"Forces," Gregor concluded. "Consider that grey suit," (Ungari glanced down at his with loathing) "regulation wear, and respect it accordingly. You'll doubtless get your greens back when I get mine."

Miles put in, "I'll be detaching the Dendarii light cruiser *Ariel* and the faster of our two fast couriers to Gregor's personal service, when you depart for Vervain Station. If you have to split off on courier duties, I suggest you take the smaller ship and leave the *Ariel* with Gregor. Its captain, Bel Thorne, is my most trusted Dendarii shipmaster."

"Still thinking about my line of retreat, eh, Miles?" Gregor raised a brow at him.

Miles bowed slightly. "If things go very wrong, someone must live to avenge us. Not to mention to make damn sure the Dendarii survivors get paid. We owe them that much, I think."

"Yes," Gregor agreed softly.

"I also have my personal report on recent events for you to deliver to Simon Illyan," Miles went on, "in case I—in case you see him before I do." Miles handed Ungari a data disk.

Ungari looked dizzy at this rapid reordering of his priorities. "Vervain Station? Pol Six is where your safety lies, surely, sire."

"Vervain Station is where my duty lies, Captain, and perforce yours. Come along, I'll explain it all as we go."

"Are you leaving Vorkosigan loose?" Ungari frowned at Miles. "With these mercenaries? I have a problem with that, sire."

"I'm sorry, sir," said Miles to Ungari, "that I cannot, cannot . . ." *obey you*, but Miles left that unsaid. "I have a deeper problem with arranging a battle for these mercenaries and then not showing up for it. A difference between myself and . . . the Rangers' former commander. There must be some difference between us, maybe that's it. Gre—the Emperor understands."

"Hm," said Gregor. "Yes. Captain Ungari, I officially detach Ensign Vorkosigan as Our Dendarii liaison. On my personal responsibility. Which should be sufficient even for you."

"It's not me that it has to be sufficient for, sire!"

Gregor hesitated fractionally. "For Barrayar's best interests, then. A sufficient argument even for Simon. Let us go, Captain."

"Sergeant Overholt," Miles added, "you will be the Emperor's personal bodyguard and batman, until relieved."

Overholt looked anything but relieved at this abrupt field promotion. "Sir," he whispered aside to Miles, "I haven't had the advanced course!"

He referred to Simon Illyan's mandatory, personally-conducted ImpSec course for the palace guard, that gave Gregor's usual crew that hard-polished edge.

"We all have a similar problem here, Sergeant, believe me," Miles murmured back. "Do your best."

The *Triumph*'s tactics room was alive with activity, every station chair occupied, every holovid display bright with the flow of ship and fleet tactical changes. Miles stood at Tung's elbow and felt doubly redundant. He bethought of the jape back at the Academy. *Rule 1: Only overrule the tactical computer if you know something it doesn't. Rule 2: The tac comp always knows more than you do.*

This was combat? This muffled chamber, swirl of lights, these padded chairs? Maybe the detachment was a good thing, for commanders. His heart hammered even now. A tac room of this caliber could cause information overload and mind-lock, if you let it. The trick was to pick out what was important, and never, ever to forget that the map was not the territory.

His job here, Miles reminded himself, was not to command. It was to watch Tung command, and learn how he did it, his alternate modes of thinking to Barrayaran Academy Standard. Miles's only legitimate point of overrule might come if some external political/strategic need took precedence over internal tactical logic. Miles prayed that event would not arise, because a shorter and uglier name for it was *betraying your troops.*

Miles's attention sharpened as a little jumpscout winked into existence at the throat of the wormhole. On the tactics display it was a pink point of light in a slowly moving whirlpool of darkness. On a telescreen, it was a slim ship against fixed and distant stars. From its own wired-in pilot's point of view, it was some strange extension of his own body. In yet another vid display, it was a collection of telemetry readouts, numerology, some Platonic ideal. *What is truth? All. None.*

"Sharkbait One reporting to Fleet One," the pilot's voice came over Tung's console. "You have ten minutes clearance. Stand by for tight-beam burst."

Tung spoke into his comm. "Fleet commence Jump, tight by the numbers."

The first Dendarii ship waiting by the wormhole jockeyed into place, glowed brightly in the tac display (though it appeared to do nothing in the televid), and vanished. A second ship followed in thirty seconds, pushing the safety limit of time margins between jumps. Two ships trying to rematerialize in the same place at the same time would result in no ships and a very large explosion.

As the *Sharkbait's* tightbeam telemetry was digested by the tac comp, the image rotated so that the dark vortex representing (but in no way picturing) the wormhole was suddenly mirrored by an exit vortex. Beyond that exit vortex an array of dots and specks and lines represented ships in flight, maneuvering, firing, fleeing; the hardened Homeside battle station of the Vervani, twin to the Hubside station where Miles had left Gregor; the Cetagandan attackers. A view of their destination at last. All lies, of course, it was minutes out of date.

"Yech," Tung commented. "What a mess. Here we go . . ."

The jump klaxon sounded. It was the *Triumph's* turn. Miles gripped the back of Tung's chair, though intellectually he knew the feeling of motion was illusory. A whirl of dreams seemed to cloud his mind, for a moment, for an hour; it was unmeasurable. The wrench in his stomach and the godawful wave of nausea that followed were anything but dreamlike. Jump over. A moment of silence throughout the room, as others struggled to overcome their disorientation. Then the murmur picked up where it had left off. *Welcome to Vervain. Take a wormhole jump to hell.*

The tac display spun and shifted, shunting in new data, recentering its little universe. Their wormhole was presently guarded by its beleaguered Station and a thin and battered string of Vervani Navy and Vervani-commanded Ranger ships. The Cetagandans had hit it once already, been driven off, and now hovered out of range awaiting reinforcements for the next strike. Cetagandan re-supply was streaming across the Vervain system from the other wormhole.

The other wormhole had fallen fast, the only way to fly from the attacker's viewpoint. Even with complete surprise on the Cetagandans' side for their massive first strike, the Vervani might have stopped them had not three Ranger ships apparently misunderstood their orders and broken off when they should have counterattacked. But the Cetagandans had secured their bridgehead and begun to pour through.

The second wormhole, Miles's wormhole, had been better equipped for defense—until the panicked Vervani had pulled everything that could be spared back to guard the high orbitals of the homeworld. Miles could scarcely blame them; it was a hard strategic choice either way. But now the Cetagandans boiled across the system practically unimpeded, hopscotching the heavily guarded planet, in a bold attempt to take the Hegen wormhole, if not by surprise, at least at speed.

The first method of choice for attacking a wormhole was by subterfuge, subornment, and infiltration, i.e., to cheat. The second, also preferring subterfuge in its execution, was by an end-run, sending forces around by another route (if there was one) into the contested local space. The third was to open the attack with a sacrifice ship laying down a "sun wall," a massive blanket of nuclear missilettes deployed as a unit, creating a planar wave that cleared near-space of everything including, frequently, the attack ship; but sun walls were costly, rapidly dissipated, and only locally effective. The Cetagandans had attempted to combine all three methods, as the Rangers' disarray and the filthy radioactive fog still outgassing from the vicinity of their first conquest testified.

The fourth approved approach for the problem of frontally attacking a guarded wormhole was to shoot the officer who suggested it. Miles trusted the Cetagandans would work around to that one too, by the time he was done.

Time passed. Miles hooked a station chair into clamps and studied the central display till his eyes watered and his mind threatened to fall into a hypnotic fugue, then rose and shook himself and circulated among the duty stations, kibbitzing.

The Cetagandans manuevered. The sudden and unexpected arrival of the Dendarii force during the lull had thrown them into temporary confusion; their planned final attack on the strained Vervani must needs be converted on the fly into yet another softening-up round of hit-and-run. Expensive. At this point the Cetagandans had few ways of concealing their numbers or movements. The defending Dendarii had the implication of hidden reserves (who knew how unlimited? Not Miles, certainly) concealed on the other side of the jump. A brief hope flared in Miles that this threat alone might be enough to make the Cetagandans break off the attack.

"Naw," sighed Tung when Miles confided this optimistic thought. "They're too far into it now. The butcher's bill's too high already for them to pretend they were only fooling. Even to themselves. A Cetagandan commander who packed it in now would go home to a court martial. They'll keep going long after it's hopeless, as their brass tries desperately to cover their bleeding asses with a flag of victory."

"That is . . . vile."

"That is the system, son, and not just for the Cetagandans. One of the system's several built-in defects. And besides," Tung grinned briefly, "it's not as hopeless as all that yet. A fact we will try to conceal from them."

The Cetagandan forces began to move, their directions and accelerations telegraphing their intention for a pounding pass. The trick was to try for local concentrations of force, three or four ships ganging up on one, overwhelming the defender's plasma mirrors. The Dendarii and Vervani would attempt an identical strategy against Cetagandan stragglers, but for a few bravura captains on both sides equipped with the new imploder lances playing an insane game of chicken, trying to put a target within the weapon's short range. Miles also tried to keep one eye on the Rangers' dispositions. Not every Ranger ship had Vervani advisors aboard, and battle arrays that put the Rangers in front of the Cetagandans were much to be preferred to ones that put Rangers behind Dendarii backs.

The quiet murmur of techs and computers within the tactics room scarcely changed pace. There ought to be a flourish of drums, bagpipes, something to herald this dance with death. But if reality broke in at all to this upholstered bubble, it would be sudden, absolute, and over.

A vid-comm message interrupted, intra-ship—yes, there was still a real ship encasing them—a breathless officer reporting to Tung. "Brig, sir. Watch yourselves up there. We've had a break-out. Admiral Oser's escaped, and he let all the other prisoners out too."

"Dammit," said Tung, glared at Miles, and pointed to the comm. "*Handle* that. Jack up Auson." He turned his attention back to his tactics display, muttering, "This wouldn't have happened in *my* day."

Miles slipped into the comm chair, and paged the *Triumph*'s bridge. "Auson! Did you get the word on Oser?"

Auson's irritated face appeared, "Yeah, we're working on it."

"Order extra commando guards to the tactics room, engineering, and your own bridge. This is a real bad time for interruptions down here."

"Tell me. We can see the Ceta bastards coming." Auson punched off.

Miles began monitoring internal security channels, pausing only to note the arrival of well-armed guards in the corridor. Oser had clearly had help in his escape, some loyal Oseran officer or officers, which made Miles wonder in turn about the security of the security guards. And would Oser try to combine with Metzov and Cavilo? A couple of Dendarii imprisoned for disciplinary infractions were found wandering the corridors and returned to the brig; another came back on his own. A suspected spy was cornered in a storeroom. No sign yet of the truly dangerous . . .

"There he goes!"

Miles keyed in the channel. A cargo shuttle was breaking out of its clamps, away from the side of the *Triumph* and into space.

Miles overrode channels, found fire control. "Don't, repeat, *Do not* open fire on that shuttle!"

"Uh . . ." came the reply. "Yes, sir. Do not open fire."

Why did Miles get the subliminal impression that tech hadn't been planning to open fire in the first place? Clearly a well-coordinated escape. The witch-hunt later was going to be nasty. "Patch me through to that shuttle!" Miles demanded of the comm officer. *And, oh yes, send a guard to the shuttle hatch corridors* . . . too late.

"I'll try, sir, but they're not answering."

"How many aboard?"

"Several, but we're not sure exactly—"

"Patch me through. They've got to listen, even if they won't reply."

"I have a channel, sir, but I have no idea if they're listening."

"I'll try it." Miles took a breath. "Admiral Oser! Turn your shuttle around and come back to the *Triumph*. It's too dangerous out there, you're running headlong into a fire zone. Return, and I will personally guarantee your safety—"

Tung was looking down over Miles's shoulder. "He's

trying to make it to the *Peregrine*. Dammit, if that ship pulls out, our defensive array will collapse."

Miles glanced back at the tac comp. "Surely not. I thought we put the *Peregrine* in the reserve area precisely because we doubted its reliability."

"Yes, but if the *Peregrine* pulls out I can name three other captain-owners who will follow it. And if four ships pull out—"

"The Rangers will break despite their Vervani commander, and we'll be cooked, right, I see." Miles glanced again at the tac comp. "I don't think he's going to make it—Admiral Oser! Can you read me?"

"Yike!" Tung returned to his seat, absorbed in the Cetagandans once again. Four Cetagandan ships were combining against the edge of the Dendarii formation, while another attempted to penetrate the center, clearly trying to close the range for a lance attack. Casually, in passing, a Cetgandan plasma gunner from it picked off the stray shuttle. Just bright sparks.

"He didn't know the Cetagandans were making their attack run till his stolen shuttle cleared the *Triumph*," Miles whispered. "Good plan, rotten timing. . . . He could have turned around, he chose to try and run for it. . . ." Oser chose his death? Was that the comforting argument?

The Cetagandans did not so much break off their attack run as complete it, in depressingly good order. The score was slightly in the Dendarii's favor. A number of Cetagandan ships had been badly chewed, and one blown up entirely. Dendarii and Ranger damage control channels were frantic. The Dendarii had not lost ships yet, but had lost fire-power, engines, flight control, life support, shielding. The next attack run would be more devastating.

They can afford to lose three to our one. If they keep coming, keep nibbling, they must inevitably win, Miles reflected coldly. *Unless we are reinforced.*

Hours passed, while the Cetagandans formed up again. Miles took short breaks in the wardroom provided for that purpose off the tactics room, but was too keyed up to emulate Tung's amazing fifteen-minute instant naps. Miles knew Tung wasn't faking relaxation for morale effect; nobody could simulate such a disgusting snore.

It was possible to watch the Cetagandan reinforcements coming on across the Vervain system in the televid. That was the time trade-off, the risk. The longer the Cetas waited, the better-equipped they could be, but the longer they waited, the better the chance that their enemies would recover too. There was doubtless a tac comp aboard the Cetagandan command ship that had generated a probability curve marking the optimum intersection of Us and Them. If only the damned Vervani would be more aggressive in attacking that supply stream from their planetary base. . . .

And here they came on again. Tung watched his displays, his hands unconsciously clenching and unclenching in his lap between jerky, thick-fingered dances on his control panel, sending orders, correcting, anticipating. Miles's fingers twitched in tiny echoes, his mind trying to get around Tung's thought, to absorb everything. Their picture of reality was getting lacy with hidden holes, as data points dropped out due to damaged sensors or senders on various ships. The Cetagandans flew through the Dendarii formation, pounding . . . a Dendarii ship blew apart, another, weapons dead, tried to scramble out of range, three Ranger ships broke away as a unit . . . it looked bad. . . .

"*Sharkbait Three* reporting," an abrupt voice overrode all other comm channels, making Miles jump in his seat. "Hold this wormhole *clear*. Help coming."

"Not *now*," snarled Tung, but began to attempt a rapid re-deployment to cover the tiny volume of space, keep it clear of debris, missiles, enemy fire, and most of all enemy ships with imploder lances. Those Cetagandan ships that were in position to respond seemed almost to prick their ears, hesitating as Dendarii ship movements telegraphed *changes coming*. The Dendarii might be in retreat . . . some exploitable opportunity might be about to open up. . . .

"Whatinhell's *that*?" Tung said, as something huge and temporarily indecipherable appeared in the throat of the wormhole and began instantly to accelerate. He punched up readouts. "It's too big to be that fast. It's too fast to be that *big*."

Miles recognized the energy profile even before the televiewer yielded up a visual. *What a shake-down cruise they're having.* "It's the *Prince Serg*. Our Barrayaran Imperial reinforcements have just arrived." He took a dizzy breath. "Did I not promise you . . ."

Tung swore horribly, in pure aesthetic admiration. Other ships followed, Aslunder, Polian Navy, spreading out rapidly into attack—not defensive—formation.

The ripple in the Cetagandan formations was like a silent cry of dismay. An imploder-armed Cetagandan ship dove bravely at the *Prince Serg*, and was sliced in half discovering that the *Serg*'s imploder lances had been improved to triple the Cetagandans' range. That was the first mortal blow.

The second came over the comm link, a call to the Cetagandan aggressors to surrender or be destroyed—in the name of the Hegen Alliance Navy, Emperor Gregor Vorbarra and Admiral Count Aral Vorkosigan, Joint Commanders.

For a moment, Miles thought Tung was about to faint. Tung inhaled alarmingly, and bellowed with delight, "Aral Vorkosigan! Here? Hot damn!" And in an only slightly more private whisper, "How'd they lure him out of retirement? Maybe I'll get to meet him!"

Tung the military history nut was one of Miles's father's most fanatical fans, Miles recalled, and until and unless firmly suppressed could rattle off every public detail of the Barrayaran admiral's early campaigns. "I'll see what I can arrange," Miles promised.

"If you can arrange *that*, son. . . ." With an effort, Tung pulled his mind away from his beloved hobby of studying military history and back to his (admittedly, closely related) job of making it.

The Cetagandan ships were breaking, first in panicked singles and then in more coordinated groups, trying to organize a properly covered retreat. The *Prince Serg* and its support group did not waste a millisecond, but followed up instantly, attacking and disordering attempted self-covering arrays of enemy ships, worrying the resulting stragglers. In the ensuing hours the retreat became a true rout when the Vervani ships protecting their high planetary orbitals, encouraged, at last broke orbit and joined the attack. The Vervani reserve was merciless, in the terror for their homes the Cetagandans had instilled in them.

The mopping-up in detail, the appalling damage control problems, the personnel rescues, were so absorbing that it took Miles those several hours to gradually realize the war was over for the Dendarii fleet. They had done their job.

CHAPTER SEVENTEEN

Before departing the tactics room, Miles prudently checked with the *Triumph's* security to determine how their roundup of escaped prisoners was progressing. Missing and still unaccounted for remained Oser, the *Peregrine's* captain and two other loyal Oseran officers, Commander Cavilo, and General Metzov.

Miles was fairly certain he had witnessed Oser and his officers converted to radioactive ash in his monitors. Had Metzov and Cavilo been aboard that fleeing shuttle too? Fine irony, for Cavilo to die at the hands of the Cetagandans after all. Though—admittedly—it would have been equally ironic had she died at the hands of the Vervani, Randall's Rangers, the Aslunders, the Barrayarans, or anyone else she'd double-crossed in her brief, cometary career in the Hegen Hub. Her end was neat and convenient if true, but—he didn't like to think that her last, savage remarks to him had now acquired the prophetic weight of a dying curse. He ought to fear Metzov more than Cavilo. He ought to, but he didn't. He shuddered, and borrowed a commando guard for the walk back to his cabin.

On the way, he encountered a shuttle-load of wounded being transferred to the *Triumph's* sickbay. The *Triumph*, in the reserve group (such as it was) had taken no hits its shields couldn't handle, but other ships had not been so fortunate. Space battle casualty lists usually had the proportions reversed

from planetary, the dead outnumbering the wounded,
yet in lucky circumstances where the artificial environment was preserved, soldiers might survive their
injuries. Uncertainly, Miles changed course and followed the procession along. What good could he do
in sickbay?

The triage people had not sent minor cases to the
Triumph. Three hideous burns and a massive head
injury went to the head of the line, and were
whisked off by the anxiously waiting staff. A few soldiers were conscious, quietly waiting their turns,
immobilized with air bag braces on their float pallets,
eyes cloudy with pain and pain-killers.

Miles tried to say a few words to each. Some
stared uncomprehendingly, some seemed to appreciate it; he lingered a little longer with these, giving
what encouragement he could. He then withdrew
and stood dumbly by the door for several minutes,
awash in the familiar, terrifying odors of a sickbay
after a battle, disinfectants and blood, burnt meat,
urine, and electronics, until he realized exhaustion
was making him thoroughly stupid and useless,
shaky and near-tears. He pushed off from the wall
and stumped out. Bed. If anyone really wanted his
command presence, they could come find him.

He hit the code lock on Oser's cabin. Now that
he'd inherited it, he supposed he ought to change
the numbers. He sighed and entered. As he stepped
inside he became conscious of two unfortunate facts.
First, although he had dismissed his commando
guard upon entering sickbay, he had forgotten to call
him back, and second, he was not alone. The door
closed behind him before he could recoil into the
corridor, and he banged into it backing up.

The dusky red hue of General Metzov's face was
even more arresting to the eye than the silver gleam
of the nerve disruptor parabola in his hand, aim cen-
tered on Miles's head.

Metzov had somehow acquired a set of Dendarii

greys, a little small for him. Commander Cavilo, standing behind Metzov, had acquired a similar set, a little large for her. Metzov looked huge and furious. Cavilo looked . . . strange. Bitter, ironic, weirdly amused. Bruises marred her neck. She bore no weapon.

"Got you," Metzov whispered triumphantly. "At last." With a rictus smile, he advanced stepwise on Miles till he could pin him to the wall by his neck with one big hand. He dropped the nerve disruptor with a clatter and wrapped the other hand around Miles's neck, not to break but to squeeze it.

"You'll never survive—" was all Miles managed to choke out before his air pinched off. He could feel his trachea begin to crunch, crumpling, his head felt on the verge of dark explosion as his blood supply was cut off. No talking Metzov out of *this* murder. . . .

Cavilo slipped forward, crouching, soundless and unnoticed as a cat, to take up the dropped nerve disruptor, then step back, around to Miles's left.

"Stanis, darling," she cooed. Metzov, obsessed with Miles's lingering strangulation, did not turn his head. Cavilo, clearly imitating Metzov's cadences, recited, " 'Open your legs to me, you bitch, or I'll blow your brains out.' "

Metzov's head twisted round then, his eyes widening. She blew his brains out. The crackling blue bolt hit him square between the eyes. He almost snapped Miles's neck, plastic-reinforced though those bones were, in his last convulsion, before he dropped to the deck. The blistering electrochemical smell of nerve-disruptor death slapped Miles in the face.

Miles sagged frozen against the wall, not daring to move. He raised his eyes from the corpse to Cavilo. Her lips were curved in a smile of immense satisfaction, satiated. Had Cavilo's line been a direct and recent quote? What had they been doing, all the long hours they must have been waiting in the hunter's blind of Oser's cabin? The silence lengthened.

"Not," Miles swallowed, trying to clear his bruised throat, and croaked, "not that I'm complaining, mind you, but why aren't you going ahead and shooting me too?"

Cavilo smirked. "A quick revenge is better than none. A slow and lingering one is better still, but to savor it fully I must survive it. Another day, kid." She tilted the nerve disruptor up as if to flourish it into a holster, then let it hang pointed down by her side in her relaxed hand. "You've sworn you'll see me safe out of the Hegen Hub, Vor lord. And I've come to believe you are actually stupid enough to keep your word. Not that I'm complaining, mind you. Now, if Oser had issued more than one weapon between us, or if he'd given the nerve disruptor to me and the code to his cabin to Stanis and not the other way around, or if Oser'd taken us with him as I begged . . . things might have worked out differently."

Very differently. Very slowly, and very, very carefully, Miles inched over to the comconsole and called security. Cavilo watched him thoughtfully. After a few moments, coming up on the time they might expect the reinforcements to storm in, she strolled over to his side. "I underestimated you, you know."

"I never underestimated you."

"I know. I'm not used to that . . . thank you." Contemptuously, she tossed the nerve disruptor onto Metzov's body. Then, with a sudden baring of her teeth, she wheeled, wrapped an arm around Miles's neck, and kissed him vigorously. Her timing was perfect; Security, Elena and Sergeant Chodak in the lead, burst through the door just before Miles managed to fight her off.

Miles stepped from the *Triumph*'s shuttle through the short flex tube and on board the *Prince Serg*. He stared around enviously at the clean, spacious, beautifully-lit corridor, at the row of smart and gleaming honor guards snapping to attention, at the polished officers waiting in their Barrayaran Imperial dress greens. He stole an anxious glance down at his own Dendarii grey-and-whites. The *Triumph*, key and pride of the Dendarii fleet, seemed to shrink into something small and gritty and battered and used.

Yeah, but you guys would not look so pretty now if we had not used ourselves so hard, Miles consoled himself.

Tung, Elena, and Chodak were all goggling like tourists too. Miles called them firmly to attention to receive and return the crisp welcoming salutes of their hosts.

"I'm Commander Natochini, executive officer of the *Prince Serg*," the senior Barrayaran introduced himself. "Lieutenant Yegorov, here, will escort you and Commander Bothari-Jesek to Admiral Vorkosigan for your meeting, Admiral Naismith. Commodore Tung, I will be personally conducting your tour of the *Prince Serg*, and will be pleased to answer any of your questions. If the answers aren't classified, of course."

"Of course." Tung's broad face looked immensely pleased. In fact, if Tung grew any smugger he might implode.

"We will join Admiral Vorkosigan for lunch in the senior officers' mess, after your meeting and our tour," Commander Natochini continued to Miles. "Our last dinner guest there was the President of Pol and his entourage, twelve days ago."

Certain that the mercenaries understood the magnitude of the privilege they were being granted, the Barrayaran exec led the happy Tung and Chodak off down the corridor. Miles heard Tung chuckle under his breath, "Lunch with Admiral Vorkosigan, heh, heh. . . ."

Lieutenant Yegorov motioned Miles and Elena in the opposite direction. "You are Barrayaran, ma'am?" he inquired of Elena.

"My father was liege-sworn Armsman to the late Count Piotr for eighteen years," Elena stated. "He died in the Count's service."

"I see," said the lieutenant respectfully. "You are acquainted with the family, then." *That explains you*, Miles could almost see him thinking.

"Ah, yes."

The lieutenant glanced down a little more dubiously at "Admiral Naismith." "And, uh, I understand you are Betan, sir?"

"Originally," said Miles, in his flattest Betan accent.

"You . . . may find the way we Barrayarans do things to be a little more formal than what you're used to," the lieutenant warned. "The Count, you understand, is accustomed to the respect and deference due his rank."

Miles watched, delighted, as the earnest officer sought a polite way of saying, *Call him sir, don't wipe your nose on your sleeve, and none of your damned Betan egalitarian backchat, either*. "You may find him rather formidable," Yegorov concluded.

"A real stuffed shirt, eh?"

The lieutenant frowned. "He is a great man."

"Aw, I bet if we pour enough wine into him at lunch, he'll loosen up and tell dirty stories with the best of 'em."

Yegorov's polite smile became fixed. Elena, eyes dancing, leaned down and whispered forcefully, "Admiral, behave!"

"Oh, all right," Miles sighed regretfully.

The lieutenant glanced gratefully at Elena, over Miles's head.

Miles admired the spit and polish, in passing. Besides just being new, the *Prince Serg* had been designed with diplomacy as well as war in mind, a ship fit to carry the emperor on state visits without loss of military efficiency. He saw a young ensign, down a cross-corridor that had a wall panel apart, directing some tech crew on minor repairs—no, by God, it was original installation. The *Prince Serg* had broken orbit with work crews still aboard, Miles had heard. He glanced back over his shoulder. *There but for the grace of God and General Metzov go I.* If he'd kept his nose clean on Kyril Island for just six months . . . he felt an illogical twinge of envy for that busy ensign.

They entered officers' country. Lieutenant Yegorov led them through an antechamber and into a spartan-ly-appointed flag office twice the size of anything Miles had seen on a Barrayaran ship before. Admiral Count Aral Vorkosigan looked up from his comconsole desk as the doors slid silently back.

Miles stepped through, his belly suddenly shaking inside. To conceal and control his emotion he tossed off, "Hey, you Imperial snails are going to go all fat and soft, lolling around in this kind of luxury, y'know?"

"Ha!" Admiral Vorkosigan stumbled out of his chair and banged around the corner of his desk in his haste. *Well, no wonder, how can he see with all that water standing in his eyes?* He enfolded Miles in a hard embrace. Miles grinned and blinked and swallowed, face smashed against that cool green sleeve, and almost had control of his features again when Count Vorkosigan held him out at arm's length for an anxious, searching inspection. "You all right, boy?"

"Just fine. How'd you like your wormhole jump?"

"Just fine," breathed Count Vorkosigan back. "Mind you, there were moments when certain of my advisors wanted to have you shot. And there were moments when I agreed with 'em."

Lieutenant Yegorov, cut off in mid-announcement of their arrival (Miles hadn't heard him speaking, and he doubted his father had either), was standing with his mouth still open, looking perfectly stunned. Lieutenant Jole, suppressing a grin himself, arose from the other side of the comconsole desk and guided Yegorov gently and mercifully back out the door. "Thank you, Lieutenant. The Admiral appreciates your services, that will be all. . . ." Jole glanced back over his shoulder, quirked a pensive brow, and followed Yegorov out. Miles just glimpsed the blond lieutenant drape himself across a chair in the antechamber, head back in the relaxed posture of a man anticipating a long wait, before the door slid closed. Jole could be supernaturally courteous at times.

"Elena." With an effort, Count Vorkosigan broke away from Miles to take both Elena's hands in a firm brief grip. "You are well?"

"Yes, sir."

"That pleases me . . . more than I can say. Cordelia sends her love and her best hopes. If I saw you, I was to remind you, ah—I must get the phrase exact, it was one of her Betan cracks—'Home is where, when you have to go there, they have to take you in.' "

"I can hear her voice," smiled Elena. "Tell her thank you. Tell her . . . I will remember."

"Good." Count Vorkosigan pressed her no further. "Sit, sit," he waved them at chairs, which he snugged up close to the comconsole desk, and sat himself. For an instant, changing gears, his features relaxed, then concentrated with attention once again. *God, he looks tired*, Miles realized; for a split second, almost ghastly. *Gregor, you have much to answer for*. But Gregor knew that.

"What's the latest word on the cease-fire?" Miles asked.

"Still holding nicely, thank you. The only Cetagandan ships that haven't jumped back where they came from, had damaged Necklin rods or control systems or injured pilots. Or all three. We're letting them repair two of them and jump them out with skeleton crews, the rest are not salvageable. I estimate controlled commercial travel could resume in six weeks."

Miles shook his head. "So ends the Five-Day War. I never once saw a Cetagandan face-to-face. All that effort and bloodshed, just to return to the status quo ante."

"Not quite for everyone. A number of Cetagandan senior officers have been recalled to their capital, to explain their 'unauthorized adventure' to their emperor. Their apologies are expected to be fatal."

Miles snorted. "Expiate their failure, rather. 'Unauthorized adventure.' Does anyone believe that? Why do they even bother?"

"Finesse, boy. A retreating enemy should be offered all the face he can carry off. Just don't let him carry off anything else."

"I understand you finessed the Polians. All this time, I expected it would be Simon Illyan to show up in person to haul us lost boys home."

"He longed to come, but there was no way we could both leave home at the same time. The wobbly cover we'd put over Gregor's absence could have collapsed at any moment."

"How did you pull that one off, by the way?"

"Picked out a young officer who looked a lot like Gregor, told him there was an assassination plot afoot against the Emperor and that he was to be the bait. Bless him, he volunteered at once. He—and his Security, who had the same tale told them— spent the next several weeks leading a life of ease down at Vorkosigan Surleau, eating off the best plates—but with indigestion. We finally sent him off on a rustic camping trip, as inquiries from the capital were getting pressing. People will twig soon, I'm sure, if they haven't already, but now we've got Gregor back we can explain it away any way we like. Anyway *he* likes." Count Vorkosigan frowned an odd brief frown, odd because not wholly displeased.

"I was surprised," said Miles, "though very happy, that you got your forces past Pol so fast. I was afraid they wouldn't let you through till the Cetagandans were in the Hub. And then it would be too late."

"Yes, well, that's the other reason you got me instead of Simon. As Prime Minister and former Regent, it was perfectly reasonable for me to make a state visit to Pol. We came up with a quick list of the top five diplomatic concessions they've been wanting from us for years, and suggested it for an agenda.

"It being all formal and official and aboveboard, it was then perfectly reasonable for us to combine my visit with the *Prince Serg*'s shakedown cruise. We were in orbit at Pol, shuttling up and down to official receptions and parties," (his hand unconsciously rubbed his abdomen in a pain-warding motion) "with me still trying desperately to talk our way into the Hub without shooting anybody, when word of the Cetagandan surprise attack on Vervain broke. At that point, getting permission to proceed was suddenly expedited. And we were only days, not weeks, away from the action. Getting the Aslunders to lie down with the Polians was a trickier matter. Gregor astonished me, handling that. The Vervani were no problem, they were highly motivated to seek allies by then."

"I hear Gregor is now quite popular on Vervain."

"He's being feted in their capital even as we speak, I believe." Count Vorkosigan glanced at his chrono. "They've gone wild over him. Letting him ride shotgun in the *Prince Serg*'s tac room may have been a better idea that I thought. Purely from a diplomatic standpoint." Count Vorkosigan looked rather abstracted.

"It . . . astonished me, that you permitted him to jump with you into the fire zone. I hadn't expected that."

"Well, when you came down to it, the *Prince Serg*'s fleet tac room had to have been among the most tightly defended few cubic meters anywhere in Vervain local space. It was, it was . . ."

Miles watched with fascination as his father tried to spit out the words *perfectly safe*, and gagged on them instead. Light dawned. "It wasn't your idea, was it? Gregor ordered himself aboard!"

"He had several good arguments to support his position," Count Vorkosigan said. "The propaganda angle certainly seems to be bearing fruit."

"I thought you'd be too . . . prudent. To permit him the risk."

Count Vorkosigan studied his own square hands. "I was not in love with the idea, no. But I once swore an oath to serve an emperor. The most morally dangerous moment for a guardian is when the temptation to become a puppet-master seems most rational. I always knew the moment must . . . no. I knew that if the moment *never* came, I should have failed my oath most profoundly." He paused. "It was still a shock to the system, though. The letting-go."

Gregor faced you down? Oh, to have been a fly on the wall of *that* chamber.

"Even with you to practice on, all these years," Count Vorkosigan added meditatively.

"Ah . . . how's your ulcers?"

Count Vorkosigan grimaced. "Don't ask." He brightened slightly. "Better, the last three days. I may actually demand food for lunch, instead of that miserable medical mush."

Miles cleared his throat. "How's Captain Ungari?"

Count Vorkosigan twitched a lip. "He's not overly pleased with you."

"I . . . cannot apologize. I made a lot of mistakes, but disobeying his order to wait on Aslund Station wasn't one of them."

"Apparently not." Count Vorkosigan frowned at the far wall. "And yet . . . I'm more than ever convinced the regular Service is not the place for you.

It's like trying to fit a square peg—no, worse than that. Like trying to fit a tesseract into a round hole."

Miles suppressed a twinge of panic. "I won't be discharged, will I?"

Elena regarded her fingernails and put in, "If you were, you could get a job as a mercenary. Just like General Metzov. I understand Commander Cavilo is looking for a few good men." Miles nearly meowed at her; she traded a smirk for his exasperated look.

"I was almost sorry to learn that Metzov was killed," remarked Count Vorkosigan. "We'd been planning to try and extradite him, before things went crazy with Gregor's disappearance."

"Ah! Did you finally decide the death of that Komarran prisoner way back when during their revolt was murder? I thought it might be—"

Count Vorkosigan held up two fingers. "Two murders."

Miles paused. "My God, he didn't try and track down poor Ahn before he left, did he?" He'd almost forgotten Ahn.

"No, but we tracked him down. Though not, alas, before Metzov had left Barrayar. And yes, the Komarran rebel had been tortured to death. Not wholly intentionally, he apparently had had some hidden medical weakness. But it was not, as the original investigator had suspected, in revenge for the death of the guard. It was the other way around. The Barrayaran guard corporal, who had participated in or at least acquiesced to the torture, though over some feeble protest, according to Ahn—the corporal suffered a revulsion of feeling, and threatened to turn Metzov in.

"Metzov murdered him in one of his panic-rages, then made Ahn help him cook up and vouch for the cover story about the escape. So Ahn was twice tainted with the thing. Metzov kept Ahn in terror, yet was equally in Ahn's power if the facts ever came out, a kind of strange lock on each other . . . which

Ahn at last escaped. Ahn seemed almost relieved, and volunteered to be fast-penta'd, when Illyan's agents came for him."

Miles thought of the weatherman with regret. "Will anything bad happen to Ahn how?"

"We'd planned to make him testify, at Metzov's trial . . . Illyan thought we might even turn it to our favor, with respect to the Komarrans. Present that poor idiot guard corporal to them as an unsung hero. Hang Metzov as proof of the emperor's good faith and committment to justice for Barrayarans and Komarrans alike . . . nice scenario." Count Vorkosigan frowned bitterly. "I think we will quietly drop it now. Again."

Miles puffed out his breath. "Metzov. A goat to the end. Must be some bad karma, clinging to him . . . not that he didn't earn it."

"Beware of wishing for justice. You might get it."

"I've already learned that, sir."

"Already?" Count Vorkosigan cocked an eyebrow at him. "Hm."

"Speaking of justice," Miles seized the opening. "I'm concerned over the matter of Dendarii pay. They took a lot of damage, more than a mercenary fleet will usually tolerate. Their only contract was my breath and voice. If . . . if the Imperium does not back me, I will be forsworn."

Count Vorkosigan smiled slightly. "We have already considered the matter."

"Will Illyan's covert ops budget stretch, to cover this?"

"Illyan's budget would burst trying to cover this. But you, ah, seem to have a friend in a high place. We will draw you an emergency credit chit from ImpSec, this fleet's fund, and the Emperor's privy purse, and hope to recoup it all later from a special appropriation rammed through the Council of Ministers and the Council of Counts. Submit a bill."

Miles fished a data disk from his pocket. "Here,

sir. From the Dendarii fleet accountant. She was up
all night. Some damage estimates are still preliminary." He set it on the comconsole desk.

One corner of Count Vorkosigan's mouth twisted
up. "You're learning, boy. . . ." He inserted the disk
in his desk for a fast scan. "I'll have a credit chit
prepared over lunch. You can take it with you when
you depart."

"Thank you, sir."

"Sir," Elena put in, leaning forward earnestly,
"what will happen to the Dendarii fleet now?"

"Whatever it chooses, I presume. Though they
cannot linger, this close to Barrayar."

"Are we to be abandoned again?" asked Elena.

"Abandoned?"

"You made us an Imperial force, once. I thought.
Baz thought. Then Miles left us, and then . . .
nothing."

"Just like Kyril Island," Miles remarked. "Out of
sight, out of mind." He shrugged dolefully. "I gather
they suffered a similar deterioration of morale."

Count Vorkosigan gave him a sharp look. "The fate
of the Dendarii—like your future military career,
Miles—is a matter still under discussion."

"Do I get to be in on that discussion? Do they?"

"We'll let you know." Count Vorkosigan planted
his hands on his desktop, and rose. "That's all I can
say now, even to you. Lunch, officers?"

Miles and Elena perforce rose too. "Commodore
Tung knows nothing of our real relationship yet,"
Miles cautioned. "If you wish to keep that covert,
I'm going to have to play Admiral Naismith when
we rejoin him."

Count Vorkosigan's smile turned peculiar. "Illyan
and Captain Ungari must certainly favor not breaking
a potentially useful cover identity. By all means.
Should be fascinating."

"I should warn you, Admiral Naismith is not very
deferential."

Elena and Count Vorkosigan looked at each other, and both broke into laughter. Miles waited, wrapped in what dignity he could muster, till they subsided. Finally.

Admiral Naismith was painfully polite during lunch. Even Lieutenant Yegorov could have found no fault.

The Vervani government courier handed the credit chit across the homeside station commandant's comconsole desk. Miles testified receipt of it with thumbprint, retina scan, and Admiral Naismith's flourishing illegible scrawl, nothing at all like Ensign Vorkosigan's careful signature. "It's a pleasure doing business with you honorable gentlemen," Miles said, pocketing the chit with satisfaction and carefully sealing the pocket.

"It's the least we can do," said the jumppoint station commandant. "I cannot tell you my emotions, knowing that the next pass the Cetagandans made was going to be their last, nerving to fight to the end, when the Dendarii materialized to reinforce us."

"The Dendarii couldn't have done it alone," said Miles modestly. "All we did was help you hold the bridgehead till the real big guns arrived."

"And if it had not been held, the Hegen Alliance forces—the big guns, as you say—could not have jumped into Vervani local space."

"Not without great cost, certainly," Miles conceded.

The station commandant glanced at his chrono. "Well, my planet will be expressing its opinion of that in more tangible form quite shortly. May I escort you to the ceremony, Admiral? It's time."

"Thank you." Miles rose, and preceded him out of his office, his hand rechecking the tangible thanks in his pocket. *Medals, huh. Medals buy no fleet repairs.*

He paused at a transparent portal, caught half by the vista from the jump station and half by his own reflection. Oseran/Dendarii dress greys were all right, he decided; soft grey velvet tunic set off with blinding white trim and silver buttons on the shoulders, matching trousers and grey synthasuede boots. He fancied the outfit made him look taller. Perhaps he would keep the design.

Beyond the portal floated a scattering of ships, Dendarii, Ranger, Vervani and Alliance. The *Prince Serg* was not among them, being now in orbit above the Vervani homeworld while high-level—literally—talks continued, hammering out the details of the permanent treaty of friendship, commerce, tariff reduction, mutual defense pact, &etc, among Barrayar, Vervain, Aslund and Pol. Gregor, Miles had heard, was being quite luminous in both the public relations and the actual nuts and bolts part of the business. *Better you than me, boy.* The Vervani jumppoint station was letting its own repairs schedule slacken to lend aid to the Dendarii; Baz was working around the clock. Miles tore himself away from the vista and followed the station commandant.

They paused in the corridor outside the large briefing room where the ceremony was to take place, waiting for the attendees to settle. The Vervani apparently wished the principals to make a grand entrance. The commandant went in to prepare. The audience was not large—too much vital work going on—but the Vervani had scraped up enough warm bodies to make it look respectable, and Miles had contributed a platoon of convalescent Dendarii to fluff up the crowd. He would accept on their behalf, in his speech, he decided.

As Miles waited, he saw Commander Cavilo arrive with her Barrayaran honor guard. As far as he knew, the Vervani were not yet aware that the honor-guard's weapons were lethally charged and they had orders to shoot to kill if their prisoner attempted escape. Two hard-faced women in Barrayaran auxiliary uniforms made sure Cavilo was watched both night and day. Cavilo did a good job of ignoring their presence.

The Ranger dress uniform was a neater version of their fatigues, in tan, black, and white, subliminally reminding Miles of a guard dog's fur. *This bitch bites*, he reminded himself. Cavilo smiled and drifted up to Miles. She reeked of her poisonous green-scented perfume; she must have bathed in it.

Miles tilted his head in salute, reached into a pocket, and took out two nose filters. He thrust one up each nostril, where they expanded softly to create a seal, and inhaled deeply to test them. Working fine. They would filter out much smaller molecules than the vile organics of that damned perfume. Miles breathed out through his mouth.

Cavilo watched this performance with an expression of thwarted fury. "*Damn* you," she muttered.

Miles shrugged, palms out, as if to say, *What would you have of me?* "Are you and your survivors about ready to move out?"

"Right after this idiot charade. I have to abandon six ships, too damaged to jump."

"Sensible of you. If the Vervani don't catch on to you soon, the Cetagandans, when they realize they can't get at you themselves, will probably tell them the ugly truth. You shouldn't linger in these parts."

"I don't intend to. If I never see this place again it will be too soon. That goes double for you, mutant. If not for you . . ." she shook her head bitterly.

"By the way," Miles added, "the Dendarii have now been paid three times for this operation. Once by our original contractors the Aslunders, once by the Barrayarans, and once by the grateful Vervani. Each agreed to cover all our expenses in full. Leaves a very tidy profit."

She actually hissed. "You better *pray* we never meet again."

"Goodbye, then."

They entered the chamber to collect their honors.

Would Cavilo have the iron nerve to accept hers on behalf of the Rangers her twisted plots had destroyed? Yes, it turned out. Miles gagged quietly.

The first medal I ever won, Miles thought as the station commandant pinned his on him with embarrassingly fulsome praise, *and I can't even wear it at home*. The medal, the uniform, and Admiral Naismith himself must soon return to the closet. Forever? The life of Ensign Vorkosigan was not too attractive, by comparison. And yet . . . the mechanics of soldiering was the same, from side to side. If there was any difference between himself and Cavilo, it must be in what they chose to serve. And how they chose to serve it. *Not all paths, but one path. . . .*

When Miles arrived back on Barrayar for home leave, a few weeks later, Gregor invited him for lunch at the Imperial Residence. They sat at a wrought-iron table in the North Gardens, which were famous for having been designed by Emperor Ezar, Gregor's grandfather. In summer the spot would be deeply shaded; now it was laced with light filtering through young leaves, rippling in the soft airs of spring. The guards did their guarding out of sight, the servants waited out of earshot unless Gregor touched his pager. Replete with the first three courses, Miles sipped scalding coffee and plotted an assault on a second pastry, which cowered across the table linen under a thick camouflage of cream. Or would that overmatch his forces? This had it all over the contract slave rations they'd once divided, not to mention Cavilo's doggie chews.

Even Gregor seemed to be seeing it all with new eyes. "Space stations are really boring, y'know? All those corridors," he commented, staring out past a fountain, eye following a curving brick path that dove into a riot of flowers. "I stopped seeing how beautiful Barrayar was, looking at it every day. Had to forget to remember. Strange."

"There were moments I couldn't remember which space station I was on," Miles agreed around a mouthful of pastry and cream. "The luxury trade's another matter, but the Hegen Hub stations did tend to the utilitarian." He grimaced at the associations of that last word.

The conversation wandered over the recent events in the Hegen Hub. Gregor brightened upon learning that Miles had never issued an actual battle order in the *Triumph*'s fleet tac room either, except to handle the internal security crisis as delegated by Tung.

"Most officers have finished their jobs when the action begins, because the battle transpires too rapidly for the officers to affect it," Miles assured him. "Once you set up a good tac comp—and, if you're lucky, a man with a magic nose—it's better to keep your hands in your pockets. I had Tung, you had . . . ahem."

"And nice deep pockets," said Gregor. "I'm still thinking about it. It seemed almost unreal, till I visited sickbay afterwards. And realized, such-and-such a point of light meant this man's arm lost, that man's lungs frozen. . . ."

"Gotta watch out for those little lights. They tell such soothing lies," Miles agreed. "If you let them." He chased another gooey bite with coffee, paused, and remarked, "You didn't tell Illyan the truth about your little topple off the balcony, did you." It was observation, not question.

"I told him I was drunk, and climbed down." Gregor watched the flowers. ". . . how did you know?"

"He doesn't talk about you with secret terror in his eyes."

"I've just got him . . . giving a little. I don't want to screw it up now. You didn't tell him either—for that I thank you."

"You're welcome." Miles drank more coffee. "Do me a favor in return. Talk to someone."

"Who? Not Illyan. Not your father."

"How about my mother?"

"Hm." Gregor bit into his torte, upon which he had been making furrows with his fork, for the first time.

"She could be the only person on Barrayar to automatically put Gregor the man before Gregor the emperor. All our ranks look like optical illusions to her, I think. And you know she can keep her own counsel."

"I'll think about it."

"I don't want to be the only one who . . . the only one. I know when I'm out of my depth."

"You do?" Gregor raised his brows, one corner of his mouth crooking up.

"Oh, yes. I just don't normally let on."

"All right. I will," said Gregor.

Miles waited.

"My word," Gregor added.

Miles relaxed, immeasurably relieved. "Thank you." He eyed a third pastry. The portions were sort of dainty. "Are you feeling better, these days?"

"Much, thank you." Gregor went back to plowing furrows in his cream.

"Really?"

Crosshatches. "I don't know. Unlike that poor sod they had parading around playing me while I was gone, I didn't exactly volunteer for this."

"All Vor are draftees, in that sense."

"Any other Vor could run away and not be missed."

"Wouldn't you miss me a little?" said Miles plaintively. Gregor snickered. Miles glanced around the garden. "It doesn't look like such a tough post, compared to Kyril Island."

"Try it alone in bed at midnight, wondering when your genes are going to start generating monsters in your mind. Like Great Uncle Mad Yuri. Or Prince Serg." His glance at Miles was secretly sharp.

"I . . . know about Prince Serg's, uh, problems," said Miles carefully.

"Everyone seems to have known. Except me."

So that *had* been the trigger of depressive Gregor's first real suicide attempt. Key and lock, click! Miles tried not to look triumphant at this sudden feat of insight. "When did you find out?"

"During the Komarr conference. I'd run across hints, before . . . put them down to enemy propaganda."

Then, the ballet on the balcony had been an immediate response to the shock. Gregor'd had no one to vent it to. . . .

"Was it true, that he really got off torturing—"

"Not everything rumored about Crown Prince Serg is true," Miles cut hastily across this. "Though the true core is . . . bad enough. Mother knows. She was eyewitness to crazy things even *I* don't know, about the Escobar invasion. But she'll tell you. Ask her straight, she'll tell you straight back."

"That seems to run in the family," Gregor allowed. "Too."

"She'll tell you how different you are from him—nothing wrong with your mother's blood, that I ever heard—anyway, I probably carry almost as many of Mad Yuri's genes as you do, through one line of descent or another."

Gregor actually grinned. "Is that supposed to be reassuring?"

"Mm, more on the theory that misery loves company."

"I'm afraid of power . . ." Gregor's voice went low, contemplative.

"You aren't afraid of power, you're afraid of hurting people. If you wield that power," Miles deduced suddenly.

"Huh. Close guess."

"Not dead-on?"

"I'm afraid I might enjoy it. The hurting. Like *him*."

Prince Serg, he meant. His father.

"Rubbish," said Miles. "I watched my grandfather try and get you to enjoy hunting for years. You got good, I suppose because you thought it was your Vorish duty, but you damn near threw up every time you half-missed and we had to chase down some wounded beastie. You may harbor some other perversion, but not sadism."

"What I've read . . . and heard," said Gregor, "is so horribly fascinating. I can't help thinking about it. Can't put it out of my mind."

"Your head is full of horrors because the *world* is full of horrors. Look at the horrors Cavilo caused in the Hegen Hub."

"If I'd strangled her while she slept—which I had a chance to do—none of those horrors would have come to pass."

"If none of those horrors had come to pass, she wouldn't have deserved to be strangled. Some kind of time-travel paradox, I'm afraid. The arrow of justice flies one way. Only. You can't regret not strangling her first. Though I suppose you can regret not strangling her after. . . ."

"No . . . no . . . I'll leave that to the Cetagandans, if they can catch her now that she has her head start."

"Gregor, I'm sorry, but I just don't think Mad Emperor Gregor is in the cards. It's your *advisors* who are going to go crazy."

Gregor stared at the pastry tray, and sighed. "I suppose it would disturb the guards if I tried to shove a cream torte up your nose."

"Deeply. You should have done it when we were eight and twelve, you could have gotten away with it then. The cream pie of justice flies one way," Miles snickered.

Several unnatural and sophomoric things to do

with a tray full of pastry were then suggested by both principals, which left them laughing. Gregor needed a good cream pie fight, Miles judged, even if only verbal and imaginary. When the laughter finally died down, and the coffee was cooling, Miles said, "I know flattery sends you straight up a wall, but dammit, you're actually good at your job. You have to know that, on some level inside, after the Vervain talks. Stay on it, huh?"

"I think I will." Gregor's fork dove more forcefully into his last bite of dessert. "You're going to stay on yours, too, right?"

"Whatever it may be. I am to meet with Simon Illyan on just that topic later this afternoon," said Miles. He decided to forgo that third pastry after all.

"You don't sound exactly excited about it."

"I don't suppose he can demote me, there is no rank below ensign."

"He's pleased with you, what else?"

"He didn't look pleased, when I gave him my debriefing report. He looked dyspeptic. Didn't say much." He glanced at Gregor in sudden suspicion. "You know, don't you? Give!"

"Mustn't interfere in the chain of command," said Gregor sententiously. "Maybe you'll move up it. I hear the command at Kyril Island is open."

Miles shuddered.

Spring in the Barrayaran capital city of Vorbarr Sultana was as beautiful as the autumn, Miles decided. He paused a moment before turning in to the front entrance to the big blocky building that was ImpSec HQ. The Earth maple still stood, down the street and around the corner, its tender leaves backlit to a delicate green glow by the afternoon sun. Barrayaran native vegetation ran to dull reds and browns, mostly. Would he ever visit Earth? Maybe.

Miles produced proper passes for the door guards. Their faces were familiar, they were the same crew he'd helped supervise for that interminable period last winter—only a few months ago? It seemed longer. He could still rattle off their pay-rates. They exchanged pleasantries, but being good ImpSec men they did not ask the question alight in their eyes, *Where have you been sir?* Miles was not issued a security escort to Illyan's office, a good sign. It wasn't like he didn't know the way, by now.

He followed the familiar turns into the labyrinth, up the lift tubes. The captain in Illyan's outer office merely waved him through, barely glancing up from his comconsole. The inner office was unchanged, Illyan's oversized comconsole desk was unchanged, Illya himself was . . . rather tireder-looking, paler. He ought to get out and catch some of that spring sun, eh? At least his hair hadn't all turned white, it was still about the same brown-grey mix. His taste in clothes was still bland to the point of camouflage.

Illyan pointed to a seat—another good sign, Miles took it promptly—finished whatever had been absorbing him, and at last looked up. He leaned forward to put his elbows on the comconsole and lace his fingers together, and regarded Miles with a kind of clinical disapproval, as if he were a data point that messed up the curve, and Illyan was deciding if he could still save the theory by re-classifying him as experimental error.

"Ensign Vorkosigan," Illyan sighed. "It seems you still have a little problem with subordination."

"I know, sir. I'm sorry."

"Do you ever intend to do anything about it besides feel sorry?"

"I can't help it, sir, if people give me the wrong orders."

"If you can't obey my orders, I don't want you in my Section."

"Well . . . I thought I had. You wanted a military evaluation of the Hegen Hub. I made one. You wanted to know where the destabilization was coming from. I found out. You wanted the Dendarii Mercenaries out of the Hub. They'll be leaving in about three more weeks, I understand. You asked for results. You got them."

"*Lots* of them," Illyan murmured.

"I admit, I didn't have a direct order to rescue Gregor, I just assumed you'd want it done. Sir."

Illyan searched him for irony, lips thinning as he apparently found it. Miles tried to keep his face bland, though out-blanding Illyan was a major effort. "As I recall," said Illyan (and Illyan's memory was eidetic, thanks to an Illyrican bio-chip) "I gave those orders to Captain Ungari. I gave you just one order. Can you remember what it was?" This inquiry was in the same encouraging tone one might use on a six-year-old just learning to tie his shoes. Trying to out-irony Illyan was as dangerous as trying to out-bland him.

"Obey Captain Ungari's orders," Miles recalled reluctantly.

"Just so." Illyan leaned back. "Ungari was a good, reliable operative. If you'd botched it, you'd have taken him down with you. The man is now half-ruined."

Miles made little negative motions with his hands. "He made the correct decisions, for his level. You can't fault him. It's just . . . things got too important for me to go on playing ensign when the man who was needed was Lord Vorkosigan." *Or Admiral Naismith.*

"Hm," Illyan said. "And yet . . . who shall I assign you to now? Which loyal officer gets his career destroyed next?"

Miles thought this over. "Why don't you assign me directly to yourself, sir?"

"Thanks," said Illyan dryly.

"I didn't mean—" Miles began to sputter protest, stopped, detecting the oblique gleam of humor in

Illyan's brown eyes. *Roasting me for your sport, are you?*

"In fact, just that proposal has been floated. Not, needless to say, by me. But a galactic operative must function with a high degree of independence. We're considering making a virtue of necessity—" a light on Illyan's comconsole distracted him. He checked something, and touched a control. The door on the wall to the right of his desk slid open, and Gregor stepped through. The emperor shed one guard who stayed in the passageway, the other trod silently through the office to take up station beyond the antechamber. All doors slid shut. Illyan rose to pull up a chair for the emperor, and gave him a nod, a sort of vestigial bow, before reseating himself. Miles, who had also risen, sketched a salute and sat too.

"Did you tell him about the Dendarii yet?" Gregor asked Illyan.

"I was working around to it," said Illyan. *Gradually.* "What about the Dendarii?" Miles asked, unable to keep the eagerness out of his voice, try though he might for a junior version of Illyan's impassive surface.

"We've decided to put them on a permanent retainer," said Illyan. "You, in your cover identity as Admiral Naismith, will be our liaison officer."

"Consulting mercenaries?" Miles blinked. *Naismith lives!*

Gregor grinned. "The Emperor's Own. We owe them, I think something more than just their base pay for their services to us—and to Us—in the Hegen Hub. And they have certainly demonstrated the, er, utility of being able to reach places cut off to our regular forces by political barriers."

Miles interpreted the expression on Illyan's face as deep mourning for his Section budget, rather than disapproval as such.

"Simon shall be alert for, and pursue, opportunities to use them actively," Gregor went on. "We'll need to justify that retainer, after all."

"I see them as more use in espionage than covert ops," Illyan put in hastily. "This isn't a license to go adventuring, or worse, some kind of letter of marque and reprisal. In fact, the first thing I want you to do is beef up your intelligence department. I know you're in funds for it. I'll lend you a couple of my experts."

"Not bodyguard-puppeteers again, sir?" Miles asked nervously.

"Shall I ask Captain Ungari if he wants to volunteer?" inquired Illyan with a suppressed ripple of his lips. "No. You will operate independently. God help us. After all, if I don't send you someplace else, you'll be right here. So the scheme has that much merit even if the Dendarii never do anything."

"I fear it is primarily your youth which is the cause of Simon's lack of confidence," murmured twenty-five-year-old Gregor. "*We* feel it is time he gave up that prejudice."

Yes, that had been an Imperial We, Miles's Barrayaran-tuned ears did not deceive him. Illyan had heard it as clearly. The chief leaner, leaned upon. Illyan's irony this time was tinged with underlying . . . approval? "Aral and I have labored twenty years to put ourselves out of work. We may live long enough to retire after all." He paused. "That's called 'success' in my business, boys. I wouldn't object." And under his breath ". . . get this hellish chip taken out of my head at last. . . ."

"Mm, don't go scouting surfside retirement cottages just yet," said Gregor. Not caving or backpedaling or submission, merely an expression of confidence in Illyan. No more, no less. Gregor glanced at Miles's . . . neck? The deep bruises from Metzov's grip were almost gone by now, surely. "Were you still working around to the other thing, too?" he asked Illyan.

Illyan opened a hand. "Be my guest." He rummaged in a drawer underneath his comconsole.

"We—and We—thought we owed you something more, too, Miles," said Gregor.

Miles hesitated between a *shucks-t'weren't-nothin'* speech and a *what-did-you-bring-me?!* and settled on an expression of alert inquiry.

Illyan reemerged, and tossed Miles something small that flashed red in the air. "Here. You're a lieutenant. Whatever that means to you."

Miles caught them between his hands, the plastic collar rectangles of his new rank. He was so surprised he said the first thing that came into his head, which was, "Well, that's a start on the subordination problem."

Illyan favored him with a driven glower. "Don't get carried away. About ten percent of ensigns are promoted after their first year of service. Your Vorish social circle will think it's all nepotism anyway."

"I know," said Miles bleakly. But he opened his collar and began switching tabs on the spot.

Illyan softened slightly. "Your father will know better, though. And Gregor. And, er . . . myself."

Miles looked up, to catch his eye direct for almost the first time this interview. "Thank you."

"You earned it. You won't get anything from me you don't earn. That includes the dressing-downs."

"I'll look forward to them, sir."

MILES VORKOSIGAN/NAISMITH: HIS UNIVERSE AND TIMES

Chronology	Events	Chronicle
Approx. 200 years before Miles's birth	Quaddies are created by genetic engineering.	*Falling Free*
During Beta-Barrayaran War	Cordelia Naismith meets Lord Aral Vorkosigan while on opposite sides of a war. Despite difficulties, they fall in love and are married.	*Shards of Honor*
The Vordarian Pretendership	While Cordelia is pregnant, an attempt to assassinate Aral by poison gas fails, but Cordelia is affected; Miles Vorkosigan is born with bones that will always be brittle and other medical problems. His growth will be stunted.	*Barrayar*
Miles is 17	Miles fails to pass physical test to get into the Service Academy. On a trip, necessities force him to improvise the Free Dendarii Mercenaries into existence; he has	*The Warrior's Apprentice*

Chronology	Events	Chronicle
	unintended but unavoidable adventures for four months. Leaves the Dendarii in Ky Tung's competent hands and takes Elli Quinn to Beta for rebuilding of her damaged face; returns to Barrayar to thwart plot against his father. Emperor pulls strings to get Miles into the Academy.	
Miles is 20	Ensign Miles graduates and immediately has to take on one of the duties of the Barrayaran nobility and act as detective and judge in a murder case. Shortly afterwards, his first military assignment ends with his arrest. Miles has to rejoin the Dendarii to rescue the young Barrayaran emperor. Emperor accepts Dendarii as his personal secret service force.	"The Mountains of Mourning" in *Borders of Infinity* *The Vor Game*
Miles is 22	Miles and his cousin Ivan attend a Cetagandan state funeral and are caught up in Cetagandan internal politics.	*Cetaganda*

Chronology	Events	Chronicle
	Miles sends Commander Elli Quinn, who's been given a new face on Beta, on a solo mission to Kline Station.	*Ethan of Athos*
Miles is 23	Now a Barrayaran Lieutenant, Miles goes with the Dendarii to smuggle a scientist out of Jackson's Whole. Miles's fragile leg bones have been replaced by synthetics.	"Labyrinth" in *Borders of Infinity*
Miles is 24	Miles plots from within a Cetagandan prison camp on Dagoola IV to free the prisoners. The Dendarii fleet is pursued by the Cetagandans and finally reaches Earth for repairs. Miles has to juggle both his identities at once, raise money for repairs, and defeat a plot to replace him with a double. Ky Tung stays on Earth. Commander Elli Quinn is now Miles's right-hand officer. Miles and the Dendarii depart for Sector IV on a rescue mission.	"The Borders of Infinity" in *Borders of Infinity* *Brothers in Arms*

Chronology	Events	Chronicle
Miles is 25	Hospitalized after previous mission, Miles's broken arms are replaced by synthetic bones. With Simon Illyan, Miles undoes yet another plot against his father while flat on his back.	*Borders of Infinity*
Miles is 28	Miles meets his clone brother Mark again, this time on Jackson's Whole.	*Mirror Dance*
Miles is 29	Miles hits thirty; thirty hits back.	*Memory*
Miles is 30	Emperor Gregor dispatches Miles to Komarr to investigate a space accident, where he finds old politics and new technology make a deadly mix.	*Komarr*
Miles is 31	The Emperor's wedding sparks romance and intrigue on Barrayar, and Miles plunges up to his neck in both.	*A Civil Campaign*